Drakenfeld

By Mark Charan Newton

Legends of the Red Sun

Nights of Villjamur
City of Ruin
The Book of Transformations
The Broken Isles

The Lucan Drakenfeld novels

Drakenfeld

Drakenfeld

Mark Charan Newton

TOR

First published 2013 by Tor
an imprint of Pan Macmillan, a division of Macmillan Publishers Limited
Pan Macmillan, 20 New Wharf Road, London N1 9RR
Basingstoke and Oxford
Associated companies throughout the world
www.panmacmillan.com

ISBN 978-0-230-76682-2

1 3 5 7 9 8 6 4 2

A CIP catalogue record for this book is available from
the British Library.

Map artwork and temple diagram
© David Atkinson 2013: handmademaps.com

Typeset by Ellipsis Digital Limited, Glasgow
Printed and bound by CPI Group (UK) Ltd, Croydon, CR0 4YY

'*Domina omnium et regina ratio.*'
'Reason is the mistress and queen of all things.'

Marcus Tullius Cicero, *Tusculanae Disputationes*

For Emma and Oliver

Acknowledgements

Though the act of writing is one generally done in isolation, there have been many people who have helped me greatly with detailed feedback and criticism of early drafts. So a big thank you is owed to: Jared Shurin (particularly for his more abusive comments), Anne Perry, Eric Edwards, Ben O'Connell, Liviu Suciu, Kim Curran, John French and Marc Aplin. Thanks, also, to my agent, John Jarrold; and to the wonderful team at Tor UK who, for some reason, keep encouraging me to write books — and most especially my editor Julie Crisp, for making this a significantly better book.

Fantastical literature nearly always draws on historical sources, whether consciously or otherwise. Though Vispasia is a secondary world, many readers will observe that it's clearly inspired by the classical cultures of the ancient world. I like to think Vispasia could sit somewhere just off the oldest maps as a hitherto unrecorded territory. So, I feel I should at least share with readers a selection of the incredible books that have helped me to understand cultures far older than our own. Some of those that have best brought such worlds to life include: Tom Holland's *Persian Fire*; Edward Gibbon's *The History of the Decline and Fall of the Roman Empire*; Suetonius' *The Twelve Caesars*; Pliny's *Natural History*; Procopius' *The Secret History*; Livy's *The Early History of Rome*; and Mary Beard's *Pompeii: The Life of a Roman Town*. Drop me a line through my website markcnewton. com and I'm sure I can recommend more.

NATIONS OF THE VISPASIAN
ROYAL UNION c.201

Tryum

DETRATA

Drobe

THERA

MARISTAN

Polonda

FREE
STATE
Free City, the
City of Gods

Zephron
Ocean

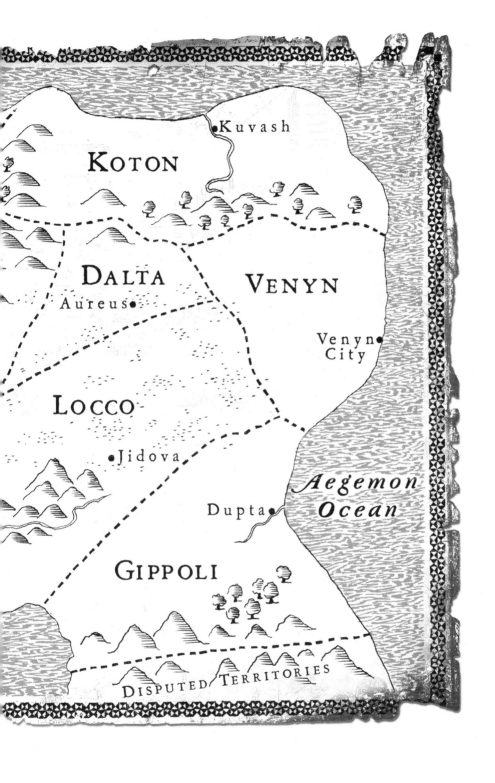

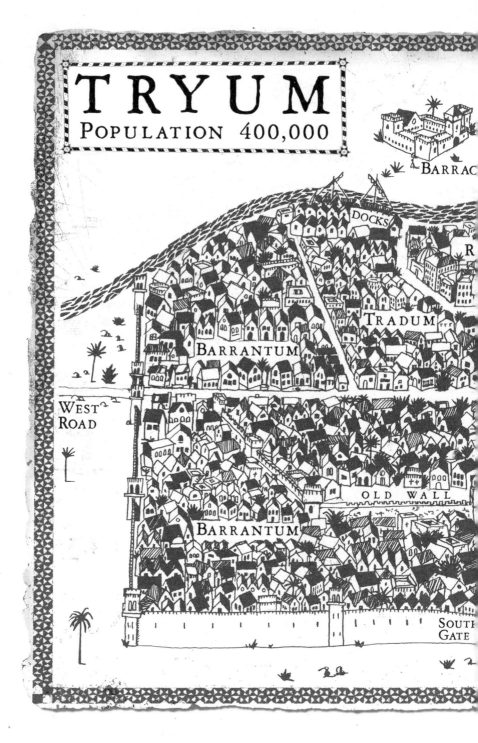

TRYUM

POPULATION 400,000

BARRAC

DOCKS

R

TRADUM

BARRANTUM

WEST
ROAD

OLD WALL

BARRANTUM

SOUTH
GATE

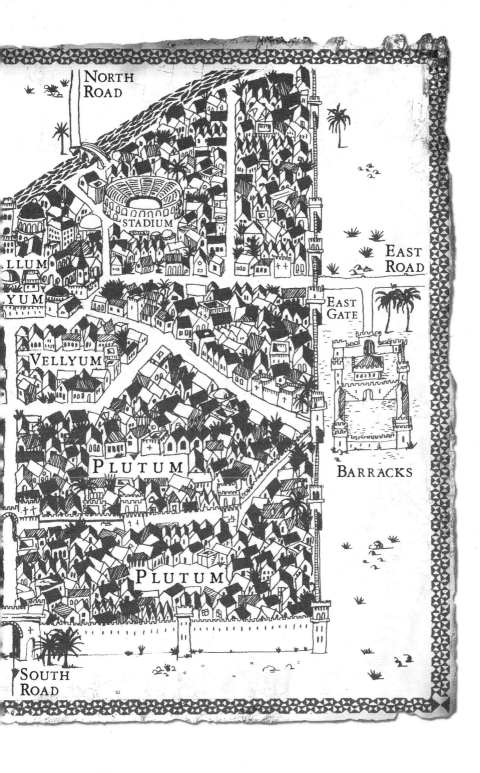

Justice Being Served

A bell called in the priests for prayer, drowning out the worst of the screams. Through wooden shutters I squinted at the vivid brightness, peering down at the men in green robes as they rushed across the paving stones of the courtyard. They surged towards the steps of an impressive temple, which was carved out of the rock-face, crowned with a triangular pediment and covered with ornate symbols. In their haste, one of the priests lost his sandal on the way and paused in the sultry heat to slip it on again. Even out here it seemed everyone was in a rush.

The man stared up in shock when the prayer bell was silenced and the sound of Cornellus' agony could be heard in all its hideous clarity.

The Temple of Procetes — a remote religious settlement hidden within a gorge — was a pleasant venue to be dispatched to for the day. It was a far cry from my usual haunts. After being in Venyn City for so long, I was happy to escape the city's dark, crowded streets. In stark comparison to the almost gaudy, luxurious architecture of Venyn, here were ancient limestone walls with clean lines and subtle decoration, modest statues of deities, and the constant waft of fragrant incense and cooling breezes from the gorge. It made for a peaceful place, and Procetes was a frugal and simplistic god. Within the settlement, decorum and diligent prayer were expected, personal ostentation was frowned upon, and the priests lived in quiet contemplation of their god.

On reflection, it was perhaps not the best place to carry out a punishment order. I wondered how long it would take before someone investigated.

Cornellus' screams continued in the next room, each one making me cringe at the agony he must have been feeling. Unlike many of my colleagues, I was less than enthusiastic about this particular aspect of the job.

Eventually, the door burst open. A balding priest in a plain woollen tunic, his remaining strands of hair slicked down with sweat across his forehead, held the door frame for support as he regarded me with a look of utter disgust.

'Do you have no respect whatsoever for the honour of Procetes?' he spluttered.

I considered that carefully before answering. 'I wouldn't want to anger your god in his own temple, of course. But you should have considered that before sheltering a known felon.'

'He claimed sanctuary,' said the priest almost spitting in his fury. 'We would have done the same to protect anyone in need. Every person deserves the right to shelter here. You told me that you would be questioning him. What are you doing in there?'

'Me personally? Nothing.'

The priest's face paled as another desperate scream echoed around the stone complex.

'As to what my associate is doing, I believe he is pouring molten silver into Gravus Cornellus' eye sockets.'

The priest glared at the brooch on my white shirt, a hollow, blazing sun made of gold: the symbol of the Sun Chamber, the institution that, in working with kings and queens, helped keep the many nations of Vispasia together in alliance and peace.

'If it's any consolation, this torture is not for me,' I continued. 'I don't enjoy seeing anyone suffer, but I must carry out my orders.'

He muttered a curse, gesturing to the heavens with his hands. 'But why? Surely an Officer of the Sun Chamber should conduct himself with more compassion. You are supposed to maintain the peace – uphold the law, protect the innocent not indulge in this . . . this savagery.'

I raised my eyebrows. 'Upholding the law is precisely what I'm doing. And it's the innocent who have been threatened by the actions of that man in there.' I gestured to the door from behind which Cornellus' screams were reaching an uncomfortable crescendo. 'Try explaining to the innocents living in the slums outside your temple gates, or the ghettos in Venyn City, why they won't receive this year's food gifts from the city's council. It's thanks to Cornellus' nefarious accounting activities. Meanwhile, he's built himself a wonderful mansion in the country and been living in the lap of luxury, eating fine foods and drinking expensive wines, not to mention the numerous whores he had visit.'

The priest flushed and glanced again as the screams started to descend into a pitiful wailing.

'You might say that it wasn't especially *virtuous*, was it? It was just as well one of our agents caught him in the act before even more people starved. Then his punishment would have been more severe.'

'Surely no one is deserving of such punishment as molten metal being poured into his eyes?' He wiped his face with his hands.

'Silver. Molten silver. We caught him siphoning off coin destined for the treasury in Free State so that he might be – and these were his own words – "surrounded by the finer things in life". So, in order for him to have his needs addressed, it was decided that his eyes should forever have fine metals imprinted upon them. Apparently one of our sheriffs possesses a sense of irony.'

'This is horrendous,' he said shaking his head. 'It is such a waste.'

'Not entirely,' I remarked. 'At least we didn't use gold.'

The priest was clearly in distress at the suffering of a fellow human and, despite my facetiousness with him, I secretly sympathized.

'You Sun Chamber people, you come here abusing your powers—'

'I'm merely carrying out my orders,' I told him. 'Anyway, I argued that his life be spared. Even this is a kindness of sorts.'

He did not seem particularly impressed by my efforts. 'I insist you finish this torture immediately.'

'It sounds like they've already ended.' The relative silence was somehow more profound now. 'You should head to the temple, priest. Cornellus will need all the prayers he can get.'

He glared at me again and left the room; shortly after he was striding across the courtyard, where sounds of holy chanting drifted, now uninterrupted, around the large enclosure. I rubbed at my eyes and felt the beginning of a headache. I'd told the priest the truth, that Cornellus' crime was a serious one, and the priest was lucky that the man's confession had not implicated the temple in any way.

The door was flung open and Maxid stepped forward, wiping his hands on a stained cloth. Behind him were Cornellus' legs, limp on the floorboards, the straps still keeping him in place – not that he'd be making his escape any time soon – and the smell of smoke drifted out towards me.

Maxid was the size of an ox and just as fragrant. His long hair was damp with sweat and every time he shaved, his beard seemed to be reborn within the hour. His brutish figure looked ill at ease in the impressive doublet and cloak of a soldier of the Sun Chamber. Despite his appearance and occupation, he was actually a mellow man at heart and a softly spoken soul.

'Well?' I asked.

'It's done.'

'You didn't kill him then?'

'Oh good heavens, no.'

'There's a first time for everything.'

'Well, I'm a careful fellow,' he said, with a level of refinement that didn't suit the rest of his image. 'You see, I only used minute amounts of silver to burn away his eyeballs. Any more would have gone into his brain.' Maxid gestured at his own head to illustrate his point. 'It just isn't any good. As I say so often, this is a job for only the highly skilled.'

'He's free to go now,' I said. 'We can release him at the temple gates, but for Polla's sake, at least give him a stick to help him, and see that he's well looked after. Cornellus was ultimately a respectable man with a powerful family, and we should treat him with all the dignity we can. We don't want to get a reputation for tormenting people needlessly.'

Maxid nodded glumly. 'Ah. I don't suppose you could do that instead? He might not wake for another hour or more, and I'd dearly like to ride back now while the sun's still high.'

'All right, I'll wait.'

'You're a good fellow.'

'What job have you got lined up next?'

'None at the moment,' Maxid said, packing some vicious-looking tools into a leather bag. 'I've a little free time. Our agents are doing good business and my skills are in high demand these days. So for now I'm going back to Venyn City and I intend to purchase some lithe young studs to bed for the next day or two, before another request comes in.'

I smiled. 'Buying love won't make you happy.'

'Who said anything about love?' Maxid replied with a small smile.

'Well, as long as it keeps you off the streets. Oh, that reminds me, this is for you.' I reached into my pocket, pulled out a purse of money and threw it over to him. 'Make sure you don't catch any diseases.'

Maxid caught the purse in one muscled hand and peered inside, scrutinizing the contents. 'Well, farewell, Drakenfeld!' He picked up his belongings from the corner of the room and lumbered straight past me.

I glanced once again at the still form of Cornellus, feeling regret at what had transpired. The law could be brutal at times – but, as I told myself so often, Vispasia would be a far darker place if there was no law.

Leana was sitting in the late afternoon sunlight, her dark brown skin glimmering in the heat. The stone seats were almost too hot to sit on, but I managed to perch alongside her. Dressed in tight-fitting clothing the colour of the local stone, and with a sword sheathed at her waist, she was watching children from the local village as they ran around a fountain, each of them waving a small wooden doll above their heads. She explained that the children were playing a game based on the birth of Procetes. Little plumes of dust rose up from the street as they dashed about with abandon, while elderly beggars watched from afar and pulled themselves deeper into the sanctuary of the shade.

'The heat, it never slows down children,' Leana commented. 'If the dolls were carved from bone, it would remind me of a game I played when I was as old as they are. Here . . .' Shading her eyes with one hand, she handed me a tube containing a rolled-up letter. 'A messenger gave me this.'

I eyed the tube in my hands. Letters were always something to be cautious about: they were usually requests for me to travel somewhere else, demands for more paperwork, news of a trivial dealing in a provincial town that needed addressing, or complaints from some nobody about the way they had been treated. But I noted the seal of the Sun Chamber in the wax, and opened the letter immediately.

Reading it, I felt a numbness hammering me. Hands shaking — just for a moment — I absorbed the information, even though none of it seemed to register at first.

Lucan Drakenfeld,

It is with regret that we must report your esteemed father, Calludian Drakenfeld, died during the night from heart failure. Your presence is requested immediately in the city of Tryum in Detrata, where you will deal with his remaining affairs and liaise with the pontiff at the Temple of Polla.

You are currently relieved of all present duties in Venyn City and a replacement will be allocated shortly.

Regards

Sheriff Balus,

Senior Administrator for Vispasian Royal Union East.

'What is it?' Leana asked.

Words felt trapped in my throat. 'My father has died.'

Rarely did I see emotion in Leana's face, let alone sympathy, but there it was — I hoped it wouldn't last too long.

'How did he pass?' she asked.

'Something to do with his heart, so it says.' I held the letter in the air before returning my hands to my lap. 'A natural death.'

'Your loss is great, Lucan. I am . . . so sorry. I will make a sacrifice to Gudan tonight to see that the spirits comfort him.'

Not now, I wanted to say, *please none of this spirit nonsense now* — but I didn't. Instead I rested my head back against the stone wall and stared up into the blinding sun.

Deep into the night, when Leana was asleep in her bed at the far end of our tavern room, after I had made my prayers to Polla and noted down the events of the day, I opened the letter and read it again by candlelight, contemplating the words, hoping they would gain more clarity.

My father, one of the greatest Sun Chamber officials who had ever lived, was already a fading memory. Greatness can be a matter of perception, however. Though he paid for an excellent and privileged life for myself and my brother, Marius, he never quite knew what to do with us after our mother died. Various people cared for us while he was busy with work. Names and faces came and went with the seasons. When he spent time with us we were beaten no more than the average child of Tryum. My brother, who was a year younger than me, took things to heart. I could never identify with his utter loathing of our father. Ultimately I felt I had more right to hate our father, after what he did to me at the time.

Despite any negative feelings, I always respected him. My only true treasured memory of him was when I was only seven or eight summers old, sitting in our garden while my father explained to me the importance of his badge of office — the one I also wear. I asked him what the Sun Chamber was and I still remember, for the first time, a softening in his voice and posture, a quiet pride that began to show. He became a different man.

The Vispasian Royal Union, he explained, was made up of the eight nations of this continent. Each royal head, with the help of elected representatives, enacted the principles of the founding treaties of the continent, the most fundamental of which was that there would be no war between nations. We prospered. There was peace and security. He looked me in the eye and said that he helped to enforce the essential laws that maintained a bond. 'We are peacemakers,' he said, 'not warmongers. The world is better for it. There is no more important job.'

It was inevitable that I would follow that path, and his affection grew for me after I made that decision.

However, I spent my later life in his shadow. My conversations with older officials throughout the Vispasian Royal Union would often involve them referring to him and his famous cases with affection. My world was often comprised of being the son of Calludian rather than a man in my own right, and perhaps that reputation would never fully go away. Death rarely seemed to end the business of the living. But this man – who I had both feared and admired, who had given me life and then dictated its path without realizing – was no more.

I was no longer Son of Calludian. I was Lucan Jupus Drakenfeld, second generation Officer of the Sun Chamber. A free man.

I watched the flame of the candle for some time, contemplating all these matters, trying to recover my memories of the buildings and people that defined my time in Tryum; moments of my childhood returned to my mind, the walls that bore my graffiti, the games we played in the street.

Eventually, as it always does, the candle sparked out.

Preparing for a Homecoming

Preparing for my return home, the following morning I headed to the merchant house by the harbour in Venyn City, capital of the nation of Venyn, to exchange my money for a receipt with the intention of exchanging it back for the local currency, pecul-las, upon reaching Tryum in Detrata. I put the receipt in a small leather tube that I hung around my neck, and walked along the seafront, enjoying the pleasant morning sunshine and the salt tang on the breeze for perhaps the last time. For who knew where I would be sent next after dealing with my father's affairs — Sun Chamber officers tended to be dispatched wherever we were most needed, though often it seemed that Leana and I had been forgotten in this city. I wrote confirmation of my travels and posted them to the sheriff, who all officers reported to, and took the long walk home one final time.

From a steep hillside, Venyn City plunged down to an estuary, which was currently cluttered with large shipping vessels. The water was murky at best, containing the scrubbed-off dirt from a thousand dubious souls. It was only further out to sea that the water became a true and brilliant blue.

Thanks to the wind, the hills facing the sea were relieved of the stifling, oppressive heat, which caused such discomfort to the city dwellers. Conspiring winds and the searing sun made the streets full of hot, damp dust that accumulated on the cracked lips of the beggars taking refuge in the shadows of decrepit buildings. Hundreds of starving dogs slunk in the alleyways or lay like the dead in whatever small shade they could find. Even the fat palm trees growing in the tropical gardens seemed to wilt in the humidity.

Over the centuries, Venyn had seemed to suffer the indifference of its gods, with invading nations plundering its spoils then abandoning its people. It had once been the centre of the grain route, but when cheaper prospects were found elsewhere the money dried up and Venyn then found itself as far from prosperity as was possible for a city. The refuge of the desperate, the debauched and the degraded, it was not a pleasant place to live any more, but somehow people scraped an existence. Legal or otherwise. It was no surprise the Sun Chamber had sent me here, a criminal base, a country of unrest. Agents and officers only tended to come together in larger numbers when a major crisis presented itself.

Crime on this scale wasn't considered a crisis when it was part of everyday life.

Despite the heat, the dirt and the stench of rotting refuse – I couldn't hate the place. I had been working here for six years. How many times had I narrowly avoided being killed on the streets in this city: escaping a mugging, loosening the grip of a desperate homeless person, or politely, then more firmly, resisting the calls of the men and women leaning out of the windows of a dockyard bordello?

The Sun Chamber had spies, but they were always on the move, always walking in circles higher than my own; and they tended to contact us only when they needed to. I could rely only upon my own skills – and later, Leana's – and that was the point. After all, it was the reason I came here in the first place, to build something of a reputation for myself.

While I wouldn't miss trying to bring order to one of the most corrupt cities of the Vispasian Royal Union, I appreciated that this often forgotten corner of Vispasia had, at least, sharpened my senses and honed my skills as an officer of the Sun Chamber. Though we had not exactly cleansed the streets of all nefarious activities, I liked to think, looking back, that where there had been disorder there was now some structure.

These dirty, ancient streets were now a more civilized place. While not being one to dwell on my successes too much, modesty being one of the precepts of Polla, having weighed up my performances I felt I could at least leave proud.

There was almost always a Sun Chamber officer stationed in every large town and city throughout the Vispasian Royal Union. Presumably my replacement would find the city still a challenge. He or she would have to build up their own local network of confidants and learn the hard way that Venyn City was tough work.

The Sun Chamber, a vast and bureaucratic organization, enforces the Treaty of Royal Blood, a two-centuries-old law that bound together the eight nations of Vispasia in union. The treaty came off the back of the bloody wars that resulted from the collapse of the old Detratan Empire, in which the continent sustained huge losses of life. One by one the nations decided it would be best for all if they maintained peace. Even to this day, royals head twice a year to the Council of Kings in Free State, central Vispasia, in order to debate matters of continental trade and politics. The alliance is not an easy one, and now and then a king may threaten to withdraw his nation from the union, but peace has been maintained. In that time, the Sun Chamber had acquired land of its own, developed a vast network of agents and officers, so much so that more senior figures, far above the rank of officer, were often depended upon to give advice on trade and commerce.

Officers worked alone, though we could hire whoever we wanted to assist us. With firm persuasion, local politicians, judges and even princes could be made to behave; and our badge of office was feared accordingly. Or so we were told during our training – more often than not, local officials didn't give a damn about deceiving their own superiors or the people they served. Generally we would bring matters to the attention of local law-makers and let the matter be dealt with internally wherever possible. Nations should sort out their own affairs – or, at least, it should appear that way.

The job sounded more glorious than it was in reality, espe-cially for someone of my level. The rich leaned on the poor when it came to doing nefarious deeds – from tax evasion to murder – so we often saw ourselves travelling into some of the darkest parts of Union and talking to the most unfortunate people, in order to report it to our superiors, who wielded great control over the ebb and flow of Sun Chamber personnel.

Sometimes I questioned the motive for being sent to various corners of the continent, though I remained committed no matter what the case in hand. For example, I did not know if capturing a man who smuggled women across borders for prosti-tution actually helped bind the nations together in political union, but I did know that it would help the lives of others, the women in question, and it certainly improved the local commu-nities. We were always told that the crimes of the lower classes were often influenced by men and women much higher up in society, and therefore an officer in his or her first few years would often be ordered into the dingiest of slums alongside the local officials in order to hone their skills. Even in the Sun Chamber, one had to earn the right to speak among the politicians and royals.

I had been brought up worshipping Polla, a truly honest and remarkable woman who later became deified, and who taught that our lives were little more than the sum of our good deeds over bad. By those criteria, my life here in Venyn City had been a good one, and in some ways I would miss the place.

The next morning, once Leana had sold our horses, and the keys to our rented dockyard offices were returned to the landlord, we set off for Tryum.

It would take us the better part of a month of travel to get away from this hole, if we cut across the continent. Instead, I regretfully opted to take a merchant ship carrying spices and cloth – at least we were told it was carrying spices and cloth – but I had spent far too long in the city to fall for such obvious tales. The captain of the ship, a lean individual with a philosophical expression, one etched permanently in place by the constant winds at sea, barely said a word to us throughout the journey. Which was perfectly fine with Leana and myself.

He mistook us twice: first for husband and wife, secondly that she was some kind of slave. Leana's scowl nicely liberated him of that opinion. Should I have pointed out that I was a member of the Sun Chamber, he would not have wanted to take me on board unless I paid twice the price. We could have commandeered his vessel, but it wasn't worth the hassle.

Besides, whilst at sea, it was wise not to anger the gods.

It is said in most religions that one of the realms one may fall into after death is a violent, dark and oppressive location. I'm almost certain that we sailed right through that place.

Seven nights we spent at sea, travelling north and east along the coastline, and it only took one night to convince me that my hatred of this mode of transport hadn't lessened with time. I vomited at least five times on the first day and barely left our cabin, if indeed it could be called a cabin; it was a small hold that was used mainly for carrying who-knew-what decaying matter in rancid crates. Leana despaired of my weakness and, impatient and anxious, spent much of her time on deck, offering her assistance, and generally making herself far more useful.

Most of the time aboard was a blur to me. I may have blanked it from my mind, or it may have been the bottle of strong wine from the captain's cabin Leana had acquired so I might drink myself unconscious – all the rarer an act considering I didn't often drink.

My one fear during the trip was that the gods would curse me again and that I might suffer a seizure of the sort that came upon me in times of trial and tribulation – a physical weakness that had dogged me since childhood. On rare occasions the seizures would strike me during the day, but it was more commonly during my sleep. But instead only one intense headache came – usually a precursor to a seizure, like a premonition, though sometimes they occurred afterwards. Leana informed me there were no episodes, however, which came as a relief.

My goddess, Polla, must have intervened with the sea gods on my behalf, for we arrived at night – alive – at a small trading town on the border of Detrata and the lush, green hills of Koton.

My only memory of that night was the captain's wild laughter as I stumbled eagerly towards land clutching my belongings, before falling with minimal dignity into a bush.

We acquired horses and set off early, moving across hilly farm-land bathed in the red light of sunrise. Gradually the styles of buildings, the crops, the living history, all became familiar once again.

Was it me that had changed, or Detrata? Now that I saw my home with a stranger's eyes, I was far more aware of its context within the wider world. Upon my departure from this country, I was a young man somewhat sceptical of such a fragile, continent-wide set-up. To me, it shouldn't have lasted for so long. Upon returning, and as I explained to Leana, I understood how Detrata fared far better within a united Vispasia than alone, even during the glory days of the Detratan Empire. There was no war to speak of and across the silent battlefields rode determined traders.

'I hear your old empire mentioned from time to time,' Leana said. 'It was a cruel place. Vispasia is still a little like that abroad.'

I considered my words carefully. 'The old Detratan Empire was a savage period. The continent lurched between extremes of maniacal dictators, civil war and famine. Wars came, then out of peace Vispasia grew, a weird and wonderful royal democracy. That said, it is the best option for people here. Stability has been maintained for two hundred years and blood is rarely spilled to the extent it used to be.'

'You have not addressed my point. All of these countries, they take their wars abroad still. They still make slaves of people from outside Vispasia. In fact, I could be one, if in life I had been even more unfortunate.'

Eventually, I said, 'I agree it's a horrendous practice, but it's better than it used to be.'

We reached the summit of the Olosso Mountains about an hour after dawn and the full splendour of Detrata was laid out before us. These famous plains became flooded with memories. The vista of rolling hills, grasslands, hamlets and tiny, stone fortifications, brought back such a strong sense of nostalgia that I did not notice Leana speaking to me for several moments.

'Are you feeling well?' Leana asked, though it sounded more of an order to be fine. 'You seem uneasy. A mild seizure?'

I slid from my horse to regard the terrain and to take a good lungful of Detratan air. It was warm even at this hour of the morning, and the cool breeze was a pleasant relief. The air was not as humid here, and the place seemed far gentler than I was used to.

I had stood at this same vantage point ten years ago. Like most young and optimistic people, I'd left with every intention of putting some distance between my father and myself, as well as making my mark on the world. At least I could say I had achieved something.

'It seems so unfortunate,' I said eventually, 'to be confronted with such a glorious sight, when I should feel only sorrow.'

Leana said nothing as she slid with skill off her horse, again making apparently athletic movements seem so effortless. She reached into her pack for a flask of water. Garbed in a similar fashion to myself, white shirt, brown leather doublet and heavy boots, she wore her dark hair tied back as if always being ready for combat, and regarded me with one of her unreadable expressions.

Perhaps that's why I found her the perfect travelling companion: we kept our wandering thoughts largely to ourselves. She took heavy gulps of water before offering the flask to me, but I declined.

'Lucan,' she said. 'Why have you not noticed the man following? Half a mile back down the slope?'

I glanced back down, following the line of the straight road along the yellow grassland until – some way in the distance – a figure on horseback came into focus. 'It's a road, like any other. He's free to pass through.'

'But you said this route was not frequently used, yet he has kept pace with us since our landing. He does not catch up or fall back. He remains the same distance.'

'You're right, I should have spotted this,' I said.

'Spirits save us,' Leana added, but made no further comment about my lapse of judgement.

'We're in no hurry. We've made good time so far. Let's hang back and let him pass. I've some bread in the bag, and some fruit – we should eat.'

'And when he arrives here?' Leana asked.

'He could be an innocent trader.'

Leana drew her sword.

'He could simply be a traveller,' I continued, 'like us. Not everyone is out to attack us. Just because we represent the Sun Chamber does not mean we can draw blood for no reason at all. We are not barbarians.'

We ate quickly, and waited behind a wind-smoothed stone outcrop as the figure came closer. Now that he could not see us, he gained pace considerably. It made no sense that someone would be after us – who in Detrata knew of our arrival?

A few moments later and the ground began to vibrate under the horse's hooves. I stepped out into the road casually while Leana remained waiting by the side with her bow, covering me. He carried a sheathed weapon and wore a scarf around his mouth, but struggled to control his startled horse. Unnerved at my sudden appearance, the horse bolted towards the horizon, hooves thumping into the sun-baked earth. His dust trails lingered in the air.

'It is possible he was sent after us, but . . .'

'Someone in Detrata does not like you much,' Leana declared.

'Or it could simply be nothing to worry about. Let's not allow paranoia to plague my return home.'

'You are far too trusting of people,' Leana replied. 'I have always said this is a problem.'

Aqueducts trailed like stone tendrils down from the mountains towards Tryum, the main city of Detrata – it was these structures that enabled life to persist. Tryum did not suffer from the humidity of Venyn City. Here the heat was drier, more pleasant, and the air was not laced with particles of sand.

But where there is life there is death, and we soon came across one of the peculiarities of Tryum, the Road of the Dead, a main causeway into the city lined with mausoleums. Flying from the ramparts of these buildings were the yellow banners of Detrata. The centre of each one featured a two-headed black falcon, along with the cross of the founding gods set within the avian's breast. On each head was a crown, and various glaives and swords could be discerned behind the wings. The closer we came to the city, we saw families sitting in wide circles on the grass, or beneath the shade of a cherry tree, eating picnics while their children chased each other around the tall monuments. Statues of the dead were constructed here in all sorts of poses: some with a book underarm to lend an air of wisdom, others in full armour for a show of strength. One or two were surrounded by images of gods and goddesses, to represent how the deceased was untouchable or blessed.

'Why do they eat here,' Leana asked, 'around the dead?'

'Just because you die doesn't mean you get out of your family duties,' I laughed. 'At least not in Tryum. Besides, it's good to keep them involved, make offerings on their behalf, light incense to purify them.'

She nodded approvingly at my response. Perhaps there were more similarities between the many religions of Tryum and her own tribal cults than I liked to give credit for.

'These are impressive statues and buildings,' she said.

'This is where the wealthy bury their dead. For the poor, the end is not so dignified. A swift pyre for the lucky. For the not so lucky, a bloated corpse in the River Tryx is the best one can expect.'

'I am not sure I will like this place,' Leana said. 'I already miss Venyn.'

'Why?'

'Such differences are not good omens, spirits save us. At least in Venyn everyone had the same chance that they would end up like a bloated corpse.'

'I'd suggest the ideal is for everyone to be buried in splendour.'

'That would,' Leana replied, 'mean a lot more people having to eat out here.'

The East Road was exactly as I remembered: first, a wide avenue of ancient poplar trees for half a mile, dappled sunlight across a busy road of traders and travellers and their belongings. Beyond stood the rectangular barracks of the King's Legion, King Licintius' private guard. When Licintius first became king as a young man, before I left, there were few soldiers in Tryum. The military was certainly out on parade today, in crests and purple tunics, their armour bright in the afternoon sun. Some were engaged in displays on horseback, busy with training regimes that they would probably never use. Others from the City Watch were marching along the edge of the road, behind the trees, offering an intimidating presence to any who would wish harm to the city.

Towards the eastern fringes, on the lower slopes of the main hill, was the urban sprawl, row upon row of newly and poorly built housing. Tryum had become more heavily populated since I had departed, and I was surprised that people could live like this. Had it always been this way?

We passed the statues either side of the road that led to a gate into Tryum. They towered up into an azure sky and were the founding gods: Trymus and Festonia, husband and wife, and Malax, the lord of the Underworld, who looked after the dead. Further along was a statue of Polla, the goddess of the sun and of the Sun Chamber — and to whom I gave a gentle bow.

Up the slope, in the distance, stood some of the most important buildings in the city, where the highest echelons of society — priests, senators and King Licintius — would mix. As we came closer to the city gates the smell was overwhelming: in addition to the strong scent of horse manure and the bitter smell of the tannery, small plumes of smoke hung above residences as the hearths cooked food, and through the haze, way in the distance to one side, were the higher tiers and arches of the Stadium of Lentus, in which games would regularly be held, and which hadn't been quite completed ten years ago.

We registered at the city gates with a young priest and an elderly censor, both of whom immediately became flustered when I gave them my name and office. They could not help me quickly enough, yet stared suspiciously at Leana. I wondered how her Atrewen profile, her elegant narrow nose and strong jawline, her skin the colour of rosewood, and her compact, muscular body would have gone down with these people. Presumably, being by the gates, they must have seen people from all corners of the world, yet they still eyed her warily.

'May we ask,' the censor said, 'about your business in the city?'

I informed them of my father's death, and that I was a member of the Sun Chamber.

'You are the son of Calludian Drakenfeld?' the priest asked, surprised.

'I am.'

'His death was a shock to us. There was not a man or woman of quality in this city who did not know of his name or his deeds.'

I felt again that same annoyance: that I could probably never be my own man in this city, along with a pang of regret that I would never see my father again. This conversation was happening too soon, so my short answers and sense of urgency saw to it that we were permitted through quickly.

A few steps later and we were inside Tryum. The wide, well-kept stone road led in a straight line through the centre of the city. Carts rocked through these immediate poorer districts, while further along livestock was being driven along the road, barging people out of the way.

All along the side streets, people lived in squalor: women sat outside houses, homeless men lay in the shade with bowls in front of them, and dogs nosed the legs of passers-by. Ragged bits of cloth were strung between walls.

'I thought you said this was different from Venyn City?' Leana asked. 'Could be the same place.'

'No city is without problems,' I replied. 'Though I never recalled Tryum's problems being quite as bad as this.

New Luxuries

The family residence was located in one of the ancient parts of Tryum. The walls of the house were made of thick stone, in the old style – a blessing in any season. But even more fortuitous was how the old buildings blunted the sound of hammering by the local smiths in the streets beyond. Set further away from the streets were the main living quarters, a simple, classy affair, with chequered stone tiles, rich red drapes, pleasant seats and rustic tables. On the walls were paintings of great battle scenes and of gods.

All of which was a step up in the world from our hovel in Venyn City.

Outside the front gates was the splendid architecture that had echoed in my dreams for so long: the colonnades, fountains, market gardens, statues, frescoes, and the bowed or domed rooftops so typical of the Polyum and Regallum quarters. In the street, two children were practising their spelling by scratching low down on the pale walls, as I used to do myself. From here the view that presented itself was of the hill leading towards Regallum, filled with temple roofs and, just beyond that, the mighty royal residence and centrepiece of that district, Optryx.

Leana had been on a brief tour of the house, investigating all the little nooks and crannies. There was a new cook who lived here also, a different one from when I lived here, and she had not left when my father died.

Her name was Bellona, named after a Maristanian goddess of food, which I took as a good portent. Older than me, she stood a shade shorter than Leana. Her nose was broad, her lips thin, her eyes gentle and intelligent – her pale, sweaty face had a welcoming demeanour. With a deep voice and a local accent, she spoke affectionately about my father and told me how handsome I looked.

I could get used to that.

After I confirmed I would of course keep her in my employment, she unceremoniously rushed forward to bow at my feet. Leana's gaze was one of amusement, and I must admit to feeling rather uncomfortable. I helped Bellona up again and asked, if it wasn't too much trouble, to prepare a little dinner before dusk.

'Of course, master,' she replied, before tentatively adding, 'though we need some coin to replenish provisions.'

'Oh, right.' I reached into my pocket and handed over a couple of silver pieces that came to ten pecullas. She seemed to gaze at the coins as if they were god-blessed. 'I'll eat whatever you eat.'

'I eat very poorly, despite my appearance,' she said. 'Cheap things, not food fit for the master of the house.'

'Honestly, I'll eat what you do,' I repeated. 'If that means you have to buy better food for yourself, then so be it.'

With a warm, toothy smile, she turned to leave.

'And please, there's no need to call me master,' I shouted after her. When I faced Leana again, she gave me that look of hers. 'You can stop grinning,' I said.

'Yes, *master*,' Leana replied. 'I tell you now, she will have you overweight within one month.'

'I'll be careful what I eat.'

'I will have to train you twice as hard,' Leana warned me as she stepped around leisurely, absorbing the place that was to be our home for the time being — not that it was known how long we might be staying.

It would only be a matter of time until her room became filled with skulls and tribal offerings, and I wondered what the upper classes of Tryum would make of such trinkets.

'So, you grew up here?' Leana asked.

'I did.'

'It is very different from that bottom-floor apartment in Venyn. I did not know your family was . . . so wealthy.'

I shrugged. 'So, what do you think of the place?'

'Far too many furnishings. Too many precious paintings. Such things make for a soft upbringing. It would at least explain your gentle nature.'

'Among other things, I like to think. Anyway, I wouldn't worry about it.' I gestured all around me. 'They're just walls. And all this art does wonders for one's soul.'

Without reply Leana meandered back into the house and, breaking the lingering silence, Bellona returned to ask what meat I'd like to eat. I exchanged a few more pleasantries with her, and enquired whether or not there were any other staff on my father's payroll. Bellona replied negatively, but she seemed coy about the subject, so I didn't press it any further. She must have been unhappy discussing money with a relative stranger and returned to the kitchen.

Only moments later, I could smell something wonderful.

I stood perfectly still in the hall, and closed my eyes to the paintings, statues, terracotta walls and slender pillars. Pots rattled in the kitchen. Water bubbled in the fountain outside. Just beyond the house — my house — carts clattered along the cobbled street. Vaguely I tried to match the noises with my youth: soon, layered above the ambient sounds, came my mother's tender Loccon voice, her sisters, my cousins. My father, for whatever reason, seemed to possess no firm memory in my mind. No, that wasn't quite true – I remembered him with a belt in his hands as he threatened to strike me over some misdemeanour. Then of course our foulest argument came back to me, when he betrayed my trust with regard to a girl I'd once known and loved.

Leana reappeared, without her doublet on, and her fitted white shirt was striking against her dark skin.

'There is a room on the north side of the building. It is the one with many green cushions on the bed, also. If you have no objections, I will take this for my quarters.'

'Why not?' I replied. With a smile, I added, 'Just make sure you don't find all these furnishings too soft and comforting.'

My very first engagement back in the city was to identify and honour my father's body at the temple, before making suitable arrangements for his burial. Over a green, silk shirt I wore a dark brown cloak, on which I pinned the golden brooch of my office.

Leana and I stood at the gates of the house, regarding the street. A vendor was frying meats nearby, while further along came the smell of pine-scented incense. The noises were startling now we were closer to the throng. Traders were packing up or travelling from the market at the forum – if I was of the right mind I would have rummaged among their wares to take advantage of the cheaper prices at this time of day.

'Will you be all right on your own?' Leana asked, pushing the hilt of her sword beneath her cloak.

'I'm going to a temple not a battlefield.'

'That is not what I mean.'

I shook my head. 'I'll be fine. Look, first, sell our horses –

we'll have little need of them in Tryum and we could do with the spare coin. Then go, explore, stay in Polyum or near Regallum,' I replied. 'Don't head too far down-city, avoid Plutum and Barrantum after dusk, and don't go finding any trouble, or you might need to ask your spirit gods for a little help.'

Leana snorted with derision. 'It will be the locals who would require the help of their gods.' As she walked slowly into the darkness of the adjacent lane, I could only agree with her.

I passed through the evening traffic towards the temple and found the humidity and crowds suffocating. Traders rolled their carts past, nearly knocking me over, before scraping their wheels on the walls or slightly raised kerb, while boys ran ahead ringing small bells to warn of the oncoming traffic. From nearby came the stench of decaying matter from whatever foods had not been sold and thrown in the gutters. Graffiti was to the point as always: no matter where one travelled in Vispasia, a hastily scrawled penis followed by a name was forever in fashion.

I walked down one familiar street where two good childhood friends had grown up, Clidus and Aetos. It was a wide, well-to-do street with a high pavement and cloth merchants folding away their wares, pulling down awnings. I lingered there for a while, half wondering what I'd say to them if they ever came by, but mainly observing who came out of the red and yellow doors from their big houses. It seemed neither them nor their families were to be seen. I asked an old man who was sitting in the sun with a cup of wine if he knew of them, and he said that he did, but they had long since left the area.

In a nostalgic mood, I continued on my way.

A farmer was attempting to drive five cows through the narrow lanes, and people had to press themselves against the wall to avoid being trampled. An attractive woman walked by and flashed me a bright smile before she was lost in the throng. Preachers leered or chanted from the relative sanctuary of decorative archways, a dozen dialects rising to my ears, whilst passers-by lit incense to offer to small statues of their gods. The sheer variety of people in Tryum was mesmerizing. From clothing to foods to the decorations on clay pots, one could almost walk the length of the continent in a single street.

The two main libraries were still here, exactly as I remembered. Their symmetrical limestone facades towered into the sky. Torches flared at regular intervals along the passageways, and philosophers had gathered on the front steps overlooking the forum, posing for the masses to see them engaged in debate, as they always did. I recalled having to bustle past them whenever I needed to study. The graffiti here was more satisfying – full of electoral slogans and statements of support from wealthy businessmen. Hardly a phallus in sight.

Loathed by many, loved by others, the street theatres were doing a roaring trade. There were several different performances on today, makeshift stages and melodramatic actors with exaggerated expressions. Further along the street, the taverns were full with all manner of clients, all the chatter here in the Detratan tongue. I tried to recall the haunts of my younger days, of conversations in the morning sunlight, of minted teas shared with a young lady on a good day, or with a dull legal scholar on an average one. They were discussions that people could lose themselves in, and which could be forgotten about soon after. It wasn't so much about what was said, but the energy, the sparring, the craft of carving out one's sense of being.

Much of my understanding of the world had developed in those establishments. In fact, I'd spent many an hour there with the one woman – though she was then a girl – the only significant romance I'd ever had. Her name was Titiana, and I wondered vaguely what became of her.

Now, looking back at the taverns, oil lamps stood on tables, shining their mellow light on new faces, none of which I recognized, even though I somehow hoped I might: the stories shared here were no longer for my ears.

People moved on, I had moved on, and that was life.

The Temple of Polla dominated the street that bordered the city districts of Polyum and Regallum. Two immense torches burned within iron cressets, framing a staircase of twenty steps. Polla's slender face set within a blazing sun was carved into the centrepiece of the facade and from her lofty position she gazed down on all those who entered.

Already I felt calm in her presence. The noises of the city fell away and from beyond the double doors came scents of incense. A serene priestess dressed in white silk greeted me in the entrance way; she asked if I could wait inside until the pontiff was prepared to see me, so I thanked her and went in.

The marble floor glittered under candlelight as people drifted past in whispered conversation. Crimson drapes hung on the walls and within small alcoves bronze statues of Polla's otherworld husbands stood. Incense, flowers or small blood offerings lay at their feet. On the side I could see a resplendent edition of the Book of Wisdom, a large text that contained details on how best to explore and interact with the world, as well as speculation on the movement of the stars and of plants and creatures that had not yet made it to Vispasia.

The senior pontiff arrived, a slender, aged man with sunken cheekbones, a minor hunch and garbed in a red robe. I returned his gracious greeting. He regarded me with a pity I didn't feel was strictly necessary.

'We did not expect you so soon,' he announced.

'I took a ship rather than coming across land.'

'Would you like to see your father now?'

'Please.'

'Come, Polla has preserved him well. The rituals are nearly over. His ashes will be ready for burial in four days.'

Together we descended to the subterranean levels beneath the temple, and entered a small chamber halfway down a dark and cold corridor that, even though it probably had little public traffic, was every bit as ornate as the temple above. Inside, the pontiff lit several candles and there in front of me, wrapped in layers of thin, resin-covered cloth, was my father's body.

I had seen many corpses in my lifetime including, as a young boy, that of my own mother. I did not know what to feel. I became strangely numb, void of thought. I simply stared, trying to connect my knowledge of my father to the body before me.

'When was he brought here?' I asked.

'About twenty days ago,' the pontiff replied.

They had done a good job of halting the decay and bad odour. 'And where was he found?'

'In his offices, not too far from here. A member of the cohorts stopped by and found him slumped over his desk – he raised the alarm initially, and our physician arrived first.'

'What was his name – the man in the cohort?'

'Brellus, I believe, but he died three days later trying to evacuate a building that was on fire.'

I glanced at the priest, saddened for the loss of life, but frustrated that I couldn't talk with this Brellus.

'Was there anything suspicious about the scene in my father's office?'

'The matter has been looked into—'

'By the cohorts?'

'Yes, and our physician. No signs of a disturbance, no markings on the body. Our physician suggests this was an unfortunate

30

occurrence and concludes that it was his heart that failed him.'

My father's face appeared far older than I remembered – his time-worn lines, saggy skin and white hair. Decay will do that to a body, of course. I placed my hand to his ice-cold cheek and withdrew it as if it had burned me. Here lay the great man of the Court of the Sun Chamber, a man whose name travelled further than mine could ever hope to. Suddenly it didn't seem to matter so much. What precisely was the point in competing with the dead?

'Your brother, Marius, visited us,' the pontiff whispered.

'Did he?' I grunted. 'I didn't even know he was in Tryum.'

'He is not. After a few months living here, he decided he'd had enough. He came here, very briefly, to pay his respects. But he's since left the city.'

'I'm sure he has.'

'He had hoped to still be in your father's will, but there were only a few trinkets for him.'

'What can he expect?' I grunted. 'They hated each other.'

The priest's sad expression almost made me feel sorry for Marius. The man's sense of pity was beginning to become too much.

'They tried to heal things, so I understand. People change. Meanwhile,' he continued, 'you received the property in full. Your brother also said for us to wait for you to return before your father's full burial.'

'That was . . . kind of him.' I glanced over the shape of the body, then beneath the cloth. Though it wasn't always easy to tell after twenty days of death, there was no obviously large gut, nothing to suggest he had succumbed to the finer things in life such as overeating.

'Your people say it was definitely his heart?'

'You find this hard to believe?'

'He always kept in good shape, exercised regularly and ate well – he'd been like that all his life.'

'Who knows why the gods decide to take us,' the pontiff replied. 'His funeral will be in a few days, once we continue the rituals here to see his soul is at peace. The necessary arrangements and notifications have already been made.'

'Oh . . .' I fumbled around for a purse of money. 'How much should the donations be?'

The pontiff waved for me to relax. 'It has all been paid for by the administration of the Sun Chamber. You will be notified before his body is to be burned. We are reading the stars each evening, waiting for an auspicious alignment.'

'And then?'

'After that, once we allow his ashes to be collected, it will be another day or so before you may have them to place within the family mausoleum.'

'Thank you,' I replied. 'I'm staying at his – my – house, should you need to find me.'

It was reassuring that my father would receive the dignity bestowed upon his office, but now that I had seen his body, something did not sit right.

With a head full of sorrow, I walked back to my residence alone, speeding through the streets now, passing the bars and taverns with their oil lamps, past the youths clustering in alleyways, and through the emptying plaza in which wind-blown litter skittered across the flagstones.

And when I eventually arrived home, there was a visitor waiting for me.

Senator Veron

'I'm Senator Veron,' he said, rising from being draped across a couch. 'You might have heard of me.'

We gripped each other's forearms in the formal Detratan greeting. He looked only a few years older than me, forty summers to his name at the most, and rather young for a senator. Veron's bronzed skin and athletic figure were also not typical of those who spent most of their time in shaded rooms arguing politics, but I'm sure his good looks didn't do any harm come election time. We stood approximately the same height, and where my eyes were brown his were a startling sky blue. His long face was handsome in the classical way, though his hair was beginning to recede a little. His easy, confident manner disarmed me momentarily; that was, until the quality of his gold-trimmed cloak reminded me once again that he was a politician. His smile seemed well practised.

'So. The son returns.' Veron's voice was remarkably crisp, and I couldn't trace a hint of dialect. He stared at me with great intensity, trying to read my expression to see what I made of him. 'A Sun Chamber official who's both a Drakenfeld and easy on the eye,' he continued. 'I'll have to watch you if you go near the

Regallum district – politicians are naturally wary of handsome professionals like yourself. You tend to win over crowds and usurp us; which, to be fair, is exactly what any of us would do in your position.'

'There's not much danger of me heading there so long as everyone's behaving themselves,' I said. 'It's been weeks since I arrested a politician.'

'That's the spirit.' Veron slapped me on the shoulder before producing a leather scroll tube, which he'd been carrying in his bag. 'This is from the Court of the Sun Chamber. As senator for this district, it was sent to my address for me to place directly into your hands when you arrived. I'm guessing your people don't trust messengers.'

'It could have been that they wanted you to be present when I read it. Any idea what it's about?'

'Sadly I worship the wrong gods to be able to read a sealed scroll – I've asked Trymus often enough, but as far as founder gods go he's not been particularly helpful.' Veron indicated that I open it, and he turned to regard a fresco to grant me some privacy to read.

I broke the seal, opened up the tube and pulled out the letter.

Lucan Drakenfeld.

You will by now have reached Tryum, in Detrata. The Court of the Sun Chamber has now consulted on the issue of your father's sudden and sad death at some length and, for the foreseeable future, and given that there is no Officer in Tryum, we have deemed you suitable for the post.

Your work in Venyn has been commended and, by order of Commissioner Tibus, you are to inherit your father's seat in Tryum. Both King Licintius' office and the Senate are being informed presently. Direct notice will be sent to the Civil Cohorts, for what it is worth, but you may investigate incidents as you see fit unless we find something else that merits your attention.

May Polla offer you her blessings.
Sheriff Goul,
Deputy Administrator for Vispasian Royal Union West.

Tibus had ordered the move – high praise indeed, coming from one of four commissioners, a high rank in the Sun Chamber.

'Good news, I trust?' Veron said.

'I appear to have a new job.'

'My congratulations.' The senator placed his strong hand on my back once again.

'Please, where are my manners,' I said. 'You must take a drink with me.'

'I won't say no if you have any wine,' he replied.

I hastily called for Bellona to see if there was any around. She shuffled away bowing to rustle up some refreshments while I urged her yet again not to call me master.

'It's always wise to keep your servants in their place.' Senator Veron nodded to me as if he'd supplied me with some profound advice.

'I'm fairly informal when it comes to such things. I've never had a servant before. Besides, angry staff will often be the first to help guide a knife into a cruel master's back. I saw it happen often enough in Venyn City.'

'A wild and adventurous place, so they tell me. You must tell me of your time there. I thrive on tales of far-away cities. The Senate can be rather dull at times – especially once Senator Chastra gets into full flow.'

We took our seats on a curved settee overlooking the fountain in the garden, and sipped on watered wine and sweet snacks. The evening was humid; the smell of vegetation was pungent. In the distance were the sounds of the city, the constant low hum of a thousand voices. Lanterns and oil lamps surrounded us, casting a mellow light. I felt myself starting to relax.

'This food is remarkably good,' I breathed, gesturing for him to help himself to the snacks.

'Not for me,' Veron replied. 'I'm looking after my health.' He patted his stomach.

'Very wise,' I replied, but consumed two of them anyway. At the back of my mind was Leana's voice berating me.

'I knew your father, Calludian, reasonably well,' Veron said. 'I've not been in the Senate all that long, just a few years, but I see to the needs of citizens from this neighbourhood, so our paths crossed now and then. His death was a great shock to us all. He will be missed. The man knew a thing or two about the world, as well as where the good wines come from.' Veron paused, with a gentle smile on his face. 'I was there the day he caught Saludus, the priest murderer, after the king tasked the Sun Chamber to help find him. At the time the city was living in fear as body after body was left hanging in public places. People were talking about the vengeance of gods and all sorts of devilry. It turned out not to be so.'

Again, another reminder of his incredible deeds, making me feel once again inferior and in awe. 'I remember when I was young all the cases he worked on seemed to affect the city profoundly in one way or another.'

'That'll be your memory playing tricks on you. I'm sure it wasn't always like that – recently he was often buried in administration and all those annoying little concerns of the great unwashed. You'll start receiving them soon enough. I'm surprised the Sun Chamber puts up with it, reporting to royals as you do.'

'We get a lot of our funding through kind royal donations, as is tradition, though of course we own a lot of land, and make plenty of money to pay for ourselves.'

'Powerful indeed. Who keeps an eye on you lot then? What happens when one of your own officers misbehaves?' He was clearly amused at this notion.

'All I meant was that we don't need royals to give us large donations these days.'

'Clever. Less dependence on the royals.'

'Yes, but it means royals can tax their people far less, and we're responsible to the people of Vispasia every bit as much as any king or queen. Though a king could ask for our help, generally we judge for ourselves what may be for the good of Vispasia. It just so happens that royals, too, are interested in the same things we are. Peace and stability.'

'And profit,' Veron remarked, smiling to himself. 'It's all quite politicized.'

'Bureaucracy, more than anything,' I replied, but wanted to change the subject. 'I don't suppose you know what my father was working on, before he passed away?'

'I believe the last case he discussed was in exposing a rather nasty little daughter–father marriage,' Veron said.

'That sounds disturbing.'

'It was. Things got a lot worse when a lynch mob found out about them and burned down their house because they didn't want the gods cursing their community. Disgusting business.'

I searched for the right words, hoping for something more considered. 'What was he really like, in the months up to his death? I hadn't seen him for years. We wrote occasionally but it was all rather formal.'

Veron gazed at me with a shadow of sympathy. 'Full of life.' He stared into the fountain. 'A vibrant sort. He was a great observer of other people, so I often felt under scrutiny in his company. A conversation could be more like a board game. But when we became accustomed to one another we dined now and then at each other's houses, but he had his wits about him and rarely said too much. Me, on the other hand, once I get a cup of wine in my hand you'd do well to shut me up.'

'Full of life,' I repeated. 'An active man.'

'Quite the athlete in his youth, so he liked to tell me. Yes, he kept active. Though, it is worth saying that in his final months he lost a little of that colour.'

'Do you think he could have fallen ill?'

The senator weighed up the question in his mind, and I grew increasingly curious about his manner: the way he'd look around the house for distractions, or pick up ornaments and eye them in the light of a lantern.

'That isn't unlikely,' Veron said. 'He was quieter. He was seen out far less often — and you know how important it is in Tryum to be sociable. We all know each other here. Social circles keep us together — they help maintain some sense of order, as we all keep an eye on each other's affairs. So, yes, perhaps an illness could well have claimed him in the end.'

'The physician said it was his heart.'

'That sounds about right,' Veron agreed. 'We had a good team of people there that day, as well as folk from the Pollan temple. I'm not a medical man, but I can tell you're curious about his death. You think it suspicious, hence the questions.'

'I have a healthy suspicion of most things.'

'You'd make a good politician. But listen, let's not talk about such depressing matters, not on your first night back in Tryum. We should be welcoming you to the city, young man. I'm glad another Drakenfeld is here to maintain some sort of order. You've good blood in you.'

'Are the cohorts any good at policing the streets?'

'They are what they are,' Veron replied. 'They change person-nel regularly, they can be flaky and unreliable, they can bring their vendettas with them and cause more trouble than they're hired to prevent. I'd like to change them if I could. They're hardly cut from the same cloth as the mighty Sun Chamber.'

'Do they report to you directly now?'

'Yes, Licintius wanted more discipline, but not the military sort — tends to offend the hoi polloi when you have men with swords running about the place. Bad for morale. Besides, despite his friendship with Maxant, Licintius isn't a fan of the military. No, each senator can organize his own policing for the district these days, which works rather well — given how competitive we all are, no one likes to have a high crime rate on their watch.'

'Which is probably why you're glad another Sun Chamber officer has arrived.'

'That's not the only reason. Your father had many good wines, too, so I'm anxious to see they're not wasted.'

I laughed and took another moment to assess the man. He seemed capable of being honest enough to be charming, though one could never tell with politicians.

'Now, I'm hungry for news — I read briefs from time to time, but they lack clarity on these matters. I've heard about an end to campaigns abroad for Detrata's army. Are all the soldiers returning?'

Veron became animated. 'Yes, and what a relief! More than that, the return of General Maxant is nothing short of a triumph. He came back to the city a night or two ago and celebrations have been scheduled by King Licintius for tomorrow evening. While the city will have plenty of food and games, there will also be the affair in Optryx. It's almost like the heady days of the Detratan Empire two hundred years ago.'

'And look how that ended.'

'Peace came eventually.'

Once the Empire had dissolved . . . It was strange how people could speak of the past as if they had actually lived through it. 'You sound rather relieved about Maxant's return though.'

'I am,' Veron continued. 'Maxant's freed up a grain route from

Mauland. Shipments are already heading our way. We've wilting fields all over Detrata – many of the senators wondered how we would feed the lower districts. Not only has Maxant secured food, but he has secured a nation in the name of the Vispasian Royal Union, and Detrata gets priority over the food.'

'So, Maxant has finally defeated the Maulanders.'

'Mauland's king is now subject to Vispasian laws. It is said that Maxant defeated an army of one hundred thousand Maulanders with a force half that. Many of the defeated warriors and communities are being shipped back as slaves as we speak.'

'A rarity for the Union,' I said.

'Think of the labour!' Veron said. 'They're all rather pale-skinned and weak-looking, so they say. It does not appear to be a particularly sophisticated culture, up in that cool northern climate. A lack of sunlight will do that to you.'

The children of Tryum were often told stories about the violent citizens of Mauland – the Maulanders would get you if you didn't study hard, or eat your supper – so to hear that the primitive society had fallen to General Maxant was a stunning concept. 'Maxant is quite the hero, then. I look forward to the celebration.'

'I'll say,' Veron replied, smiling. 'King Licintius was almost weeping when he announced the news to the Senate. King Licintius and his old friend General Maxant have given Detrata a flavour of old times. The king needed it, too – there's a vicious streak of republicanism developing in the Senate, so this will ease his woes.'

'Are you of a republican persuasion?'

'I can be. I can be a royalist too. I find if one is more versatile in beliefs, one's career lasts longer, but there's a strong desire in the Senate to return to past glories.'

'Empire building?'

'Perhaps. I've not seen anything myself, but the rumours are strong that neighbouring royals are nervous. Maxant has taken an army to the edge of our world. If I were them, I'd be nervous too. Anyway, more immediately, we'll have street tables throughout the city with whatever food can be spared from the city's stores – which will do his popularity no harm.'

'If I was feeling suspicious I'd say such offerings would be to buy public favour – just like those old imperial days.'

Veron gave a hearty and warming laugh. 'With such cynicism you could easily have a place in the Senate alongside me.' He took another sip of his wine and contemplated the fountain for a little longer. His smile never left his lips.

We spoke of political matters a little longer, of the importance of Maxant's return from Mauland, of King Licintius' sister Lacanta, who was said to be eyeing up Maxant for marital union.

We said our goodbyes and he invited me to his large house on the side of Polyum that bordered Regallum, a phenomenally wealthy street – he took the trouble to tell me that fact.

It was getting late. Leana had not yet returned, but she was more than capable of looking after herself. I stood at the front gate of the house a little longer after Veron left, smelling the city air, gauging the mood of the streets, and watching those intoxicated with alcohol navigate their way along the pavements.

Finally it was time to head to bed. I'd chosen to convert one of the guest rooms into my own – my childhood room had long since been transformed into a pantry, and it didn't seem right to sleep in a dead man's bed. It was a quiet spot at the rear of the house, nearest the gardens, with a small window high up in one wall. A candle glowed beside my bed, and the rest of the room remained unfamiliar and in shadow. Lying there, contemplating the day's events, something did not sit well inside me. It was very probable that I was experiencing some form of denial about my father's death — he was, after all, a man who stirred up such odd and conflicting feelings — but it did not seem right that he was dead.

A Blade to the Throat

Leana shuffled towards the table as I was eating breakfast. Sunlight streamed across the spread of bread and spiced lamb; the early morning aromas from the garden were heady and vegetative, and the ripple of the fountain was soothing. The sun in this garden was always peculiarly intense. There were no high buildings nearby, and the roof was low, meaning that one could find a deep warmth in every corner at most hours of the day. Quite often the shadows of birds sitting on the roof could be seen around the edge of the fountain and, as a child, I had fun guessing – nearly always incorrectly – the species in question.

This was a much more pleasant set-up than the fish odours and curses of tradesmen that constantly afflicted my ground-floor apartment in Venyn City. In comparison I felt like a king.

'I didn't hear you come back last night.' I smiled as she struggled to sit on the nearby wicker chair in the shade. She was wearing just a white shirt and black breeches, none of her light armour, and she seemed unwilling to face the light.

I popped a piece of bread in my mouth and took a sip of water. 'Am I to take it from your rather unresponsive presence that you had a good night?'

She could barely meet my eyes. 'My apologies, Lucan. It is not in my nature to overindulge.'

'Nonsense, this is a new city for you. I expect you to have fun from time to time. One of us has to.'

'Your wine here in Tryum . . . Spirits save me, it is so strong.'

'The staff were always tight in Venyn City and they watered it down. Here you must suffer the consequences of fine hospitality.' It was amusing now to be especially cheerful and loud.

'What is our plan for today?' Leana gestured towards the bread and I nodded for her to help herself.

'There are a few affairs I must set straight before we do any-thing else. My father had rented offices towards Regallum, only a few streets away from the king's residence, so I need to check if they are still in the family name. But before that, I'm heading out to discover all the secrets of the city.'

'What do you mean?'

'I'm going to get my hair cut and have a shave.'

Leana gave me a blank look. I grinned, drank up my water, scooped up my cloak and headed out into the morning sun.

Human memory is a curious thing, about as reliable as a myth.

Often I would lie in my ground-floor apartment in Venyn City, reconstructing these dusty back lanes and plazas in my mind. The roads walked mentally were littered with echoes of emotions or events, but they seemed well beyond reach, a fading dream. Today my route was deliberately taken at a very slow pace, so that I might retrace my past and locate these places in my mind, but what could be gleaned from my observations was that friends had moved on, shops had closed down, and noth-ing was how it used to be. While I was busy outgrowing my home, it was busy moving on from me – and I was fine with that.

Tryum was firing up for the day and everyone moved about with purpose. Stone walls glowed in intense sunlight and already the heat was becoming uncomfortable. As the sun climbed higher, the streets thinned out and people ventured indoors, into cafes or brothels, standing under awnings or stepping into offices. My white shirt, grey doublet, black trousers and boots were too much for these temperatures.

The salon was located on a dusty street on the edge of Polyum, which faced the slightly poorer district of Tradum. It looked in good health: a freshly painted green sign bearing the name *Lillus*, with a stall jutting out from the front that sold fabrics of all colours. Someone was busy washing the flagstones outside. The walls were covered in the scratched reports of satisfied customers. I headed inside into the cool shade.

'Well then,' said the old man with a thick moustache and a balding head, as he turned from arguing with one of the water boys. His skin was a little lighter than Leana's. 'Well, well. Do my eyes deceive? Is this . . . ?'

'It is,' I said, stifling my laugh. I quickly glanced around and nodded to the two customers on the benches, and observed that behind them the faded frescoes of sporting heroes had not changed in the slightest. Light from the open-roofed hall passed through another doorway, and nearby there were several purple paper lanterns. In a back room, pine incense was burning.

'Lucan Drakenfeld, my boy!' He turned to his assistant on one of the chairs by the window. 'We have an honoured guest – a member of the renowned Sun Chamber!'

Lillus shuffled over to me and took my face in his palms. I bent down and saw the accumulated years in his dark face, though the creases came from smiles and not scowls. That was all I needed to know.

'Lucan, it is so good to see you,' Lillus breathed. 'So very good. The boy has become a healthy man.'

'You're looking well too, Lillus.'

He waved away my comment. 'Listen to this! I am an old man with not much left to give. But I try. I keep busy. But you – you have good skin, brown like a polished table. You look every bit like your mother's people of Locco, though it takes a skilled eye to match you up with them. Your eyes – dark, yes, but they dazzle me so! It is a good thing I have no wife, as I would keep her far away from you.'

'If you keep talking like that I'll start to believe your flattery. Anyway, are you telling me you're still not married?'

'Ha! Fonce, listen to him.' He turned to one of his younger staff members, who looked so similar to Lillus he could have been a son. 'Married indeed – no, I am still unattached and as charming to the ladies as ever. If I am lucky, many of them are charming in return.'

'You're a randy old goat,' I said grinning.

'Lucan, I am interested in simple pleasures, simple things. The ladies – they tell me much.'

'Then tell me, Lillus – as I've been away for many years – what do your ladies have to say about Tryum?'

'Always after information,' he whispered softly, and our conversation took on an entirely different mood. 'Come, we will head to the room at the back, where it is much cooler and no one can hear us speak.'

After the initial exchange of pleasantries, and catching up with family histories, we came to the subject of my father's death.

Lillus paused at this point to apply the shaving cream with a thick brush, licking it across my face with seriousness. I sat back in the same old chair I'd used as a child – though back then it had been with a board to raise me up. Despite a few rips in the upholstery, it had stood the test of time, much like Lillus himself. Up on the ceiling I noticed an elaborate latticework of spiders' webs, behind which drifted the blue smoke of incense. In the windowless room, shadows were chased into the nooks and crannies by the soft lantern light.

'I confess your presence has been somewhat expected.' Lillus was more focused. 'Your father recently asked me to pass on a piece of information when you returned. He would not say what it concerned and it seems to me more riddle than fact. But he said that you must revisit a childhood place, one which stored many memories. He also asked me to help you out should you ever need it – as if he needed to say so. Does this mean something to you?'

'It does,' I replied, not entirely convinced that it did.

'Then my work is done. Your father paid me well, you know, over the years – far more than he should have. It is a shame I did not see him for some time before his passing.'

'You always acquired such essential information for him.'

He waved his hand. 'People like to talk to their barber, do they not? I merely harvest the gossip. It was for him to sift through such words for that golden nugget of truth.'

He brought his razor to the edge of my jaw, and proceeded to make firm, precise strokes down my neck.

'Tonight is the big night,' he announced, then leaned in to whisper. 'The general returns from abroad; a success, so they say, and that will please the bloodthirsty. The city criers have been announcing a festival for many nights. King Licintius will be there, with his sister Lacanta, as well as the general and his family and so on. Men and women of the Senate will be there: Chastra, no doubt, close to the heart of operations – cynical as always. Veron, the man who governs your district, a man I haven't yet learned to trust. I hear tell that Senator Divran, ever since she lost her husband, has turned to dark ways, dark gods . . . magic. She will also be there.'

'Magic?' The razor scraped along my jawline again.

'Only rumours. I cannot vouch for them. But, yes, the wife of Senator Trero – a man of many dubious businesses – suspects her husband is being drawn into the dark arts by Divran, who is said to be the witch of the Senate. It is said she conducts strange rituals. She tries to raise the dead.' He paused and leaned in a little closer. 'Divran blames Lacanta for having driven her husband to suicide.'

'Is there anything in that?'

'Lacanta is an attractive lady, and has ways of charming people, and frustrating them also. I cannot say what went on between her and Divran's husband, but it is said he simply fell from a window by accident. Anyway, all of this magic talk, it is probably nothing more than a few dubious sacrifices and wishful thinking. It happens from time to time.'

'Who else is going tonight?'

'Most important people. You know how these things are. Maxant's success comes at the right time for the politicians. He has unlocked not only fresh labour, but more importantly a new grain supply.'

'Good news then.' I didn't let on that Senator Veron had visited last night. I wanted to hear what Lillus had to say, someone who was not a senator.

'An understatement,' Lillus whispered. 'The lower districts, Plutum and Barrantum, they are really starting to suffer. The first grain shipments arrive within the week. Maxant is not a slow man. No doubt he will hand out the first bowls of grain himself – the people's hero. It is said he could be lining himself up for a place in the Senate. I have heard many anxious voices. Politicians are under great strain. We were probably weeks away from food riots, though you would not hear such talk broadcast about the city. It is whispered, along the roadside in Polyum, Tradum and

Vellyum, that Maxant is asking for land for his veterans, too, but what land will remain for them? Sun-baked clay is not much use. That may cause trouble, should King Licintius not oblige – though I think he will. He is a very good and old friend of Maxant.'

'What are the senators' wives saying?'

'Or husbands – we have several female senators these days. Dalta's Rule.'

'Ah, thanks to the charming Queen of Dalta. She who owns such precious resources gets to have a say in the laws of Vispasia.'

'Behind the scenes, there is pressure to reward hard-working impoverished families with land further afield. Detrata has prospered and now we are too big – that has led to rumours that the Senate wishes to expand our borders somehow. The king resists – he knows the value of Vispasia. New aqueducts are nearing completion to bring water, despite the old ones in the city being broken in places. There is demand for bigger projects, though King Licintius is not of a mind to spend money on such things, and nor is his sister, for that will mean more taxation – they had been unpopular enough.'

'How old is she now?'

'Twenty-four summers, I believe, and an incredibly well-read woman, so they say. She is more beautiful than one can imagine, growing the wonderful curves of womanhood. That is how the statues are carved, but apparently she does look like them.'

'I would've thought a man like Licintius would have used her to seal some commercial pact with another nation, especially if food was scarce. It's not unlike a king to do that, no matter how abhorrent for the lady.'

'That's true. As for Lacanta – she . . . she is not well controlled, it is fair to say.'

'Is that a problem?' I asked. 'Surely she has her own will?'

'Yes. But her status requires that her life is not her own, as does the king's status. Lacanta likes the company of many other men and women, so the rumours go. One by one, she steals their hearts and then their minds. Not inherently a bad thing, of course, but it causes tensions where there should be as few as possible. Licintius cannot stop her, though I suspect he doesn't really care, as he is making a good job of causing scandal himself ever since he became a patron of the theatre.'

'That would explain the number of street productions I've seen.'

'What's more, he has permitted the formation of the Guild of Prostitutes. Such attitudes are frowned upon, though I like it myself.'

'No bad thing that they have some organization and protection,' I replied, remembering how unsafe life could be for the oldest trade.

'Many in the Senate disapprove. It is easy to forget that this is still a conservative city, full of conservative morals. And with Licintius bringing in labour from abroad to build the aqueducts and complete his temples — at the expense of the poor here, I should add — and with Lacanta busily corrupting marriage after marriage . . . well, it is simple to see why many wish to see the royal brother and sister no longer in such a powerful position. There is talk of Maxant being shoehorned in as a republican leader, someone who can begin campaigns abroad, but will the people support a military dictator? Who can tell? Besides, as I say, Maxant and Licintius are old, old friends.'

'We live in complex times, old friend,' I said.

'We do. And it makes life all the more interesting, I find.'

Lillus finished his shave and threw a hot towel across my face then commenced to trim my hair. For a little while longer he talked of the arts, of scandalous affairs, of suspected orgies, of missing people, of immigration and nationalism, and of the resurgence of gangs ever since Licintius inherited the throne – though he claimed the latter was due to senators using whatever methods they could to influence their own neighbourhoods.

A visit to Lillus' was never dull but, more importantly, never without gain. One did not pay merely for a haircut – the costs included information about the fabric of the city. My years away from the city no longer seemed important: my studies of contemporary Tryum were complete.

'Now, here is the handsome boy I remember,' Lillus announced, stepping back and offering me a small mirror to look at myself. He'd done a wonderful job – my hair was only a fraction shorter, but far neater, and my skin felt incredibly refreshed after the shave.

'Not so much a boy any more,' I said. 'My bones ache a little more each day.'

'Nonsense. They ached when you were a boy, too – you just cared less.'

'Thanks, Lillus.'

'I've missed the Drakenfeld smile, young Lucan,' Lillus called after me. 'Your father's tended to fade towards the end.'

'How so?'

'He would never speak of it. But there was a sadness in his eyes. After knowing him for so long, I could tell these things.'

'You've no idea what could have caused it?'

Lillus shook his head. 'Not even I could find that out.'

I paid him, bid farewell to the other members of staff, and headed through the front door into the intense heat, shading my eyes from the sun.

Lillus' conversation still echoed in my mind. I headed home immediately, to investigate the childhood places that my father had mysteriously discussed with him. Those words already felt like some premonition, a vague confirmation of my suspicions that all was not as it appeared.

There were only a handful of areas to search around the house. The pantry that was once my old room was the likely place. There, I knew of one large and loose tile behind which I used to hide my childhood delights. It was surprising that my father would have remembered this place at all.

With a spoon I levered up the black tile in the furthest corner of the room, underneath the small window that overlooked the garden. Sitting down on the floor, I moved the tile to one side and reached down into the gap. I drew out a small wooden box and pressed back the lid into the past.

'What have you there?' Leana stood in the doorway, leaning on the frame with her arms folded.

'Your head is clear?'

'Let us not discuss that. What is it?'

I showed her the box and invited her down next to me. 'Only me and my father knew this was here.'

'You said he hardly knew anything about your childhood.'

'It seems he remembered something at least.' Inside the box were small items from when I was young, including dice and a wooden dagger. I drew out a small figure made from clay. 'I last played with this when I was no more than five or six years old. He gave it to me as a present one birthday, but when I was older I just kept it safe. Wait . . .' There was a piece of paper under the doll, which I flipped out with my finger. Underneath that was a key.

'What does it say?' Leana asked.

I unfolded the thick yellow papers and read the script out loud.

Lucan,

You will most likely find this under less than happy circumstances. Here is a key and contract to the rented office near Regallum. The landlord will probably say that the contract is void, but you can see that here it meets the legal conditions of the city. He will claim I owe him far more money than is true, though in truth there is still — regretfully — a debt to be paid. I am also convinced that he has been sending gang members from Plutum or Barrantum to this house in an attempt to threaten me.

Things have not worked out as I would have liked.

But should anything happen, please know that I am sad for how we parted. Do with this key as you will, and make of me what you will.

Your father, Calludian.

The second page of the letter was in fact the rental deeds to his offices.

'It's like he speaks to you from another world,' Leana observed casually.

'It suggests that he knew he was going to die, doesn't it?' I said. 'It is as if he made preparations for my coming home in the event of his death, but he couldn't quite bring himself to admit it. He always was a proud man.'

'You are becoming convinced he was murdered.'

'I feel as though he was. Just look at what he's saying — "a debt to be paid".'

'Some kind of money trouble?'

'Unlikely. I mean, look at this place. This is a house in Polyum. He was renting offices for his work with the Sun Chamber, but . . .'

'Had he ever been that way in the past?'

'No, never. Well, I think — and this is a hazy memory at best — that he and my mother argued over his ways with women. He spent a lot of money on women and drink at one point, but that was a quarter of a century ago, when he was a younger man. But she never spoke ill of him to me when he'd gone, and their conversations were kept away from my ears. He should have no need for money troubles now.'

'No one needs to be in money trouble,' Leana said. 'It can happen to the best of us.'

My father's offices were already unlocked when we arrived. The shabby door pushed back with ease; beyond it lay musky darkness and an aroma that could only be generated by old legal texts. The place was almost empty, as if someone had begun to move out. There was a door to one side and a bookcase that had seen long service. Dust motes floated notably near the arched window. The view from it was over a bustling street market. Across the way was a small temple, though I couldn't see which god or goddess it glorified.

Suddenly, people started to come down the stairs. Leana placed a hand to her short sword, though I waved for her to be cautious. Loud voices suggested that, whoever was coming, they weren't bothered about being heard. One of them knocked the door back with his buttocks, and cursed as he dropped one end of a large trunk.

'Who are you?' I called out.

'What's it to you?' The man was in his forties; he was a foot shorter than me, with wide shoulders that looked out of place on his otherwise lean body. Skin sagged down his face, which was burnt by the sun. His shabby brown tunic was a size too big for him. The other man, just behind, was actually much younger, clearly the man's subordinate.

'My name is Lucan Drakenfeld,' I declared. 'My father rented this office and I've come to inspect it.'

'Aye, Drakenfeld,' he spat. 'Never paid his bloody rent.'

'It was all paid for.' I produced the contract and waved it in his direction, but he made no move to read it.

'Master said otherwise. Did well not to chuck him out earlier.'

I approached the trunk that the two had been carrying and opened it. Leather-bound legal texts were piled within. 'Where exactly were you taking these?'

'Out.' The man scratched his crotch and spat on the floor. 'To the master. He can deal with 'em.'

'Was this everything?'

'Nah, we took another trunk yesterday evening.'

'I want it sent back. Who's your master?'

The man was starting to look thoroughly annoyed, as if I'd just ruined his day. 'We work for an intermediate, so we hardly ever see him — chief does all that. Owns a hundred properties and only cares that he gets his money each month.'

I wrote down the location of my house and handed it to him. 'This is where I live. If your master wants to come for dinner to talk about this, he's more than welcome.'

'You rich types, you do everything in dinners, don't you?' He waved away the paper. 'I suppose you'll want these texts keeping here then.'

'If you could just move—'

'Cock off,' he grunted. 'I ain't lugging this back upstairs. Someone can sort it out later.' Wiping his hands on his tunic, he and his colleague sauntered to the door and exited into the busy street.

I opened the trunk and lifted out one brown tome, a fine collection of legal essays by a long-deceased philosopher, and placed it on the desk. The other books here seemed much the same, though each one a little outdated.

Once again, I wondered how my father, a man rarely short of coin, could have become so poor that he struggled to pay the rent on his offices.

I was in no mood to enjoy the festivities that night. My mind had too much to process. Leana did not head out into the city either, despite my urges for her to find out what was going on during the grand feast organized by King Licintius. But she declined. Though she would never say it outright, I suspect she felt a little guilty for her hangover this morning.

Instead we ate in a companionable silence out in the gardens while we watched the sun fall behind the rooftop, before eventually heading inside to our separate rooms. There, I concentrated hard on the conversations that my parents had within these walls, trying to discern something about the past that might inform the present. My parents didn't really have arguments – they were both too intelligent, and instead they might have reasoned debates over issues. However, my father could be just as domineering over her as he was over his children. As an adult, I never had the chance to understand him completely – having somewhat avoided that challenge for the most part. Putting a continent between us would do that. Had he been someone who lived recklessly though? It seemed hard to match up, though perhaps deep down I wanted to remember him in death as a good and honest person.

Despite the celebrations of the city, which could be heard loud and clear at this hour, and despite the new mystery of my father's debts, I managed to drift off into a heavy sleep.

A banging on the main door woke me up.

The noise was followed by Bellona calling my name from the other side of the house. I peered out of the window, but could only ascertain that it was the middle of the night. However, it sounded like the festivities were still ongoing.

I dressed hastily and ran along the corridor, almost slipping on the slick tiles. Bellona directed me towards the open door. Just outside, on the step, stood several cloaked men. One of them was carrying a torch, the flames casting a sinister glow on their faces. It was obvious that there was a sense of urgency and restlessness about them, something clear even in this dim light.

'We wish to speak to Lucan Drakenfeld,' one man declared, a thickset individual with a neat beard. He looked at me with intense eyes, and he wore the silver sash of the Civil Cohorts – the citizen police of Tryum – across his shoulder.

'That's me.'

They all seemed hesitant now they knew my name, wondering who should speak next.

'I'm . . . My name is Constable Farrum,' he eventually said, affecting a much calmer and crisper accent. 'From the cohort – Civil Cohorts. As Officer of the Sun Chamber, your, uh, presence is required. It's urgent.' He sounded like an actor forgetting his lines.

'Well, Constable Farrum, what's happened?' I asked.

'Someone's dead,' he said.

'OK,' I replied, 'so where is the body?' Murders occurred all the time, of course, but it wasn't often that a murder required so many people to disturb me like this in the middle of the night.

'Optryx.'

'A killing in King Licintius' residence?' I asked.

'Yeah and we ain't allowed into those halls,' Farrum said. 'The likes of us don't get told the day's password. We were urged to get you. This means I'll get beatings if we don't do that, so I'd appreciate it if you hurried along. Sir.'

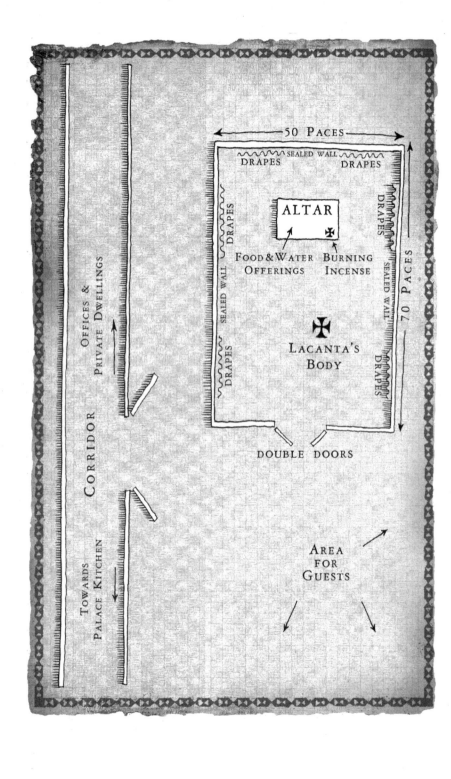

The Locked-Temple Murder

The men from the Civil Cohorts gave Leana a brief look of suspicion and surprise when she stepped outside with me, but she shrugged it off, as she always did. We were both armed, both wearing cloaks to keep off the chill, though I made certain my golden brooch was in plain view. We were marched through the backstreets of Tryum, which were still full of energy: drunken crowds in masks flowing from place to place; home-made shrines and private ceremonies under oil lamps; exuberant, torchlit fan-dances.

Soon we entered the relative calm of the Regallum district, where soldiers from the King's Legion had been stationed along major junctions, though a few were hurrying past in pairs — and in haste. Their orders echoed sharply around the street, and a few citizens were being stopped and roughly searched in the shadows.

Heroic statues stood tall, their expressions lost to the night. Pillars defined the nearby buildings; there were no cheap stores lining the streets here, no traders harassing passers-by to buy their dubious wares.

The men from the Civil Cohorts were joined silently by some of the King's Legion, who guided us along a road that led behind

Optryx, an immense, intimidating building without much light. We banked upwards towards the royal residence; from here in daytime, it would have been possible to look down over most of the city. Only a couple of temples were positioned on higher ground than this, to be closer to the gods.

The cohort was halted at the door. Eventually, after some fuss and security checks, Leana and I were guided into one of the most impressive buildings I had ever seen in my life – and I had seen a few.

As a child I often wondered what it would be like to live in Optryx. Back in those days I imagined it to be simply sumptuous, though perhaps with wild animals and spirits gallivanting through the hallways; in my version of this place there was a constant stream of performers, jugglers, singers and acrobats. There would have been a thousand soldiers standing in polished golden armour patrolling the rooms. Though it was the whimsical fantasy of a boy, I never imagined I'd be visiting the place as a grown man for work.

Domed ceilings, each with intricate hollow panels, towered into the shadows some fifty or sixty feet above my head. Cressets burned from lushly decorated walls, candles were perched on central columns; their light cast down on the multicoloured mosaic floors and on thick, pink marble columns. Every other wall was painted with rich frescoes of the heavenly plains of existence – a logical trend in the arts, of which I approved – as well as gods, kings and emperors of the past. The colours used here were well beyond the everyday palette, and would have cost a small fortune. Here was a bold statement of power and wealth indeed. The rooms through which we were taken – each one equally as large as the predecessor – forcefully humbled whoever walked through them.

My pulse quickened as we passed through gold-plated double doors and into a room packed full of people. It was obvious that this was no longer a celebration – it seemed more like a wake for the dead. People muttered to themselves in small groups, seated on the floor, their expressions glum or exasperated. At regular intervals along the walls, and in larger numbers by the door, stood soldiers in bright armour. Two of them gestured with their spears for me to pass through the doors. One of them paused as Leana followed, but I stressed that she was my assistant, and she was permitted soon enough.

Senator Veron veered towards me wearing his finest red robes of state, which contained incredible gold details and religious motifs. Stepping carefully over more people sitting on the marble floor, or simply shoving through clusters of those who were still standing, he arrived somewhat shaken.

'Drakenfeld, I'm glad you've made it.' We shook, gripping each other's forearms.

'You were the one who sent for me?'

'I certainly was. I thought you might be available to cast some light on the matter. This isn't one for the lawyers either – at least, not yet. I only hope you're half as good as your father.' Close up, I could see that he was clothed splendidly in a fine, crimson tunic, and both his belt and boots seemed to be of sublime craftsmanship. His expression was far more serious than that of the light-hearted senator who'd visited my house.

We turned to face the room. 'What's the situation?' I whispered, suddenly aware of the volume of people around us. 'All I've heard is that there's been a death.'

'I'll say. This way.' Veron steered me through the glum faces of the guests. Nearby the guards were closing the door, as if to make sure no one could escape.

'Can you tell me anything else about the situation?' I asked.

'Best if I showed you,' Veron said turning back.

For some time we walked through the throng — a good few hundred, all in all, each in their most opulent clothing. Platters of food were discarded on side tables, having been pillaged long ago. A low-level muttering had replaced lively chatter; more than once we stepped through deep silences as conversations suddenly paused at our approach. Along the walls, bright banners of Detrata, each one bearing either the image of the double-headed falcon or the cross of the founding gods, hung down from an impressive height.

Towards the end stood two copper-coated statues of Trymus in different dynamic poses, and we passed between them and into a small corridor with rooms branching off either side. The aesthetics remained the same: continuing the bright and bold displays of wealth, the marble, the gold leaf, and the over-the-top artistic statements.

Then before us stood a structure set within a large hall. It was marked by a much larger set of doors, above which stood a stone carving of the god Trymus — wild eyes and big beard. A solid wall extended for some way on either side, and there were no paintings on this — merely the pure unadorned limestone. Soldiers and a few high-ranking officials were loitering here — the crowds had been kept well away.

'This is a private temple of Trymus,' Veron informed me. 'Maxant's ceremony was to be held here, they were due to enter the temple at midnight, but the temple had been locked. The door had to be broken down by Maxant's soldiers so that they could get in. And when they did . . .'

I frowned. 'Did they not have a key?'

'They didn't expect it to be locked. They tried to fetch someone to get another one, but they were running out of time. It was General Maxant's privilege to open the door at midnight — as part of his triumph, so that he could receive the blessings of Trymus and wear Trymus' mask for the evening – and his men urged him to get in there before the midnight deadline passed and the stars moved out of alignment. The ceremony loses its essence and Trymus may not have been able to receive contact. Besides, the sooner he did, the sooner we could all get drunk. A few of Maxant's soldiers then tried to knock the door down. It took four of them a good while to prise it open. And when they did . . .'

Veron nodded to the brutish-looking guard who cautiously pushed the door open for us. The senator led the way; Leana and I followed him inside.

In the centre of the temple, laid on the floor, was a woman's body covered in blood.

'This is Lacanta,' Veron whispered. 'The king's only sister, second in line to the throne – and now dead, Trymus help us all.'

It was dark in the temple, so I asked for torches to be brought closer, and eventually two soldiers obliged.

Lacanta lay on her side, on one arm, with her other extended out to one side at a right angle to her body. Her face had been beaten, and was bloody and bruised, but bad as those wounds were, they were not what had killed her: there was an unmistakable deep wound around her neck that showed where her throat had been cut.

'This is horrific,' I said, louder than intended.

She had been wearing a brilliant blue dress, with small gemstones around the hem, and this was stained with her blood, as were the long waves of her dark-blonde hair. She was a voluptuous woman, someone who indulged in the pleasures of life from the look of her, and her jawline was very well defined. Jewels and gold rings remained on her wrists and ankles, so this did not look like a robbery, though one could never be certain.

'And none of her things have been taken?'

'Not that we're aware of.'

'Has a weapon been found?'

Veron shook his head.

'Are you sure no one has taken one away for safe keeping?'

'The room is exactly as we found it.'

'Who's we?'

'At first Maxant's soldiers and himself. A few senators piled in pretty soon after, but not as many people as you'd think. Twenty at most. No one has touched a thing, and most of those twenty were ushered out by the soldiers who then dealt with the panic throughout the rest of the building. Hysteria tends to build quite quickly.'

I looked at the body and noted how her clothing seemed to have been pulled out of place. 'Does anyone think she has been sexually tampered with, in any way?' I asked somewhat hesitantly.

'I'll get permission to make such enquiries,' Veron said.

I nodded. 'I'd appreciate it if the king's physician – if he has one – could look over her, once she's been cleaned up. I'd like his or her opinion for it might tell us more about what happened here, and the type of murderer we are dealing with, if she had taken poison, or whether or not she's been planted here like this, after being killed elsewhere.'

'Planted?'

'It's distinctly possible.'

Though it seemed unlikely. There was blood here, of course, but if she had been planted, there must have been blood somewhere else outside the temple. I put this to Veron and he sent one of the soldiers to clear the area even further, so we might assess the scene better.

I moved around to her outstretched arm so that I might get a better look at her skin. It had not yet begun to turn purple, though her hands possessed a touch of blue. I took the liberty of trying to move her arm, to check that stiffness had indeed not yet set in, which put the time of death well within three or four hours, though it was impossible to tell when exactly. These things differed between people and climate.

'What else can you tell me about the scene, when she was first discovered?' I asked. 'Just the facts.'

'The temple had been locked,' Veron continued. 'When we came in, it was said there was a key in the lock on the inside There's no other way in or out of this place, except through those doors.'

'No one saw anything?'

'No. Waiting on the other side were hundreds of guests, who'd been standing there for about an hour before the room was opened in the climax of the ceremony. Not one of them saw anyone come in or out.'

'I may need a few moments.' I made a quick inspection around the room and asked for Leana to do the same, inside and out. As we did, a few officials and senators came to observe what we were doing. I felt their gaze upon me, and wished they would go away so we could concentrate.

The temple was at least fifty paces wide, austere for a place of worship perhaps, and in stark contrast to the rest of the building we had just experienced. The flagstones were all made from white and blue marble, and seemed secure enough – I could perceive no trapdoors, no holes. The walls were composed of thick limestone. Some were covered by rich, beautiful red drapes, and I peeled them back in case there was another door – but there was nothing. I took the hilt of my blade and bashed it against the fat blocks like a hammer, but along all sides both high and low the sounds were as I expected. I moved over to the damaged door to see that the heavy iron key was indeed still on the inside.

Outside, however, there was no sign of blood on the floor or walls.

There were no windows here, no open roof. The only light came from candles and paper lanterns – of which there were many. Several votive offerings of food and cups of water lay on an altar and incense was burning. To one side lay the mask of Trymus, a garish, white and purple chequered object with gold trim.

'Maxant was to wear that for his triumph,' Veron commented when I paused by it. He added dryly: 'Soldiers aren't known for their sense of fashion.'

'Who lit the incense?' I asked, examining the smoke. Gentle blue wisps carried the deep woody aroma around the temple. Several small, unlit pyramids stood to one side. 'It's been burning for some time now.'

No one seemed to know the answer to my question. I inhaled the smoke, noting that it was the same kind of sandalwood that could be found in any temple in Vispasia.

'It must have been like that when everyone entered,' I continued. 'This incident occurred around an hour or so ago, it seems, and may I confirm that no one had come in for some time beforehand?'

Veron consulted with one of the soldiers from the King's Legion, who stood resplendent in his purple robes and polished armour. 'Not even so much as a pontiff,' he confirmed. 'As I say, none of the guests saw anything.'

'I have many more questions, but let me summarize to be clear: around midnight, the king's sister Lacanta was found with her throat cut. The weapon is not here. None of her jewellery has been removed and she has – I will assume for now – not been tampered with. The temple was locked and sealed, and the key left in the door, on the inside. There's no other way into the temple unless one was a god; no way out, apart from through those doors.' I pointed towards them. 'There is no blood outside that we have seen thus far and, finally, it appears that whoever was in here with her lit incense at the altar of Trymus.'

Leana moved in closer. 'All of this on the night of a big cele-bration.'

'Maybe the killer wanted to scare the guests,' Veron offered.

'Perhaps, though there are more subtle ways of scaring people.'

'The killer might worship Trymus.' Leana indicated the statue and offerings.

'Another possibility – it's a rather morbid sacrifice, if it is one. It's not uncommon for his temples to receive blood donations, though it is usually from oxen, goat or chickens. How long do you think Lacanta has been dead?'

Veron moved to stand next to us. 'One of the soldiers claimed her body was still warm when we found it, though it is a hot night and this temple rarely gets cold. Obviously it's colder now and she's becoming fixed in place by Malax in his Underworld.'

'The gods don't hang about. We're going to have to get state-ments from as many people as possible,' I said.

'I wouldn't have thought that will be a problem,' Veron replied.

'Who had access to the key?'

'There are a few copies kept in the back offices, copies are kept for every lock in the building. Though it's a private temple, Trymus grants access to all. This section of Optryx isn't any-where near as secure as the other side, where the king resides.'

I made a note to ask the temple's pontiff about copies. 'Where's King Licintius? I take it he's aware of this?'

Veron gave a sad laugh. 'Poor Licintius followed the soldiers into the room when they found her. He fled to his private quar-ters in an immediate rage. I've never seen him so angry. General Maxant first sent his soldiers to close all the doors in Optryx and to stop people leaving, and then went up to join the king. I don't think any of the soldiers have the nerve to approach him just yet – in his mood, he might well turn them into eunuchs.'

'So this is Calludian's son,' came another voice. A small, hunched old man shuffled towards me, pushing past the guards on the door with a scowl on his cleanly shaven face. Thin wisps of hair clung to his sweaty head, and he used a stick to prop himself up as he walked. He gave me a look of utter contempt. 'I never did like the Sun Chamber. Ideas above your station, if you ask me. No one votes for you.'

'It's a pleasure to meet you, sir,' I offered. 'Please, don't come too close to the body, you might contaminate the scene.'

'See what I mean?' the man scoffed to Veron. 'Ideas above his station in life.'

Veron looked apologetic. 'This is Senator Chastra. Senator, this is Lucan Drakenfeld, Officer of the Sun Chamber.'

'I've heard all about him and his dark bodyguard,' Chastra muttered, examining Leana with his bright green eyes and a sneer on his face. His mind was still active, even if his body wasn't up to much. He turned to face me. 'A woman, too. That must make you feel quite effeminate.'

'If you're keen to prove your masculinity, you could always challenge her to a fight.'

Veron placed his face in his palms at my reply. Leana remained impassive.

'I wouldn't want to dirty myself with foreigners,' Chastra replied. 'Besides, the only fighting I do is with my words.'

'He certainly does,' agreed Veron. 'You should hear him in the Senate – he still gives a rather devastating speech on occasion.'

'Senator Chastra,' I said turning to face him. 'Presumably you're not here to dazzle us with your charm. You are a man of words so what have you to offer about this incident?'

'All I have to say on the matter is that it's unlikely you'll find the killer. This one was struck down by the gods. Struck down for living an immoral life. A murder in a place like this brings bad omens to the city.'

'Is that so?' I asked.

'Look around you. Solid walls and a sealed door. Struck down by the gods. I'll be damned if I can work it out.'

'That's why you're not in the Sun Chamber,' I replied, noting a rare smile on Leana's face as she continued to examine the temple.

'If it isn't the gods, maybe Senator Divran is right with mutterings of magic. But I'll wager some divine power was at work.'

'Did you see Lacanta at all tonight?' I asked.

'Of course,' Chastra spluttered. 'We all did. Earlier this evening she was mingling with her brother and General Maxant, talking to Veron, me, half a dozen other senators. In fact, some of us saw her – and were conversing with her – no more than a few moments before the temple doors were opened. A matter of minutes.'

'Ridiculous, if that's what you claim,' Veron declared. 'People were standing just outside the door as part of the celebrations for the better part of a whole hour. Dozens would have seen her killer leaving the room if the murder was so soon after you saw her.'

'You might think it impossible,' Chastra said more calmly, 'but I saw what I saw.'

Not impossible, I reassured myself – just baffling.

Impressed by the clarity of his recollection, I listened to what the old senator had to say, and began to patch together a narrative timeline of the evening.

As was clear, Licintius had been holding a huge celebration for

General Maxant and his conquests. The two of them were practically inseparable all evening, the king proud of what was happening to his nation, bringing it more prestige and power within the Vispasian Royal Union. Lacanta had been with them for a short while, before going on to blend in with the crowd, regaling people with her tales, using her charm on many of the male senators in front of their own wives. She was, by all accounts, not only rich and alluring – but beautiful, too, a powerful combination of traits, yet her antics, getting thrills from playing mind games, seemed at odds with the other aspects of her personality.

Veron commented that perhaps it was a way to feel vaguely human in her position, but Chastra scowled at him for such naivety. 'She was a manipulative bitch, plain and simple. Her brother's no better.' He waved down Veron's protests. 'No, I'm too old to care for the consequences of what I say, and I have little time for royals, but I am not surprised in the least that she ended up this way.' He gestured to her corpse with his free hand, his other firmly on his cane for support. 'The gods will punish the wicked.'

I noticed the derogatory way the old man spoke about women, his patriarchal and archaic attitude if they did not conform to his beliefs of how they should behave.

Chastra's account of events continued. There had been small theatrical productions all evening, improvised shows in alcoves. Many of the senators had apparently grumbled at having to share this grand event with mere thespians, who then had the audacity to try to talk to guests who were far above them in social ranking.

'So there were a lot of people from all walks of life in the building,' I offered. 'People who would not normally be permitted.'

'Everyone had been given the password,' Veron said. 'Security had to be relaxed tonight, but usually there's a new password each day, known only to a select few.'

'We had many different types of people here, many of whom could wield a blade to cut a throat. Even a senator could do that. Even one as old as you.'

'What are you suggesting?' Chastra spluttered. A part of me enjoyed his enraged expression. 'I have committed no murder. Such crimes are for the young and ambitious.'

'You said it was the gods a moment ago,' I said. 'Now, I'd like the soldiers present to take details and accounts of people's movements this evening.'

Chastra's face reddened as he glared at me. 'This is outrageous. A god of some sort has clearly seen to it that this woman's life was not to be. I am a senator—'

'And a potential suspect in a murder investigation,' I reminded him. 'Of course, your reluctance to conform to protocol will be noted.'

Names and addresses were taken from those who were still here, which I would later match against the guest list I'd asked for. I requested that those soldiers in the King's Legion who could write put down any useful information. Those who could not write, I asked to continue searching the building. Eventually, people grew tired and protests came from the heads of powerful families to be allowed to go home.

I didn't want people leaving immediately, not when things were fresh in their memory, though I did not mind if anyone came to me later with information. Faces or snippets of conversation could crystallize in the mind days, even weeks after a crime, and still prove to be useful. Afterwards, my details were circulated to anyone in a position of authority in the room.

People could not be kept on site for much longer, despite my efforts, and the sun soon began to rise on a new day. When the guests commenced their exodus, I returned once again to the outer doors of the temple of Trymus. Leana was still there, sketching out the inside on a piece of parchment.

'I am convinced it is sealed,' she said. 'No way in. No way out. Apart from that battered door.'

'You would have thought we'd have a few days to relax before being thrown straight into a murder investigation,' I remarked, staring at the temple door.

The face of Trymus looked down upon me, his severe expression somehow appropriate for the mood.

'What does Trymus even stand for?' Leana asked. 'I never can understand why there are so many gods. You people have a fixation with them.'

'Trymus and his wife, Festonia, built Tryum. They are the god and goddess of war, among other things. He made himself king and defended the original settlement against waves of strange invaders. Apparently during the Detratan Empire one couldn't move for his temples. He's seen as a blessing in wartime – and for agriculture. No doubt in times of food shortages, like now, people make as many offerings as they can so that he'll heal the crops.'

'It does not seem to have done much good,' Leana remarked.

I eventually came to an agreement with some of the senators that we would return to Optryx later, after everyone had rested. If the killer was in the building, the soldiers stated in no uncertain terms that they would find them – though given the amount of skills he or she might possess, I doubted that. If the killer had indeed escaped, they were likely to be far from Optryx by now.

As we were about to leave, Veron informed me that he had arranged, with the administrative staff of the residence, for me to be granted a meeting with King Licintius later in the day.

What would my father have thought about all of this? Would he, too, be making the same decisions?

The matter needed to be resolved as quickly as possible – it was a chance to prove myself to the people of Tryum.

First Steps

Though the remainder of the night was humid, I slept peacefully enough, and dreamt of falcons soaring over my house in a most unnatural manner.

After waking, I was prompted to make an offering to the small shrine to Polla, which my father had kept in immaculate condition. There, in the corner of the open hallway, with a cool breeze passing across my back, I muttered the purifications in an attempt to clear my mind, channel some of her essence, and to think logically.

How had Polla coped in a crisis? When she had been alive all those centuries ago, before she had become a goddess and assumed a position of power, she had been a remarkable lady, living through times of deep religious and political strife, when women were treated abysmally by their societies, and never failing in her quest to understand the world better, to fathom her position within the universe. Praying to such a figure each morning was always inspiring.

Bellona provided a hearty breakfast: despite the events of the previous night I was famished, and devoured the minced pork and flatbreads. Leana had been up for a little while and joined me just as I was finishing. She had been to the Forum to see what people were saying of the murder, but it seemed no one had even heard the news yet. Or if they had, they were too afraid to talk about it.

After breakfast, I took a moment to walk around the house trying to familiarize myself with my past once again — it was an uncomfortable process because in some ways I didn't like to be reminded of the person I had once been. The small details were fascinating: indentations in chairs that had come from years of sitting; the well-worn wooden surfaces on the sides of tables. The echoes of my father lived on in these areas of wear and tear.

Also, I noticed that an item had gone missing from a table in my father's bedroom. There was a square within the dust that indicated something had stood there once, but had been taken away. Perhaps a few weeks ago, since some dust had settled in its place. Was it significant in any way?

While Leana worked through some martial exercises in her room, in my study I looked at the sketch she had made in the temple on the night, examining the structure and dimensions, where the shrine was located, where the body of poor Lacanta had lain, and where the doors stood firmly barring entry to the chamber.

So Lacanta had been spotted moments before she had been found dead. That meant, in five or ten minutes, someone had managed to break her away from the celebrations in the main room, steer her into the temple, and kill her, before going back outside. But the celebrations were at their height and, as Veron pointed out, at that point those temple doors would have been watched by guests right up until the moment General Maxant entered to don Trymus' mask. What's more, the door was locked on the inside and murderers do not just vanish into the air.

Who had one of the keys to the temple?

Tracking Lacanta's final moments last night was going to be crucial. It was essential to find out who she had spoken to in the evening, who was nearby, who might have been following her, whether or not there were any strange occurrences. Perhaps the witness statements would prove fruitful. It would require a good day or so ploughing through their observations — that is if the soldiers could be trusted to record a reliable account.

Also, I needed to get a better idea of who would want Lacanta murdered, though that would not be an easy task. By Lillus' account at his barber's shop, a concise summary of rumours, she was both popular and despised, depending on whether or not one was the recipient of her alluring gestures.

Conscious not to be late for my appointment with King Licintius, I washed, changed and made to head out into the morning sun. But before I did I asked a favour of Leana: to see if the people of the city were talking. So often a lead had come off the back of local gossip that turned out to be more than just idle chatter. It was also useful for Leana to begin exploring the more marginal parts of the city, the hidden taverns and the backstreet dice dens, which might develop into useful points of contact in future.

We were going to be around in Tryum for a while.

The soldiers manning the entrance to the open courtyard in front of Optryx were not interested in my badge of office, though I did need to give the day's password, which Veron had told me last night. Security was tighter now — was this a reaction to the murder? If indeed it was, it had come far too late.

The building was quiet, not at all what I assumed would be the bustling residence of servants, administrative staff and politicians in full flow. Senator Veron met me and steered me towards a small side room with a highly polished desk, marble floor, and shelves full of books. Judging by the abacus, it must have been some kind of accounting or stocktaking room.

Inside was a dark-haired man in his early forties wearing military garb, a deep red tunic, leather breastplate, and with a sword sheathed at his side. Dark, short and well-oiled hair, and with a wide yet lean face, he was muscular, confident and relaxed. Reaching out with his right hand, he stood to greet me. His forearm was incredibly solid, and it had been a while since someone had gripped my own arm so tightly. Though I was a relatively tall man, he looked down on me. Small scars of battle were dotted about his face.

Senator Veron conducted the introductions: 'General Maxant, may I present to you Lucan Drakenfeld, Tryum's new Officer of the Sun Chamber.'

Maxant stared intensely with his bold, hazel eyes. His manner was proud. 'The son of Calludian returns home.'

The words sounded like some kind of accusation. 'You knew my father?'

'Not well, but we met many years ago. I remembered him to be a good man. Honourable, reliable. Keen eye for detail. I hope this remains a family trait.'

'As do I. I'm sorry to meet you under such circumstances.'

He turned to the desk and gestured to two pieces of paper. 'We matched a register taken last night to the guest list. Everyone is accountable. Everyone has at least another to vouch for their presence. Everyone who was invited remained here until released.'

'Very effective work by your soldiers, general,' I said.

'Good men, my lot. We've been through much.'

I could only imagine the exertions of a long campaign. Maxant's army had been abroad for years. They had lost ten thousand men over that period, had fought many battles and skirmishes, and at one point faced starvation. For them to have stuck at it so long would have required a phenomenal sense of loyalty and leadership. Indeed, they had been through so much.

I looked at the guest list. People had been arranged into classes of status, from the men and women of the Senate through to respected citizens of the city. 'These weren't the only people here last night. Where are the lists for the staff, the soldiers?'

Maxant nodded. 'We will get a list of them and let you know if there is something of note. As for the actors—'

'What access did they have?' I asked. 'What were the productions, how long were they in the building?'

Maxant looked to Senator Veron, who shrugged. 'I'll ask around. We'll get the answers – don't worry.'

'I would appreciate that.'

'King Licintius wishes to see you shortly,' Maxant announced. 'We have a few moments yet before we must go.'

Senator Veron moved to the shelves to glance at the books. 'How's he been since last night, general?'

'How do you think?' Maxant snapped. 'Licintius is devastated. He loved his sister deeply. Their bond was strong, and who else can he really trust? Everyone thinks they can do a better job. Him and his sister were left in powerful positions at a young age with only each other for confidences, so I suspect he feels utterly alone now.'

'Indeed, it's very sad, very sad,' Veron said. 'Still, at least he has his general back now to confide in.'

'What's that supposed to mean?'

Maxant stood a little taller as if to express his dominance in the room. Veron seemed oblivious to the fact, merely raising one eyebrow at the now-bitter tone of the general.

Veron shrugged. 'Only that you're an old friend, and no doubt he'll be glad you're back to help him through this.'

Maxant grunted and turned his back on the senator.

'The Senate will discuss the matter shortly,' Veron continued. 'We must see to it that we establish some firm facts before the rumours spread across the city. Of course, if Drakenfeld here is as sharp as his father, hopefully we'll have no need to worry about rumours.'

No matter how sharp I might be, it wouldn't stop people talking.

We exited the room and were absorbed into a larger contingent of officials and soldiers, twelve of us in all. Hushed instructions passed back and forth: 'You wait for the king to arrive. You fall to two knees – not one, do not bow – two knees. Do not look him in the eye until he has spoken.'

Our group passed through the marble corridors and under the immense domes once again, which were even more impressive in the light of day. We did not walk by the temple. I wanted to return to the scene of the crime in the hope of working out the mechanics of the incident without the distraction of others.

The huge chamber we entered next left me awed. I had never seen such artwork adorning plaster like this – not in quantity, style or clarity. Every vacant wall space was covered in hugely expensive hues, great vistas or scenes from the myths of our lands – that looked so real they could have been alive. Large windows pierced the walls. Through one of the lower ones could be seen the rooftops of Tryum, and the little plumes of smoke from domestic hearths. A city as yet unaware of the crime that had been committed against its monarch.

We were instructed to stand in the centre of the room. The floors were made of highly polished white marble; bold red pillars lined the chamber like a temple, leading to steps up to a cushioned throne. Made of dark wood, the throne was carved in such detail that it couldn't be appreciated from where we stood.

Nobody spoke. The faces of the others betrayed their anxiousness, although Maxant seemed relaxed.

Moments later, after the clattering of a few doors, two soldiers of the King's Legion led a man into the room.

Those around me fell to two knees while I, a Sun Chamber officer, needed only to fall to one – a quirk of Vispasian law that left me on a par with the greatest citizens of Tryum, but more nervous than it should have. Those nearby had their gazes fixed on the marble floor. Even the mighty General Maxant did not look up, though both he and Veron were on one knee also.

'Please rise, all of you,' Licintius called out. 'You know I tire of ceremony when matters are of a serious nature.' His voice possessed a lovely timbre, but was weighed down by melancholy.

Everyone rose to their feet while an aide to one side whispered in Licintius' ear. His blond hair was wavy, in the style of the military heroes of the old Empire, and he was dressed in a purple tunic that, on closer inspection, contained a spectacular amount of subtle detail in the stitching. His highly polished boots were light brown, matching his belt. There were a couple of items of jewellery around his wrists, gold bangles, a surprisingly effeminate decoration for a king. Everything about his composure, the slight upturned angle of his jaw, the way he held his arms, all suggested years of practice to perfect the look of noble dignity.

Licintius nodded and regarded the rest of the room, moving his gaze across the gathered faces. 'Lucan Drakenfeld?'

Being in the presence of kings always made my heart beat just a little faster. Licintius stepped forward to meet me. His eyes were a piercing jade colour and he gave off complex scents, reminiscent of jasmine and citrus. Close up he looked a little older, but he couldn't have been many more years advanced than me, perhaps in his mid-thirties at most. His face was broad and lean, much like Maxant's, yet Licintius was a slight man, and not anywhere near as tall.

We did not touch in any formal greeting, but surprisingly he placed a firm hand on my shoulder and gave me a sad smile. 'Your presence is indeed welcome here.'

'I'm honoured, but regret our meeting is under such circumstances. You have my deepest sympathies, sir.'

'Sympathies . . . Yes, you do understand, don't you? A lot of people have been saying that word to me without really meaning it, but you lost your father recently, did you not? We share in our grief.' He looked back to the others and called over to them: 'Please, talk amongst yourselves while I see to business with the Sun Chamber.'

Licintius steered me to one side, far away from the ears of the curious. 'You will find whoever did this to her, won't you?' he whispered urgently. 'You will see that they are brought to justice?'

'I'll do my very best, sir,' I answered. 'However, it is a puzzling mystery.'

'Witchcraft,' the king breathed. 'I have heard of dark matters in the Senate in recent months. They have tried to harness the powers that belong only to gods.'

'It is one option.'

'I have another,' the king added. 'That she was assassinated.'

'Was anyone a threat?'

'Who was not? Foreign princes were lining themselves up, and she turned them all down.'

'Her marriage was not your decision, then?'

'No. I'm no northern barbarian. She could choose her own path.'

'Are there any such foreign princes you think might have been responsible?'

'A royal wouldn't have done it himself. He'd have an assassin do his bidding, of course, but I'd place money on the attack having derived from Maristan.'

An old rival of Detrata, and one that had suffered greatly under imperial rule, Maristan stood just to the south of Detrata.

'What will it take for you to find the killer?' the king asked. 'What help do you need from me?'

Taking a deep breath, I rapidly weighed my options. 'If it isn't much trouble, I would like to see Lacanta once again, though perhaps after your physician has seen to her.'

'Of course, Drakenfeld. I'll have my physician meet you after this and you can go with him.'

'Thank you. I'd also appreciate two other things, if I may be so bold as to ask.'

With a tilt of his head he indicated for me to continue.

'One is access to the Temple of Trymus once again, just to take another look at the scene. The second is to have access to senators, and over the next few days I'd like to speak to those who attended the party last night.'

'You think one of them is responsible?' The king looked concerned by the implication. 'I know they like to stab each other's back — figuratively, of course. Not here. Not in Tryum — this is no tribal backwater. We are a civilized people.'

'I'd like to keep my options open.'

'I'll see to it that you are granted free access and I will address the Senate personally on this issue.'

I gave a short bow of thanks, but wanted to ask him more. 'I may also have a few extra questions for you to help locate Lacanta's murderer. No one knew her as well as you did.'

Licintius gestured with upturned palms. 'If you have something to ask, please go ahead.'

I glanced back to the whispering crowd behind us. Maxant towered silently at the back next to Veron, who seemed to be smiling at one of the women nearby.

'Did anything last night strike you as particularly out of character for anyone? An argument perhaps.'

Rooted to the spot, the king descended into deep concentration. He looked almost angry, and his momentary silence made that all the more potent.

'Nothing odd, as such,' Licintius said. 'No. There were a few people upset at the actors I brought in, but that is to be expected when the classes mix. It does them good, though, whether they like it or not.' I noted the promise of a smile, but nothing more. 'There was a row. One or two of the grander families did not appreciate me bringing foreigners into Optryx. They don't like those from abroad – they don't trust our neighbours.'

'What happened after that?'

'Nothing. It all quietened down thankfully.' The look of sadness on his face grew. 'I do wish people would be more open-minded in this city.'

'But other than that – there is nothing that comes to mind? Nothing in the days leading up to the event? Please, anything you suggest could be vitally important.'

He reflected on the matter for some time before saying, 'Two nights ago, while out riding in the country, one of my men pointed out two meteors to me – one following another, and each with a large tail. Do you think it could mean anything? My astrologers suggested it meant the gods were displeased. Do you think such things would be connected to her death? Why else would it have occurred in the temple, if it was not the business of gods?'

'I am afraid such matters are out of my area of expertise,' I sighed.

Licintius glanced down at the floor and his silence was profound. 'I will send a messenger to find you when I have more time for you to ask your questions, Drakenfeld, and we will talk in private. Now, sadly, I have too little time to grieve. Others demand my attention.'

With a look of profound weariness Licintius marched back to the group. In a quiet, firm voice, he enquired who was next.

Would She Have Screamed?

I waited on my own, sitting on the floor beneath the altar of Trymus, just in front of the spot where Lacanta had been found dead. No hard evidence remained now, of course, but I could clearly recall the position in which she had been found. What must she have been thinking in her final moments?

Some people preferred to see out their time surrounded by statues of deities, but they had usually lived a long and successful life; they had the luxury of choosing how their time would end. But not Lacanta.

Would she have screamed? Would anyone have heard?

The room was solid, and there had been a celebration in process, potentially loud enough to drown out any noise that might have left her lips. If one was intending to murder to make a statement but not be discovered, this was an ideal location.

Standing up, I looked at the bearded stone face of Trymus, and wished that, as the only witness to the crime, he could speak to me right now. But communicating with the gods was the job of priests; I'd have to rely on my own investigations.

The double doors were crafted from a very fine wood, possibly oak, and the grain was heavily polished. There were gold-leaf shapes pressed decoratively in a thin, rectangular line around the edge, and in the centre the ornamentation was of trees or flowers. The key was still in the lock, on the inside. There were no signs it had been tampered with. The other door bore the brunt of the damage from Maxant's men — a testament to the strength of the lock — and had splintered where the bolt had been.

'It seems only Trymus saw what happened last night.' A short man, garbed in a green shirt, brown trousers and black boots, approached. He was balding, the remaining strands of hair left to him slicked across his head, and stood with the slight hunch of a man who had spent many years as a scribe or at a work-bench. A short ornate dagger hung by his waist, though he didn't seem nimble enough to use it. He gripped my forearm lightly and we shook. 'You're a tall one, I'll give you that. We'll just have to see if altitude reflects intelligence.'

My face must have shown my confusion.

'Didn't anyone tell you I was coming?' He shook his head and looked to the gods. 'I am Yago Boll, the king's physician.'

'Ah, of course, I'm delighted you could meet me so soon.'

'Oh, a pleasure. Anything to get away from his insufferable majesty at the moment. He is not one to cope well with his sis-ter's death, it seems. But you don't see the rage like I do. At least he's accepted it this morning. You'd better solve this soon or I'll be forced to bring more cases of wine from the kitchens and drown my sorrows.'

Licintius hadn't been at all angry with me, though his face certainly showed the potential for such rage. Maybe he was calmer because I could help him, or maybe his long history with the physician exposed the man to purer emotions.

'Did you look at Lacanta last night?'

Boll regarded me as if I'd asked a ridiculous question. 'No, this morning. I deal with the living, for the most part. Let priests handle the rest, I say. Only the servants have been washing her body since then, so she's easier to examine.'

'May I see her now then?'

'Yes,' he sighed, 'this way.'

On Licintius' orders, Lacanta's body had been laid out in her room and cleaned and dressed in her finest clothes and jewellery. Her hair had been arranged to flow down across her shoulders and a well-placed thin scarf covered the grisly wound that had been the killing stroke. The room was bright and airy, presenting a glorious view down the hill and over Tryum's rooftops. Pale yellow walls, a polished marble floor, a ceiling painted with deities, it was a pleasant place to be. A huge amount of perfume filled the air.

'Best not to ask questions about why she's in this room again and not resting in a temple,' Yago said, shaking his head. 'It isn't right; the gods will not like it. King's orders though. Now, come then, Sun Chamber boy, son of Calludian, tell me what I cannot see for myself.'

'I get the idea that you're not much impressed with me.'

'I don't like people telling me about my job.'

'I'm not here to do that. I want to know what you think, as it happens – please, talk me through how you think she was killed.'

'Isn't that obvious?'

'Tell me what you see,' I replied.

With an exaggerated sigh, though with notably more energy than before, Yago Boll lumbered across to the other side of Lacanta's bed.

Leaning over the body, his fat hand pulled aside the scarf. Only when he glanced up at me did I realize how wild his eyes were. 'This cut across the throat would have done the serious damage. It caught a major artery. Secondly there have been four further slashes across the face, causing minor disfigurement. She received further knife wounds to her chest and stomach, and a stab wound in her right side, though none of these were deep enough to have been the finishing strokes. The servants haven't done a bad job of covering the damage, to be honest.'

'It all seems rather vicious when a neck wound would have been sufficient,' I said.

'I cannot tell you if this was because of a struggle or something more ritualistic. There do not seem to be any wounds or bruises that suggest she put up a fight.'

'What kind of blade would have done this?'

'It wasn't a big weapon — I'd say a hand-knife, possibly even something one might find in a kitchen, easily concealed.'

'You're quite sure about this?'

He looked proud of himself, as if his years of expertise had built up to just such a moment. 'I would say it is more likely than not. Fruit knife, even. Something sharp enough to create these cuts one can see here. A sword would have made more of a mess.'

'Not something an assassin might carry?'

He shrugged. 'Not really, but it depends on the assassin, of course. You think this might have been a professional job.'

It came as a statement not a question. 'Something the king said about Maristan. Lacanta rejected the advances of one of their princes.'

Yago Boll shrugged. 'I try to stay out of such matters. Those things do not interest me.'

I nodded and contemplated the scene. 'Out of interest, did she suffer from any other illnesses? Did you ever have to treat her for anything?'

He shook his head and moved across next to me again. 'Lacanta was the picture of good health so I hadn't seen her in three years. Apart from the king, I tend to deal with senators mainly these days – a paranoid lot. I generally just prescribe the occasional starling or hare when they need the entrails. Lacanta ate rather too well, if you ask me, but her evening antics probably kept her from becoming excessively overweight, if you follow.'

I did not approve of his sneering tone, but it reminded me to ask, 'Had Lacanta been assaulted in a sexual manner before she was killed?'

'No, that was certainly *not* the case,' Yago Boll confirmed.

'Did you see her, casually, at all last night?'

'No. As I say, I haven't really seen her for years. And, though I was invited as a guest last night, I would not be permitted within ten feet of her unless she suffered illness.'

The lack of ostentation in the room was surprising, considering her high position in society. Drawers revealed clothing, jewellery, strange trinkets and so on but nothing particularly expensive or luxurious. There were a few books on the bookshelf by the window, arts and travel, enough for a thorough classical education but, again, nothing out of the ordinary, nothing to fit such a flamboyant lifestyle, if the rumours were to be believed. From the paintings on the ceiling to the choice of bed linen, everything was of conservative taste, seemingly reflecting a woman who understood and appreciated her position in life – but didn't flaunt or rebel against it. There weren't even any notes from a lover. The room was rather dull.

Something seemed out of place. There was a shape within the dust on one of the side tables; something had been removed. The object looked to have been around two handspans long, and rectangular – like a book.

I addressed Yago Boll once again. 'Though you had few dealings with her, may I ask what you heard about her private life?'

'Oh, Trymus' balls, where to start,' he said, looking down at her finely dressed corpse.

'How about last night? People must speak.'

'From what I heard, she was the same as ever. Flitting like a butterfly from person to person. She knew how to work the room. She was tempting enough to make any sane person behave out of character.'

'Do you think that someone could have been jealous of such behaviour? Was there anyone serious in her life?'

Yago Boll shook his head and scratched his breastbone. His shirt showed signs of perspiration as the day grew hotter.

'Can you give me any names of men you saw her with on the night?' I asked.

'If I did, you'd spend the next few days of your life speaking to them all.'

'You exaggerate, surely.'

'I never exaggerate.' His manner darkened. 'There could have been perhaps ten, eleven men I saw her flirting with – and that was just at a casual glance, I was not going out of my way to keep track of her.' He gestured to the bed dismissively. 'Who knows how many men – or women for that matter – had the privilege of seeing this ceiling.'

'Indeed,' I replied, somewhat curious. The rumoured outlandish behaviour of Lacanta just didn't seem to match the simplicity of her bedroom.

Later, Veron handed over a large box full of statements from the party guests. He suggested that I might want to take them home with me to comb through for intriguing facts.

'I tell you one thing,' Veron added shrugging, 'and that's if you solve this, you'll be as famous as your father. You're well known already. So why not stop by at mine to dine tonight? Oh, and bring your servant . . . Leana, I think you said? I want to invite a few other guests and they'll be fascinated to see someone as interesting as she is. You say she can fight?'

'She's not some wrestler or some gladiator.' I gave an awkward laugh. 'There are plenty of people just like her across Vispasia. I'm sure there's even a community of Atrewens in the city, if you cared to look.'

'They must have taught you some bizarre things in Venyn. Where did you find her?'

'I didn't find her.'

'Buy her?'

'She's not a slave.' I placed the box to one side while I explained how I'd met her.

I had been on business in Atrewe, beyond the southern seas and the borders of Vispasia. My investigation took me to one of the Vispasian Royal Union trading posts. There, tribes were fighting to secure a mineral deposit — there were bloody massacres, and it was like the gods of hell had taken vengeance. The loss of life — and of such remarkable ancient relics — was painful to witness.

Leana had been one of the few members of her tribe left alive after one such massacre, somehow managing to survive the violence in which twenty thousand people were slaughtered. What I didn't tell Veron was that, as I stepped among the ruins of a broken temple away from my entourage to gather my thoughts, Leana tried to kill me. Her sword missed my neck by a matter of inches as I knocked her weapon aside.

I shouted something at her, I can't remember what, but when she snapped at me in broken Detratan I was taken aback. She accused me of scavenging among the dead for trinkets, and I said what dead? That was when she led me to the bodies of her people, a sight I'll never forget — Leana won't either.

She asked me for work, said there was nothing left for her.

That she wanted to get away, to put a sea between herself and these horrors. As it happened, I had recently lost my previous assistant because he wanted to stay at home to care for his family. Even if the gods had arranged it, it seemed like a good idea at the time. Both of us benefited from the deal.

'Well, it's a splendid tale,' Veron sighed. There was something about the man's mannerisms that suggested he longed to be far away from here. 'You must both come tonight then. It's absolutely settled. My guests will love such a story. We will have good wines, artisanal breads, unusual meats, and music while you provide entertainments.'

Smiling awkwardly, I picked up the box of statements again, wondering if everyone in Tryum was this superficial.

Before I left, though, I asked one final question of the senator. 'I don't suppose you know where Senator Divran lives, do you?'

'I'd stay away from that mad old witch if I were you. What do you want her for?'

'Answers as always. Does she live far from here?'

'Not at all. Only a few streets away as it happens.'

The Witch

Senator Divran's house was a surprisingly small building located on one of the most expensive streets in the city. There were no shops, no reason for normal citizens to stray down these roads. Soldiers made reassuringly regular patrols. A few domestic cats trotted about with the authority of lions. It seemed every bit as secure and well kept as one might expect of a district where the senatorial class resided.

Divran's house was slender, but judging by the surrounding architecture it went some way back. The wooden shutters were closed and for a moment it appeared as if no one was in, but when I knocked on the door a young maid in a soft blue gown answered.

'Is Senator Divran at home?'

'She is,' the maid said, hesitating for a moment. She seemed someone whose face was normally disposed to happiness, yet something was very uncertain in her mannerisms. She glanced with wild eyes to the large box I was carrying, and must have wondered if I was selling something.

'Well, can I talk to her?' I asked, explaining my position.

'Yes. Please, if you wouldn't mind waiting for a moment in the study.' She led me through rooms that had little in the way of natural light, and fetched me a cup of water before leaving me among Divran's books and papers.

Placing my box to one side, I glanced across some of the tomes, noting some very esoteric titles coming from all over Vispasia. There were papers bound by string on subjects such as natural sciences and ancient religions. Vast lists and strange diagrams that looked more like maps. Some of them displayed stains, what could have been flecks of dried blood – certainly not ink. On some, calculations had been written, based on very old numerical systems, pre-dating the Empire by several hundred years. What could they have been?

Cupboards, shelves and small drawers, each made with exquisite craftsmanship, stood against one wall. Curious, I nudged open one of the small doors to see the skeletons of small rodents arranged on a shelf. In another was the partially decayed carcass of what appeared to be a crow. What reason could there be for a senator to possess these bones? Was every single drawer and cupboard filled with decaying creatures?

Aware that Divran would soon arrive, I moved across to the sole bright spot in the room. A small window looked out over a courtyard plastered in decorative frescos, scenes from nature that seemed an artistic extension of the garden. For a moment I lost my mind in its wonder.

'Good afternoon, Officer Drakenfeld,' a voice said.

An attractive woman in her late forties or early fifties stood before me, with auburn hair, a broad face and brown eyes, wearing a vibrant high-necked blue dress. She was slender, in an athletic way, and she looked at me as if my mere presence delighted her in a primal sense, like an animal that had wandered into a trap.

'Senator. Thank you for seeing me.'

'Well, it was only a matter of time before you came, wasn't it?' she sighed. 'Let's get it over with.'

'Was it?'

'Of course,' she replied. 'The witch, Senator Divran, must have something to do with that mysterious murder. Isn't that what they say?'

'Who do you mean by "they"?'

'Oh, come now, Drakenfeld, I've been in the Senate for long enough to realize what goes on.'

'And are you a witch, then?' I gave a smile.

'I would be arrested if that was the case, surely?'

'The law's not always clear on such matters, even if you were — though that is depending on what you might have done.'

'You seem vaguely amused by me, officer. Do you find the matters of the supernatural amusing?'

I didn't answer her, uncertain of my own opinion. Though I was generally sceptical about such things, it wasn't a subject on which I wanted to be proven wrong. 'I'd like to know your activities on the day and the evening Lacanta was murdered.'

Divran told me: she was working in the Senate trying to drum up sponsorship for a team of writers to categorize the natural systems of the world, though few could be bothered to open their purses. Plenty of witnesses could vouch for her every move. At first she didn't feel up to celebrating the deeds of 'a thug' like Maxant, but she was eventually persuaded to attend by some of her friends in the Senate. She remained with them at all times, with no interest in the temple — until, of course, there was a murder.

'Now I am as fascinated as you are,' she concluded. 'I have an active interest in documenting the things that cannot yet be explained, as you will see by this library.'

She gestured to the books and scrolls around her, unaware that I'd seen the animal remains as well.

'I don't think the supernatural has anything to do with the murder,' I replied.

'What makes you so sceptical? Why not a ghost, or a spirit who can move through walls – such things are common throughout the world.' Then she added with a smile, 'I've seen them myself. A ghost could easily have entered the temple.'

'That may be so, but if it was supernatural, why be so brutal? Why leave a key in the door? Why wait until there were so many people around before killing her? The incident has too much ego involved, and too many flaws to be anything other than a human incident.'

'Such foolish confidence.' Divran was restraining her obvious anger. Here was someone who had strong opinions and who didn't like them being rejected, but who was skilled enough not to fight back on the issue. 'Don't think such things aren't likely to be down to the unknown. I've witnessed more strange things than you care to dream of.'

There was a finality to her statement, and she regarded the garden now, silhouetted in the bright square of light. A bird flittered about one of the bushes by the window, bringing a sense of tranquillity to proceedings.

'Your husband passed away recently,' I said. 'I'm sorry for your loss. Did he have anything to do with Lacanta?'

Divran's body froze, her shoulders became tense – just for a moment – until she released them and became calm once again. She still did not look at me. 'He killed himself because of her. He threw himself out of a window because he couldn't have her.'

'There was no love between the two of you any longer?'

'There never was at all,' she said bitterly. 'I always loathed him. He married me for money and for my family ties.'

She spoke then of his pitiful attempts at furthering his own career in the Senate, of his own 'pathetic little interests' and of his sudden affection for Lacanta.

'It didn't go anywhere,' she said. 'It was never going to. Still, some men are just like that, aren't they, once these little infatuations take root.'

She spoke of how he died, having thrown himself from a window at a party one night. The height of the fall was enough to kill him, much to the dismay and disgust of the guests. In the lead-up to his death, his behaviour had become suddenly very nervous. He was a paranoid man. He was concerned the authorities were out to get him because of his overtures towards Lacanta. This would all be easy to verify, of course, but something unsettled me. It was the way she described it: hinting at darker forces behind his actions, the possibility of a curse being placed upon him. It was obvious this is what she believed.

She let the doubt hang there: if I chose to believe her story, then I had to accept her supernatural abilities.

'Do you miss him?' I asked, watching her reaction carefully; but she gave nothing away.

'If others say I am a witch, then I can still talk with him.' She chuckled to herself. 'It's even said that I commune with other dead husbands, enabling them to walk about the city. People say a lot of things.'

'I'm not interested in what others say right now, senator. What do you say?'

'I say that the dead have ways of still being with us, whether we like it or not. Walk among the tombs sometime, officer. It will do you some good.'

Divran was no more enlightening and always mysterious, enjoying the attention I was giving her. So I left.

When I arrived home, somewhat disturbed by my encounter, a messenger had left notification of my father's funeral, which was to take place shortly after dawn the next day. I hoped that the pontiff back at the temple had put up a public notification to inform other people.

There was another note from Bellona: a priest had stopped by but left no official message of his business.

With a heavy heart, I tried to clear my mind and set to work.

The statements from the guests were spread out before me, waiting to be sifted through in order to divine some kind of truth. It was an impossible task: the guests would all have vaguely similar or vaguely conflicting statements; families would, most likely, say that they had seen Lacanta at slightly different times before the temple was opened; people would no doubt vouch for each other.

Before that task, I had to send a letter to the Sun Chamber headquarters in Free State, detailing my investigation of this crime and the king's insistence that the case be resolved swiftly. Someone had gone to great lengths to kill Lacanta and I suspected that it could cause further political tensions. I requested also that any unattached agents be sent to help me, but that was unlikely – they operated in ways that I barely understood.

I took a brief break to sip some herbal tea whilst regarding the sunlit street from my front door, once again familiarizing myself with the city, the passers-by, my neighbours.

It may have been my mind playing tricks on me, somehow layering the past over the present in my imagination, but I could have sworn that one of the women who walked along the road was familiar. It was just a glimpse, no more, but enough to release a shiver up my neck – though I stopped short of walking out to get a better look.

Perhaps my encounter with Divran had encouraged strange thoughts in my mind, but it seemed like someone I once knew. Who I once loved.

Shaking my head, I finished my tea and resumed work.

Leana returned moments later looking as cool and calm as ever, despite having spent time rummaging around the more questionable parts of the city.

'The word is out,' she announced. 'Everyone in Barrantum knows. Even the slums. By the way, this city has some dire places.'

'I know. So what were people saying? I like to think there might be truth in rumour on occasion.'

'They say a ghost or god did it,' she replied.

'A ghost?' Perhaps Divran had been spreading rumours.

Leana shrugged. 'It is only what I heard. This is not the truth you wanted?'

'There seems to be a lot of superstition in the city. Anyway, we both have dinner plans later.'

'What, me also?' A look of concern came over her face.

'Yes, you also.'

'That sounds suspicious,' she sneered. 'What do they want with me? I am not dancing or getting naked for any men. I will cut their c—'

'There's no need for that,' I interrupted. 'As if I would expose you to that! You'll be present as my guest, that's all.'

'Your guest. This still sounds odd, but someone needs to keep you out of trouble. You will be drinking lots at this party I take it?'

'No, of course not – it is my father's funeral tomorrow morning. Come to think of it, we probably shouldn't even stay out all that late.'

Leana nodded thoughtfully. 'What have you got there?' She indicated the parchments on the desk.

'Statements from the guests.' I told her about my visit to the palace, but my mind wasn't forming any connections at that moment. Light was fading from the sky, it was early evening and I needed to rest before tonight's activities.

'You should know also,' Leana said, walking away, 'that I have seen three different men over the past day loitering outside the main gate. One hid a knife up his sleeve. When it was clear to him that no one was going to leave the house, he walked into the crowds and spirited himself away.'

'Do you think they were anything to do with that rider who was following us before we came to Tryum?'

'Hard to say from what they were wearing. I do not remember his face,' Leana replied with nonchalance, and turned towards her room.

It was only then I noticed the small collection of bones she had been holding behind her back.

'I see you've found something to put towards a shrine for Gudan,' I called out after her.

Leana paused momentarily before I saw a flicker of excitement in her composure. 'On the edge of Plutum I found a herbalist from Atrewe. An old woman who left long ago, because of the troubles. She makes a living from selling herbs, trinkets and very authentic clay pots.'

Visibly happy, Leana strolled into her room.

It came as something of a relief that Leana had made a connection. She had come with me from her homeland – not that she ever showed much sign of wanting to return. Our relationship was hard to explain to most people: we expressed our bond in our shared silences, our unspoken gestures. We learned to live side by side through rough periods and rougher places, slowly understanding the way each other operated, building a trust that I doubted could be replicated with anyone. Her presence offered protection and security; sometimes I doubted what I could offer her and hoped that, deep down, it went beyond money and a way to escape bad memories.

And I recalled the contradictions of Tryum: indeed it was a

city of many cultures, and many new accents and dialects; yet from what I had gathered, people feared foreigners more than ever. This was strange – even in the deepest days of the Empire, it was said that Detrata and Tryum especially welcomed people from all over the continent. We considered them Detratan even though they had not been born here.

Had things changed in the harsher conditions? Had the lack of food led to a natural distrust of people who were not local? Were the senatorial classes sowing seeds of fear so that it might be a popular act to invade other countries? No doubt we would soon find out.

A little while later, in our finest clothing, we left for the event at Senator Veron's house. We took no more than seven steps out of the front gate before we found ourselves in trouble.

Veron's Party

They were waiting for us in the shadows, three men wearing hooded tunics and cheap sandals. I couldn't tell much about them from their faces, but they were soon crowding around us, steering us back against the red wall surrounding my property. Leana had her short sword in her hand before I even thought to draw mine.

Leana crouched, grabbed some dust from the ground and flung it into the nearest assailant's face before striking the man next to him with her blade, drawing blood. She then turned her attention to the first man, who was still wiping his eyes, and jabbed the blade into his thigh. Screaming, he crumpled to the ground clutching his leg. I went for the man Leana had injured, making a few lazy jabs and eventually managed to knock his blade to one side. I punched him in the centre of his face, feeling his nose crunch. He, too, fell to the ground; I smacked him over the back of his head with the pommel of my sword and then he lay still.

The other grounded attacker received the same treatment while Leana dealt with the final standing assailant, who seemed more skilled in the arts of violence. Never wanting to miss any action, a small crowd had gathered to watch, cheering Leana on.

Realizing this she delighted in making some utterly unnecessary show moves, delivering rapid punches to her opponent's face and stomach and kicks to the side of his leg.

While she revelled in what she did best, I called for someone in the crowd to bring some rope. After being handed some I quickly tied the others' hands behind their backs. Leana finally finished, much to the admiration and cheers of the locals. I tied up the last of them, and lined up the three attackers side by side outside my front gates.

'You were slow,' Leana declared, out of breath but with a grin on her face. 'Bellona's cooking will only make you worse.'

'I'm out of practice, that's all,' I said.

They were poor, not particularly well-nourished men – clearly the bottom of the chain, as far as I was concerned. Perhaps their employers would seek me out in other, gentler ways. I sent for the Civil Cohorts to come and clean up.

Constable Farrum arrived on the scene quickly, in his silver sash and brown tunic. I noticed crumbs in his beard.

'Sorry if I disturbed your meal,' I said, and he started to brush out the crumbs. I told him what had happened, pointed out the crowd of witnesses, and asked him to identify who these men were and what they were doing here.

He seemed nervous and excited as he checked a few trivial details with me, before calling out to some of his own men. A handcart lumbered forwards and the attackers were hauled up on board, still unconscious, before being taken away. There were very few gaols in Tryum – it seemed that the city didn't consider dedicating resources to prisoners particularly worthwhile when matters could be dealt with privately, but I instructed Farrum I'd pay him for his troubles.

'Every other day we found a fight in Venyn City,' Leana commented. 'I am surprised just how quickly we got into it in Tryum.

You told me this was the most civilized city in the Vispasian Royal Union.'

'It is,' I replied.

'It seems much like others,' Leana said, 'if you ask me.'

It was dark now and, though keeping time in Tryum was a loose concept, we hurried because we did not want to appear too rude to our host.

'I am . . . nervous,' Leana admitted.

'You just won a fight with three men and now you're nervous?'

'Spirits save me, you are not helping my mood.'

'You'll be fine. It's just a party.' I laughed. It seemed absurd that Leana could be intimidated by the grand approach to Senator Veron's mansion and yet easily handle herself when threatened.

'Easy for you to say. You live and breathe such social circles. Me, I belong with ordinary people.'

'I enjoy being with people from all walks of life.'

'So you like to think,' she replied. 'You were born into this higher life. Me, I must keep silent when they talk to me, lest I betray my background.'

'Let their words wash over you. Most of it is a lot of pretentious nonsense. Anyway, you've not met them yet – you might decide you like them.'

'Just why must we go to this stupid thing?'

'For work and for pleasure,' I replied. 'Many of the highest levels of Tryum society will be gathering under one roof. There's every chance one of them will be able to tell us something about the murder, or at the very least open up some useful routes of enquiry. It's why we should be glad that Veron has welcomed us into his social circle – that man is giving us quick access to the great and good of Tryum, whether or not he realizes it.'

Two heavily built servants admitted us into Veron's wonderful rectangular garden, which was rich and sensuous, filled with wide-leaf plants that weren't domestic varieties. A dozen scents were being emptied into the evening sky, jasmine, marjoram . . . smells that blended with cooking aromas coming from the house. From inside came laughter and gentle music from a lyre. It seemed ridiculous that a house could be so big in Tryum: built on one level, it was set back from the streets, and designed in the city's typical style, with regular columns, a symmetrical facade, decorated with thin lines of painted details, but it was too dark to perceive the full array of colours.

Cressets burned outside and above the entrance way, bright yellow beacons against the indigo sky. There were braziers lit amidst the foliage throughout the garden, encouraging exploration and secret conversations in the half-light.

We were welcomed by two more of Veron's serving staff, each garbed in a rich silk tunic, before the senator himself came forward to greet us.

'Ah, Drakenfeld! And . . . Leana, isn't it?'

She nodded.

'Thank Trymus you're here, Drakenfeld,' Veron said, his annoyance plain to see. 'Ever since General Maxant arrived he's been boasting of his bloody conquests. We need some intellectual stimulation. Quote a philosopher or two. Make something up about the stars. Anything to redirect the conversation away from savage topics.'

'I'll see what we can do,' I replied.

There were at least three dozen people scattered around Veron's mansion, many of whom I recognized from the night at Optryx. People were gathered in their fineries, in gold-trimmed cloaks, plush tunics, beautiful dresses and necklaces. Faces soon turned to regard us as we mingled. I noticed how the walls of Veron's house were well painted, with scenes of cities from the myths, where the gods dwelled. Mosaics were many coloured, the lanterns crafted from bronze. It was clear that Senator Veron had great personal wealth and I wondered idly where it came from. Incense mixed with the scent of spiced meats, which were carried about on trays by attentive servants. General Maxant was there, dressed in his military finery and his deep-red cloak, accompanied by two women who appeared to be in awe as he spoke to them.

Veron pointed out one man, dressed unusually in crimson breeches and a bold red tunic, with all sorts of delicate decorative details, as Cettrus the Red, one of the riders from the Blood Races. 'Now I know people will frown on us cavorting with people so far down the social scale,' Veron said, 'but the riders are popular men. It adds a little excitement to proceedings – not to mention making me seem an eccentric host.'

'Is your wife here?' I asked.

'Atrella? No, no – she's away on business. She's left me with the much harder job of entertaining this lot. Did you meet Senator Divran, by the way?'

'I did, yes.'

'Doesn't she send a shiver down one's spine? Did she do it then – murder Lacanta?'

'No. I don't think so. Do you know how Divran's husband died?'

'Oh yes, quite a scene – not to mention a mess.' Very briefly, Veron confirmed Divran's descriptions to be accurate, though he added his own particular sense of colour.

There was a strange hush as we were guided through the house, many people stopping their conversations and openly staring at us. I could feel Leana tense at my side.

Veron clapped his hands for the lyre player to cease.

'Please,' I whispered, 'no need for formalities on my account.'

'Nonsense!' Senator Veron announced me with my full title, as the new Officer of the Sun Chamber for Tryum, son of Callu-dian, and assigned to investigate the murder of Lacanta. He then introduced Leana as my assistant and gave a brief version of how we met. 'We will expect more details of such a story tonight!' he finished, then turned to me as the chatter rose again, and spoke slyly. 'You're not wedded in any way, you two?'

'No,' I confirmed quickly, as I noted the outrage in Leana's face.

'Good,' Veron replied. 'There are several women here who have been dying to get their hands on you.'

'Oh, I'm not really looking—'

'No one ever looks,' Veron said, 'but if the gods decide it's the right moment, there is no need to fight against their cosmic will.'

As Leana smirked at my discomfort, Veron steered two young women into view, one a black-haired lady with olive skin and wearing a green dress, the other with lighter hair, yet piercing blue eyes, and wearing an outfit that matched them. The women immediately began talking to me – or rather, talking at me. This had not been my plan for tonight: I did not come here to seek a bride, but answers. Yet they did seem rather charming . . .

I felt a sharp nudge in my ribs from Leana and a look that told me I'd better not be distracted from the case or abandon her to these people, but before she could glare at me too long, Leana was then guided towards one of the trays of food by another guest.

It turned out the women Veron forced upon me, Aemilia and Messalina, were wealthy daughters of senators and lining them-selves up for the Senate one day. They seemed pleasant company, but I could tell they were more interested in my position within the Sun Chamber than me personally. There was a wide-eyed look about them that made me feel as if I was just another rung on a social ladder.

When they said they were at Optryx the previous night I steered the conversation immediately to the murder. They had both been disturbed by the events. I asked them if they knew Lacanta in person and, as predicted, they replied in less than favourable terms about her behaviour in the company of men.

'She liked to break hearts,' Aemilia confided. 'It could have been any one of fifty men who killed her – and any one of fifty women, for that matter. Though most likely it was someone using illicit magic. It could quite easily have been some servant hiring a soothsayer or curse-trader, someone who has nothing better to do than dredge up discredited gods. Disgusting.'

'Why do you say it was magic?' I asked.

'Illegal cults,' Messalina replied, and leaned in as if we were conspiring. 'I've heard tell that such cults brought a farmer back from the dead – from the very hands of the gods, wouldn't you know? It just isn't right, if you ask me.'

'You've heard tell,' I said.

'You don't seem convinced?' she asked. 'Oh I know, I know. I've met people like you before, people who don't believe in the other realms.'

'Though I admit my job can make me question matters too much, I believe there are many mysteries,' I replied. 'But in my goddess's writings, we tend to apply logic first and foremost. Only then can we begin to delve deeper into the unexplained – once reasoning has been ruled out. It is how she differs from, say, Trymus, whose followers deal mainly in faith first, questions later – if at all. That is why she remains the only god associated with the Sun Chamber.'

'Be careful,' Aemilia said, stepping back from me as if I'd been cursed. 'It is simply not wise to speak ill of the gods.'

'I respect everyone's faith and everyone's gods,' I said. 'We live in a cruel world, so if people can find comfort, so be it. Trying to play gods, though . . . that's something else entirely.'

'Well, you might rule out magic, but who are you to say it doesn't go on?' Messalina asked. 'And it seems that Lacanta associated herself with such dark arts, given the number of marriages she ruined.'

I still could not match these descriptions of Lacanta's public life with her more austere, private chamber. It was as if she had been putting on a show — but why would that be?

'Was she ever caught in the act with anyone?' I asked.

'Oh no. Never. She was too cautious for that.'

I asked for names of those individuals with whom Lacanta was most intimate, but the ladies could only provide gossip and rumour based on lingering glances and suggested dalliances — none of which could provide the foundations of a solid investigation.

In the corner of the room, Leana was involved in a conversation with Veron and a crowd of guests. 'I should really see if my assistant is coping.'

'We saw she came with you. Are you comfortable doing business with something like that?'

'Like what?' I demanded, noting how they viewed Leana with some disdain.

'Oh, you know.'

Indeed, I knew. Making my excuses to the two ladies, I walked across there, just in time to hear Leana finishing her account of how we met.

'How extraordinary,' one of the older men wheezed, captivated by the tale.

Veron was looking at Leana with more than a hint of lust. I felt on my guard — not that he would harm Leana, but that she might harm him.

'Wonderful accent, isn't it, Drakenfeld,' Veron said, catching my eye. 'The way the vowels are extended, that each word is pronounced with consideration. I know you taught her Detratan, but what does she speak usually?'

'Sarcasm, for the most part,' I replied. 'No, she speaks our own tongue – at her own insistence, as well as our convenience – but she's been known to curse me in Atrewen from time to time. I think she's reached a good level of Detratan. She's even schooled me in Atrewen, though I'm not sure she's taught me how to swear. She saves such choice words for herself.'

'It's all so fascinating,' Veron replied. 'Now, I think it's time you told these people some proper tales from the road. We long to know of the wider Vispasia. I long to know of anything from beyond the Senate building. What wonders have you seen?'

Though I was not looking forward to discussions with Veron's guests, I did not exactly dislike being surrounded by people eager for me to speak. I had been schooled well from a young age in rhetoric – as was essential for all of us in the legal profession – and it was not just a boon in the law courts. People loved a good story.

'I once met the Gold Queen,' I began, to audible gasps. 'It was deep in the heart of Dalta, a nation where women have far greater rights and privileges than men.'

'Nonsense,' a man said.

'It's true. As a man it makes me really understand the position of women in our own nations – having experienced the opposite. The Gold Queen is the heart and soul of the Vispasian Royal Union, with much of the mineral wealth – and she knows it. She's more arrogant than any king, and more beguiling than any lady I have set eyes upon. She dresses in nothing but gold-coloured cloth, and her body is weighed down by her excessive jewellery so that she rarely leaves her immense bedchamber. She sleeps there, eats there, bathes there, and dictates the entire business of Dalta from a horizontal position.' I smiled at one of the more prudish-looking ladies nearby. 'She experiences a lot of her pleasure at the same angle. When she needs to inspect the provinces of her country, to check on local officials and accountants, a good number of slaves carry her there on her golden bed.'

'Were you on a case when you saw her?' a woman asked. I took her to be a senator, too, judging by her stately clothing.

'Did you see her in her bed?'

'Was she clothed?'

I smiled at this bombardment of questions. 'I like to think she took a shine to me, but as for the rest, I'm afraid I'm not allowed to say . . .'

I repeated similar pieces of information – how I saved Prince Bassim from an assassination attempt in Venyn City, of the Ziggurats of Locco, the Skeleton Prince of Gippoli – pausing in all the right places, allowing for natural drama to fill the gaps in what I had to say, leaving them waiting on key moments so that they would remain interested, and trying my best to recall my rhetorical training. This was, after all, partly why Veron wanted me here, so I did not wish to let him down after he had been so kind to me during my return. Even Cettrus the Red seemed impressed, though he did not speak to me.

They were most impressed by my having travelled to Free State, a neutral yet heavily fortified territory; there once a year, within a sprawling village comprised largely of temples, all the kings and queens of the Vispasian Royal Union gathered to discuss the affairs of the world and hold each other accountable for their own nation's contribution to Vispasia, to pass new laws and to remove old ones. From that nation, everyone's futures were to be decided. Though they seemed in awe of my travels, they seemed to be rather dismissive, if not fearful, of other nations, particularly those closest to the border, Maristan and Koton. They quoted the king on his dislike of Free State, too, suggesting yet again a desire to return to the days of Empire.

The guests – some of whom were very high-ranking clerks and officials – could not get enough of the tales, so it wasn't until a little later in the evening that I gladly broke free.

At that point, my throat was dry and I badly needed a drink.

Suitably replenished, I managed to take Senator Veron to one side. 'My apologies for getting down to business on a night like this, senator, but do you have the names and addresses for those actors who were present at Optryx?'

'Yes, of course,' he said. 'I managed to speak to the Censor earlier today, and he noted them down for you.' He slipped away into the crowd, then a moment later returned with a cup of wine and a scroll of paper, which he handed to me. 'The Skull and Jasmine theatre company,' he said. 'They're rough sorts, from a rough part of the city, but name me a thespian who isn't a dodgy fellow.'

'Thank you.' I slipped the scroll in my pocket.

'What do you think of the ladies?' He gestured around with his cup. 'Charming, aren't they?'

'Yes, but—'

'Not your sort?' Veron frowned as if I was some puzzle he needed to decipher. 'If you want a male companion, we can set you up with one of those. One just tends to ask about women in the first instance – an old habit really.'

'Neither will be necessary,' I insisted.

'Are you certain you and your assistant aren't wed? I rather admire the darker-skinned women. Much more adventurous. They'll let you—'

'Quite certain,' I said.

Parties turned people into strange creatures. I don't know whether or not Veron was drunk, but he was starting to remind me why I had been so happy away from Tryum all these years – that, at night, and in these circles, people would reduce each other to sexual commodities. 'I'm afraid my career permits little time for affairs of the heart,' I said.

'A great shame,' he spoke into his wine, 'there are a dozen women here who would be all over a handsome fellow such as yourself. At least three have told me so tonight, in explicit detail. I envy you, being free and single. It's been years since someone spoke of me in explicit detail.'

'Perhaps after I find Lacanta's killer, I may be able to enjoy such matters, but not at the moment.'

The reminder seemed to sober him, and his countenance grew more serious. 'Indeed. Now go on, mingle, and you will have some more wine, won't you? I've purchased many amphorae for tonight, and it all needs to be drunk, else people will say I am a bad host. I might be many bad things, but a bad host I am not.'

'I'll not drink too much,' I replied. 'My father's funeral is after dawn tomorrow. It probably wouldn't be all that respectful – to him or the gods – if I turned up reeking of wine.'

Veron smiled and placed a firm hand on my shoulder. 'You are your father's son.' Then he turned to mix with his guests once again.

'No,' I promised myself. 'I'm more than that.'

A handsome middle-aged lady approached me when I was on my own, and talked about love like she knew what it meant. I'm not sure what she wanted of me – I'm not even certain that she knew herself – but she soon left me alone again. I talked with one of the other guests – a good-looking young man – one who had been close to Lacanta.

'How close?' I asked, and the look I received was innuendo enough. The same individual then questioned me gently, touching my arm, and asked me if I would like to return to his house afterwards. I politely declined, without trying to bruise his ego, and he seemed to brush off the rejection well enough.

Such attention might have been flattering, but I saw that many of the guests here were looking for reasons to disappear with another. Parties could on occasion be pointless for a Sun Chamber official, but when there was a case going on, they could also provide fascinating details as wine liberated people from their inhibitions, and secrets were spilled. At least I could begin to get a picture of Lacanta's social scene, which was a boon for someone unfamiliar with contemporary life in the city. She was hated and loved by many; there was no shortage of narratives winding around her life.

There seemed to be an air of desperation about tonight's conversations. Many people would often whisper in brief, urgent moments away from the other guests. I suspected that, with so many senators in the room, political manoeuvring was the topic of the night, yet I had heard nothing of note, only the occasional muttering about foreigners, about borders, about the glories of old – and of military expansion. More than one individual expressed an interest in purchasing Mauland slaves, too.

Eventually, a little later into the evening, I managed to speak to General Maxant. We stood in the large garden by the fountain, enjoying the balmy Tryum evening. Tonight he was wearing two metal bracelets on one arm, of the kind awarded for bravery on the battlefield.

'How goes the investigation?' he asked.

'I'm listening to what people have to say for the moment. All I've heard so far concerns either ghosts or magic.'

He grunted something that could have been disapproval, but I knew Maxant had spent too much time away from the city to know about such things.

'You were on the scene of the murder before anyone else,' I said. 'You and your men opened that door to the temple.'

'With some difficulty.' He stared into the fountain. 'We are not weak men, Drakenfeld, and it took a lot of us to break open that door.'

'And even though you were among the first to gain entry, you saw nothing at all? No one who might have been hiding in the shadows. No one who could have sneaked out when the moment was ripe.'

'If we had seen a man, Drakenfeld, his head would now be sitting on a spike outside Optryx,' he replied angrily. 'We are not the kind of people to dither on such matters. You might not like our kind of justice, but it's quick.'

'I meant, rather, that something might have been at the periphery of your mind. Maybe it could have been the strange movements of those around you. Someone stepping in behind who you did not think should be there. A figure out of place perhaps.'

'We're the best soldiers in Detrata. Highly trained. Alert at all times. Back from a glorious campaign. There were eight soldiers present, eight who entered the room ahead of a surge of senatorial types and I'm telling you that none of us saw anything in that room other than Lacanta, on the floor, covered in blood.'

Two guests walked by, badly pretending not to have heard the general. I considered if one of the soldiers had done the deed in a rapid move, but it might not have been at all possible. Even if it was, the general wasn't going to say anything. Was he involved himself? I thought back to what Yago Boll had said about the murder weapon being a small blade — not the sort of thing that a soldier would carry. Even now Maxant's sword was at his side.

'A tragic situation,' I said softly. 'I think all we can safely say is that Lacanta's death was not suicide. At least, not with those wounds.'

'Suicide is a cowardly way out,' he grunted. 'The gods don't look kindly on such matters. Especially Trymus – he abhors such things. Lacanta wasn't the type to resort to suicide.'

'I've seen the most unlikely figures kill themselves,' I said. 'Our heads are complex instruments.'

Maxant shook his head. 'She wouldn't have done that.'

'Did you know her well?'

'I knew her – not well – but I knew her. I've been good friends with Licintius for much of my life. Admittedly much of what I know of her is through his eyes.' Maxant paused for a moment, then continued more softly. 'He held her in great affection. That's enough for me to know she was a good sort.'

'She seems not to be as popular as I would have thought,' I said, 'for a good sort in such a prominent position. People here offer a somewhat different view.'

Maxant chuckled. 'Depends on who you speak to.'

'Well, now I'm speaking to you.'

'I'd no problem with her, if that's what you're getting at. She was probably too scared of a rough old thing like me. Tend to attract certain types, we soldiers.' He grinned bitterly. 'Not that attraction means much in a marriage in Tryum.'

'You were not one of those susceptible to her charms?'

He swigged from his wine cup. 'She was a fine lady. No doubt about that. But I'm someone who can spot tactics a mile off.'

'What kind of tactics?'

'Plenty of questions tonight.'

'It's just about my only annoying habit. So, what tactics?'

Maxant grunted a laugh. 'The kind she uses in the Senate. To persuade people to back the king's policies over the years. Licintius will miss not only his sister, but a great ally in that respect. And he knows it, too. She was vital to furthering his ambitions. Many times he'd have trouble getting something passed through the Senate. Lacanta had the ways to nudge an unpopular policy through. Knew how to play the games without anyone knowing she was even in the arena in the first place. I admired that.'

'A lady of politics,' I whispered, knowing this complicated matters immensely. There were no longer jealous lovers who might have the urge to kill her, but political rivals as well. The number of motives and suspects grew ever more complex. 'Do you think it could have been an assassin from a nearby country?'

The general looked surprised at the comment. 'I am not up to speed with local politics, outside of what letters I've read while abroad, so I cannot comment on the tensions between our nations – I am merely a servant of Detrata. As for an assassin? It was certainly a thorough job. But how did they escape a locked room? As soon as you've a suspicion, tell me who you think did this. Licintius is like a brother to me. I can't stand seeing him in such pain. I'll help you where I can, send my soldiers in to surround a building, whatever it takes, you hear?'

I gave a nod. 'Where can I find you?'

'I'm staying at my villa along the coast. It's less than half a day's ride, but the sea breeze is good for my spirits.'

'Not a city man then?'

'I like my sleep,' he remarked.

'The sounds of the city can get to all of us,' I smiled.

'It's not that. It's the coastal air – very soothing. If you'd seen what I've seen in Mauland, then you'd need it too.'

There was a sudden, distant look about the man.

I thanked the general for his offer and left him alone in the garden with his thoughts.

Inside, Leana was still reluctantly the centre of attention and, by the sound of it, facing a barrage of patronizing questions. She was relieved by my presence. We thanked Veron for his hospitality, made our excuses and finally left the mansion.

Exhausted, we headed through the dark streets in relative silence.

It had not been an entirely wasted night, I decided. At least I had some addresses to go on, and would soon be able to ascertain more about the Skull and Jasmine group.

We turned down a relatively empty street, moved across the stepping stones to the other pavement, something that was never that simple in the dark.

The two of us moved towards the light from a couple of braziers, and I could suddenly smell something potent, like vinegar, when . . .

. . . Leana was standing over me with her sword drawn. I was lying on my right side, my head supported by my cloak. Even in the darkness, I noticed the scratches across the back of my right hand, caused by the stone of the pavement.

'How long did it last?' I asked.

'Not long. I counted a little over a hundred heartbeats and you began to show signs of settling.'

I wasn't confused, just a little disorientated. I knew exactly what had happened. 'Did anyone see me?'

'No,' Leana replied, sheathing her sword. She helped me off the ground. I felt unsteady for a moment, my body aching mildly from having been so tense. The sensation soon passed. In a few breaths I was able to relax a little.

Once again I looked at the scrapes, this time in more detail. 'I must have been shaking quite a bit this time.'

'No more than is usual.'

'The gods were lenient this time,' I replied and folded up my cloak. A hundred prayers to Polla echoed around my mind. 'Thank you, Leana. As ever.'

Leana regarded me with perfect neutrality. I didn't like a fuss being made over my seizures. I didn't even like anyone knowing, but Leana had so often stood over me protectively until the sensation passed.

Leana alone could do this and not think it a slight of the gods — how could she if she did not believe deities could possess such powers?

A light sleeper, she would occasionally come into my room if the seizure happened during my sleep. Over the years I could think of no more trusting act than for her to stand over me while I suffered the vengeance of the gods. It was one of many reasons I could not cope without her.

'Any visions?' she asked.

'No,' I said. 'Never have. I don't think I ever will.'

'A shame. In my tribe you would be deemed a notable shaman for such things.'

'It is a pity I'm not in Atrewe then.' Besides, even if I was experiencing visions, I could never remember a thing from a seizure. 'I'll need to make some offerings to Polla when we get home.'

'I can sit by your bed later,' Leana asked, 'in case it happens again.'

'I . . . would appreciate that. In this city more than any other, Leana, it is important no one ever finds out. In Venyn it might not have mattered so much, but here people frown heavily upon such things. There are strict procedures, strict social etiquette. People are conservative. Few would ever trust me again.'

Leana nodded. 'If you like, I will show you an apothecary tomorrow — I saw one down towards Tradum from your house, on a very thin street. Maybe there is advanced medicine in Tryum also?'

'There is, but what can an apothecary offer to protect against the deeds of bitter gods? No, I can only change this through prayer and by trying harder to please them. Come on, it's late. We should at least get some rest before our early start. I can only hope that I don't suffer from a headache during what's left of the night.'

Debts

Swinging incense in a large silver burner, the pontiff led the small entourage down the steps of the Temple of Polla. Every priest and priestess had their face covered in a pale-blue paint, as was the wrapped body of my father, who was being carried along on a wicker throne.

The sight was painful yet I couldn't help but feel strangely detached from the scene. It was happening — indeed I was very conscious of it — but it seemed so otherworldly, as if it was some mythological play, a story concerning the gods themselves.

It was just after dawn and the light was weak. Tryum was beginning to wake, but the funeral process had begun even earlier than this: two priestesses came to my house so that they could dismiss any bad spirits with their brushes. I hadn't slept properly, the grinding wheels of carts making their way through the city's streets made me want to flee to a villa deep in the countryside. Maxant had the right idea with his coastal retreat.

Even at this early hour, dozens of people had come to mourn as my father was carried to his funeral pyre, and I found the gathering to be touching. A rather hungover Veron was there, as was Lillus the barber, who nodded sadly to me across the way.

Men and women from the Senate had come, but I had simply no idea who some of the others were. My father had been a man of some renown — so, for some, I'm sure there was a certain morbid fascination to see how the mighty are fallen.

Leana stood beside me, her hand moving to the hilt of her sword, scanning every face with great attentiveness.

'Is something wrong?' I asked.

'I am convinced we are being watched,' she whispered. 'At least, there is some unwelcome presence here. An angry spirit.'

'Surely no one is likely to try something in such a public space.'

'Concentrate on mourning — that is your job. I will make sure we remain safe.' Leana resumed scrutinizing the faces leaning out of windows, and those standing silhouetted on top of the nearby aqueduct. I noticed how one part of the structure was badly in need of repair, judging by the gaping hole in its masonry.

My father's wrapped body, which would have been coated in a flammable balm, was carried into a small enclosed courtyard, where the rest of the pyre stood waiting for him, and his wicker throne was hauled up on top. The pontiff began a melancholic chant of the tale of Polla, as the goddess of the sun, she who shone light into the darkest of places. It was into the light that my father's body would be sent. Polla was not one for blood offerings.

Torches were brought forward and the pyre was lit in several places; the flames soon began to spread, engulfing my father's body. I felt a lump in my throat, but forced away any unsavoury emotions as masked dancers commenced the ritual of the Passage through to the Underworld. Their graceful, wide-armed movements were comforting, a welcome distraction. Only because I had travelled through many countries, and seen many different peoples, did the notion of ritual strike me as curious

— that much of such displays was more about symbolism and tradition.

The flames became more ferocious and burned consistently, and for a long time. The painted faces of the priests and priestesses standing behind were soon blurred by the shimmering heat.

The sun banked higher in the sky and my father could no longer be seen. Later his ashes would be gathered into an urn, which the pontiff would then secure in the family mausoleum outside Tryum, his final resting place. Though that would not happen until the priests had conducted further rituals.

The blue-faced pontiff slowly gathered up the remains, and his priestesses came forth with brushes to cleanse the courtyard of evil spirits. People began to drift away, a few old friends lingering till the very end. One or two of them nodded to me, though I could not recall their faces — evidently, they knew who I was. Everything seemed strangely quiet, now, but that was how funerals were done in Tryum. No celebrations of life like the Atrewens; just a simple acknowledgement of death and a show of respect to the gods.

And that was that. Well, apart from the fact that Leana was right about the fact that we were being watched.

'Where next?' Leana asked. 'Are you to continue to contemplate your father's passing at a temple?'

'No, we've not got the time,' I said. 'We should head down into Plutum, but before that I want to find out why there was an attempt on our lives last night.'

We headed to Constable Farrum's house.

Cutting through a small plaza, we passed where vendors in wine-coloured tunics were selling cinnamon sticks and hot chickpeas. Either side of them, two stores specialized in theatre equipment, masks and the like. A wood yard stood at the far end, its operations spread over three precarious floors, and next to it was a large stonemason's building, with various examples of craftsmanship on display out the front. Several stone busts glowed in the morning sunlight.

'Let us not be slow,' Leana said. 'I cannot see who it is, but we are now being followed.'

We continued towards the stonemason's, slipping down an adjacent alleyway.

I heard their steps closing in behind us while, up ahead, two men jumped down from an open window, blocking our path.

We were surrounded by six individuals. Each of them wore a mud-coloured tunic, and only one was rich enough to sport boots. At least one face had been at the funeral. Judging by the curved blade in his left hand, he wasn't about to pay his respects.

'Lucan Drakenfeld, son of Calludian, Officer of the Sun Chamber.' One lanky man spoke slowly and stepped towards us with an arrogant swagger. With more than thirty summers behind him, his beard still appeared like that of an adolescent. 'You owe us money.'

I withdrew my short sword a moment after Leana had drawn hers. 'If you feel you're owed something, why not come closer to collect it?' I called back. For good measure, I let him know what I thought of his beard.

'Let's not spill blood,' he spat, having momentarily lost his calm. 'Hand over what we're owed and we'll leave you in peace.'

They weren't going to kill us: it would be tough getting money out of a corpse. 'How about this for a deal: leave now and still keep your life. Or stay and be butchered.' Sweat trickled down my back and I longed to ditch my cloak.

The man shook his head. 'See, this is no way to talk. You're from a family of good standing. Should be showing us an example of pretty manners, right?'

'Who's your employer?' I asked. 'If I have debts, tell me who they're owed to – otherwise I remain ignorant of what you claim.'

'You don't know about your debts?' The man laughed, as did the others. 'What family is this that don't talk?'

They came closer still, two in front, four at the back.

'I've only been in the city for a few days,' I called out. 'I know nothing of a family debt.'

'The money is owed by a Drakenfeld,' the lead figure said. 'We do not care who pays it, only that the account is settled. Or we spill blood, which I don't wanna do.'

'You're not going to kill me,' I replied.

'Who said anything about killing? You can still pay with only one hand.'

Leana threw a dagger into one man's neck; he dropped his sword and collapsed, but by the time he'd hit the ground she'd already sliced the arm of the ringleader and then opened his throat before any of us knew what was going on.

On seeing this display, the four men behind us ran back into the plaza.

I stared at Leana, who set about retrieving her dagger.

'What?' She freed it from the body and wiped off the blood on his clothing. 'You spend so much time talking. At least this business is over with now.'

'We'll have to report this,' I replied. 'We can't just go about killing people and walking away without letting the authorities know.'

'They are scum. No one cares.'

'I care.'

'Why are you so annoyed?' she asked, sheathing her blades.

'I was hoping to get answers.'

'You got a few. Your father owed money. These people were

not going to tell you who the money was owed to, they just wanted you to hand over coin. With only one hand, if they had it their way.'

'I do not pay you to kill people needlessly. A life is not ours to take away unless absolutely necessary.'

She regarded me with an anger that made me question if I'd gone too far. Our understanding of the topic differed greatly – I had not seen the atrocities she had witnessed growing up. I had not seen all my friends and relatives butchered, my entire community left to rot in blood.

'OK,' she said, seemingly more relaxed. 'But you should know that people from your culture do exactly the same when they go abroad. It is only you who thinks in such a soft way.'

I couldn't fault her on that.

Sometimes it felt as though I was the only person in the whole of Vispasia, irrespective of culture, to abhor killing. Perhaps my seizures, too, made me sensitive to the well-being of others, though truthfully anyone who took to heart Polla's teachings would also share the view that life is precious, not something to be taken away so easily. Other cultures long before our time had given edicts on the fair treatment of others, and sought to preserve life wherever possible, so to the discriminating it seemed we now lived in more barbarous times, where a man casually being hacked down in the street had become the way of things. I even struggled in my work for the Sun Chamber, when skilled torturers would walk someone close to the Underworld before bringing them back to consciousness. How could we defend civilization without dignity?

No, removing a life is the business of the gods only, and I could live by no other code on the subject.

The visit to Constable Farrum's house was humbling. It was situated in the relatively safe region of Tradum, a zone of Tryum that had been commandeered by the merchant guilds and their thousands of members. Over the years Tradum had swelled into tenement blocks extending upwards from some of the more industrious smiths and grain merchants. There was little art or finesse to be found in the architecture, only simple columns and bland facades, little in the way of colours, and the suggestion that two or three streets away a stranger might find themselves in a very rough part of the city.

Along the fringes of the district, facing Plutum and Barrantum, more esoteric cliques and entrepreneurs could be found. There were soothsayers, curse-dealers and moneylenders; a few prostitutes, male and female, paced under the arch of an aqueduct. Grubby, vacant faces regarded me from the cool shade of doorways.

From my youth I remembered the practice of illegal and – so my friends always claimed – ancient magic carried on in some of these back alleys. Curses were traded on tablets, and dubious, non-approved gods were worshipped by those seeking to profit over the vulnerable. It was a dirty trade but one that Tryum seemed to thrive on.

I had clearly grown accustomed to the fineries of Tryum, even after just a few days here. Stepping into Farrum's simple home was disarming. His wife, a wiry, dark-haired lady in her forties, greeted us with such grace it seemed as though we were royalty. Politely I asked her to stop bowing. There were four barefoot children standing sheepishly in the corner, dressed in grey tunics that seemed a size too small, and I wondered if they should have been attending school at this hour – Farrum should surely have been able to afford it.

Farrum came to meet us and led us through to a back room.

'There was a fifth and sixth, but they both died of fever in the spring,' Farrum said. 'Still, losing only two, that's a good record for the city, especially when there's so little food. Some people go without for days.' I was shocked by his calm manner when explaining the loss of his children.

Were things really so bad in Tryum?

The downstairs living quarter was a kitchen, hall and dining area all combined into one reasonably large room. The only natural light came in through the open door, while lanterns hung unlit from meat hooks on the ceiling. The walls were cracked and herbs had been wedged in the gaps for either storage or an offering. A small shrine to Festonia, the female co-founder goddess of Tryum, stood in one corner, decorated with beads, trinkets and a bowl filled with scented water. There were probably just one or two rooms upstairs.

Farrum shoved a heavy oak table to one side and gestured to a trapdoor; he had kept the three offenders in a pit underneath the floor.

'Shouldn't you have some safer quarters,' I asked, watching him unlock the door, 'away from your children?'

'Costs money,' he said, scratching his beard. 'The Civil Cohorts get a decent wage, but it doesn't pay for things like that. Besides, this lot are not going to cause me no harm here, sir.'

'Before you open that up, we've some information.' I registered the killings earlier, and informed him where we had left the bodies. I apologized for their deaths.

'Why? You're an official, they are thugs — it's the way of things.'

I gave him an accurate impression of the earlier scene. 'Do you know who they might be?'

'Possibly. I got a hunch they were related to the buggers below.' He stamped one foot to indicate the captives.

'Do they talk much?' Leana asked.

Farrum shook his head.

In the dusty half-light, Leana moved over to the trapdoor as Farrum unlocked it. After he flipped it open, Leana reached in and grabbed one of the offenders by his bound wrist, and then hauled him up and onto the floor. She kicked him in the ribs, sending him sprawling, then she grabbed him by the hair and yanked him upright.

'Enough,' he spluttered. 'No more. Get this witch off.'

'Hear that, Leana,' I laughed, 'he thinks you're a witch.' I leaned over his squinting face. 'She's far worse than that, my friend.'

Leana unsheathed her short sword and crouched down on one side of him.

I followed suit and pointed to the blade. 'See the small markings near the hilt? Venyn metal, this blade. I'm afraid Leana here left her sharpest sword at home. Venyn steel, it isn't so good. It's not as sharp as some blades. This won't do a good job cutting through your flesh – it will mess you up quite a bit. If it doesn't kill you, you'll likely get gangrene, and you probably don't want any of those things to happen. Am I wrong?'

'N-no,' he spluttered.

'Now, if you would be so kind as to tell me what we want to know, we'll not harm you at all. We'll even let you go scurrying through the streets back to whatever hole you crawled from.'

He locked eyes with mine.

'You don't have to talk,' I continued, thinking of some of the well-used lines I'd relied upon before. 'But I should inform you that Leana here has killed two men this morning already and, in her tribe, the number three has great significance. Your dying would have meaning to me, too, as I'm almost certain throwing your corpse into that pit would encourage your accomplices to talk instead. Answers will come, soon enough, and I am a patient man.'

'What . . . you wanna know?' he spluttered.

'The name of your employer,' I urged. 'The person who sent you three to the gates of my house last night.'

He looked from me, to the blade, to Leana, and then back to me again.

'You'd be doing me a favour,' I continued. 'Farrum here has a good house, a good family, and they don't need to see me clean away so much blood just after breakfast.'

He nodded. 'Don't get paid enough for that,' he said. 'Top boss, his name is Veldrum Hecater.'

'Excellent, and what does Veldrum Hecater want?'

'Money. Money that he's owed. That's all.'

'From whom?' I asked.

'Calludian Drakenfeld.'

'Why?'

'How should I know?'

'Where can we find Veldrum Hecater?'

'He's got a large house. Along the border of Vellyum and Plutum. Near to the Seventh Temple of Malax.'

I stood up and Farrum nodded to me. 'All right. You've been very helpful.' I nodded to Leana who threw him back into the pit, and he landed in the darkness with a grunt.

Veldrum Hecater? Who in Polla's name was Veldrum Hecater?

Constable Farrum locked the door and gave me a look of admiration. 'What shall I do with them, sir? Do you wish to bring about a private prosecution? It'd be a pleasure to arrange that with the courts in your honour.'

More figures would come after me if these were brought to the courts. The only way to stop them would be to get to the source of the debts. 'No, not this time. I'm happy for you to let them go, one by one, but don't cut their restraints. They're not a threat to us, but they need to leave here thoroughly humbled.'

'Right you are,' Farrum replied.

'I'm interested in this Veldrum Hecater — what can you tell me about him?'

'I've not come across him personally, I'll admit, but I've heard tell his legitimate trade is as a moneylender. Course, that don't necessarily mean he's not got an illegitimate trade on the go as well.'

A moneylender? As I knew him, it was improbable that my father would have needed the services of a moneylender. But even in death he had already started to surprise me.

Heading Down-City

I knew better than to let personal matters interfere with my professional schedule, but even so, on the way back from exploring the addresses of the Skull and Jasmine troupe in Plutum, my destination was Veldrum Hecater's residence.

The frustration of this case was starting to burn me up inside – there were too few clues, too many potential suspects, though little reliable motive. And from my dealings with royals and well-to-do folk, they tended to want things to be resolved as quickly as possible. Given that no one had anything significant to say about Lacanta's death that night, it really was time to start eliminating some of the many possibilities and to narrow down my focus.

Unfortunately, that was easier said than done.

Since it remained difficult to discern just how the murder was carried out, all I had to go on were the suspicions and suppositions of others.

But perhaps the actors had seen something.

'You know the way, I take it?' Leana asked.

'Of course,' I replied. 'Well, nearly.'

'Not one bit.' Leana smiled.

'Roughly. Finding one's way around Tryum is not always easy, even having grown up in the city.'

When Tryum was a dominant player in the city states of the Detratan Empire, two hundred years ago, it not only expanded through architectural ingenuity, but the military pillaged other nations, bringing back their structures, their essence and, most of all, their treasures.

As a result, parts of the city were a mishmash of stolen cultures, thrown up in quick succession during the years of expansion – and, it has to be said, without much consideration for city planning. Over several decades, Tryum became a mess of streets. The city's royals, in the more logical districts of Regallum, Polyum and Tradum – and to an extent Vellyum – tended to demolish anything that didn't please their eye, and permitted architects and businessmen to step in to fill the gap with something altogether more satisfactory. The problems became more apparent when it was realized that different rulers had radically differing tastes – so schemes were cancelled and new designs requested. It also meant that these days tourists never understood the nuances of the streets, and could often be found stumbling down an alleyway in a dangerous neighbourhood, never to be seen again.

With more luck than judgement on my part, we managed to find our way quickly into Plutum, one of the two poorest regions of Tryum.

The buildings here were taller, closer together, and constructed with little care for safety. It was often said that people should walk in the middle of the street in case crumbling masonry or decaying roof tiles fell down on top of them. It had been known to happen.

Streets became narrower, more illogical in their direction and filled with even more people. Those caught up within the traffic were noticeably poorer, their clothes more austere: ripped trousers, no shoes or boots in some cases, grubby tunics, and there was not a single piece of metallic jewellery on display.

Carts rolled by carrying meagre supplies of grain; amphorae were being filled with water at a fountain; prostitutes stood chewing tree gum in open doorways, idly regarding the street beyond. The graffiti above the head of one lady – featuring the addition of a large phallus, I should add – suggested that one could indulge in all sorts of activities within the room behind her.

Here were merchants, coppersmiths, blacksmiths, a vegetable store, which couldn't have been doing much trade situated right in the middle of the pervading stench from the sewers. Beggars drifted towards us with outstretched hands, pleading in a variety of dialects. Leana unsheathed her blade in a display that made them step away.

'It's all right,' I cautioned. 'They'll give us no trouble – the gods have been unkind enough to them as it is without us creating a scene.'

I felt the gazes of unseen people, each one observing our steady progress through the streets. People wore a nervousness, and continued on their business with a discreet urgency. Many clearly didn't want to hang around for longer than they had to, in order to get their daily shopping or to travel elsewhere. The lower regions of the city were not places to stay unless you were unfortunate enough to have no other choice.

'It does not seem the type of place for kings to visit,' Leana said.

'I couldn't agree more,' I said. 'Though this place could provide good lodgings for actors, I wonder how it happened that people from here managed to work their way up into Optryx?'

'Is society split in Tryum, so that rich and poor must not live together?'

'It's like that throughout most of Vispasia,' I replied. 'Wherever one finds cities, one finds divisions forming.'

Walking in the midday heat through the dusty streets, I unfolded the paper that Senator Veron had given me, containing the address of the Skull and Jasmine theatre company – but there seemed little hope of me finding the exact spot. Addresses in this part of the city tended to be based on descriptions of how to get somewhere, but even with this it seemed unlikely we'd actually find the place.

We passed a tavern situated roughly in the right area, surrounded by tenement housing. Its sign had long since faded, as had the colour of its wooden doors, and there were two rusting braziers on each side.

'Your buildings are so tall,' Leana said.

'Walls were built to mark the limit of growth. The only way to build now is up.'

We stepped under the green awning into the darkness inside. It took a moment for my eyes to become accustomed to the lack of light, but at least it was much cooler here. The ceiling was wooden, supported by several thick beams, the floor made from large stone tiles, and there was a hearth at the far end.

A gang of young and old men sat playing dice in the corner to our left, with a pile of coins about the value of five pecullas before them. There were a couple of business deals going on to our right, judging by the ledger book, and next to them sat what looked like a foreign priest, naked from the waist up, gorging himself on a loaf of bread. I smelled cooked food and bad wine. A few shafts of sunlight worked their way through from the shutters behind, but otherwise the place was lit by candles on the tables. Everything about the place said it was a fire hazard.

All in all, there wasn't much of a refined atmosphere to be found here.

'Reminds me of Venyn,' Leana observed. 'I bet more than a few nights here have ended in blood being spilt.'

'Hey!' shouted a man serving wine to a customer, 'this is my tavern you're talking about.' He was a bearded, skinny fellow in his late forties, and wore a loose-fitting pale shirt covered in stains.

'Do you own this place?' I asked.

'I lease it. But I consider it mine, yeah. Who're you?'

I stepped nearer, showing my golden brooch. 'My name is Lucan Drakenfeld, Officer of the Sun Chamber.'

He frowned as if trying to remember the name, then his composure fell away completely. 'Oh no, we don't . . . look, this may not be the finest of places, but I pay all my bills on time and we don't get anywhere near as much trouble as we used to.'

'Relax,' I said. 'I'm not here because of you. I need your help in finding an address.'

'Yes . . . of course. Though it might be easier if you gave me a name – addresses change with the winds in Plutum.' He laughed awkwardly. Everything about his posture suggested that events occurred here that were not fully within the limits of the law.

'I'm not seeking an individual. I'm looking for the residence of people from the Skull and Jasmine theatre company.'

He looked quickly to those behind me. I made a hand signal to Leana to be on her guard.

'Skull and Jasmine, you say?' the man repeated.

'If you're about to warn any members of your establishment behind my back to attack us, I can assure you the matter will be dealt with quickly and that one of the more careless Sun Chamber torturers will have the chance to practise their craft on you. Am I clear?'

The tavern manager simply shook his head. Nothing was said

for a moment, and in that silence rats could be heard scurrying across the stone tiles. The gang members by the entrance all took their seats again and began staring into their drinks as if nothing had ever happened. Meanwhile the sweaty priest just kept on filling his mouth with bread.

'Good,' I said, and regarded the manager once again. 'Now why would you have us threatened?'

'They're protection, that's all,' he said, his voice almost faltering on every word. 'We gotta look after ourselves down this way. Nothin' personal.'

'I think I see,' I said. 'You've paid protection money for them to keep your place in order? More fool you if you want to get into that business, friend.'

'What choice does someone like me have with the gangs?' he whispered. 'Those senators let them run these districts to keep the peace. It might be all right for someone like you, with your connections, but I have to make do with them.'

I shrugged. 'Now, please, it seems you've heard of the Skull and Jasmine troupe. Tell me more. I'm particularly keen to know their recent movements.'

He sighed and drew a chair up to one of his round tables. Leana and I remained standing – I didn't have any intention of remaining there for longer than I had to.

'Actors is actors,' he sighed and spread his hands out on the table. 'Weird bunch at the best of times. Can't understand any of the fancy Detratan-style shows that you often see. You know, real culture lovers' stuff. But the Skull and Jasmine's more popular with the public you see – they do things involving recent happenings, and the likes. You know, they do plays of local news or gossip, that sort of thing. I like them stories – real easy to understand.'

'Have you seen many of their performances?' I asked.

'Couple. There's a tiny amphitheatre only a few streets away. A lot of the travelling performers go there before they perform in the likes of Polyum and Regallum. Keeps them in touch with the common folk, they say, but I'm sure that's because it's cheaper to drink and bed someone around here, heh!'

'Has there been any behaviour that you might think was odd, or out of character?'

'You tell me what's odd for the likes of them!' He started laughing but when he saw how serious I looked he began to concentrate. 'Well, it's funny you say this about their behaviour. As a matter of fact, there's been all sorts of gossip in here. Weeks ago one of them, so I've heard tell, was spreading gossip of how he was all intimate with King Licintius. Tell you what, that'd explain why at his age Licintius ain't found a wife.'

It was common knowledge that Licintius had quickly divorced his first wife many years ago after she had an affair. Would he be the sort to turn to the affections of an actor? It seemed unlikely – though not improbable. There had been more eccentric royals in the past, but one didn't often see them mix with the lower classes.

'What were this man's assertions?' I asked. 'In fact, what was his name?'

'Can't remember what he was called, but this was just talk – you know how it is sometimes. Some of them were bragging about it beforehand, saying how they were getting paid a lot of coin for this production at Optryx – we're talking in the hundreds of pecullas.'

'This place doesn't seem to be the regular haunt of a king,' I said.

'Aye, I've no idea how their paths crossed.'

'What have you heard since the night at Optryx?' I asked.

'Since Lacanta's murder, you mean? That why you're here?' His expression betrayed his hunger for gossip.

'Answer the question.'

The man looked down at the table with a wry smile that soon faded. 'No one's heard much since, it's as if they've gone into hiding. It's all a bit strange, but then I've always said, these actors are weird people. Worship strange gods. Their lives are full of debauchery. They all bed each other, taking it in turns or going all at the same time probably, I don't know.'

'Who they choose to bed does not make them strange people,' I replied. 'It depends on one's preferences and one's gods, of course. Why do you honestly think they were strange?'

'Just their behaviour, like. You know. Always going around drunk, being everywhere and then — all of a sudden — being nowhere. That's strange for them, at least.'

'Do you think they left the city?'

'Not to my knowledge. Think they're just staying quiet. If they killed anyone, they'd need to stay out of sight if you ask me.'

For such social creatures to cease being social, something must have happened, but what could it have been? At last, I felt we might have found a genuine lead. I reached into my pocket, drew out the folded-up paper and placed it before him. 'How far away is this place?'

He scrutinized it in the half-light. 'You're reasonably close.'

I looked to Leana with a smile. Sometimes I could gain no end of pleasure in proving her blunt doubts to be wrong.

'Guesswork,' she said.

I turned back to the manager. 'Well?'

'Two streets down if you head left out the door. Turn right at the broken fountain and walk about a hundred yards down the lane. There is a place large for the district, and the Skull and Jasmine actors all live in there together.'

'Thank you.' I was about to leave when I thought I would test out the name. 'Oh, I don't suppose you know of a Veldrum Hecater, do you?'

The panic in his face told me all I needed to know.

'I can't help you there, mate.'

He wouldn't make eye contact after that. 'I appreciate your time,' I replied.

We turned and left the tavern, heading back out into the bright, hot day. Compared with the relative calm inside, the street seemed a dozen times busier than previously.

'That was good,' Leana said. 'You did not even have to bribe him.'

'He was so scared, he'd tell anyone anything they wanted. I don't know how much to trust him given how quickly he wanted us out of there.'

The Skull and Jasmine House

A river of stone, the buildings and streets of the city were constantly transforming. Everywhere around were statues or structures either in various stages of decay or being constructed with bright, new stone; though as we moved further down-city we saw much more of the former.

We followed the tavern keeper's directions to the broken fountain, which three men were repairing while another was rebuilding the road around it. There on the corner of the street, side by side, stood crumbling statues of the gods Trymus and Festonia. They were posed to represent the story of the founding of the city, where these two gods — man and wife at the time — established the first few buildings that would eventually become Tryum. Together they organized a small army to fight off strange creatures that besieged the settlement, and their heroic sacrifices later made them become gods. Though the statues had lost their shields and swords, they still stood tall and defiant, inspiring everyone in the neighbourhood on to greater acts.

Leana bought a quick snack from a street vendor and offered me a bite, but I never wanted to eat at a time like this. I prepared myself to be ready for whatever these actors would do. The house turned out to be on a quiet street. There was a battered red awning outside and on the door was a painting of little white flowers curling in an S-shape with a skull set on top.

They looked over the looming, pale stone structure. As the tavern keeper had said it was large for the district, which made me think the Skull and Jasmine troupe were not doing as badly as many actors. I suspected that royal money might have gone into helping them live here.

'No windows or doors anywhere down the side,' she said. 'This seems the only way in and out, from the front at least. Do you think they'll run from us?'

Memories of Venyn, where every other person we sought out tried to flee on our arrival. 'I doubt it. Not if they're in favour with the king.'

Knocking on the door, we stood back and waited. At the end of the street a priest walked by chanting his morning prayers. A dog sifted through the detritus that had gathered around the base of the buildings.

Leana moved in and banged the door again with her fist several times. Eventually someone came to unlock it.

A young woman stood there, black-haired with a heavy fringe, wide-eyed and dressed in a once-ornate blue gown that had clearly seen better days. She stood a little shorter than me and was thin to an unhealthy extent. She stared at both of us, her gaze lingering on Leana for a moment longer. The girl was giving nothing away in her expression.

'It's early. What do you want?' Her voice was surprisingly crisp and confident.

'My name is Lucan Drakenfeld, Officer of the Sun Chamber. I need—'

'An officer? I was wondering when you'd get here.'

'You know of me?' I asked.

'No, I've no idea what the Sun Court—'

'Sun Chamber.'

'Sure,' she continued. 'I just figured that someone would come along sooner or later, someone official, and I reckon you're someone, right? Everyone looks to the low-downs first.'

'This is an awfully big building for a low-down,' I replied, and she gave a slight smile. 'Please, I'd like to ask some questions.'

'Sure, come inside. The place isn't exactly clean — that's what living with others does for you.'

We followed her inside into the musky darkness. The house was similar to many good homes in Tryum: there was a large hall with a small open roof, adjacent rooms in which to dine and a kitchen. I assumed there were sleeping quarters higher up. But everything was run-down: many floor tiles were cracked or covered in grime; the paint on the walls was peeling. There was a strange smell, much like that of the bar, and there weren't many windows. Clearly this was a building that had once been a place of beauty, and it was sad to see it in this decayed state.

'What's your name?' I asked.

'Clydia. What's your name?' she asked addressing Leana directly.

Leana moved forward and introduced herself, seemingly amused at the young girl's attitude.

'So,' Clydia continued, 'Lucan Drakenfeld and Leana. How's your day been?'

'Well, I attended my father's funeral this morning, but things are starting to improve.'

'Oh. Sorry to hear that,' she replied, possibly even sincerely. 'I'm guessing you must really enjoy your work to still be out today.'

'Something like that. I'm after information, and I think you might be able to help me.'

'I'm guessing you're going to want to know at least two things.' Clydia reached down for a clay jug beside the table. 'Wine?'

I shook my head. 'It's too early.'

'Suit yourself. As I was saying, you're going to want to know what we were doing the night of the murder, and you're also wondering how a bunch of people like us get to know the king.'

'If the acting doesn't work out, with a mind like that you could try for a career in the Civil Cohorts.'

'Pah, I'd trust them less than I'd trust an actor,' she sneered.

'Why do you say that?'

'Low-downs. More often than not, men from the cohorts will accuse us women of all sorts, get us in some dark alleyway and then try to lift our dresses. Life's shit at the bottom, not that someone like you would know. Just look at the way you dress. Fancy fabric, 'n all. Such a lovely voice. A nice education, no doubt.'

'I am not here to judge,' I said, 'I'm simply here to find answers to my investigation.'

'What's she here for then?' Clydia indicated Leana, then slumped on a cushion near the wall, alongside two fine-looking amphorae.

'Leana helps when the answers aren't as forthcoming as I would like.' I gave a gentle smile.

'That a threat?'

'Not yet.' I hoped Clydia wouldn't give me too much trouble, and it seemed to me that her tongue was likely to be her most offensive weapon. 'What exactly is the Skull and Jasmine?'

'I've often wondered that myself.' Clydia chuckled as if noting some private joke. 'We're a loose group of nine actors, from different parts of Vispasia.'

'You have a local accent – you're from Tryum, I take it?'

'Close. I'm from a small town further along the coast. Tryum seemed to absorb me somehow. Came here five summers ago, when I was fourteen, but the Skull and Jasmine didn't really come together until two years back.'

'How did it happen?' I spotted a couple of stools next to the table, and drew them up for Leana and myself.

'We were desperate people. Had little in the way of money. We all fell in love with street theatre – how could we not? – and started putting on little productions to spread the word of the older cultures.'

'How did you get on?'

'Not well. We didn't make much money.' Clydia shrugged.

'What happened?'

'Instead, people wanted more and more popular tales instead of art. They wanted to hear stories of what General Maxant had been up to in Mauland, stories of popular heroes, gods, comedies . . .' She took a sip from her cup and sighed sadly. 'There's not much art to that, but it paid our rent and food for a while. People don't come to see us to learn, they come to forget, to dream.'

'Dreaming still requires thought. So somewhere along the line you fell in favour with the king.'

She smiled, shaking her head with amusement. 'Strange isn't it, people like us – a girl like me – suddenly finding ourselves in that big residence.'

'It is a rather breathtaking place,' I remarked.

'Seemed like it was made for the gods. And there we were!' She was much less aggressive now. Her face became vibrant, her attitude far warmer than before. 'We were good friends with the king.'

My look of surprise didn't seem to go down well. Clydia rolled her eyes, as if she'd seen that reaction a hundred times before. It must have been annoying, if she'd had something to brag about, that people didn't believe her. 'It seems unlikely . . .'

'King Licintius likes to visit the city at night. Course, if you even mention it to him he'll deny everything, but he liked to visit his people, only . . . not as himself. He dresses up in disguise.' Her expression was perfectly serious.

'You're not actually joking, are you?'

'Course not. That's how he found us. I think it's a good thing, too – how else is a king to know his people? From senators whispering into his ear? No. He'd heard about several theatre groups, but wanted to meet one for himself – away from the life in Optryx, so he said. We were new, we had little in the way of a following. So one night, with ten armed guards in civilian clothing walking up and down the street outside one of our performances, the mighty King Licintius came to pay us a visit.'

I raised an eyebrow. 'That seems . . .'

'Hard to believe?' Clydia finished. 'I know. Could scarcely believe it myself. Came in here, he did – right where you're sitting. Dressed almost like one of us. He's a handsome man up close – did you ever see him?'

'I have spoken face to face with him, yes.'

'When he's in his royal fineries he's like a god, but when he dressed like us he seemed almost within reach. I wanted to touch him to see if he was real. I made a drunken pass at him once, I think. A girl in my position's got to try these things.'

'I take it he didn't accept your kind gesture,' I said.

'Nah, he wasn't interested.' Clydia gave a warm laugh. Her moods seemed to skip between extremes within the same sentence.

'So what did he actually do with the Skull and Jasmine, when you were all together?'

'Do? We acted, of course. He wanted to join in. Wanted to have some fun, the kind he couldn't have up there.'

'You're telling me the king simply came all the way down here, putting his life at risk, to have fun with some poor actors.'

'Poor doesn't even cover the half of it. We were massively in debt – we couldn't even afford the rent on our tiny little apartments at the time, let alone this place.'

'Do you have any evidence of these assertions? Forgive me for asking, but it seems remarkably unlikely and, as you say yourself, the king will deny such occurrences. Where is your proof?'

With her free hand she gestured to the room around her. 'This place. How in Tryum d'you think we could afford to live somewhere like this? We're not renting any more – this is ours.'

'Licintius' money paid for this building,' I said.

'And the rest,' Clydia said. 'For a small time we dined like kings and queens. Well, not quite, but we had mushrooms and pheasants at least. He wanted actors to enjoy a little luxury so that they "might refine their craft free of worries". It meant we could finally perform the plays that we wanted.'

I absorbed what she had told us and contemplated this large house in one of the poorest districts of the city. It seemed so unlikely, yet here we were. The only other possibility of them owning such a place is that they were operating criminal activity on the side, yet there were none of the rough types on standby for protection, none of the questionable social circles that build up around it. At the moment, there was just one girl.

'Where is the rest of the Skull and Jasmine troupe?' I asked. 'I'd like to speak to them.'

'Upstairs asleep. Same as I was before you arrived.'

'It's midday,' I observed.

'What's your point?'

It appeared her spirited half was about to return, so I decided to ask her about what happened the night of Lacanta's murder at Optryx, all the while scanning her face for signs of evasiveness.

Clydia spoke calmly, clearly and with a surprising amount of detail, all of which matched up with what had been put forward in the written statements of the guests that night. She discussed the play they were putting on, a rendition of 'The Gods and their Conquests', an old play that dated back to the beginnings of the Detratan Empire hundreds of years ago. It was the king's choice that they perform this particular piece, as it would high-light the importance of Maxant's own triumphant conquests in Mauland.

As for the murder of Lacanta, Clydia explained they had not been in a position to see the Temple of Trymus; the play was conducted in a private outdoor theatre within the grounds of Optryx – one of the most beautiful places Clydia had ever per-formed in.

I asked her whether or not all the actors were present in the same place all night, but she explained that they'd mingled with the party guests – much to the disgust of some of the senators. She gave a smile at that last point. All in all, there was nothing in her statement that didn't tally with what we already knew, nothing to suggest she was lying and, unfortunately, nothing to suggest she knew anything of value concerning Lacanta's killing.

'Who's the leader of your troupe, the one who everyone seems to know as your figurehead?'

'You'll be after Drullus then.'

I gave a nod; she gave a sigh.

'Drullus. He managed to get pretty close to the king, didn't he?'

'How d'you know that?' Clydia didn't sound surprised, but I hoped she was.

'I'm the one who's meant to be asking questions,' I replied.

'That's a shame.' She drew her knees to her chest and took another sip of wine. There was something distant in her gaze that I couldn't quite fathom. Despite living with so many others, she seemed quite alone. 'Yeah, Drullus could charm his way with anyone. Even me.'

'But Licintius and Lacanta?'

'Not her, just him. Drullus managed to appeal to the creative side of the king and – somehow – the king expressed an interest in anything Drullus had to say. Drullus was like that, though. He always promised the world and the heavens to someone, but never came good.'

'Licintius and Drullus – did they ever sleep together?'

'What a sweet way of saying it, Drakenfeld. You mean, did they fuck?' She laughed at me. 'I never knew and, strangely for Drullus, he never said. He usually boasted about that sort of thing, whether with men or women. He wasn't fussy. But not with Licintius – didn't reveal anything. But we didn't mind though, we were all just happy for the money and comfort.'

'I'd like to speak to him – can you wake him for me?'

Concern manifested on her face and she became nervous. 'Drullus hasn't been here since the murder.'

Was this a lead at long last? Drullus' disappearance made finding him all the more pressing.

'Can you describe him for me?' I demanded.

'About as tall as you,' Clydia said, 'skinny, bronze skin, dark-blond hair that came down to his eyes. He sometimes wore it plaited.'

'Have you any idea where he might be found?' I asked. 'Any old addresses, relatives or friends?'

She moved forward to say something, but hesitated.

'Go on,' I urged her. 'If you know anything . . .'

'I don't. Not exactly. You heard of a gang called the Snake Kings?'

I let out a deep sigh and made a small prayer to Polla.

'Right after we left Optryx,' Clydia continued, 'he told us he was going to them. I knew about that gang, but didn't know Drullus even had connections there.' She described the location of where I might find the Snake Kings, but repeated that she had no idea where Drullus might have gone now.

I asked her to fetch the other members of the troupe, and one by one they all shuffled down the stairs, most of them young men, though there was one other woman. All were dressed in weird and wonderfully coloured clothing, though one man wore just a pair of trousers and seemed happy enough to parade around semi-naked.

They seemed fit and handsome people, and I imagined they made quite a lively bunch when they were all properly awake. A few slumped on the floor, a couple of them stood to talk with me. After my requesting it, Clydia told the others what she had told me so far. It was less confrontational coming from her; and meant I could watch their reactions to see if Clydia had been lying to me.

None of them showed signs of surprise; a couple of them were so tired they barely showed signs of life. Further questioning during Clydia's conversation didn't bring anything further to light. The actors' only connection to one another was their profession – they were a disparate bunch, from wildly different backgrounds. None of them had become close to Drullus in any significant way. Though they shared interests as well as jugs of wine, it appeared that Drullus had kept himself to himself.

Frustratingly, none of them could tell me anything about the night at Optryx that Clydia had not told me already. One of the men had seen Lacanta and remarked how attractive she was, and that he, too, had seen her moments before she had been found dead. When he saw her she had been full of life, smiling and laughing with other guests, as if she didn't have a care in the world.

One thing I did find interesting was that the king had constantly wanted them to perform certain plays – ones glorifying Detrata and establishing the king as a noble leader and the nearby nations as friends, not enemies. They explained that the king liked to create a mood whereby people of the city would feel more secure: satisfied by the conquests, and that they would want no more. When pushed on this, the actors suggested that the king actually preferred peace to war, stability to uncertainty, and that he was pro-Vispasia – unlike, it was said, many in the Senate.

The sudden appearance of the king down here was not as odd as I had assumed. Perhaps along with other reasons Licintius was using these actors for his own propaganda to boost his popularity around the city, and to spread his messages.

Of Drullus, it turned out that the other woman and two other men had slept with him, but nothing turning into anything serious. Drullus was not, they said, a man who liked to commit to anything other than the theatre. At last I told them they could go, but asked them not to leave the city. A few of them headed back upstairs, the other woman included. There was a tension between her and Clydia but I didn't think it was connected to the case.

As I was about to leave, Clydia stepped forward and touched my arm. 'Do you believe us?' Her eyes revealed a sudden panic. 'I don't want anything bad to happen to the troupe because we know the king. We just wanted to perform plays and not starve . . .'

'If you're telling me the truth,' I replied, 'then I see no reason for you to be afraid.'

As we left and continued back through the sunlit street, Leana said, 'And do you think she is telling the truth?'

I considered the matter and contemplated just what the actors might have gained from lying. 'She might be boasting a little, or they might be protecting themselves, but I believe she was being genuine enough — it was her fear at the end that persuades me. Why be so scared if she was making it up?'

The Snake Kings

Clouds had massed, darkening one half of the sky leaving the other in ochre tones. It started to rain. This was not just any kind of rain though, it was the kind that had received the full backing of the gods. I'd heard rumours that the city's priests had been conferring in the shadows of temples, praying to any god inclined to listen, in an attempt to help relieve the people of the city from the intense heat and surrounding crop failures. Street astrologers, hedge witches and those of the more dubious arts, had also been making sacrifices, casting runes and studying the stars in an attempt to bring rain.

Perhaps it was the will of the priests, priestesses, pontiffs and their clerics uniting in secret prayer that helped produce this downpour. Or, as I was inclined to believe, perhaps it was just the natural rhythms of the world, things that were simply beyond the control of even the gods, let alone priests.

Whatever the cause, the rain came as a blessed relief to the people of Tryum.

If the sun could not always reach down to these shaded lanes because of the height of the surrounding buildings, that did not stop the rain. Drummers stood on street corners as people danced barefoot in the mud. Children headed outside, their arms outstretched, and ran in circles while their parents laughed on from the shelter of an awning or doorway. A few traders were hastily erecting covers for their produce and wares, but even they did so with a beaming smile. In the poorest streets of the city, as we marched slowly across from Plutum to Barrantum, the mood of the populace grew increasingly happy. Tensions were dissolving before us in the rainwater.

I hoped the Snake Kings would also be in a better mood because of the weather.

The Snake Kings were a legendary gang of the lower districts of Tryum, mainly Barrantum if I remembered correctly, but who had some dealings elsewhere in the city. Of all the rival factions the Snake Kings had their fingers in most pies, including that of the Civil Cohorts who rarely intervened in any of their business.

And what a business it was. Coins, looted from private dwellings by their thieves, were melted down and sold back as ingots to those higher up in the city at a knock-down price. They charged commission to moneylenders who needed a little extra force to recover stubborn debts. Snake King members were more often than not responsible for trafficking young women — and young men — into the sex trade. The gang even possessed influence in the political sphere, helping to rig votes by keeping people away from the count, or in ensuring that graffiti against certain factions of the Senate was removed from the city walls.

They were not the only gang in the city — gangs were the silent shame of Tryum. Nowhere was free from their influence, and it was difficult to attach blame to their acts, much to the eternal frustration of my father, who would frequently curse their names.

Anyone who had an interest in furthering themselves in the

city liked to keep on the good side of the gangs. This meant that if the actor Drullus was indeed hiding behind the Snake King's protection, life might become very difficult for us trying to track him down.

'You honestly believe her?' It seemed Leana did not notice the rain. I had drawn up the hood of my cloak, but she had merely flipped up the collars of her jacket, continuing as normal, with water streaming down her face.

'Who?' I asked.

'Clydia.'

'You think I shouldn't believe her?'

'She is an actor,' she replied. 'She performs.'

'Everyone performs – some people are more honest about it than others. I'll grant you, the parts about the king's antics down here do seem a little improbable. But it is worth reminding ourselves that there were many leaders of the Detratan Empire who bedded men as well as women, and many a ruler who had no shame in associating him- or herself with those more unfortunate than people of their position.'

'She could be playing a game,' Leana said. 'Why are we here, in this part of the city? She may be sending us on a chase through the streets so we keep out of the way.'

'That may be so. But I'd rather that than have no chase whatsoever.'

It was getting late in the afternoon, but I felt we were at least closing in on something. I had a nagging suspicion at the back of my mind that no one was quite telling me the truth about the murder. No one seemed to have seen a thing out of the ordinary on the night of a seemingly impossible crime. That the king went to the lower regions of the city to express himself creatively did appear to me to be slightly fanciful. That a man had gone on the run, however, was not. That a man might also have been bedded by the king threw the case open to many new questions.

Clydia had described the location where the Snake Kings might be found, on the border of Barrantum and Vellyum, a street just off the main thoroughfare, which led down to one of Tryum's massive gates. It was a building of four floors beside a wood yard, with whitewashed walls that had seen better days. The sun had come out again, and there was a dark smear across the horizon where the clouds had moved on, looking like a volcano had spewed its contents to the heavens. Puddles sparkled in the afternoon light and the air felt a lot fresher. People had stopped working outside, for a moment, so the city was as calm as I'd seen since my arrival.

As we approached the door of the building, it was already ajar. Leana cautioned me, unsheathed her sword and pushed the door slowly back.

I followed her inside to a small room. Aside from the stone floor, the place was constructed entirely of wood, with thick beams crossing the ceiling. A strong smell of urine came from somewhere; perhaps we were above some sewers or near some operation that gathered the liquid for reuse. There was no one around, and there was only a stairway in front of us.

'What do you think?' she whispered. 'Head upstairs?'

'There's nowhere else to go,' I replied.

Leana led the way with me following on her heels. The place wasn't quite what I'd expected to find as a safe house run by a leading gang of the underworld – it felt abandoned.

We approached the top of the stairs and stood side by side, listening for any signs of life. There seemed to be conversation coming from further along the corridor, so we both took a few steps forward—

The floor gave way and we both fell into darkness.

*

'A trapdoor,' I said, looking up at the opening above us. How very embarrassing it was to fall through it — to fall for it.

'It could have been worse,' Leana grunted. 'You could have landed on the stone floor instead of falling on me.'

We found ourselves in a room on the ground floor. It was a crude cage of sorts, albeit the metal mesh was only on one side — the rest of the room was made from thick panels of wood. There wasn't much to be seen, the place was dusty and we were in the company of two rats. Testing the mesh got us nowhere; it seemed firm, but there was a lock.

'Do you have a pick?' I asked.

Leana reached down to her belt and handed over a pin. 'This do?'

'I'll see.' The lock possessed an impressive mechanism but I pushed my fingers through the mesh of the cage and manoeuvred the pin into the key mechanism. It wouldn't take me too long — when training for the Sun Chamber we often spent many hours working on the various types of locks found throughout Vispasia. This one was a particularly common variety, a cheap but usually effective lock, and remembering how its insides functioned it only took a few moments before there was a click.

'There we go.' Handing the pick back to Leana, I grinned and pushed the cage door open.

As soon as we set foot outside, there was the sound of people approaching. We were on our guard as the door to a room opened, revealing two figures silhouetted by the cresset light behind. Short swords glimmered in their hands.

'Stay where you are,' they cautioned.

Leana showed them her own weapon. 'Two of them, two of us,' she sneered.

'I'm happy with those odds,' I added.

'All right,' a figure said. 'We don't want no blood this afternoon.'

'A man after my own heart,' I replied.

'Lay your weapons down,' the man grunted.

'And you,' Leana snapped. 'Put down your swords.'

'What's going on down there?' a more aggressive voice shouted, possibly their boss.

'Now look, this is not a particularly pleasant welcome,' I called out, hoping to defuse the situation. 'Is this how simple guests are treated in Tryum these days?'

'Who the hell is talking like that?' The figures parted revealing another slightly shorter man.

'If we had some proper light down here you might be able to see who,' I replied.

'Listen to the rich boy speak,' the man said. 'He's got a lovely voice, don't he? Shame to lose a tongue like that. Ruin a handsome face. We could sell him as a whore and make a lot of money.'

'You would die trying,' Leana interrupted.

'Easy, lads. I like women from where she comes from. Atrewe, ain't that so? I'd remember that accent a mile off. You're a long way from home, black lady.'

Leana didn't move but I figured it was only a matter of time and while I had no issue in principle with this man being erased from the city, I hoped to Polla she would not kill anyone, not when we needed answers instead of corpses.

'Thoughtful people, you Atrewens — could kill you in the morning and write a poem about it in the afternoon,' the man continued admiringly. 'You don't talk as much as we do in case the spirits hear you, ain't that so? I spent some time there in my younger days, when I was stealing ships around the coast. Good days they were. Atrewe is a big place. You come all the way here with a man like him?'

'Get to the point or I will open your stomach and leave you to the rats.'

There was a silence in which he assessed us.

'Rich man, what's your name?' he called out.

'Lucan Drakenfeld, Officer of the Sun Chamber, newly stationed in Tryum. This is Leana, my peace mediator.'

He snorted. 'Man with a sense of humour. I like that.'

'It helps to pass the time.'

Another figure emerged and stood alongside the others, blocking what little light there was and probably our only exit too.

'Is this the home of the Snake Kings?' I asked.

'One of them.'

'Good. Are you their chief?'

'One of them.'

'That's a start,' I replied.

'Shouldn't we be asking the questions, since you've fallen through our trapdoor?'

'You just asked a question right there.'

The shorter man stepped closer. 'You talk far too glibly for my liking. Tongues that quick are best removed. What're you doing here?'

'We're looking for someone, an actor named Drullus.'

'Drullus.' He turned to his colleagues and said, 'I've never heard of a Drullus. Have any of you heard of a Drullus?'

'No,' came the reply, all well rehearsed, and all of this pitched to steer me towards bribing them.

'Let's get to the point. How much do you want?' I asked.

'A thousand pecullas.'

For them to request so much meant that Drullus must have paid them something near that figure to keep his whereabouts quiet. It was a lot of money, more than a year's earnings for most people – and certainly more than anyone in Plutum would probably see in their lives. All of this begged the question of how an actor could possibly get his hands on that much cash. Of course, it wouldn't be an issue if he had friends in high places . . .

'What would we get for a thousand pecullas?' I demanded.

'A specific location. Whether you find Drullus there or not, we can't say.'

My eyes were growing accustomed to the darkness. The leader's face was broad, though without an ounce of fat, and his eyes narrow. He was certainly a good head shorter than me, though he looked nimble, as if he knew how to fight and flee.

Leana was outraged. 'A man came to you for protection, for shelter, and you're willing to sell him out? Where's your honour?'

He grunted. 'I'm running a business here. What's honour got to do with it?'

'I'm a member of the Sun Chamber pursuing an investigation. You could be held accountable for withholding information,' I told him.

'My gang might say otherwise.'

'You realize I could bring an army to this place – you've heard of the Sun Legion, haven't you? Five thousand of the finest and highest-paid soldiers in all of Vispasia could come straight to Tryum and wipe the Snake Kings from the collective memory of the city.'

'That would mean you had to get out first,' he sneered.

'Your trapdoor and lock didn't hold us. Are you sure you like your chances against an angry Atrewen warrior and myself, a trained Officer of the Sun Chamber?'

He paused considering.

Leana took a step closer to him and whispered, 'I will kill your men quickly, but before I send you into the afterlife I will first skin you with breath still in your body.'

He grunted a laugh.

'She means it,' I assured him. 'She's killed a few people already today. However, the other option is that I pay one hundred pecullas and have the money delivered here before noon tomorrow. You get your money, I get my information. And I promise that no harm will come to your client.'

'Five hundred.'

'One hundred pecullas.'

'Three,' he bargained, 'and the offer of a network of good men should you need it.'

I waited in silence, considering that I'd have to request authorization for a bribery receipt later to recover the money. How I hated administration. However, having a network such as the Snake Kings to hand was worth the effort.

'Three,' I agreed. 'Delivered here before noon tomorrow.' I offered my hand and forearm and he shook it.

The tension in the room seemed to vanish.

'My name is Yadrix Velor.' He smiled widely. 'And I'm glad to make a connection with an Officer of the Sun Chamber.'

Drullus' hideout was not too far from the Snake Kings and, after the brief interlude, we continued through the streets once again. Unfortunately Yadrix could offer no further information about Drullus, especially on why he was seeking a hideout at all.

'People seek help from me all the time,' Yadrix had commented. 'I do not ask for their secrets − I do not care, as long as they can pay. There is a lucrative trade to be found in such things in this city.'

I hated making deals with people like Yadrix as they were people who profited from misery, but sometimes it seemed the only way of getting what was required.

Relieved not to have engaged in another fight, and glad − as ever − that Leana was by my side, I asked her if she was all right after Yadrix brought up the subject of her country, Atrewe, with that niggling guilt that I had dragged her far from her home.

'You mean, do I want to go home to Atrewe?' she replied. 'No. I am happy here.'

'Are you sure?'

'Yes,' she replied.

'Do you miss Atrewe? I never ask.'

'I am happy. Few people in Tryum – in Vispasia – would ever meet someone from Atrewe. From what I understand in Venyn, many think us bad, stupid people. Here so far I have been treated as a novelty. I can change those thoughts – they will respect Atrewens. I believe that will do all Atrewens a favour in the long run.'

Leana and I had shared so many experiences over the years, been in so many scrapes together, that much of my life was framed by her reassuring presence. We'd faced street executions by Venyn gangs; we had uncovered treasure hoards on the eastern Vispasian coast. We had been in the presence of priestesses and bishops, of kings and queens. We'd eaten snake as the sun set, purpling the skies of the desert regions, in our relentless hunt of a multiple child murderer. We had witnessed armies clash on a beautiful glade, turning it into a bloodbath, before moving in to arrest the victorious general with just a hundred men of the Sun Legion at our side. It was difficult to imagine my role without her. And yet, despite all of our shared experiences, she rarely opened up to me. Perhaps it was a cultural quirk, but I felt she knew me far better than I did her.

Bad weather had come again since our brief time with the Snake Kings, and rainwater still trickled downhill. The refreshing smell made the journey to the location somewhat more pleasant. It was the middle of the afternoon and hunger was setting in, so we stopped off at a pastry stall and purchased food to eat on the way. As the rich flavours filled my mouth, it made me realize just how much I'd missed the local cuisine, though it had never cost this much. The vendor muttered only that the city was over-crowded, and that there wasn't enough food in Detrata.

The house we were seeking was right on the border of Vellyum, situated on a surprisingly pleasant street. A good family with an honest trade might wish to live somewhere like this. There were low-level structures with shops facing the street, much like in Tradum and Polyum, though not as refined. The roads needed a little more repair, the walls were plastered with more graffiti than was possible to read, and there was the overpowering stench of urine – but it was a good street, with a man nearby wearing the sash of the local Civil Cohorts keeping the peace.

Beyond the store selling cloth, we headed through into the narrow alleyway and down the side of the building, the gap only a little wider than my shoulders. We continued along until we found the red door we'd been directed to.

'This is it.' I moved to try the door, but paused, considering my options.

'Knock it or kick it?' Leana asked.

'Kick it. He wouldn't open it unless it's to someone he knows or is expecting. If we knock, he might slip out of another entrance.'

I took a look around the alleyway to check no one was about. This wasn't exactly the way we did things in the Sun Chamber. Leana had been a bad influence on me. But there was little here except the high walls and stone pavements, only a washing line stretched at the far end between the two buildings.

Back by the door, we both took a couple of steps, then struck the lock-side of the door together, and it shuddered back. One more determined kick from Leana and it smashed open com-pletely. I rushed inside to confront our suspect while Leana stayed back to see if he would make an exit from a window.

Inside the long, thin corridor was empty but decorated with cheap frescoes and mosaics. Wondering whether our bird had already flown, I moved quickly into the next room, which was a kitchen, before running up the stairs into darkness on the floor above and entering another room. It was filled with a cloying and all too familiar stench. I reached across to open the wooden shutters.

There, sprawled on its side with bent knees, a corpse became illuminated by the hazy afternoon light.

The Stench of Death

When Leana arrived she put her hand to her nose. 'Spirits save us, are there no more windows to let in the breeze?'

'None that I can see.'

The pervasive stench indicated that the man had been dead for some time. His blood had pooled and dried on the floor. Dressed in casual garb, which seemed loose-fitting on his slender frame, his skin was lightly bronzed and his hair was dark-blond: he fitted the description that Clydia had given us.

'Leana,' I said, 'I need you to find your way back to the Skull and Jasmine house. Though we've travelled a long way around the city, I don't think it's too far from here. We need Clydia to come here and identify the body. Tell her she can bring a couple of the other actors if she needs them.'

Leana nodded and left the room, and a moment later I spotted her sprinting through the street.

With the sounds of the busy community outside, I set about assessing what had happened.

There was no blood to be found on the walls and in fact not even around the edges of this room – which implied there had not been a struggle. There were no signs of a fight, no broken jars or pottery, all of which were still standing by chairs or on tabletops. There was an uneaten loaf of bread, a bowl of olives and two apples on the table, laid out for a solitary dinner with one wooden cup of water, and two silver peculla coins next to it.

One of the other rooms was his sleeping area, a dark bare chamber with a couple of unlit lanterns and, aside from a small bag of clothes, there was nothing for me to go on. Everything was incredibly neat and tidy, the picture of an everyday man living alone.

The state of the room where the corpse lay suggested two things: either the man had taken his own life, or he was killed by a professional. Yet, it couldn't have been suicide. Not only was there no blade nearby, but if this was Drullus, he had paid a lot of money to hide away here in order to keep his life, not to give it up. But if it had been a murder, then the victim must have known his killer to have let him in. Either that, or we were dealing with a highly skilled operator, who could move about the streets with quiet grace and stealth, and could gain entry to this building without force. In many respects, it was not unlike the case of Lacanta's murder. I double-checked the rest of the house, especially the windows, but there were no signs of anything being amiss.

I reached down and turned the body over, noting that the stiffness of death had long since set in. There was just one clean but very deep cut along his throat. Had the blow been a rapid slash from in front, or a careful slice from behind? The knees were bent, too, which indicated he had been kneeling down before his killer as his throat was opened – as if he had submitted himself for execution. Drullus may have known there was no point in running away: this would have been a pitiful death for the poor actor.

There was a dark thread no more than the length of a finger, which had been caught in his nails as if he'd been clutching at his attacker, pleading for mercy. A piece of thread this common could tell me very little, but simply added to the broader picture of what may have taken place.

There were no signs of a head wound, not even any bruising to the flesh. So he hadn't been beaten or attacked, pointing again to a professional hit rather than a break-in or robbery gone wrong. His tunic was drenched in blood, but I didn't yet want to strip the clothing to examine the rest of his torso, not until Clydia had formally identified him and confirmed my suspicions.

Leana returned with Clydia and two of the other actors; young attractive men, one with a slender frame, one with broad shoulders, both with cropped black hair – they looked similar enough to be brothers. One wore a grey tunic, a dark cloak and sandals, the other had dressed in tones of dark green. Clydia, in her long blue cape, was dressed for the rain.

Crouching down, I peeled back a blanket I had found to cover the body, revealing his face, trying to hide the worst of the injuries from them. Clydia immediately let out a wail. She turned into the shoulder of the slender actor and sobbed and heaved repeatedly while he stroked her hair with one hand and stared aghast at the scene.

The one with the broader shoulders stepped forward and crouched down next to me. 'That's him all right,' he breathed and shook his head. 'Poor, poor Drullus.'

Poor Drullus indeed. So here before us all was the most promising lead in the case of Lacanta's murder, and he was dead in his own safe house.

'I'm going to ask some routine questions and I'd be grateful if you can answer truthfully.'

The actor nodded.

'When did you really last see Drullus?' I asked.

'I honestly didn't see him after the performance at Optryx – and we left before the ceremonies started to reach a climax. We tend to come and go out of our house, so don't really pay much attention to each other's movements unless there's a production looming. But I'm pretty sure it was right after that evening's performances, when we went our own way.'

'Do you have any idea who might have done this, perhaps an enemy of the group?'

'There were people we all upset, and often. Actors aren't exactly loved in Tryum. We're treated like whores a lot of the time.'

'But could anyone you know have come in here and slit his throat? I ask this, because I'm inclined to believe Drullus knew his killer and let him in.' I explained the few signs of a disturbance and that the broken door was our doing.

'I honestly don't know. I don't think so. I don't even know what this place is – your lady –' he indicated Leana '– told me he was hiding out. I've no idea why. He made no mention of it before. He just went out, but we didn't think it important because he could be gone for a couple of days at a time.'

The other man, his arms still around Clydia, nodded to confirm this point.

'Well,' I continued, 'it seemed he intended to remain here for a while at least. Look at the food on the table.'

'That's Drullus' diet all right. He liked to look after himself – said that his physique and complexion would improve.'

'He didn't even drink wine, not like we do,' Clydia added.

'You . . . you don't think we're in trouble do you, sir?' the slender man asked. 'Will whoever did this, will they come after us as well?'

I shook my head. 'Drullus came here on his own, knowing that it was he alone who was being hunted. And he was right, too. So I do not think you are in immediate danger. I would, however, remain vigilant. If you have friends, go and stay with them. Don't go out alone. Being cautious will do you no harm.'

I pulled the blanket back across Drullus' face, and stood up once again, noting that the afternoon sun was sliding from the sky. It was time to let these actors get back home. They would not be much help now so, after giving them my address in case any information should surface, I told them a message would be sent when Drullus was available for burial.

Once they had gone, Leana stepped alongside, by Drullus' corpse. 'You look unwell.'

'I'm fine. In a way, I grieve for him. Here was a handsome young man with potentially a decent life ahead of him, where he could enjoy his work. And it was cut short, for what reason? What did poor Drullus do exactly?'

'It could be connected to Lacanta somehow?'

A dead royal and a dead actor, both now in the Underworld with help from a blade. Their lives crossed in some way, potentially, but I suspected that only King Licintius would know how. 'Before I can really say, we need to see the king. I want to watch his reaction to the news of Drullus' death.'

As we headed out of the room, I noticed something by the door frame and crouched down to pick it up.

'Have you found something?' Leana asked, leaning over me.

I twirled a leaf around in my fingers. It was still green, indicating it had not been a dried import, and it was generally an oval-shape with several acute points. 'Henbane, I believe. I could be mistaken.'

'Here.'

I stood and handed it to Leana, who confirmed my suspicions.

'Now,' I said, 'what would an actor be doing with a leaf of henbane?'

'Maybe he made a drug from it to get visions? It could be some creative thing. You know what these people can be like.'

'Henbane is also a poison,' I replied, standing up. 'And you heard what the actors told us — he liked to look after himself.'

'Well, he didn't die because of this leaf — unless it is as sharp as a blade,' Leana remarked, running her finger along the edge.

'Indeed not,' I replied. 'But how did a fresh henbane leaf get here?'

Veldrum Hecater

We checked with the locals along the street enquiring where we might find a herbalist but there were none nearby and certainly no one could be found selling henbane on the nearby market stalls.

While we were in this part of the city, I felt it prudent to pay a quick return visit to Yadrix Velor and the Snake Kings, to see if they knew anything about Drullus' death. So much for the protection money he had paid them.

Yadrix was in a much more welcoming spirit this time, as he was hopeful of a connection with the Sun Chamber, but he knew nothing of what had happened to Drullus. He claimed that his job had been merely to provide a safe house for the actor, and it was Drullus' own fault if he let in his own murderer.

I also asked him if he dealt in henbane, in any form, but he shrugged. 'There are stronger poisons available if you want to kill someone,' he claimed, 'and more effective herbs if you want to escape reality for a few hours.'

It was time to head back up-city before the evening fell, but via a route that would take us past the border of Vellyum and

Plutum, which was near to the Seventh Temple of Malax. In that area was the house of the moneylender Veldrum Hecater.

My father's supposed debt to him had been at the back of my mind all day. With that matter resolved, perhaps my mind would settle more, allowing me to focus on the murders. At the very least, he could stop sending people to attack us. If money was owed, the debts would be paid, but just how bad had the situation for my father been?

A couple of shopkeepers nearby were starting to pack up for the day. After asking one of them which was Veldrum Hecater's door, they pointed to a splendid gated property set back from the street.

'You should do this on your own,' Leana said. 'It does not look to be a terrible place. I know that this is a private thing for you also.'

'That's very considerate,' I said. 'I'll meet you back at our house.'

She nodded and started to walk swiftly back along the high pavement.

The gates to the property were open, so I took that to be a welcome gesture and headed straight for the main door. The gardens, in the late afternoon and after the rain, were magnificent to walk through, and I noted a handful of species I had seen on my travels, some even all the way from Venyn, and a handsome fig tree.

I knocked on the large double door and called out for Veldrum Hecater. A moment later a hatch slid back and a foreign woman asked for my name. I gave that and my title, suspecting that it would already be a familiar one in this household.

The door opened and two servants ushered me inside to the hallway, where they told me to wait. Sunlight slid through the open roof at an angle, illuminating a vibrant red fresco beyond.

The fountain in the centre of the room had collected a lot of water. There were many great works of art here, and statues of several kings and queens – including a fine one of Licintius himself, which didn't look all that unlike him.

'Son of Calludian,' came a voice. A slightly hunched man shuffled towards me, wearing a black tunic, light-grey trousers and slippers, and he carried a cane in his right hand. He must have been at least fifty years old and the expression that time had carved into his face was one of utter satisfaction with the world.

'Are you Veldrum Hecater?' I asked.

He nodded once, and smiled. 'You look . . . rather unkempt, young man. Have the gods been unkind today?'

I had no answer for that. 'You've sent several men of little skill to my house recently – and if not to my house, then to hunt me through the streets like an animal.'

'Ah. That is true.'

'All I received from these men was a garbled message about my father's debts. If you had a problem, you should have talked to me personally. I'm a reasonable man and I always follow the law.'

'You know how these things go, a man of your standing,' Veldrum replied. 'Delegation. A message goes down the chain and before long it becomes rather confused. I'll see to it that someone's punished. I'm sorry my men bothered you, but . . . we were owed rather a lot of money.'

'So I understand,' I said. 'How much?'

'Let me see. Please, let us move to a more private room, away from the curious ears of my slaves.' The old man gestured for me to follow him. 'Can I get you a drink?'

'Water would be most refreshing, thank you.'

'Nothing stronger?'

'Not at this moment,' I replied.

'As you wish. I will see one of my slaves brings it to my study.'

Again, he stressed the word 'slave' as if he wanted to make a point of owning them. It was rare to see slaves within people's houses these days – they were illegal unless brought in from overseas. No doubt Veldrum Hecater would be among those seeking to purchase slaves fresh from Maxant's victory in Mauland.

His study was lined with ledgers, and a large desk stood against a small window that faced across the gardens. The place was a bit of a mess, with piles of paper all over the black and red tiled floor. Veldrum lifted a hand abacus from one wicker chair and asked me to sit while he rifled around in one of his drawers. A milky-skinned young man in plain clothing came in to hand me a cup of water, and I thanked him. Veldrum did not even seem to notice he had come in.

Veldrum drew out a heavy ledger and, with focus and caution, flicked through the pages while muttering about the quality of the paper. It seemed absurd that, for this man, something so profound in my father's life – these apparent debts – could simply be reduced to another line of information in a book.

'Here we are,' he announced, hunching further over the book as if to better understand his own handwriting. 'Now, your father borrowed twenty thousand pecullas and, with interest, the deal we agreed on was for him to pay back thirty thousand within a year.'

I nearly spilled my water, but managed to place the cup to one side. 'Thirty thousand pecullas?'

'That is correct. It is one of my larger loans, but he was in a good position in society and had a stable career, and the rate of interest was very competitive. I don't always make such pleasant deals.'

'How much did he pay back?' I asked.

'He made regular payments of five hundred pecullas a month, which would have taken him a long time to cover the full debt, and which may well have ended in more interest if the contract became invalid.' Veldrum followed the lines in the ledger once again. 'That said, he did make one rather large payment and very nearly managed to clear the debt . . . Yes, here we go. He made a payment of twenty-one thousand pecullas.'

'In one go?'

'That is correct. Three months ago, to be precise. I remember it because it was just before the Festival of Festonia.'

'How much is left on his account?'

'He needed to pay four thousand pecullas to settle the debt, which, of course, falls to you to pay. I have all the paperwork here — all signed in the presence of a witness.'

He showed me the documents and, true to his word, there was my father's signature and the family seal in red wax alongside it.

'I'll pay the four thousand,' I sighed. Taking into account the bribe I'd have to pay from this morning, it meant all of my remaining savings, all the money I had transferred across from Venyn, would be gone. I still hadn't received any salary payment this month from the Sun Chamber, but it could not arrive soon enough.

'Oh, that is good news.' Veldrum Hecater reached for a reed pen to make a note in the ledger. He blew for the ink to dry and set the book on his desk. Meanwhile I started wondering just how under Polla's blessed gaze I was going to make ends meet. I would have to send urgent messages to a Sun Chamber station post to transfer money in my name to Tryum. Perhaps one day I could sell the villa — I barely had enough use of all the rooms in one house let alone another one standing empty.

'I'll have the money sent to you by nightfall tomorrow,' I said.

Veldrum Hecater nodded and sat back in his chair.

'There's just one small matter that I don't quite understand,' I continued. 'Why would my father come to you, a moneylender down-city? I do not mean to cause offence, sir, but there are far more respectable establishments in Polyum and Tradum that he could have sought. Banks themselves, perhaps.'

Veldrum broke into a peaceful smile. 'He came to me for the same reason anyone would, young man. Shame. Shame certainly helps a person feel humble. Whatever his reason, he was too proud to go to someone in his own neighbourhood who might know him. Gossip does tend to spread like wildfire in Tryum. However, I can't help you out with the question of why. That is one mystery you will have to solve for yourself.'

'The debts will be settled. Will you call off your men?'

Veldrum nodded. 'I am sorry they have been rather rough. Many of them are not in my employment directly – we tend to outsource to private groups from time to time. I don't like all that nasty business, but people will go about the city believing they can take money from others but not give it back. The world cannot operate in such a way.'

I said my goodbyes to the moneylender and headed back out into the streets, which were bathed in the soft red light of sunset and, pulling my cloak around me, I strolled back along the busy main roads towards Polyum, wondering why my father needed the money and how someone in a position of responsibility could have ended up in this kind of trouble.

The Apothecary

Early in the evening I decided to take a bath, and felt all the better for doing so.

A small, private bathroom was such a privilege. The floor possessed a lovely pattern of bold red and blue mosaics, and there was a metal-lined base to the bathtub itself, under which hot coals were placed to warm up the water – though one had to be careful the coals were not too hot, else they might burn.

There were many public baths scattered throughout Vispasia, of course, but they were very social places, where senators, councillors, traders, soldiers and bureaucrats would hatch their plans. This comfort was such a contrast to life on the other side of Vispasia. It was easy to see how wealth might easily spoil someone.

Bellona, Polla bless her, had already heated a few coals and placed lanterns around the room creating a mellow and relaxing atmosphere. In this quiet solitude I could gather my thoughts – and there was no shortage of things to be thinking about.

Lacanta's death echoed through my mind. Her seemingly impossible murder and the still-burning incense – was that possibly some kind of offering to Trymus? The locked door niggled me incessantly. Then there was the room that suggested she was, at heart, rather a quiet person, and not the scandalous figure portrayed in public. Were her affairs all some kind of act? A way to work her political charms in order to steer Licintius' policies through the Senate?

The king, too, seemed to be more of a mystery than he first appeared. There was potentially the air of a love affair surrounding his relationship with the deceased Drullus. I still couldn't work out why someone wanted to hunt down and kill Drullus. Perhaps he had seen something that night, or even been the killer. Was it an act of passion — jealousy driving him to kill the one person closer to Licintius than he? It felt like a long shot. Finally there was that leaf from the poisonous plant henbane, which seemed so out of place in Drullus' hideout.

On top of all this loomed my father's mysterious debts. It seemed so out of character for him. What was he doing that required him to borrow so much in the first place? He managed to keep Bellona on staff despite this, though it was well known in our family that he couldn't cook for himself. I called for Bellona, who briefly made an appearance at the door, though wouldn't come into the room.

'Was there anyone else who worked here?'

Her reply came as a whisper, 'Another cleaner, but your father had to let him go.'

'Could he not afford him?'

'He would not say. Please, I must attend to dinner.'

'Thank you,' I replied, listening to the soft sound of her slippers across the tiles.

So the sad truth was that I had never really known him well enough to be a decent judge of his true character. Just as the rest of the world had seen him, all I witnessed was the urbane investigator, more concerned about closing a case than spending time with his family. Perhaps if I'd visited more, if I'd written to him more often . . .

So many 'ifs'.

I would have the rest of my life to worry about being a more considerate son, but for now I slipped down the bathtub and buried my face under the warm water, hoping it would wash away my concerns – if just for a moment.

Leana later asked if she could use the bath after me, refusing my offer that she could use fresh water, with an admonishment about the waste 'so typical of this godforsaken, sinful city'. There were times I wish she wasn't quite as adept with my language – or as colourful – as she is.

While she was bathing I informed her of my plans to go out into the city to pick up a few supplies. She didn't question me, thankfully, and agreed to my request that she saw the bribe was paid to Yadrix Velor. I left the necessary money in a purse on her bed. In the corner of the room stood her wooden Atrewen idol, a representative of the spirit master Gudan – he was not a god exactly, since there were no definite gods in Atrewen culture. Gudan was a legendary figure to Leana, a man who could converse with the spirits, and someone on whom her spirituality could be focused. It prompted me to take a moment to pray to my goddess.

Finding the shrine that Bellona had moved into the hall, and bowing before the statue of Polla, I requested her aid in cleansing my mind and strengthening my powers of logic and intuition. Polla was a gentle goddess, her human form one of exquisite beauty and modesty – unlike many of the other gods and goddesses in existence. With the subtle, knowledgeable tilt of her head, and the Book of Wisdom open in her hands, the statue was deeply inspiring. Lighting some incense in a small burner and waving the smoke over my face, I lost myself in the ritual, letting her cool logic and calm presence fill me.

A few moments later, wearing a green cotton shirt and a decent pair of black trousers, I threw my cloak around me and headed out into the night with a spring in my step.

Walking out of my gates with a pocketful of coin, the city seemed pleasantly cooler after the rain. Where to tonight? The niggling sensation of the seizure last night had remained at the back of my mind all through the day, and though I had prayed to Polla, I did wonder if a more earthly solution was possible.

Leana had mentioned there was an apothecary nearby.

It wouldn't hurt to take a look.

The apothecary seemed to be one of those shops that never quite looked either open or closed. And it was on one of those streets that meant a lot of people had to be asked before I was directed to the right place. But sure enough, under a sign with long-faded gold lettering, stood the apothecary. I was glad of its concealed location.

This street was just about wide enough to get a horse through; it wound tightly down a gentle slope, with two-storey structures on either side. Several cats sashayed back and forth before me, pausing to nose the air as if my presence had somehow ruined the ambience.

I knocked on the apothecary's door, making certain my face remained in the shadows. All around were the sounds of the city moving into its evening alter ego, while on the next street along was yet another cart grinding its wheels against a wall or pavement, and at least three local residents cursing at the driver.

The door opened and a woman in her forties, wearing a smart grey gown, stood there. 'Oh, I'm afraid I'm just about to finish for the night, sir.'

'Perhaps I should come back some other time then. I don't wish to impose.' My voice felt uncomfortably frail and I turned away quickly.

'No, please, come in,' she said rather jovially, placing a hand gently on the side of my arm. She looked me in the eye and had such a determined look about her. 'It's been a quiet day and I could do with the trade. Besides, you actually seem as though you are avoiding me, which I find curious. Please, put yourself at ease.'

Laughing awkwardly, I followed her inside and closed the door behind me.

The smell was incredible: a whole array of herbs, spices and oils blending together, some on a small stove, others sitting in open jars. In the light of a couple of paper lanterns, I was able to take a better look at the woman. She was maybe a bit younger than I first thought, her hair a pale blonde rather than grey – the kind of colouring found in people from the far north. Her eyes were an intense shade of green, and set in a narrow face. Her gown covered a grey woollen tunic that was splattered in stains, much like that of an artist. She also seemed to have a surprisingly good posture, and not that of someone who had spent years hunching over a table.

Thick wooden shelves held up ledgers, one of which was open on a desk, next to a candle. From my quick glance, I noted long lists of complex plant names with observations alongside them, much like those of a physician. This was promising: there seemed to be the satisfying air of logic about her profession.

'So how can I be of help?' she asked. 'It is not often I have a gentleman of such lofty upbringing visiting me.' Her voice was soothing. I could have listened to her talking all night long.

'Is it my accent?' I wondered if I sounded out of touch with people who lived even a few streets down from my own.

She gave a gentle laugh and walked behind her work desk, on which stood glass jars and wooden trays with little dividers. 'Your boots, actually. I've not seen boots that well made for a long time.' Her gaze moved up and down my body, keenly assessing me.

'I'm here because I need something to calm the mind.'

'Could you be more specific?' she asked. 'Is it a headache?'

'No.' I watched her grind some seeds or herbs with a pestle and mortar.

'It's OK, it really is,' she said. 'I don't know who you are; you don't have to tell me either. I won't even tell you my name, if anonymity is important. But I can't help you unless you tell me the specific symptoms. I'm not some countryside witch. There's a considered process to my methods. Now, are you having strange thoughts or dreams?'

'No more than anyone else,' I replied.

'Well, we can rule out trying a mage to read them for diagnosis then. Tell me more.'

'It's my father. He suffers from seizures. I'm concerned I might have inherited such things, though I've shown no signs of it. I'm worried that I too might be cursed by the gods.'

'Who is your god?'

'Goddess,' I replied. 'Polla.'

She nodded. 'The lady of knowledge – I've read her texts and can see why your mind matters to you. But tell me about your father's symptoms.'

We probably both realized this was a charade, but I revealed what I could under the guise of my father: that the seizures occurred, sometimes in sleep; that they came and went with no reason nor rhyme; that he could remember nothing about them at the time; and that the experience was certainly not one conducive to visions. I added that he was used to them – that they were

182

part of his life now, and he accepted them and the headaches that sometimes came with them, but he would certainly appreciate them to strike less often so that he could get on with his life.

When I finished the description of the affliction, the apothecary stopped what she was doing and nodded. 'I've heard of such seizures before. Sometimes they come after an injury to the head, sometimes they come after a great illness. I'm afraid I have nothing that can stop them for ever. However, I have heard of some remedies that can – for some people – lower the risk of these seizures occurring, so that may be of help to your father as well as yourself, if you are worried such things are hereditary.'

I nodded and leaned on the edge of the table. 'You're certain they'll work?'

'Some people of this city will claim opening up a rabbit's entrails will help you understand the world better. Some people think they can divine things from the skies. Who am I to argue if they believe it to be helpful to them? All I know is that I have made years of studies – as did my mother, and as did her mother. I keep honest notes of what I do. As a man of Polla, I'm sure you appreciate such methodology.'

I let out a gentle sigh. 'I'll take whatever I can.'

She moved to her shelves and began looking for certain jars, picking them up one by one. She laid them out on her workbench and began transferring the contents into a tiny wooden box.

'How much do I owe you?' I asked.

'Ten pecullas,' she replied and, after seeing my reaction, added, 'prices are going up each year due to demand for herbs. It's the same all across the country.'

Funny how we only appreciated the true cost of items when we could barely afford them. I reached into my pocket, counted the coins out and handed them over. She passed me the small box. 'Make a tisane from these — just three pinches in each cup. Drink it as often as you can.'

'What's in here?'

'Mainly gingko biloba, which is a known aid for matters of the mind, but I have put in three or four exotic species in addition. I would like it if you could let me know if your father improves at all.'

This felt like an illicit transaction, but I nodded, thanked her, and without making eye contact moved towards the door then paused. 'I don't suppose you would know what henbane could be used for, do you? All I know is that it's a poison.'

'And a deadly one, too!' She gave a brief laugh, though her expression grew to one of anger. 'You don't want to take any of that. Trust me.'

'No, I'm not going to. I just wondered if there may be other uses for it.'

'Some claim to use it in making alcoholic brews, but mostly it's used as a poison.'

'Do you know the nearest place where the plant grows?'

'Certainly not near Tryum. I know of suppliers who can fetch some in from further afield, but the nearest grower would be in Maristan at the very least, and that's a few days' travel. The poison tends to be created out of the city and imported. You should take care not to acquire any, stranger. Many a good man has died from encounters with that plant.'

Perhaps Drullus was one of them.

Perhaps Some Dancing

'Drakenfeld!' Senator Veron marched towards me in his smart evening attire as I approached the front gates of my home.

'Senator Veron. You're dressed for a night out in the city, I see.' I indicated his rich brown cloak, red tunic and polished boots.

'I am,' he replied, clasping my arm. 'And you're coming with me.'

'I am?'

'You are.'

'Where are we going?' I asked, as he guided me along the street.

'For drinks, and perhaps some dancing.'

'Oh, I'm not really the dancing type.'

'We're not the ones who will be doing the dancing.'

'Any particular reason for this?'

'No one should have to spend the night of his father's funeral alone,' he declared. 'So I've taken it upon myself to cheer you up.'

'You have?'

'And you can thank me later.'

✻

As we passed through the busy streets, he casually asked me how I was getting on with the case and whether or not my investigation of the Skull and Jasmine troupe produced anything of note.

It became apparent, very early on in our relationship, that Veron was something of a gossip and a socialite but his flamboyant charms were entertaining. Tonight he clearly wanted information to satisfy his own curiosity, and use it in whatever way he could to gain an advantage over other senators. It would do no harm to keep him on side, so while I did not reveal my knowledge of Drullus' death, my adventures in the lower city seemed more than enough to keep him interested.

'I've come also with a message for you,' Veron announced. 'The king wants to see you tomorrow, and he requested that I let you know. He's after something of a progress report – he's been rotten company since the murder. His mood has been foul and, on quite unrelated matters, he's ordered his personal guard to beat a priest and a judge – though the latter had it coming to him, to be fair. Anyway, Licintius wants the head of Lacanta's killer on a spike at the earliest opportunity.'

'That's fortunate,' I replied, contemplating how calm he'd been in my company. 'I'd actually hoped to meet with the king soon, and to revisit some of those rooms in Optryx.'

'You think there may be something useful there?'

'It wouldn't hurt to explore the place further, to get an idea of any potential hiding places the killer could have used.'

'You lead an exciting life, Drakenfeld. It's a world away from legislation. Let me know if you need further access around the city and I'll do what I can.'

'I appreciate it, senator. So, where exactly are we going?'

'You'll see,' he replied, with a devilish smirk. 'You've made it perfectly clear that you are a man who does not want to settle down with a woman—'

'Despite your best efforts,' I laughed.

'I have cousins, distant relatives, who are still unattached and you seem a worthy match indeed.'

'Are you working on commission for them?'

'There's a business worth exploring!' he replied. 'Anyway, as I was saying, if you're not in the market for a wife, then you are a man who must like the pleasures that an unattached life can offer. Therefore, we are going to one of the more . . . shall we say, exclusive taverns in the city.'

'A tavern . . . with dancing?'

'The finest women in the city, no less.'

'You mean a brothel.' I shook my head. It was no secret that everyone in Tryum was fascinated by such matters — apart from me, who had better things to do. There were brothels of all kinds, for all purses and all tastes. Sometimes the business of sex never even made it indoors, and around some districts one might see furtive transactions being made behind crumbling colonnades.

'By Trymus, no,' he said. 'You don't approve of such places though? Not in the mood for women? I know of a place for men — good, strong young men, so it's said. One or two of the senators openly use them when their wives are away. The women are more discreet about it when their husbands are out of the city, and have the men come to them.'

'Wherever we are going will be fine, so long as it's not a brothel.'

'That's the spirit!' he declared. 'You won't regret it.'

I already was.

'Besides,' he continued, 'the tavern is a rather good place, since it is secluded, dimly lit, and will permit us to talk openly. Now that the only Sun Chamber officer in the city is in my neighbourhood, I want to pick your brains about better policing.'

From indulging in prostitutes to examining legal matters, the range in the man's morals did not seem apparent to him, but I did not mind too much. To be honest, the drinks and bright company would be a blessing tonight. Veron was correct in thinking I had not wanted to be alone.

Located on a good street, the tavern looked rather impressive, much like the private residences on either side of it, with a grand facade made up of regular columns, each one possessing remarkable detail.

As we passed through the iron gates, a couple of alleyways led away either side, but I couldn't see any assailants or anyone wanting to collect a debt, only puddles glinting in the light of several cressets. So far, the moneylender was keeping his word.

Inside, the building was luxurious, and it didn't strike me that the place could be considered a crude tavern. Then we passed through to a large room beyond, which was an assault on the senses. The walls were gaudy with colour, a mix of deep reds, purples and blues. There were quite a few people here, many having conversations in booths lit by candles, or lounging on long, circular couches, with hostesses perched nearby. Across a marble floor, drinks were being carried by busy serving staff, while men and women of good standing chatted as if this was any ordinary party. I could only speculate at what was happening in the rooms beyond, where women led men away by the hand. At the end of this long room was a stage, on which women were dancing to the slow, tribal beat of a drum. Needless to say, they were not wearing much, just a few strips of cloth.

Cressets burned, incense was heavy in the air, and everyone but me seemed glad to be there. Veron strode about with an ease I couldn't quite share. He led us to a small table in front of the stage, where he applauded the three scantily clad female dancers.

Each of them wore a mask, possibly for artistic reasons, but I wondered if it was also so that the many hungry eyes around the room could not identify them.

'Does your wife approve of you coming to this place?' I asked Veron.

'Oh, yes – this is one of the milder establishments. She's probably doing the same sort of thing wherever she is.'

'Atrella isn't in the city?'

'No, she's out and about doing a few business deals with people in nearby nations. Our children have grown into fine young men and women, and are living their own lives. Well, when they're not bringing shame on the family, that is. My wife being the really smart one of us has stepped in for me, in order to finish off negotiating various trading deals. It was said I couldn't be trusted, but I don't know. Hopefully this business will be enough to see that we live well in our old age. Don't worry, she's quite safe – she's taken twenty former military personnel with her for protection.' He paused to stress the fact. 'That's if they're not busy roughly taking her at her insistence.'

Veron didn't even seem annoyed by the prospect of infidelity. He just kept on grinning to himself. Beyond his carefully orchestrated facade, I got the impression that he'd crossed a point in his life where he just didn't care any more, and that he would now forever drift between islands of sensual pleasure. While I'd had my suspicions about Veron, I felt rather sad for him, suspecting that he might actually be a rather lonely man.

I said nothing while he ordered drinks and motioned for me to sit. After wine was brought to our table, he spoke in the half-light about how often he came here, that he used the cordial atmosphere to negotiate business contracts and trade rights for the city, but most of all he came to escape the Senate.

'Do you enjoy your work?' I asked.

He gave me a sly glance. 'You question me as if I'm a part of an investigation. I know how it works. Get people talking.'

I smiled. 'I'm merely curious about the life of a politician in Tryum. It's been so long since I've had the opportunity to liaise with someone of such a lofty status.'

He picked up his glass and took a sip of wine. 'People in the city talk a lot. They like to criticize the role of senators.'

'Oh, I wasn't criticizing . . .'

Veron waved my apologies away. 'I can sympathize with such sentiments. We senators do not always possess a perfect reputation, but many of us do good work, Drakenfeld. We bring money into the city and we honestly try to look after the people. Things are a lot different since the days of the collapse of the Detratan regime. There is fairness and light where there used to be a ruthless rule, though that's probably why some want to re-create those days. The money's being spread about more on public services, and not on lining someone's coffers. Me? I'm happy when people leave me alone, and if that means building a better sewer or public baths, so be it.'

'And how will recreating the old days work precisely? Remove Detrata from the Union? Risk the wrath of a continent?'

Veron held his hands in the air, grinning. 'I merely speculate, Drakenfeld! It's Senate talk, you know me. People talk of a lack of space here, of the need to stretch our wings a little. I'm sure Mauland's capitulation to us will help on that front. The frontiers are a little safer, the nation can be proud once again.' He paused to take a sip, one eye on the nearest serving girl. 'Which reminds me, I wanted to pick your brains about policing.'

'Ask away,' I replied.

'The king's applying gentle pressure to shake up the cohorts, which means we senators have to deal with them. There is still much crime in the city, and our cohorts, who report to senators individually, are under a great deal of strain, or so they tell us. Between you and me, they seem a remarkably disorganized bunch, and I dare say many of them are corrupt as hell, taking all sorts of illegal payments, working with the gangs and so on, which means the people of Tryum do not trust them. What advice do you have from what you've seen so far? I know you've not been here long, but I would like a fresh pair of eyes to evaluate matters for me. I have a report on my own district to make to the Senate and I'd like to see if I can improve things not just there but across Tryum. To make it a proud city once again, to recapture some of that discipline from the Empire days . . .' He gave me a satisfied look on that final point.

I sipped my watered-down wine before giving him a considered answer.

Constable Farrum kept prisoners in his own home, I explained, in front of his children. The cohorts had so few resources to hand, and gained little respect from the people of the city. In my experience in other cities, this often meant that they preferred to make money on the side. They needed more public resources and a stricter code of training – something to make them feel proud. I suggested Farrum was a good man, ultimately, and that he just needed support.

'I have seen no evidence of criminality on his part,' I finished.

'That's because he's in awe of you,' Veron laughed. 'It must be rather lovely to be envied.'

'I don't see how – I don't see why.'

'It's rather simple. Not only are you an Officer of the Sun Chamber – a station which even the most honest of them could only ever dream of obtaining – but you're also a Drakenfeld. Your father did more to help this city than any of those cohorts combined will achieve. His name carries prestige, and you carry that same name.'

Wearing an eye mask, a girl danced slowly on stage, rather near us, moving her arms through the air as if she was swimming deep underwater. It was an utterly enchanting move, but seemed to be technically brilliant as well.

'I'm sorry,' Veron continued, 'his name must be a lot for you to live up to.'

'Only in Tryum.'

'You're working on a case that is the talk of Tryum, at least. And speaking of the talk of Tryum . . .' He leaned in a little closer. 'It seems our glorious General Maxant will be entering the political arena very soon.'

'He seeks a place in the Senate?' I replied.

Veron nodded. 'With Lacanta gone, the king will need a new figure to help him influence senators, someone with a bit of presence in the absence of Lacanta's skills behind the scenes.'

'He doesn't strike me as a man of politics.'

'It's the only way for him to go. The people are fond of him. He has significant financial resources at his disposal now. He'll do well. The king is going to have him by his side at the Stadium of Lentus in a couple of days' time – you're welcome to accompany me to that, by the way. In fact, I insist.'

'I'd be delighted to do so, thank you. I haven't seen one of those races in years. Are they still as brutal as they used to be?'

'A little more so now the rules have been relaxed even further. Perhaps they're the perfect way to honour a general who has been away on a brutal campaign for years, though I believe it will also feature a funeral speech in honour of Lacanta. You'll want to attend for that reason alone, no doubt. But before this, Maxant will be making a speech tomorrow afternoon.'

'To the Senate?'

'No, to the people,' Veron said. 'His streets are going to be in one of the lower regions of the city – possibly Vellyum – to help the king establish even more popularity with the poor.'

A cynical move, but perhaps good tactics on behalf of Licintius. 'I may wish to hear what our victorious general has to say for himself on political matters.'

'I thought you might,' Veron replied, but he wasn't looking at me – he regarded the women on stage.

My gaze followed his. Of the three women who were now dancing, I thought I recognized one of them – it was the woman I saw walking by my house recently, the one who'd strolled straight out of my past.

Initially it was only because of a scar on her back that I recognized her, but then her movements and the shape of her limbs confirmed who it was. Watching a little more attentively, I could hardly believe who I was seeing. She wore a green eye mask, and a green wrap of cloth around her breasts and waist, and I was absolutely certain it was her.

Titiana.

I watched her dance right in front of me, her face tilted away as part of the routine, but soon she came within touching distance. Her bronzed legs were almost precisely as I remembered, as was the rest of her lithe body, currently arching back over. When she rose to the top of her pose with her dark hair spiralling down, she looked right at me – and froze.

The music continued, but she didn't move for several heartbeats.

We continued staring at each other and she realized she had lost her place, falling far behind the other women. Her dark eyes were just as incredible as I remembered; they possessed an intensity that made me feel guilty just for looking at her. She tried to compose herself and rejoin the others, soon hiding the fact that she had ever been out of rhythm in the first place.

The song finished, the music stopped and the woman I was convinced was Titiana turned to escape behind the stage and out of the back of the room. I leapt up and tried to pursue her, but two hefty-looking men wearing short daggers intercepted me. No one wanted a scene here. I heard Veron muttering something to me, but all I could do was babble that I'd be back shortly.

Where was the damn exit? I ran past all the guests towards the entrance, and back outside. The streets were cool, thronging with the energy of night and all that might entail for the people of Tryum. I hurried around the side of the building into one of the alleyways, just as the back door to the bar opened up – and that was where I dashed.

'Titiana.'

She slammed the door, breathless, and slowly turned to face me. No longer wearing her mask, I knew for certain it was her and no other.

In a rapid move, Titiana slapped me across my right cheek.

That really hurt.

'I probably deserved that,' I breathed.

Her face was heavily made up for the stage, and I wished she would wash it all away to reveal who she was. She moved to strike me again; I caught her wrist this time. Titiana moved her other hand and I grabbed that, too. 'I heard you were back, you bastard.'

'You can't still feel such hatred for me?' I asked, exasperated.

'I can – and I do,' she replied.

Whether she pulled me or I pushed her gently back against the door, it was impossible to tell, but it was certainly mutual. Her lips moved to within inches of mine, and we just remained there, knowing exactly what to do, but uncertain of the consequences.

Titiana shoved me back and said, 'We can't. Not again. I'm a married woman now – a lady of Tryum.'

'You were the last time,' I replied. 'Or at the very least, you were on your way to being one.'

'It's different now. And you can't tell anyone you know me.' No longer could she focus on my face. Instead her attention was taken by anything either side of me, anything other than me.

Our foreheads touched gently. 'I'll not breathe a word of it. Why would I want to share this good secret? I'll happily come back and pay double for private dances. Triple even.'

'I didn't think the Drakenfelds were the type to come to such places.'

'Admittedly this isn't my usual night out. It was Senator Veron who brought me here. For a moment I was worried he was going to drag me into a brothel.'

'I've heard about him,' she replied. 'The senator who spends more time at dinner parties than engaged in Senate business. He comes here a lot.' She paused for a moment, her anger gradually diffusing. 'So what are you doing back in Tryum? I thought you'd gone for good.'

'I came to attend my father's funeral,' I said.

Titiana's expression grew sorrowful and for a moment she seemed lost for words. 'I'm very sorry for your loss. I heard he had passed away. He was a good man. But how long have you been back?'

'Only a few days. I've since been attached to the Lacanta murder.'

'Really?' Her awe came and went like a puff of wind. 'So, you're still with the Sun Chamber . . .'

There was a bitterness in her voice. Conscious she was hardly wearing anything, I took off my cloak and put it around her.

'We should not be here, Lucan. What if somebody sees us?'

'This is one of the least suspicious acts in the vicinity of this tavern. What if someone saw you in there?'

'I take such a risk each night.'

'Why do you need to work here?'

'Because of the money. It pays well and there isn't as much danger as you'd think. I'm an attractive woman and all I have to do is dance and occasionally speak pleasant words to gullible but rich old men. There's nothing else involved – people go down-city for more.'

'I know the types that come to these places. You're a smart woman – you could be doing something safer for the money.'

'I could have, but not after what you did.'

The guilt hit home, but I tried to ward it away in my mind with the logic that ultimately she was the one who had broken the law. 'Let me take you out for something to eat tomorrow. I want to speak to you more. That's all I want. Simply to talk.'

'Then what?' Titiana snapped. 'Sleep with me until you're satisfied, and leave me in the middle of the night?'

'You know that's not what I would ever intend to do, and if I did when I was young, that was because it was mutual, and we didn't want anyone to find us together.'

We said nothing for a while, though it wasn't awkward and didn't seem to matter. The contours of her face seemed so familiar, which in itself was a strange sensation.

'I must go,' she whispered eventually.

'Tomorrow. You know my old house?'

'I can't exactly forget it,' she replied.

'You'll come then?' I asked. 'Tomorrow evening, at sunset.'

'OK.' Titiana opened the door behind her. 'But I really must go.'

With that she disappeared back inside the tavern, closing the door behind her.

Veron was standing outside waiting for me, his hands in his pockets, and he was grinning like a child who had just discovered the taste of sugar.

'So,' he declared, 'finally there is a woman who gets the blood pumping through the veins of Lucan Drakenfeld. And a dancer, too! Now I'm jealous. You know, I was starting to think you possessed the libido of a statue.'

'You're going to want to know who she is, aren't you?'

'I am.'

'I thought you might,' I replied. I looked up and down the street, and it was busy with evening activity. 'Let's go back to mine – it will be a lot quieter there.'

'As long as there is wine to go with this story of yours, I do not mind.'

Nostalgia

In the calm sanctuary of my garden, we sat on the edge of the fountain, regarding the shadows beyond the regularly spaced columns. Leana had gone out for the evening, and Bellona decided she would light some cressets and candles on our behalf. Despite saying that we didn't mind the darkness, she was terribly keen to impress our visitor.

Class divisions weren't that noticeable during my time in Venyn, but in Tryum I felt guilty every time I spoke with Bellona. For many, to see a senator, king or queen could seem like walking with gods. It wasn't right, it was something which even Polla had disapproved of, but how could an entire culture be changed?

We settled in. I gathered my thoughts.

Senator Veron reached down to scoop up the cup of wine by his feet and, once he'd taken a couple of gulps, he motioned for me to tell the story, as if I had become his entertainment for the evening. 'When you're ready, Drakenfeld.'

My mind travelled back all those years, to simpler times, when all I cared about was my studies, listening to a good tune played on a lyre and feeling the body of one girl in particular against my own.

'Everything I know about love I learned from Titiana,' I began.

'Just the one teacher?' Veron smiled.

'I was twenty summers old, and she was seventeen. I'd completed my third year of training for the Sun Chamber that very year and was shadowing my father on some of his minor work, when our paths crossed at a festival celebration. She was the daughter of a cleric who worked under Licintius' father, and came from a reasonably well-to-do family. Her father made the mistake of being caught in private discussions with a non-royalist faction of the Senate, and found himself booted out. That meant Titiana and her family were soon fighting for their status. So her father lined up Titiana for marriage to the son of a senator.

'That didn't stop our affair, however. Perhaps I hoped we could be something more, but that was not for us to say — that was for our mothers and fathers to decide. My mother might not have minded had she been alive. She was from Locco, near the deserts, and attitudes on sexuality were more relaxed there. If you loved someone, you could choose to marry them, as strange as it sounds. Anyway, the life of someone attached to an official of the Sun Chamber is not always a happy one given our often constant movement about the continent. Our passions were confined to sudden, discreet moments, wherever we could find them. We knew it was wrong.'

'That often makes it all the more interesting,' Veron commented.

'I don't know what it was about her that appealed so much. There were so many qualities. Perhaps it was her stubbornness, a wish to be her own person, a refreshing change for the families of this city. Perhaps it was the way we could converse about the great poets of the past, as well as speculate on the meaning behind the stars. Perhaps it was—'

'The fact that she possessed the beauty and body of a goddess?' Veron interrupted.

I smiled. It was some effort to pretend I was above all that, but that would have meant lying to myself. 'You never got to see her eyes. Such big oval eyes. You'd think they were the colour of chestnuts at first, but there were so many shades beyond. I could stare at them all day and never reach the other end.'

'My gaze didn't get that far,' Veron replied.

'So there we were,' I continued, 'two young lovers of Tryum doing the things that young lovers do.'

'And what happened to this great passion?' Veron asked. 'She was betrothed to someone else and that was that? You left the city, jaded, never to return?'

'Not quite,' I replied, and sipped my cup of wine.

'Well, what else could it have been?' Veron laughed. 'You didn't arrest her, did you?'

I said nothing.

'You did arrest her.' Veron clutched my arm with excitement. 'By Trymus' tomb, you're certainly efficient, Lucan Drakenfeld, I'll give you that much.' He sat back still chuckling to himself. 'I can't believe you'd do that to your own lover.'

'No, it wasn't like that,' I protested. 'Not quite anyway. Let me explain. Her family was starting to suffer and they were losing money. Titiana and her sister took it upon themselves to make money for the family funds. Her sister took to sleeping with senators and selling their gifts, while Titiana stole from well-to-do houses, family connections and so on. I caught her with jewellery she'd taken from a lady in Tradum and she confessed everything. I didn't have the money to help her, since all I had was an allowance from my father. I didn't know what to do. So

200

foolishly I turned to my father for help, hoping he could lend me the money and . . .'

'Did he not help?'

I snorted a laugh. 'He informed the Civil Cohorts, who later arrested her, took her confession and let due process take its course. What surprised me was that the lady whose jewels Titiana had stolen actually decided to go ahead and prosecute her, rather than forgive her, despite my efforts at reasoning with the old bag.'

'Well, she was fully entitled to do so,' Veron observed.

'Though I didn't think she would to a young woman whose family had fallen on hard times.'

'And her punishment came shortly after?' He seemed to enjoy this story, thriving on a bad story that had happened long enough ago for him to bother with sympathy.

'She was to be whipped in public. It was not as brutal as it could have been, thank the gods, but it was enough. I tried to help out, once justice had been administered, but understandably she wanted nothing more to do with me. The last time I saw her, she ripped off her dress in public and showed me the wound on her back, which was so raw. She told me that I had done that to her.'

'Nonsense,' Veron said. 'She brought it on herself.'

It was my father's fault, I told myself, though in my darker hours I felt the blame ultimately belonged with me. 'At the time, Titiana was not in the mood to discuss the technicalities, which was perfectly understandable. We never spoke again. Shortly after that I decided that there was nothing left for me in Tryum so I ventured across Vispasia.'

'To forget about a woman,' Veron added.

'Not entirely, but she was a large part of that decision to leave. There was nothing here for me other than the shadow of my father and a woman who wished me dead.'

Veron clapped me on the arm. 'I guess that explains why you're in no hurry to find a wife. It's a fine story, Drakenfeld.'

'And I wish none of it was true,' I sighed.

Politics

We talked a little more about love, something that Veron and I both admitted was a distant memory. People did not marry for love in Detrata, not unless it was coincidence or the gods smiling upon them. Marriage was to bind families and their businesses, to bring stability where there was none. A happy, loving union could develop from time to time, of course, but generally with luck a good partnership could be formed and a strong bond forged between families. It was, Veron confessed, how he and his own wife had been paired up.

Deciding to change the topic I asked for more details about Lacanta's dealings with the Senate. Veron mentioned again the king's desire to influence senators, and that Lacanta was his only effective method of persuading others.

This bold, political Lacanta was the one who everyone knew, but it couldn't have been the whole picture. Next I intended to explore the Senate, just in case Lacanta's actions there had caused bitterness to rise up against her. Could she have delved too far into the dealings of others to warrant being killed?

'Lacanta's murder,' I continued, 'has so far taken me to the lowest regions of Tryum, but that doesn't feel right. Most murders tend to happen between people who know each other, people of the same class – such as political rivals. Unless Lacanta regularly cavorted with the poor, I feel I've been looking in the wrong place. My investigation ought to focus up-city.'

Veron nodded and gave my words some consideration. Somewhere in the far distance I heard a group of people singing.

'What were your dealings with her?'

'Oh very subtle,' Veron said.

'I'm curious, senator,' I replied, in good humour. 'I have little idea who she actually was as a person.'

'We rarely spoke, if it means much. As I say, I'm not one for tensions. I float around from faction to faction, not committing, not protesting too much. It makes for an easy life. She had little interest in me, since I almost always sided with Licintius. Say what you will about him – and others do – he speaks a lot of sense. For a king he has the common touch.'

'What do those in the Senate think of her?'

'Some people called her Licintius' witch,' Veron confessed. 'Not in the same way as Divran being a witch. More metaphorical. Senators are tricky individuals – forming allegiances or groups, but always to further a cause. Sometimes that may even be a good thing, but at other times it can be disastrous. There are those who seek agrarian reform, those against it. I've hinted that there are some who would like Detrata to free itself from the laws of the Vispasian Royal Union – laws, as a Sun Chamber officer, you help to enforce – so that we might return to the old days of the Detratan Empire. Some even wish us to turn into a republic, without a king. And some who speak on behalf of certain religious cults, or who represent the interests of bankers. There are as many factions as there are senators.'

'How did Lacanta fit into this?' I asked, wondering if he'd

provide a similar story to the one that Maxant had told me. 'Can you give an example?'

'There was a bill recently, from Licintius, concerning the resettlement of Maxant's veterans from his campaign in Mauland. A goodwill gesture, and a thank-you from the Senate for the military's work in enriching Detrata. To you and me that all sounds very reasonable, of course, but a strong faction in the Senate said there was simply not enough land to go around anyway . . . and so on. They suggested that the policy was to do with the king looking to help out his old friend – all the usual excuses, most of which are based on emotion rather than fact. The bill was ready to collapse. What's particularly strange is that these senators are the very ones who love the military – they were doing it just to spite Licintius.'

'And Lacanta changed things.'

'Absolutely. Lacanta worked her powers on some of the key opponents of the bill, and before any of us knew what was going on the bill had managed to pass through the vote. I didn't think it would, but it did – and I was glad it had done so. Despite my demeanour, I like to think I have some faith in the democratic process, and abhor such seedy influence in the Senate. That's why many of the senators call her the witch – because it seems like magic had been used by her to control people. Some are convinced that it is genuine witchcraft, too – it's not merely a word to be used as insult.'

'Have you seen anything to suggest there were darker forces at work?' I asked. 'I keep on hearing about such matters, but I find it hard to believe, despite all I've seen over the past few years. When I grew up, the only dark art I could remember was the trade in curses. Some of them even worked too.'

'There is talk – there's always talk – but I've not seen anything. Well, at least not until the day she was found murdered. If anything could be an act of summoned ghosts, then her murder could be evidence of that. I tell you what, Drakenfeld – I would not like to mess in the affairs of such entities.'

I finished my cup of wine and regarded the night sky. The stars were out, clear and sharp, and there was a pleasant tang of woodsmoke in the air. Closing my eyes, it seemed like I'd never left the city.

'Veron, can I trust you?'

After a long pause he replied, 'No, probably not.' Veron chuckled, acutely aware of his own self-depreciation.

'Then you're the most honest politician I've met.'

'But that doesn't mean we can't be friends.'

And it seemed, beneath the layers of the suave politician and the man who was faintly disappointed with life, I could at least believe that. 'Could you give me the names of specific senators to interview?'

'Plenty,' he replied, 'but it depends on what you're hoping to discover.'

'Who were those closest to Lacanta? Who could she bend around her finger, who was she sleeping with? I don't care if I have to speak to every member of the Senate and it takes me months.'

'I'll write down some names for you before I leave,' Veron said. 'Be careful you don't interfere too far – senators are powerful people. Not quite as powerful as the king, mind you, but we still wield a lot of influence.'

'I'm sure they will all be aware that if I was killed, that would be the second Sun Chamber officer to die within a month. With two officers out of action so soon, I have no idea what the Sun Chamber might do.'

'Are they really that sensitive, the Sun Chamber?'

'Absolutely,' I replied seriously. 'We have to write a weekly report – if nothing is heard of us for a month or so, officials would flood Tryum to find out what was going on. So if someone in the Senate tried to get rid of me, we'd come back in droves.'

'Such power,' Veron remarked. 'Such administration. Has your father's death not created more of a fuss back at your headquarters in Free State?'

'No, it was declared as natural causes. The priests and pontiffs, and the Pollan physicians, did not suggest otherwise. Just as well really, as the Sun Chamber gets nervous easily, and I would not like to see them so upset.'

After another cup of wine, which we drank in a pleasant, companionable silence, Veron bid me farewell and left me with his list of names. With a good amount of alcohol inside him, he shambled back through the evening streets a relatively happy man. I headed indoors, whereupon Bellona handed me a scroll of messages and another tube, apologizing for not handing them to me earlier.

When Bellona left for her sleeping quarters, I headed into the study and opened up the scroll. Bellona had written the note and I marvelled at how neat and precise her handwriting was. It was heartening to know she had received a good education and I wondered if my father had helped her in any way, perhaps to give her more of a chance, or to aid him in matters of administration. In that moment it occurred to me how little I knew about the woman.

The messages largely consisted of more people asking for help. The owner of a local gem store claimed he had been robbed and wondered if it was possible for me, instead of the cohorts, to investigate the matter.

A priest had tried to speak with me, apparently for the second time. He said he would visit me again. What could a holy man want with me? Since it could have been a matter of a spiritual nature, I made sure to inform Bellona to take a full message from him should he call again, lest the gods get angry with me.

A clerk's daughter had gone missing late last night and not come home in the morning; and three youths had been spotted harassing a senator and the official in question wondered if I might be able to do something about it.

I shook my head despairingly. Any other month and I would perhaps be in a position to try to help these people, but these were rather trivial matters and I could not afford to lend my time to them. These were issues for the cohorts.

Finally I inspected the tube, which was sealed in wax and stamped with the emblem of the Sun Chamber. I opened it up with a knife and was relieved to see a letter in response to mine. The roads around Detrata were in a good state and a reliable messenger could travel for dozens of miles in a day without much trouble. My initial correspondence had been with the Sun Chamber station at the Three Nations border post, situated where the territories of Detrata, Theran to the east and Maristan to the south all meet, and which is at the other end of the country from Tryum.

The reply had come from a senior official, who acknowledged the importance of my case, approved of my summary and my intentions, and asked whether or not I would like military assistance to be brought closer to the borders, given that the case dealt with the senatorial classes. I exhaled deeply and stared into the distance, contemplating my options.

In no mind to answer such matters, I decided to lay down my head and get some much-needed rest.

A Glass Vial

I woke with the sun, having enjoyed a pleasant night's sleep, and spent my first moments thinking entirely of Titiana.

The way she had moved on that platform seemed to have left an echo in my mind, a sight that simply would not shift easily. I began, as always, to over-analyse her gestures and her second glances, weighing up the meaning behind what may well have been utterly without purpose. Long ago I'd realized that I did not expect answers from such mental anguish, but it was good to exercise such old emotional muscles once again.

The clarity of daytime did little to assuage my concerns of her having chosen this lifestyle. There was no shame in what she was doing – dancing was a celebration of the body, after all – but I had seen many times just how badly people could be treated in that profession, and I worried for her safety.

Even though I had absolutely no right to do so.

After consuming a light breakfast I set to work, first examining the list of senators' names that Veron had provided for me, and later combing through the witness statements again. Leana joined me and confirmed that she had made the payment via the gang leader, who had given her no trouble. In fact, they were too pleasant; they wanted her to stay longer, to buy her drinks, but she wisely decided not to hang around too long and instead absorbed the sights and sounds of the city.

'Did you have a good night?' she asked.

I wanted to tell her about Titiana, who I had once mentioned to Leana when we were out working on a case in Venyn. At the time the conversation was purely to take our minds off the gruesome task of cleaning up after a smuggling crackdown had gone wrong, to open up to Leana and show her I was not an emotionless soul. Not that she particularly cared either way.

'I bumped into Senator Veron,' I said, 'who was his usual lively self. We now have a list of senators with whom Lacanta was involved – and possibly intimately so.'

'This is good,' Leana replied. 'But I do not understand him. He seems too friendly, no?'

'I wouldn't worry,' I said. 'He's just a politician, hoping to discover gossip or to bank a favour for future usage, but he's opening doors for us to expand the investigation.'

'It could be that he is guilty – he comes to find you on the night of the murder to put you off the scent.'

'I've thought about that, but he has witnesses that can vouch for his presence before the incident. A good few people within these statements talk about how he was causing a great deal of fuss because he didn't like the wine.'

'Hmm. Will today be as busy as yesterday?' Leana asked.

'I hope not. First I'd like to visit the money temples. We need to book an armed escort to accompany the large payment of cash to Veldrum Hecater, and I also need to cash in the remains of my credit note from Venyn – all of it, in fact. Then I will have finally cleared my father's debts, which should then guarantee we don't receive further attacks.'

'Good. That is one less thing to worry about.' Leana grabbed an apple from the table and bit into it.

'And after that,' I continued, 'it's straight to Optryx, where—'

There was a banging at the door. Bellona came shuffling through the hallway, wide-eyed, but seemed hesitant to open it to such a vicious pounding. Leana strode over to see what the matter was and, with Bellona, they both unbolted and drew back the heavy door.

I stood up, hearing voices in loud discussion. Presently, three men marched into the room, two of whom were hefty-looking fellows carrying a large trunk; another, much older man followed and he promptly began to order them about.

'Place it down there, lads,' he said, gesturing to the middle of the room with his polished walking cane. He was taller than me, at least two decades older, with long grey hair, thin lips and sunken eyes, and he walked with a slight limp that he tried to disguise with his cloak.

'What's going on?' I demanded. 'And what in Polla's name is that?'

'You're the Drakenfeld boy?' he snapped.

'My name is Lucan Drakenfeld, and I haven't been called a boy in over fifteen years.'

'Means nothing to me, boy.' He tapped the trunk with his cane. 'You can keep your father's shit here.'

The trunk was similar to the one from the rented office, which I had not yet had the opportunity to revisit. 'We were legal tenants—'

'Who have not kept up repayments. I don't care what deeds you have, or whatever legal terms you folk like to throw around, you're no longer welcome in my property. Everything that was in those offices is in this trunk – books, papers, and other bits and pieces – the lot.'

'Now, just wait a moment,' I began.

'What? Don't tell me you actually want to keep renting? Not

on your life, sir! I've had enough of your family to last me a lifetime. Consider your contract to be terminated.'

I decided not to pursue the matter. Another office was such a
waste when I had more than enough space in this house. 'Why
do you hate my family so much?'

'Your father did not exactly set the best example,' he grunted.
'Now, out of here, lads. We've much to do today.' He turned to
leave and the other two men scuttled out of the room.

'Wait.' I stepped forward to casually block the man's path, cautious that it did not appear to be a threat. 'I know so little about
what happened with my father, let alone what concerns his
debts.'

'Just as well if you ask me,' the man snapped.

'Why?'

'Got into gambling, didn't he? A bad habit, that.'

'Gambling?' The word seemed to physically hit me and I sat
down on a wicker chair, dumbstruck.

'Aye, one of his sons led him down that dark road some time
ago, though he's long cleared out of the city.'

'My brother?'

'Probably. Don't you keep an eye out for each other?'

'Not my brother, no.' Marius kept himself to himself, and life
was all the better for it. He loathed our father. 'Did he mention
what my brother had done?'

He shrugged, before continuing as if he was now enjoying
himself: 'Opened up old wounds, so I understand. Gambling.
Women. Drink. Didn't just happen right away, but over time.
Lad had his own debts and came scrounging from his father. Calludian did a grand job of keeping it quiet, but not from the likes
of me. Pleaded with me, you see. Explained his problems. Tried
to tell me to hang on, that he'd deliver the money sooner or later,
to have a heart and all that. Very poor form.' The man jabbed

212

his cane in my direction. 'Even had the money to pay it off, so he eventually claimed — pay all the debt in one go. So he did for most of it. But he was still in arrears. Never trusted him after that. If you'll excuse me, Tryum is only just waking up and I've several other matters to see to before people leave for work. Too many scroungers and people in debt for my liking. City didn't build itself on scroungers. Put the lot of them in the army.'

The bitter man limped his way out into the hazy daylight, and Bellona closed the door behind him.

I called Bellona over, and she froze on the spot. 'Please, there is no reason to be shy. Have I offended you?'

She shook her head. 'You are highborn . . .'

'Don't think me somehow better than yourself.' I could just about recall my mother once reminding me about that fact, that I should always remember I had been born into privilege, and not to abuse that position.

It didn't do much to soothe Bellona, but Leana guided her to the table. I took this opportunity to ask her if she knew anything of my father's debts and his gambling habits. Despite my soft tone, she was visibly distressed. Leana, even though she was hesitant, did a better job than me in soothing her. Eventually all Bellona managed to say was that, from time to time towards the end, my father had difficulties making ends meet, which is why there was now only the one member of staff. Eventually she calmed down, and her words came with considered clarity.

'He never spoke of money. Sometimes he said to buy cheaper bread, sometimes no meat or fish. He never said why. I'm just the cook. It is not my place to know these things.'

'And my brother Marius?'

'I didn't really see him. He took the master out from time to time, into town at night. Those nights they came back late and drunk, but your brother never stayed in the city for long. I overheard once that he was on the run from debt collectors himself, and didn't like to settle in one place.'

So my brother's gift for my father was to lumber him with debts and bad old habits. My family's past, my father's old misdemeanour, once again echoed through my mind. Perhaps some people never forget their old ways.

Bellona clearly didn't like being involved in such affairs, so I took her hand between my palms, looked her firmly in the eye and told her that no harm would come to her while she was under this roof. She offered me a warmer smile than before and then stood up.

'I must get back to work. Big houses don't clean themselves.'

As she left the room, Leana turned to me with a look of surprise. 'Your father gambled?'

'Apparently so. My father – who everyone in this city speaks of like he was a god – turns out to be human after all. No doubt my brother played some role in leading him down such a path, for the few nights he decided to hang around.'

'You never mention him.'

'For good reason. He's never had respect for any of us, and rejected anything of a proper lifestyle. Polla knows what he's up to now, other than getting people involved in gambling.'

'Not a good start to the day.'

'No, it is not,' I sighed. 'But at least that provides more of an explanation for the debts.'

'Be positive,' Leana said. 'You have your father's possessions back, do you not? In Venyn this would have been opened long ago, the contents for sale in some market.'

'You make a good point,' I sighed, stepping over to the trunk.

I levered it open and stooped to peer inside. Several heavy ledgers lay underneath writing instruments, an abacus, three or four ornaments, and a smaller, polished wooden box. I lifted the latter out, opened it up. Inside were a couple of peculla coins, and a small stone that could have been used as a paperweight. What caught my eye, however, was the empty blue glass vial, which was no bigger than my thumb, and shaped with a long, thin neck. A tiny cork was stuck in the end.

'What is that?' Leana asked, stepping closer.

'I saw vials similar to this at the apothecary . . .'

We held eye contact for a moment.

'You went to one last night.' Leana possessed a sudden look of pride.

I nodded, but wasn't going to say any more on the subject.

'So what do you think this was?' she asked, nodding towards the vial.

'I'm not entirely sure. I wonder if he was on a form of medication?'

'Did he suffer from seizures also?'

'No. Well, not to my knowledge – not unless he hid it.'

'You say his heart had stopped,' Leana continued.

'That's what I was told.'

'Perhaps he used a herbal concoction to soothe his pains? It is not out of the question. Where was the box likely to be stored?'

'Probably in a drawer,' I replied. 'Somewhere out of sight, where he kept a couple of coins . . .'

Leana nodded. 'Perhaps you should go back to the apothecary and ask if they know about where such vials are sold. They might know other traders who deal in such things.'

'That could be worth a go.'

A child looked up from smashing walnuts on the side of the kerb, shading his eyes from the sun. I said hello to him, but he either did not hear me or did not care. Behind him stood a pepper merchant dressed in fine silks, who was hawking his wares rather forcefully to passers-by.

Leana and I continued through the busy streets outside my house, and upon entering the next street saw an elderly man wearing the robes of a priest strolling serenely through the gates to my property. Was this the one Bellona had referred to in her message? There was no time to go back, but I had left firm instructions to get more details. We headed deep into the district of Regallum. Protected by armed personnel, the banking building was in fact a refurbished temple, one dedicated to a god no longer in favour with the Senate. It was an impressive structure, with eight ornate limestone columns on its front, and a brazier either side of a stairway leading up to the main entrance.

Building work was taking place along the shaded side, where a stonemason stood on a ladder making some fine adjustments higher up another column. As we approached the main door, the soldiers, whose armour was concealed by heavy black cloaks, examined us closely. I made sure my Sun Chamber badge was on full display and let it be known Leana was clearly with me. They stood back and watched us impassively, with only a quiet nod to indicate that we might continue through.

Inside the bank, on the marble floors under an ornately painted dome, where people spoke in hushed, almost spiritual tones, I cashed in my credit notes from Venyn and arranged to transfer money in coin to Veldrum Hecater. They knew him well, it seemed, and I half expected some comment as to my father's affairs – though none came. They were curt, efficient and exceedingly dull individuals, who tried to negotiate a higher fee at every transactional opportunity.

I could not leave soon enough.

Optryx

'Well, that's finally dealt with,' I said. 'I've just about enough money to last a few weeks, but unless we get a salary payment delivered soon, we will be licking limestone blocks for dinner.'

'Then you should find a way of getting more money,' Leana said.

'And how do we do that?'

'I do not know,' Leana replied. 'You are supposed to be the thinker.'

As we walked up the gentle slope towards the king's residence, I felt a sudden relief having put my father's debts behind me, and the family name cleared once and for all. I imagined him trying to work, to solve the riddles of some crime with such financial problems on his mind. To have no money was bad enough, but to owe others such a fortune would have been torturous. To very nearly pay it off would have been an immense relief, and suspicious in itself.

When we arrived at Optryx and gave the day's password, we were permitted inside the building. I spoke with the administrative staff about the king's desire to see me this morning. While there it seemed a good idea to examine other parts of the building. These officials, who wore beautiful green and cream silk gowns, seemed more than willing to help, so it was not long before we were ushered through a double door, along a bright marble corridor, and beginning the preparation to be in the company of King Licintius once again.

We waited in a small, private room. I perched on one of four long, cushioned seats that had been arranged in a semicircle around a window overlooking the internal gardens. For a while Leana and I sat in companionable silence, enjoying the warmth of the morning sunlight on our faces, watching the tops of the plants stir in the breeze. From my casual glance, there was no henbane there.

The door opened without warning. A small armed escort from the King's Legion led Licintius into the room and I knelt to one knee, Leana to two. His expression changed to one of surprise when he saw her, but he made no further comment.

'Drakenfeld, please — on your feet.' The king seemed genuinely glad to see me. His outfit was breathtakingly ornate, a cloak comprising of both blues and purple silks, and a rich yellow tunic embroidered with the black falcon of Detrata. It was luxurious, a stark contrast to the armour of the four soldiers, who took precise and slow steps to take their places along the side of the room.

I introduced Leana, but after that, for the rest of the conversation, he hardly acknowledged her presence. I enquired how he was coping with the matters surrounding his sister's passing.

His expression changed and beneath the royal glamour was the look of a tired man. Licintius simply shook his head and gestured for us to take a seat on one of the couches. It was only when the sunlight reflected off his jewellery that I realized quite how much he was wearing.

'Let us start on a more positive note,' he sighed. 'Tell me how your investigation is proceeding. I've been eagerly awaiting your report.'

I explained where my investigations had taken me so far: to the Skull and Jasmine troupe, as steered by the suspicions of many of the guests that night. I felt it had been the will of the people to send me down there to investigate the most suspicious but least likely individuals — though I did not tell him that.

'You do not believe the actors are truly implicated in this?' Licintius asked, gazing across his gardens. 'I enjoyed their company very much. They seem good people, of which there is a shortage here.'

'It's too early to say, sir. However, the leader of their troupe, a man called Drullus . . .' I paid close attention to the king's expression, waiting to see just how much of what Clydia implied could be seen.

'I know Drullus,' the king replied. 'What of him?'

'He was found with his throat cut in a small hideout, further down in the city.'

I saw, briefly, the signs of distress in Licintius' face, his creased brow, the gaze at me — right through me. 'Oh, what a waste.' Licintius shook his head. 'I must see to it that his body receives an appropriate send-off.' He waved over one of the nearby soldiers and muttered something into his ear. The man left the room, presumably to set the royal wheels in motion.

A king would not see to the funeral requirements of someone so low in the city without there being some kind of bond between the two of them.

Continuing my report, 'I had hoped Drullus could tell me more about what he saw that night, but it was not to be. If indeed he was somehow involved, that line of enquiry has been ruled out. You requested the Skull and Jasmine to perform – did you know much of their work?'

'I saw one or two performances,' the king said, as if still numbed by the news. 'They occasionally show up at the larger theatres, but they possessed a genuine love of the arts not often seen in the well-known troupes. One could see the quality of their acting.'

I nodded, waiting for him to continue, but he did not say anything else. It could not have been a great time for the man, with his sister and – potentially – his supposed lover having been killed.

'With your permission, I would like to make a more thorough examination of the residence,' I said. 'I'd like to look at more rooms, to get a feel for things as they may have occurred that night, to see if anything else can be found. This is a vast building and I can only cover so much at any one time. But, most of all, I would like to get an impression of what it was like for Lacanta on her final day. I'm sure a better picture might form in my mind.'

'By all means.' The king turned his sunken eyes towards me. 'I will let it be known to all staff that you are granted access without question.' After he regarded the garden again he said, 'The Sun Chamber is very famous to educated souls, and no one knows better than we royals about the gravitas of your post. But though your dealings are more for the benefit of Vispasia, you will find whoever's doing this, won't you? This is a personal request. I'm sure there are wider benefits for the nation. Lacanta was well liked by people.' There was more than an edge of desperation to his words.

'I will do my best to find out what happened, sir,' I replied.

'For a man of your experience, who has seen many things throughout the world, how many murders go by without justice being issued?'

'Honestly?' I asked, and he nodded. 'Very many, I'm afraid. Often in big cities lone killers are seen committing the act by witnesses, which is why I'm surprised that no one saw anything on the night Lacanta departed this world. But as I say I will do my very best to find whoever did this and bring them to swift justice.'

He clenched his fists, his manner transformed entirely like a man possessed. 'And when you find them, I will have their bodies flayed in public and their heads will be left to rot on spikes for the rest of my days. I am of a mind to send my personal guard through the city knocking on every door until we find out who is responsible. Just tell me where to look and I'll send them.'

There was a violence about his mood that seemed every bit the king I had expected but not yet seen: determined to show action rather than explore the calmer, more considered route.

'I can understand your fury, sir,' I replied. 'But I fear soldiers tramping through the streets may do more damage than good. I suspect it would be a good thing to ensure soldiers of the City Watch keep vigilant. The Civil Cohorts have been briefed to keep an eye out. However, if you could spare the personnel, it may be prudent to send some of your staff to other nearby towns in order to find out if there are conversations going on that suggest the killer is elsewhere. One of my concerns is, if we are dealing with an assassin, then they may be far from here already.'

'I will do this immediately,' the king said. 'I'll arrange for some of my finest agents to move into all major settlements in Detrata, Maristan, Theran, and Koton to see what they can find. An act that is entirely within Vispasian laws, of course.'

'Of course, and that would be very useful,' I replied. 'And in the meantime I will continue to do my best to root out any suspects here — even if they're in the Senate. When will Lacanta's funeral be held?'

'Very soon,' he sighed. 'Which is why, in an ideal world, I would have liked her killers located and punished while her spirit was still within her body. She would more peacefully join the afterlife if that were the case. I do not like to think that her soul may stray.'

If her god was Trymus, as was to be expected of royals of Tryum, what the king said meant a lot to him. Trymus' followers believed that resolved deaths were beneficial in the afterlife, otherwise their ghosts may return to the land, forever attempting to attend to unfinished matters. Murders were not just about the death but about helping people beyond that border to rest peacefully in their new world. I had to bring Lacanta's killer to justice not just for the king, but for Lacanta herself.

His mood picked up and a new light came into his eyes. He became a proud man once again.

'The races at the Stadium of Lentus in a couple of days, which were meant solely for General Maxant, will now also be held in her honour,' he said. 'This will be the moment where we formally announce her death to the people of Tryum, so we can all mourn in unison – royals, senators and the people alike. After that I will hold a more private engagement. She would prefer it to be that way.'

'A wonderful plan.' There was that contradiction again: even in death Lacanta seemingly led a double life as someone who appreciated the bigger stage as well as the more intimate event.

The king stood up, and we followed suit as was expected. 'If you will excuse me, Drakenfeld, I have trade matters to attend to. I have little time to mourn, frustratingly – Tryum does not stop, even if our own lives do from time to time. In the meantime, please explore this residence as you wish. Lacanta's body is lying in another Temple of Trymus within the city – it would be indecent to keep her in the very room where she was killed. Her room has also been cleaned since the incident – hopefully the gods will be pleased with our treatment.'

'Do you know, sir, in the cleaning of her room, if anybody noticed that objects had gone missing?'

'I am not aware of any.' Licintius frowned, and looked towards me with expectation. 'Why do you ask?'

'Purely to be thorough.' I remembered the shapes in the dust when I was in her room last and wondered if anyone had reported anything. 'It would help my investigation a great deal to know that all paths have been explored. If something had been reported as missing, it might help to find whoever did this.'

'To my knowledge nothing has been taken and, from my moments alone with her to mourn, I noticed nothing out of place.'

The king walked to the door and the guards snapped in line to follow, their armour rattling as they did so. Licintius turned to face me.

'You are free to explore Optryx. I ask only that my private bedchamber and the meeting room in which I will greet an official from Gippoli be left in peace.'

'If it is your wish, so be it,' I replied, before adding a formal farewell.

The king and his soldiers departed, and I could finally relax.

The Bookshelf

Trymus looked down upon us as we entered his temple. We weren't going to find any more clues there, especially since it had been cleaned up long since, but it still irked me that someone could be found within a locked room after having been seen only moments before outside. Perhaps a fresh look under a different light might help to ascertain some key method in spiriting Lacanta's body in here.

Something, that is, other than the excuse of magic.

Though gods were rational beings, I could not trust magic at all. Magic was about people trying to control their own environment, rather than leaving these effects to the will of the gods. Magic was comprised of curses, charms and the like, without the divine right to use them properly. People should not play at being gods.

I had seen or heard many strange things in my time that I could not explain: I'd witnessed a regiment of skeletons march through the desert night, but was warned from stepping too close to examine it clearly; a good friend of mine was convinced that he saw a woman with snakes for arms killing a trader in Locco by strangulation, though I could not satisfy my own curiosity on the issue. But was it possible for someone to tamper with the fabric of our worlds, to transport a body through walls, and could the gods have permitted such treacherous acts in their own temple? Sometimes I found it most difficult to bring together the mysteries of the world with my desire for reason.

All I could think was that whoever had killed Lacanta was simply very smart. That the key had been found on the inside of the door was still a problem for me.

Leana brought over the royal pontiff, the king's private priest, who had been involved in the procession that night. A slender man with something of a goat-like face, he told me that, as a rule, there were several copies of the key so that the temple would be free for anyone to worship, whenever they liked. He told us it was well known that these copies were kept in various offices, and disappeared to find one. I recalled how there had been an urgency to open that door so that the festivities would happen at precisely the right time and that the soldiers were too impatient to wait.

The pontiff returned several minutes later in possession of two keys, but said that he had expected to find a third. 'I have no idea where it could be. I'm always misplacing them though!'

The key was a curious point but it did not resolve the problem that it was still impossible to get Lacanta inside the temple in such a short space of time – merely a matter of minutes from when she was last seen – with so many of the guests watching the point of entry.

Was the key merely a decoy, something designed to deceive people after the murder?

Next to the temple were smaller chambers, formal reception areas, a library, and various meeting rooms. I had to request that some of the rooms be unlocked, and since no one person possessed the key to all of the rooms Leana spent just as much time finding the necessary member of staff as I did exploring the rooms. The whole process was time-consuming and took us the better part of the day. Still, as Leana commented, today was at least more relaxing, despite having been in the presence of the king.

There were fourteen rooms down one long, echoing corridor, not too far from the temple, and while we rooted around the area we frequently received many anxious or suspicious glances from the royal staff. I was impressed at the sheer number of people who passed us: clerks, servants, soldiers, priests, trading officials from around Vispasia. It was an incredibly busy building. Even on the night of the murder, there were hundreds of people present.

So why had no one witnessed anything happening that night?

Everyone had of course seen Lacanta mingling with guests, and plenty of people had seen her corpse, so what had happened in those precious, final moments between? Had she been ensconced with a lover, or been involved in some heated discussion?

Away from the temple were smaller rooms, private quarters perhaps, and a kitchen. Next to the kitchen was a room I took to be a pantry at first, but noted a large number of plates stacked to one side with food in gradual stages of decay. When we unlocked it and entered we disturbed two rats, which scurried past us and out into the corridor, scaring the male cook in the next room. There wasn't much in the room, simply a strong smell of food that had gone off. However, on the far wall, next to a stack of discarded hessian sacks, was an engraving of an upright hand with an eye in the centre of the palm.

It was the Offering of Light, a symbol of Polla's brother-god

Ptrell. He was a rare god indeed, barely worshipped this far west. I hadn't seen it at all in the city, so what was it doing here in a room buried within Optryx? Who had taken the time to engrave the symbol of Ptrell into the wall? It appeared to have been done recently, too.

Somehow, perhaps because of his association with Polla, discovering this symbol seemed to reassure me. I felt, through him, Polla might be trying to tell me that I was on the right track, to tell me to keep looking.

Invigorated by this sign, we headed to Lacanta's room, which was a good deal more pleasant, as it had been aired and incense had been lit to rid the place of the stench of death.

'Incense, just like in the temple,' Leana observed. 'Except that could have been as part of an offering.'

'What if that incense had not been part of an offering at all, but an attempt to rid the temple of the smell of death, just as it has been in this room?' I remarked.

'You mean not sacrifice, but it could be the act of a . . .' she searched for the word, 'calculated killer?'

'Not of a calculated killer. Corpses do not give off a smell immediately and a calculated killer would have known that.'

Leana stepped towards me. 'So it could be their first killing, and they were trying to hide their tracks, even though they had no need to so soon?'

'Exactly. Or it could have been a distraction for whoever was to investigate the case. Or people might have been encouraged to believe it was a religious killing. The incense could mean something or nothing, such is the curious nature of this crime.'

'What was it you said to the king,' Leana said, 'about missing objects?'

'When I first came in this room, because of a space in the dust on one of the tables . . .' I marched over to the small piece of furniture. 'This one, in fact. It looked as if an object had been removed from it. Now, not a trace of evidence remains.'

'You think it might be significant?'

'Everything could be significant at the moment,' I sighed. 'At the time I was too preoccupied with her corpse and the royal physician to contemplate the situation. I should have paid more attention. If there was something missing, we'll probably never know. Judging by its shape I assumed it might have been a book or a storage box. Much like the one missing from my father's room – though in that case I have a suspicion it was the base of a statue that might have been sold. Anyway, whatever it was, it has been moved.'

'In the night, the killer might have gone back to her room to remove something,' Leana speculated. 'Or one of her lovers might have come back to take an item that they thought could make them look guilty.'

'She certainly led a complicated existence.'

I continued searching around the room and decided to take a closer look at some of her reading material, which was in the far corner of the room, up on a high shelf. There were four large books piled on top of each other, as I remembered the first time, volumes in blue or green leather. I lifted each one down in turn and opened them up. Two books were on Detratan mythology: famous classics that most of the wealthy homes in Tryum were rarely without. It took a while to make out the writing on the spine of another since it was so old; but when opened it was revealed to be on the natural wildlife that could be found in a coastal province called Destos, which I remembered fondly from my childhood as a rural holiday area for the rich. It seemed to have been read many times. Inside a book of plays there was a hand-drawn map containing the sketched names of places – it was difficult to work out where, but it might have been important because the paper was reasonably fresh and potentially drawn by Lacanta herself. In fact, the lines and symbols didn't seem unlike those in Senator Divran's study.

Was Lacanta interested in the dark arts? I put the paper in my pocket while no one was looking.

'Now this is interesting.' The final book was a volume of plays by the famous, ancient Maristanian writer Locottus, which seemed to fit neatly with the idea that both Lacanta and Licintius were appreciative of the theatre, but it was inscribed to her as 'a gift from Nucien'. I reached into my pocket and drew out the list of names that Veron had provided. There were only ten names written down and a man called 'Nucien Malvus' was one of them.

'Is it the same one?' Leana asked.

'We have a match,' I replied. 'It's about time we made our presence known in the Senate – this will give us some further purpose. While we're there we can go through as many of the names on Veron's list without creating a bad name for ourselves as hunters of senators.'

I put the books back and took one more look around before leaving unsatisfied.

I made my formal requests with the staff to visit the Senate building, but it turned out that all the senators had already gone home for the day. Only then did I realize just how much time we'd spent looking in every nook and cranny we could find in Optryx.

Noting that the sun was low in the sky, we hurried home.

On the walk back it seemed right to explain to Leana who I was meeting later, and we briefly discussed what had taken place while Veron dragged me out.

'You found her then,' Leana said.

'I have. I'm not sure what to do though.'

'I am not,' Leana continued, 'the best person to give advice on this subject. She will not distract you from the investigation, I hope?'

'You know me better than that.'

'I do. Your people here seem preoccupied with love and sex, as if it is all that matters in the world.'

When we arrived home, a message had been left for me from the pontiff at the Temple of Polla: now that the various rites had been performed on my father's ashes, they would become my property in the morning, to take to the family mausoleum.

After washing, changing into my smart attire – a deep blue tunic and cloak, my best black trousers – I made myself smell fresh for the evening using what little fragrance was available.

And waited for Titiana to arrive.

Sunset came and there was no sign of her. I paced the hallway, convincing myself that it was stupid to expect anything to happen, that it was ridiculous to even hope for forgiveness. Clearly Titiana had come to her senses. If that was her decision, I could not blame her.

Presently there came a knock at the door and I managed to rush there before Bellona. Titiana stood on the doorstep, a vision worth the journey across the continent. She wore a wonderful cream and red dress, with just one small necklace, nothing flamboyant, and her dark hair was hanging loose around her shoulders. She was a few years older than the figure who had been preserved in my memories, but somehow she seemed to be even more alluring.

'I was starting to think you wouldn't arrive,' I said.

'I was starting to think I shouldn't,' she replied.

'Yet here you are.' I stepped outside and closed the door behind me. Now that I knew that she didn't detest me quite as much as she could have, a sudden awkwardness came over me. Even when imagining this scene from the other side of the continent I hadn't really planned what we would say or do.

'I don't know about you, but I'm famished,' I said. 'I've not been in the city for a long time. Can you recommend a good place to eat?'

A Small, Underground Tavern

We wandered through the backstreets, away from prying eyes. Titiana was, of course, a married woman, so secrecy was essential; I'll admit that was something of a thrill.

Tryum's citizens seemed to behave strangely at this hour. Half-veiled figures drifted in and out of doorways, as if on some illicit business. The city changed its texture completely, as if a new cast of characters had been brought on stage. I half-expected Senator Veron to be following in the distance, swigging wine from a cup and cheering me on.

Titiana led me slowly across the neighbourhoods of Polyum, to an establishment she had always wanted to eat at, but could never afford. She told me that, since I was the one paying, she wasn't going to miss the opportunity to eat there.

The tavern was a remarkably charming place, a subterranean establishment built beneath a temple, right on the border with Regallum. Inside there were hundreds of candles, mirrors, ornate coloured glassware, beautifully crafted wooden furniture, with plenty of happy guests drinking and enjoying its relaxing ambience. From its location, and assessing all these fine decorations on display, I had the impression that a lot of senators might dine there, and I could only imagine the kind of deals that had been struck in the alcoves.

We were seated at a table at the far end of the tavern, a small booth tucked away from the hubbub. A jug was brought over by a serving girl and, as she poured wine into two cups, she told us the owner would be with us shortly to talk about tonight's dishes. The place was heady with the smell of delicious food, the kind that seemed a world away from what I'd happily snacked on in Plutum and Barrantum.

A man at the table beside us, handsome, but dressed in a shabby brown tunic and unshaven, didn't seem to fit in with the other drinkers and diners. He had by him a small drum and I wondered if he was a busker. He looked up at me and gave a warm and toothy smile.

The tavern owner strode over to welcome us; he was a middle-aged man of ample proportions, dressed in a wonderfully ornate red tunic. From memory, he proceeded to list several of the dishes that were available. I had been used to austere meals in Venyn City and was amazed at the delights on offer, but in the end I opted for the simple spiced fish dish. Titiana said she would have the same, and the tavern owner left us alone. He turned to the table nearby, where the man with the drum was finishing up and they were discussing payment.

Titiana smiled and looked around the tavern, and the lack of conversation between us was not at all awkward. It was as if we were slowly remembering how we used to act together. From the other table I overheard a discussion between the two men. The man with the drum was asking for forgiveness for not being able to produce enough money.

'My deepest apologies, I assure you,' the busker said. 'I have coin at the home where I am staying – it is but a short trip. Please, if I leave this drum here with you, as insurance, I will retrieve it and return.'

'That instrument?' the tavern owner asked, dissatisfied with the offer.

'The drum, yes. It's very precious to me – it is my employment around the city. Without it, I'm nothing.'

'All right . . . But you'll get back quickly?'

'Before the night is done I will return,' the busker urged. 'I need my drum for tomorrow where I am playing for an important family in Polyum.'

'Hurry up,' the owner warned.

'Of course, of course.'

I turned to watch the tavern owner holding the drum while the shabbily dressed busker headed out of the door. Shaking his head, the owner turned to walk past us.

'Sir,' I called, and whispered, 'that drum in your hand.'

He leaned in closer. 'This thing?'

'The man who gave it to you is about to con you,' I said.

'Never!'

'I'm afraid so – it's a very old trick. He'll most likely be working with a partner, someone who will be in the tavern tonight, and probably very well dressed. He or she will then tell you that this instrument is worth a great deal of money, that it is a Detratan collectable or something like that, and they'll then try to convince you to let them buy it off its owner for a large sum.'

'What are you on about?'

'He'll then hope you buy it from the busker, who doesn't know the alleged true value of the instrument, for a much smaller price. You're meant to think you can sell it back to the well-dressed man for a huge profit, but all that will happen is that you hand over a lot of cash for what is, ultimately, a cheap drum. Meanwhile, they'll have shared the coin and not even be in the same neighbourhood by the time you notice.'

'You seem very sure,' he laughed.

'I have seen it done in many other taverns in cities across this continent. You're not the first. You'll not be the last. It is a very old trick.'

'You're a cynical man,' he replied. 'People are better than that!'

'That may be so, but keep hold of that drum and wait to be approached – then you can comment fairly on my nature.'

With a cautious glare the tavern owner nodded and took his drum to the countertop nearby, placing it beside the sacks of fresh bread.

Titiana frowned at me, and gave a short laugh. 'He's right, you seem very sure of yourself.'

'With the drum, I am, at least. Not so much with you it seems.'

'You were confident enough last night.' All I was getting was a half-smile, but I had waited for years to see just that much. 'Yet you claim to struggle with me now?'

I shrugged. 'Love makes things more difficult.'

'Love. You said you loved me right before you gave me the wound on my back.' The half-smile remained on her face. 'If that is what you think of love, then you're better off without it.'

This wasn't going to be easy. Over the years I had speculated on this imaginary conversation, of how it would go and how we would both act, but in my head my words had come out effortlessly, and she had been a lot less hostile. I was better off sweeping away criminals from the streets of Vispasia, than trying to form pretty sentences with her.

'Titiana, you might have married and started a new life, but I never really moved on. I've never had the opportunity to find a partner, or start a family. I've simply travelled from city to city, from street to street, dealing with those at the edge of the civilized world.'

'You made your choices,' she replied. 'I notice that you can't seem to apologize for your actions.'

Was it only pride from making me do so? 'I am sorry for what happened, and for my part in it. I'm truly sorry.'

It didn't seem that difficult, after all, to say the word.

Though we sat in silence for a few moments, it felt as if a tension had been ever so slightly dissolved. We could relax. The serving girl brought over a complimentary bowl of olives and a tiny loaf of sourdough bread, a refreshing gesture that would probably be reflected in the final bill. As she left a smartly dressed man in polished boots and a rich silver tunic with gold hem approached the tavern owner. After a moment of easy-going conversation, he pointed towards the drum.

Titiana must have caught me looking. She leaned forward, her face caught in the warm glow of the candlelight. 'Now that it seems you're right about this busker, are you going to be as unbearable as I suspect?'

Smiling, I shook my head. 'I'm certainly not as bad as I once may have been. I've been involved in rather more important matters than this – which is simply one of the oldest confidence tricks going. It's fascinating. Watch him: he's full of charm, wearing the finest clothes, in order to gain the owner's trust. It's all very well planned.'

We observed the conversation between the men for a moment longer. Eventually the man in the crimson tunic walked out of the tavern.

The owner approached our table with a haughty look on his face. 'Consider your meal free if you can tell me what happens next and, more importantly, how to make sure I am not conned out of any coin!'

I leaned back in my chair. 'You're OK for now. The busker will return, but all you really need to do is make sure he pays for his meal, and then you simply hand back the drum. He may seem hesitant – surprised, even – but simply concentrate on making sure you collect payment for his meal. Accept nothing else. He should leave you alone after that, and will probably head off to attempt this again in a more unlucky establishment.'

He nodded and turned to Titiana, gently pressing down on her hand. 'If you ask me, you should keep hold of this fellow – in Tryum, there are too few like him.'

The expression on her face alone was worth the price of a dinner.

We ate our meal in a more pleasant mood than I could have possibly hoped for. What's more, I couldn't remember eating more flavoursome food: the taste of the fish was so intense and tender.

We talked, and I tried desperately to make her laugh in order to hear what it sounded like again. A hundred memories flashed back before my eyes. I didn't know how accurate they were, given the layer of sentiments within them, but those moments from our younger days returned: day trips riding out to the coast; making love in the garden of the Temple of Festonia; long, hot days where we'd go swimming, then wade onto the shore where I'd proceed to kiss her skin under a ferocious sun. It didn't really matter where we went or what we did, just as long as we had each other's company, and our affair lasted for months without anyone ever knowing what we were up to. Was it any surprise I hadn't really moved on?

Gradually, Titiana opened up to me – not much at first, but enough for me to know she no longer loathed me. Which was, ultimately, progress. It turned out she was living in Vellyum, which wasn't as bad as things could have been. Her husband was a wine merchant for the middle classes, and spent much of his time out of the city ensuring the trade was running smoothly.

He was still out of the city, as it happened – and I did ask to make sure.

She had two children, a girl of four and a boy of five, who were staying with her husband's sister, though she did not dwell on the subject too long. The feeling left me with happiness for her, and an emptiness inside myself. I had once imagined what it might have been like to raise a family together. No matter how much I asked her about her life, she seemed awkward talking about it, which was perhaps understandable. Her tentative gestures made me start to feel guilty that I had dragged a mother away from her family simply so I could entertain my senses of love and lust.

Titiana asked me of my adventures and I told her of the things I'd seen across Vispasia. Unlike Veron's party, this time it was about the struggles of the people throughout the continent, of the damage left over by the old Detratan Empire that still, two hundred years later, left its mark on the world. I spoke of tribal wars, of political factions going rogue, of the delicate cohesion of the Royal Union. Finally, I commented dryly that the Sun Chamber was now my only family.

'Still, the continent is all the stronger for being united,' I continued, 'even if the nations cannot always agree on the most harmonious paths at times.'

'You walk in a different world to the rest of us, Lucan,' Titiana sighed, as if partly jealous and partly proud of me. 'More wonderful than mine.'

'Each of our own worlds is challenging enough,' I remarked. 'It's all a matter of context.'

The busker returned to the tavern for his drum and, true to my instructions, the tavern owner returned it to him and took the money for the meal. With a disappointed look on his face, and no longer smiling when he glanced at me, the busker trudged out of the establishment a disappointed man.

The owner approached our table once again. 'I make a point of not disturbing lovers too much—'

'Oh, but we're . . .' Titiana said.

The man palmed the air.

'Let the man speak, Titiana,' I said grinning.

The owner burst out a laugh. 'You should say that to my wife – she constantly tells me to shut up! No, consider your dinner paid for tonight. When you dine here again, you ask for Kollans.'

We finished our meal and stepped outside into the mild Tryum evening. Cloud cover had come in from the eastern skies, obscuring the starlight. I didn't know quite how late it was, but I told Titiana that I ought to get to bed soon.

'Do I bore you now?' she said, teasing me. 'Is your life now too exciting to bother with the likes of me?'

My own grin soon faded. 'No, tomorrow I will be claiming my father's ashes so that they can be buried in our mausoleum, south of the city.'

'Oh.' She took my hands, I momentarily held my breath. 'You needn't do a thing like that alone,' she said. 'If you need support you only have to ask.'

'If you're willing, I wouldn't mind the company.'

'You're not the only one who could do with the company,' she replied.

'That's settled. I'll meet you around two hours after sunrise.'

'I'll come to your house.' Titiana leaned forward, and her lips touched mine so softly I could have mistaken them for a gust of wind. She whispered to me, 'You still owe me a dinner, because I don't believe you actually paid for that one.'

As Titiana turned to walk back slowly through the streets of Tryum, I contemplated how so little had changed between us – the way we interacted, our similar disregard for social norms, my efforts to make her giggle – and the realization of this was somehow rather comforting. I stood still longer than was necessary, watching Titiana walk around the corner, vanishing into the night. A moment later, an old woman shuffled by and regarded me with either a grin or a grimace, it was difficult to say. At least I was smiling.

The Mausoleum

'Lucan . . .'

Leana's soothing voice woke me. The first rays of the morning sun poured in through the tiny window and met high up with the opposite wall. Brightness warmed my vision and I remembered that I wanted to be up early: another busy day lay ahead, another day in which to try to find Lacanta's murderer. My groggy vision settled on the small bone charm Leana was wearing around her neck, some unfathomable creature's skull pale against her skin.

'You had a seizure during the night,' she said.

'Did I?' I sighed. 'For how long?'

'One of your longer ones. You settled soon enough.'

She was already dressed, ready for another day's work, while I remained in a dream-like state, not yet fully awake. To be so punctual and in control of one's sleeping habits . . .

'It seems the apothecary's little potions were no use,' I said.

'You took what she said, before you fell asleep?'

'Well, uh, no.'

'Spirits save me, you only have yourself to blame.'

'You make a fair point, Leana,' I replied. 'Actually, I wanted to

241

go to the apothecary today anyway, to check whether or not the blue vial had contained poison.'

'Would you like me to come also?' Leana asked.

'No, I'd like you to do me a favour. General Maxant is making a political speech to the people in the lower districts today. I would like it if you could just track the movements of his people beforehand.'

Leana faced me, more attentive now there was a firm plan for the day. 'What are you hoping to find?'

'It's more out of curiosity than anything related to the murders. While we won't hear anything but a well-rehearsed speech when he's presenting his case for election, I'd be interested to see what the preparations are like . . . see just how keen he is on being elected to the Senate. In the meantime, I'll be off to the mausoleum.' I spun my feet onto the floor. 'And Titiana will be coming with me.'

'I see,' Leana replied. 'How did it go?'

'We had a pleasurable evening,' I yawned, casting my mind back to the most minute details, smiling inwardly. 'Nothing happened, if that's what you're thinking.'

'I am in your employment only – your own life remains yours. You need tell me nothing more.' She moved to the doorway.

'You know I think of you more like a sister than someone I employ,' I said, 'and normally I'd tell you more. All I can say is that I don't think she hates me any more.'

'Then you must have been trying very hard,' came the reply, before she left the room.

Many people would think it unbearable to work with someone who liked making such comments, but I rather enjoyed them. In her own way, she was keeping me in check.

After arranging a rendezvous point with Leana for the afternoon, I wrapped the glass vial and put it back in my pocket, before heading out through the brightening streets. The route was more obvious in the pink light just after dawn, but the narrow street was still concealed nicely from the thoroughfares. I enjoyed being out and about at this hour: it was as if this was how Tryum wanted to be seen, calm and cool, without the throng obscuring the wonderful mishmash of architecture or crowding the temples. One could appreciate the smaller details of buildings, or the arrangement of statues along a colonnade.

Eventually, as I reached the apothecary, the scent of some blissful concoction wafted up the street towards me. There was a small rack of her samples standing on the tiny window ledge. I knocked on the open door, announcing my arrival.

The same blonde woman was there; she was smiling as she stood over a pan of boiling liquid and wore the same dirtied robe she had worn the other night. Herbs and bottles were spread about the place, just as before, and the ledgers were more neatly arranged now. There was an acute sense of peace in the room.

'Welcome again.' She looked up once before regarding her pan again. 'How's your father coming along with the treatment?'

'He forgot to drink some yesterday,' I replied, 'and suffered a seizure in the night.'

'Oh that's not good! He'll need to take it regularly if it's to be of any help at all.'

'He can be a bit forgetful, you see, but I haven't come today to talk about his treatment.'

'You have another ailment?'

'Not exactly.' I considered the best line of approach and thought it was about time I started being more honest with her. 'My employment is as an Officer of the Sun Chamber.'

She paused and gave me a quick look of concern, before returning to work.

'You're in no trouble, have no concern on that matter. I'm actually here for your advice.'

'Tell me your question, lawmaker.' She continued to stir the liquid in slow, precise movements.

Law-enforcer, I wanted to correct her, but that would have been petty. I reached into my pocket and took out the blue glass vial, holding it in front of her by its long neck. 'This is related to an investigation I'm working on. I don't know where it comes from or what it originally contained, but I would like your expert opinion.'

She took it from me and brought it under the light from the window, rolling the vial between her thumb and forefinger. While she did this, I glanced quickly at a piece of paper to one side, which looked like something attached to a delivery – it contained the address of this place and featured a name at the top: *Mordia Lapmus.*

There was no expression on her face to suggest she knew what the vial was – until she unplugged the stopper and raised it to her nose. She jerked it as far as she could from her face, placed the stopper inside again and, angrily, handed it back to me. 'Where did you get this?' She thrust it back into my palm.

'I'm afraid I can't say. But I take it you know what it is?'

She laughed incredulously. 'Oh yes. I do. It is hemlock.'

My eyes widened in astonishment. 'Are you quite certain of this?'

'One cannot be completely sure with poisons, but I would say this probably contained a poison made from hemlock. I was schooled early on in my life to recognize such vile odours.'

'Is it easily available?' I asked.

'If you know where to look, anything is easily available in Tryum,' she replied.

'No, I mean are there many apothecaries in Tryum who

genuinely trade in such things? Other than the quite legitimate Mordia Lapmus, of course.'

Her eyes widened at the mention of her name, and she opened her mouth to reply, but seemed to consider her words more carefully. 'It was certainly not me. I specialize in making people feel better, not in the arts of death, though there are those who practise such things in Detrata. The last time you came here, you mentioned henbane, and now you bring hemlock. If you work with death, I'd rather you took your work elsewhere.'

'I'm sorry,' I said. 'I don't deal in such sinister arts myself and I share your appreciation for the living. But with a little help I might be able to track down who sold this or, more importantly, who bought it.'

'Whoever buys hemlock wishes to kill another – or themselves,' Mordia replied. 'It's very simple. No good comes of the substance. There is no justification for owning it.'

'OK, so do you know who might sell similar blue vials? Or is there anyone who trades in hemlock in Tryum?'

'The vial is not common,' Mordia said. 'But neither is it rare. I wouldn't be able to match it, off the top of my head, but I can give you a list of other apothecaries who work in the city.' She paused, and looked around with impatience. 'I will write down a list for you. I only ever know the reputable traders, though – it may well be that your search will put you in contact with more unscrupulous traders.'

She reached across to one side and, with a reed pen, scrawled on a ledger, while I regarded the vial once again. What would my father be doing with poison? Had his personal situation become so bad, had his debts caused him so much anguish, that he felt the need to take his own life?

'There.' She ripped out the thick page from the ledger, folded it up and thrust it at me. 'I know only of seven other apothecaries who may be able to help you further. If there are illegitimate tradesmen, which there may well be, then I make a point of not knowing them.'

Many of the addresses were situated in the higher or mid levels of the city. None of them were in Plutum or Barrantum.

'Thanks for your time, Mordia.' I moved over to the door. 'I promise not to bother you any more.'

'Just make sure your father keeps drinking his tisanes,' Mordia replied, more warmly than before, but now distant – utterly focused on the contents of her pan.

Seeking to hire a horse, I wandered the backstreets of Tradum to the biggest of the city stables, a large, noisy and pungent court-yard. An array of tradesmen, blacksmiths and armourers laboured around the perimeter of the structure, forming a lively, self-contained community.

I examined some of the remarkably ornate signs and chatted to the workers. Paying fifty pecullas for the day, apparently, I could be riding a wonderful brown stallion fit for the military. But given my finances, instead I paid ten pecullas for an old white mare with a huge personality. She seemed happy to go any-where today and I was happy to ride with her.

From there I rode down to the Temple of Polla, where the pontiff was waiting for me, to collect my father's ashes. In the shaded entrance he gave me the key to our mausoleum, which was stored safely within the temple. A smell of incense pervaded from the never-ending fire. Calludian Drakenfeld's ashes were contained within a large urn, on which a battle scene from the Visions of Polla, with relief lines around Polla herself, was painted. There was a remarkable level of skill involved in its creation – this was a beautiful send-off for my father. Two rings lay buried within the ashes, the pontiff told me, which were found on his body at the time.

I thanked the pontiff for his assiduous and respectful preparations, wrapped and placed both the urn and the key within a shoulder bag, before heading back to my house.

While I waited for Titiana, I took a quick look around my father's room to see if there were any other items to take to the mausoleum with me, something that might make for a good send-off. He had not been a great collector of trinkets and my mother would always hassle him not to hoard useless items. In the end I settled on his Sun Chamber brooch, which was located in a drawer, deciding that it was more than appropriate.

But then it struck me: if he was wearing his rings at the time of his death, when he was found in his offices, why was his brooch of office here in a drawer? What was the reason for him taking it off?

I placed the brooch within the urn, sealed it once again and tucked it away. The knock on the main door moments later was Titiana. She stood before me in a long blue tunic and black cloak, her hair tied in thin silver bands and brought forward around her neck; her sensual, olive-brown skin seemed to glow in the clarity of the morning sun.

On seeing her I realized how grateful I was not to be taking my father's ashes to the mausoleum alone.

Mausoleums, crypts, tombs and exposed sarcophagi – the houses of the dead were scattered throughout the hillsides near Tryum in all directions, and my father's lay to the south-east. In that way, it was deemed that the dead should surround the living, ensuring we did not forget their presence. I could certainly vouch for the effectiveness of that plan: my father's own departure through to the Underworld and beyond had certainly overshadowed my arrival in Tryum. Even in death he managed to be

247

sending me about the city and, for better or worse, I felt I knew him more in death than when he was still alive.

With Titiana sitting behind me, we rode towards the south gate and the day was already starting to get hot. The road was full of tradesmen and shoppers, wanderers and home-comers. Aqueducts towered across neighbourhoods, casting even tall buildings in shadow. Plutum lay to our left, Barrantum to our right, the south road dividing the poorer districts in two. Not that anyone would notice a difference between them — poverty did not discriminate, after all. But it was heartening to witness at least two priests wandering the slums and giving alms to the poor.

Pairs of soldiers from the City Watch marched up and down the wide road at regular intervals, maintaining the sense of order here, though a glimpse into the streets beyond would suggest there was very little order to be found. The old city wall, built during the Detratan Empire, had long since been looted for stone, and stood as an impotent barrier, where only two watch-towers now remained. Tryum had bloomed over the years and the resplendent new city wall loomed in the distance in all its lime-stone glory, cracked and weathered already, but a good deal more robust than its predecessor. It was reassuring to see such scrutiny from the soldiers as they assessed who was going in and out.

Eventually we managed to head out of the gates to the coun-tryside beyond. The mare was a reliable companion for us, and she soon picked up her pace once she was free of the streets.

Titiana held on to me. A decade disappeared in an instant.

As the sun rose ever higher, we continued on the road through farmland. Hills shimmered and in the distance were the outlines of the monuments to the dead. The yellow and black banners of Detrata rippled in the wind above them. Such structures, for reasons I never fully understood, tended to cluster around auspicious hilltops that were important in Detrata's history, or for religious reasons that had largely been forgotten. It's strange, sometimes, how rituals become established practice and no one ever knows their true origins. We just do what we're told, and act in certain ways, until it's engraved on our souls.

The weight of the shoulder bag, which contained the urn, seemed greater with every few yards of travel.

'This is it,' I said.

Found by the hill of Four Gods, the Drakenfeld mausoleum was a tiny structure compared to those nearby. Our family was wealthier than most people of Tryum — and I was conscious of my good fortune on this matter — but it was clear that there were a great number of people who were richer than us. This gap was especially obvious when looking at family monuments.

The first Drakenfeld to be buried here was my grandfather, who was the first senator to gain his position based on his exploits as a general in the military, rather than because his fortune was large enough to bribe the right people to prove he was a citizen of good standing. I never knew whether or not he approved of his son, my father, joining the Sun Chamber — the subject wasn't one that was raised all that much. He built up his wealth yet remained true to his mild-natured and humble roots: this small, domed mausoleum contained just four pillars no taller than me, and a relief of Polla. The elaborate structures either side featured intricate facades and bold architectural statements.

Nearby a few people walked with offerings in their hands through a ruined colonnade, and a family was dining at the foot of one nearby structure, chatting merrily in the sun.

'What an incredible place.' Titiana gestured to the row upon row of fascinating monuments surrounding us, each one unique in some way. 'This really is a whole other city just for the dead.

They say on auspicious nights that such places become alive with ghosts, and figures of bone lose themselves in the surrounding hills.'

'That's why we make sure to keep the mausoleums locked,' I said and smiled. 'I can't be doing with dead relatives hassling me in my sleep.'

'I'm serious,' Titiana said, with the wonder of a much younger woman. 'All stories have their roots in truth. Besides, I've used such tales more than once to make the children behave and go to bed on time.'

We dismounted from the mare and for a moment simply ambled along the path in separate directions, each in our own world of awe and respect. Titiana seemed happy enough so I wandered among the stones noting the family names and trying to recall their position in the city.

Suddenly a figure caught my eye walking among the structures, and following me. He – at least, it was dressed in the clothing of a man – wore a tattered and ripped cloak, but otherwise his tunic seemed fine, if a little colourless. He looked at me, wide holes in place of his eyes; and no sooner had that thought registered, than he turned to flee through a wide avenue of mausoleums. I moved quickly to catch up with him, but could no longer see him.

Senator Divran told me to walk among the tombs and a small part of me wondered if the figure had been her creation. Shaking my head, I retraced my steps – I knew better than to believe in such fantasies.

Titiana was waiting by the mare, but didn't seem interested in where I'd been – she was too entranced by my family's mausoleum. I reached into my bag for the urn carrying my father's ashes, and passed it to Titiana momentarily, before pulling out a heavy key. After unlocking the iron gate, which had rusted somewhat, we stepped into the dark sanctuary of the mausoleum.

I left the key in the lock, out of the way.

After the brightness of the daylight it was difficult to see the details at first, and there was a prevalent musty odour. Beneath our feet was a yellow mosaic floor featuring the two-headed falcon. Alongside it was the icon of the cross of the founding gods, representing where both Trymus and Festonia marked on the ground the very position where Tryum would be built. I searched around for the right spot, slid back a stone cover and placed my father's ashes down alongside my mother's.

'You rarely spoke of your mother,' Titiana said.

'I hardly knew her, if I'm honest,' I replied. 'She died when I was no more than five summers old. I know far too little about her, because my father didn't often mention her name. An aunt once told me that it was because he never really let her go after she died. I have memories of her, though, glimpses that come back to me now and then.'

'What was her name?'

'Mawya. She came from the deserts – from Locco. People often told me she possessed such beauty that passers-by would stop her in the street to tell her so. I think people's memories can be kinder than the reality, but I'm reassured she was kind and gentle-natured, and always thought the best of people no matter how they treated others. I vaguely remembered her singing songs of the desert to me but . . . well, after that my upbringing was with my brother and my father.'

'That would explain your inability to talk plainly with women,' Titiana joked, and I was glad of her lightening the mood. 'Will you be buried here one day? That must be a sobering thought.'

'So long as there is someone here to remember to bury me – and someone who can be bothered to bring my ashes all the way up that hill, then yes.' Solemnly, I drew back the heavy stone lid and set it in place with a clunk.

We stepped outside into the daylight once again. With my mind somewhat exhausted by now, I lay down in the long grass with a sigh, regarded the pearlescent blue sky and enjoyed the warmth. The leaves and branches of a nearby tree stirred in the soothing breeze. Titiana lay down next to me, resting her head against my shoulder, her sweet floral fragrance drifting over me.

I wanted never to rise from that spot.

When the sun reached its zenith I felt it was time to return to Tryum. I decided to take one last look at the mausoleum to preserve the image in my mind, as I did not know when I would return, but then realized the key was still in the lock with the metal gate closed. It hadn't locked – of course it wouldn't, because the key had not been turned – but for a moment it looked as if the ghost of my ancestors had placed the key there.

Placed the key.

Of course.

A Bloody Business

We strolled down the gentle slope towards the horse. The city stood before us and, from here, we could clearly see the clash of architecture of new and old, the harsh contrast between itself and the farmland surrounding it; and the river that stretched out towards the sea a mile or so beyond. On a day like today, I wished to immerse myself within that deep blue liquid.

'How is your investigation going?' Titiana asked.

'I'm afraid I'm not able to talk much about it,' I replied.

'I see. Lucan Drakenfeld, keeper of state secrets.' Titiana laughed warmly.

'No,' I said, 'it's more for your own protection. The fewer people who know about my life, the fewer lives are in danger. I wouldn't want you to lose any sleep because of something I said.'

'I'm not afraid.' Titiana linked her arm through mine, and I missed a breath feeling her skin brush against my wrist. 'Besides, the whole city is talking about it. Rumours in the markets suggest all sorts of fanciful possibilities. I've heard priests say that the spirits of former Detratan emperors were responsible because they disapprove of the newer royals.'

'I would have trouble arresting a ghost.' I gave her a very

limited account of what I'd seen so far — enough to satisfy her curiosity, I hoped, but nothing that would be the seed of gossip. The last thing I wanted was for rumour to spread in one quarter of the city, attracting the king's interest. I knew how fragile his mind was over this situation, and I was reluctant for him to send his soldiers chasing gossip.

'That wasn't so hard, was it?' Titiana said.

I contemplated the view once again before glancing at Titiana, beguiling Titiana. Words could not express all my hopes and frustrations right then. I had of course lain with other partners in the past, but either because my life was one continuous journey or I could not let go of the past, none of them really compared to her — or at least my memories of her.

'Where do we go from here?' I asked. 'I want to see you again, but you're married. That said, you're certainly someone who seems to care less about being seen with me today than she did last night. Does this mean I am forgiven?'

'You apologized to me for what you did,' she replied eventually. 'That was something you were too proud to do the first time around.'

Titiana pulled back on my arm as I was about to step up onto the horse. Her eyes seemed even more enchanting in the light of the midday sun. I felt an awkwardness develop between us.

'You're married,' I said. 'It's as simple as that. I get it. You have a reputation to protect, as do I.'

'It doesn't matter. I wear a wedding bracelet and nothing more.' She faced away from me now, and towards the city. 'I barely see him. I barely see anyone but my family. They say if you're a rich woman you can rise to the Senate these days. Well, not from where I am you can't. A woman's place lower down the city is confined to her husband's shadow.'

'It doesn't have to be like that.' I longed to tell her of what it was like for women in places like Locco, where men and women shared the responsibilities of raising a family, lest it bring shame on him; even Dalta, where women ruled the nation, not just the home. Not everywhere was reluctant in leaving behind the ghost and structures of its empire. 'Titiana, right now I can promise little more than I did all those years ago. At least, not until the Lacanta murder is solved. After that, who knows? I have money now and no parents to dictate my actions.'

'Will you ever find the killer though?' Titiana brushed her hand along the side of my head and I held her wrist in place, hoping she would never let go of me. 'The way you speak about it, you might as well be looking for a ghost.'

'Perhaps I am.'

Her lips rushed to mine and I felt the surge of intensity in my chest. For that endless moment, on that hillside with the dead looking on behind us, nothing seemed to matter. The years fell away and it seemed as if I was enjoying the carefree times of my youth – no pressures, no concerns, just the present moment.

My hands moved down to her waist and I pulled her against me. Meanwhile the breeze came in tenderly from the sea, bringing with it the invigorating scents of the landscape.

We rode back in a comforting silence, Titiana in front of me, my arms around her waist. Occasionally I would kiss the back of her neck and she would tilt her head forward to permit me access.

Her tunic was of an impressive quality and I wondered if she had brought out one of her better garments today. Sometimes one could read too much into what a potential lover might wear, constantly divining for truth in the slightest of details.

She said that she wanted to make her own way back, alone, to her neighbourhood, so I left her just inside Vellyum, on one of the better streets. I asked where she lived but she wouldn't tell me 'in case I turned up drunk one night pining for her company'. She was smiling, but it was clear that I was not to go with her, and I thanked her for coming with me this morning.

She disappeared through the hectic lanes before I even had the opportunity to ask when we could meet again. I imagined – and hoped – that she would find me soon enough.

The final stretch of the journey, to return the horse and reclaim my deposit, was spent in melancholic thought. Titiana's departure had left me feeling rather isolated and I quietly prayed to Polla that my goddess might spare some of her light for me.

Leana was standing in the shadow of a Temple of Festonia, a block-like building quite unlike the other temples in the city, and one that was in much need of renovation. The two-headed goddess had lost one of her arms, though I assumed the statue's angry expression was carved before someone broke it off. It seemed a shame to treat the gods with so little respect, but that was the least of the district's problems: a couple of crippled old women limped by, while skinny, almost-naked men prostrated themselves before tavern owners or merchants for coin – the men of business standing over them were the new gods in this district.

'How did it go?' Leana asked, still examining the people milling about the courtyard.

'I've put my father to rest now,' I replied. 'Anyway, what have you seen today?'

Leana walked me around the area in which General Maxant would be making his declaration to the neighbourhood about his intention to go into the Senate on their behalf, all the time explaining what she had seen.

'He is to make his speech from a balcony behind the local Temple of Trymus.'

'So Maxant moves to prove his loyalty to the city's founding gods,' I suggested. 'A safe tactic.'

'You can see the recent graffiti on these walls,' Leana continued. 'There are political slogans about his conquests and his suitability for the role. Look carefully around the paint; there is writing that is insulting to other men.' She showed me one example, which suggested, in rather more crude terms, that a man called Gerrantus liked to commit sexual acts with animals. 'Gerrantus is the senator of this contested neighbourhood. More over here, also.'

Leana showed me several other pieces of graffiti along these lines, and some with the curious allegation that Gerrantus was responsible for killing Lacanta by summoning evil spirits.

'I'd have to check, but I don't recall his name being present on the list that night,' I replied. 'He's certainly not on the one Veron gave me, of those who were close to Lacanta.'

'It would not be the first lie on these walls,' Leana said. 'More.'

We walked behind buildings, away from the main traffic of the city, towards a cluster of men who were loitering beside a pastry stall, eating and generally laughing and joking in an easy-going mood. They were dressed in the kind of everyday clothing that people wore around these parts, grubby tunics, ripped trousers and sandals.

'What are we looking at?' I asked.

Leana moved me to a position alongside a rusted brazier. She kept her back to them while I faced them. 'Pretend we are friends or lovers, smile at me, and keep watching.'

I glanced up every few moments, until another man came along, dressed the same: they stood taller as he walked up to them, and they exchanged nods before he marched on.

'Maxant's veterans?' I whispered.

'Yes,' Leana replied. 'I only noticed them when I saw the same group of men walk by the same point three times.'

'They're patrolling the place to make sure any rivals are kept at bay. I suppose they'd have every interest in their general making it into the Senate, where he could start granting them all sorts of pensions or extra land. Maxant is no fool.'

We strode back towards where the full spectacle was building up, and kept ourselves in the shade of the ruined temple to observe the event.

Large whitewashed buildings, their facades blighted with age, loomed up either side of us, three storeys high. An old woman was hanging her washing from out of a top-floor balcony that seemed so precarious it might collapse at any moment. A huge vulture flew over the courtyard in the direction of the coast, each wing longer than I was tall.

I thought about how Maxant was making a calculated move towards establishing his political career. Once no one was within listening distance, I discussed the matter casually with Leana, suggesting that I might trust him even less than other senators.

'Why?' she asked.

'The key.'

'The key to the Temple of Trymus?'

'Yes,' I replied. 'The realization only came to me earlier today. I have a hunch, but it is no more, that whoever entered that room first was the person who put the key in the lock on the inside of the door. We have always been led to believe that the door was locked from the inside, making it impossible for anyone to either enter or escape that room. But what if the key had been put in there deliberately after the door had been barged open? Whoever had the confidence to do such a thing must have known, beforehand, they'd be among the first to enter the room that night. And no one else but our beloved, celebratory general could have possessed such a confidence – because he was destined to open it for his own ceremony. He knew precisely when it would open and precisely when everyone would see Lacanta. Seeing all his operations here highlight that he is a superb tactician both on and off the battlefield. I'm sure he could have managed a simple key trick.'

'But Lacanta and Maxant were both seen by many people just before the body was found. Maxant especially was the focus of attention that night.'

'I didn't say that he killed her,' I replied, 'merely that he was the first to gain entrance to the temple – and knowingly threw people off the scent. The rest remains a mystery, though if his men are this organized . . .' I paused. 'It all must have happened so quickly. The planning would have to have been so thorough, precise to the last heartbeat.'

'Could he risk sharing such a matter with his soldiers?' Leana asked. 'If they battered the door down with him, they may know more.'

'If such a pact was ever revealed, that they killed a royal, it would mean the end for Maxant – so he may not have wanted others knowing. He may have worked alone. But say he did put the key in the lock – he would also have to be very confident that his soldiers would be distracted by the blood-soaked body of the dead royal . . .'

'Why would he kill her?'

'I don't think he'd really want to kill Lacanta and not even our glorious general, fresh from the field of slaughter, would be swift enough to be the cause of her death that night. But look at what he might achieve as a result.' I gestured to the gathering throng below us, all of them waiting to hear what Maxant was about to say, many of them desperately eager to catch a glimpse of a man whose achievements would mark him out for legend. 'Senator Veron suggested that with Lacanta out of the way, Licintius may need to rely on Maxant's popularity. He implied nothing, of course, but it's possible that Maxant felt Lacanta was in the way of his senatorial career. Not just that, but Maxant was after land for his veterans. Think of his extra power if he had strong influence in the Senate – think what he could achieve. Come to think of it, if other senators had dreams of Empire, then they'd certainly get behind him.'

'An unlikely conclusion,' Leana said.

'It is, and I don't fully believe in it myself, but the man we're about to watch possesses a far more cunning streak than I've previously realized.'

The anticipation of the crowds was something to behold and I tried to explain to Leana their desire to see General Maxant. To these people, he was not merely just some politician – he was a war hero. They were all too rare these days, having largely been confined to stories. Not only that, but Maxant had travelled north to lands beyond the limits of their understanding. Mauland's people were so far away they were almost like mythological beings. Maxant might as well have ridden his warhorse to another world entirely.

The general had returned victorious, having secured the colder, northern frontiers, placated a savage culture and brought with him all sorts of treasures. Though the gods existed in the heavens, to the people of this neighbourhood General Maxant would be as close as they might get to seeing a god. And no doubt, in centuries to come, he would be deified and his name would be uttered with the likes of Trymus, Malax or Festonia, and become part of the city's heritage.

But to me he had now become a suspect in a murder investigation.

We were standing only a dozen yards or so away, down one

side of the courtyard, still on the temple steps, which offered a perfect view of the scene. I hoped we might be able to hear his every word. There were a good three thousand people within this courtyard now, leaning out from windows, huddling on balconies or sitting precariously on rooftops, all engaging in a lively, peaceful banter with one another. They lined the streets and alleyways beyond so that it was impossible to move around. Up on the steps, where Maxant would be appearing, a few of his soldiers were standing, wearing only the bold purple tunics of the military, but no armour. At least, these were the only soldiers wearing uniform – no doubt there were many more milling around the perimeter of the courtyard or within the gathered throng itself.

We waited so long it was as though we would be here until nightfall, but presently the victorious general came out onto the platform, rising up above the masses with his arms out wide. A priest of Trymus stood behind him, bathing the general in incense. The noise became ferocious, as if a war had spilled into the courtyard.

Maxant was clearly enjoying this position. Wearing the same purple tunic as his men – as if to signify that he did not consider himself superior – he accepted the applause he received before waving for silence.

Flanked by soldiers, he addressed the crowd.

'Citizens of Tryum!' His voice was full of the command I expected from a man of his position. It must have carried the full length of the courtyard and a few streets beyond. 'In the presence of Trymus, you bless me with your presence. You are the people who contribute to the structure of this city. You are as essential as the aqueducts or the grain supply. You make Tryum.' A predictable roar went up and everyone applauded him. Flattery only enhanced his popularity. He held his hands aloft for silence once again. 'But

your neighbourhoods are in need of support. Your current representative, Gerrantus, has not served you well.'

There was a scuffle within the crowd. A man was trying to
shout something, his voice muffled, and soon he appeared to get
dragged down to the ground.

Maxant carried on regardless. 'No. Gerrantus hasn't served
you well at all. He leaves dead bodies to rot on the side of
the road. He lets pathetic thieves stalk the streets, destroying
the lives of hard-working families by taking their valued possessions. There is too little order, but I can deliver military discipline and make your streets safe again. I have travelled far, with
these men beside me.' He gestured to his comrades. 'And we have
brought discipline and civilization to the wild places of the
world. Gerrantus, they tell me, has barely walked beyond the city
walls.'

The crowd seemed to like that. Maxant gave a confident smile.
Though his posture was formal, his manner was anything but –
his composure was pitch-perfect for the occasion: proud and
humble, jovial and serious. He continued for several more minutes listing his priorities for the district, which included greater
access to grain, a minor relaxation of taxes and new units of the
Civil Cohorts to be formed, all of which would receive the blessings of King Licintius. He listed his credentials: a man who was
born not four streets away, who climbed the ranks of Detrata's
army, who through grit and steel led the finest warriors in the
kingdom to regain the pride of the Detratan Empire. I never
expected quite the cheer that the last point received. I did not
realize just how much these people still longed to live in a con-
quering nation.

'I will bring discipline and order and safety for the hard-
working people of Tryum,' he repeated. 'All I ask of you is a
show of hands come election day, on the morning after the next

full moon. Come, friends, support me – and I will support all of you in return.'

That was that. Maxant walked off the platform and out of sight, the priest and his soldiers following him. The masses were jubilant and optimistic.

But it was the men who were not cheering, however, that caught my eye. I indicated a couple of large groups of them to Leana. Some I recognized from earlier, but others I took to be either supporters of Gerrantus, or merely hired thugs.

'Things are about to get bloody,' I said to Leana.

'Shall we stay to watch?'

'Yes, let's hang back a little longer.'

Now that people were beginning to move on, we stepped back a little deeper within the sanctuary of the crumbling temple. I spotted a member of the Civil Cohorts stood by idly a few yards away, clearly not aware of what was about to happen.

'Be careful.' Leana placed her hand on the hilt of her short sword.

The crowds gradually dispersed, and the two groups of men became more defined. Once they did, the mood changed dramatically and the rest of the stragglers hurried their pace. There were about two dozen on one side, nearly all men, and twice as many on the other; each wore roughly similar clothing, grubby tunics of varying shades. The outnumbered set of men were physically superior to the others; I took these to be Maxant's soldiers.

Situations like this pained me. As a member of the Sun Chamber, all I could do was observe the confrontation and report it to the correct authority figure. I could not stop it without any soldiers to hand, and neither were we powerful enough to subdue it.

Quite a few people were still lingering around the fringes of the courtyard, watching the spectacle from a street corner or from windows.

Blades were drawn. Two leading figures stepped towards each other and spoke in the centre, the soldier standing a good head taller than the other. After a short while, it seemed to transform into a relatively calm debate.

And then Maxant's man slit the other's throat so quickly, I barely saw it happen.

The victim collapsed as the other men surged towards the soldiers, who proceeded to form a disciplined line.

The melee was fast, violent and efficient; blood spouted in thick gouts as skin was ripped open. There were rapid punches and crippling kicks, but no sooner had it all started than the remaining attackers, or victims, fled.

Standing with their weapons still poised, the remaining soldiers regarded the courtyard, which was so badly stained with blood. With a professional calm, they gathered up the corpses and dragged them to the perimeter of the yard, before proceeding to vanish down a side alley.

'Is this how politics is done in Tryum?' Leana remarked. 'This is your version of democracy?'

A Way to Make Money

Another beautiful evening lay ahead. The sun was just passing beyond the rooftops and birds skittered about in the clear, purpling skies. Smoke drifted about on the breeze, having come from the stoves being fired up for the evening, which mixed with the scent of jasmine flowers from a nearby bush. After the excitement and emotional range of my day, there now seemed to be a wonderful stillness, and a sense of peace.

I took another moment to look at the hand-drawn document acquired in Lacanta's room. It was incredibly vague, so much so that I started to believe it could have been something else entirely – a sketch perhaps, or strange esoteric notes that had manifested in this way. The words were indecipherable, which didn't help, and there were various triangles scattered about. Maybe it was an encoded drawing from a lover?

Bellona had prepared a nourishing meal of freshly caught fish covered in pepper, bread and vegetables from the market gardens of the city. She turned to leave us, but I nagged her incessantly until she sat down to dine with us. Reluctantly, and eventually with a heavy smile, Bellona agreed, but she would not touch a drop of wine no matter how watered down it was. She ate tentatively at first, with great pauses between mouthfuls, though with time she relaxed – and only then was I satisfied.

'I've been thinking,' I announced, after chewing on some bread. 'I have a plan which solves three small problems, and I'd like your thoughts on the matter.'

Leana's glance was non-committal, but Bellona's face seemed full of concern.

'This house stands empty for much of the day and there are many rooms that simply aren't being put to good use. Meanwhile, many people in this city can't even afford to feed themselves. It simply doesn't feel right to me. That's one problem.'

'You want to move house?' Leana asked.

'No,' I replied. 'Now, another issue I'm concerned with is our safety. Bellona, our work brings us into contact with very dubious characters indeed. You'll know what it was like for my father of course.'

She nodded, and though I waited for an answer none came.

'The third issue is money,' I said. 'I know you don't like to talk about my father's money situation, Bellona, but the matter is resolved – have no fear of that. However, that has left me without much in the way of savings, and I don't wish to get into the same situation.'

Leana took a sip of water. 'And your plan?'

'I'd like to use some of these rooms as offices. I think this could become a station of the Civil Cohorts. Daytime offices for the most part – it is a private home, ultimately – but I'm sure we could have a nightwatchman too. Senator Veron gave me the idea, as he's looking to improve things for the neighbourhood. He could transfer some of the money to me to cover the rent and so forth. In the meantime, it would mean all these rooms aren't wasted, we're protected, and we have a little extra income. The most important thing, though, is that the surrounding streets will be improved even further by the presence of a team that I can mentor, to some extent. What do you think?'

Leana considered my words before declaring, 'This is a good plan. Not that you need it, but it has my support.'

'Good, and Bellona, you'll be happy with more people about?'

'Is it simply more stomachs to feed?'

I laughed. 'More or less, I guess. I'm not sure exactly. The place could get a bit messy with so many people about. I'll be able to pay you more, of course. Say, another few pecullas a week? That's on top of expenses for food. You'll probably need to manage a bigger household budget, and if you need more help I'll entrust you with finding whoever you'd like – a quick-running lad to go on errands perhaps. Also, I noticed you have good writing skills – should you need any additional tutoring in numeracy or other languages I'm sure that would be easy enough to arrange. You'll be able to manage your own small empire before long.'

She nodded eagerly, with wide eyes and a smile to match. 'Thank you, sir. Your father paid for me to learn to a certain level, though I am not as fine with words as I would like.'

'That's settled then. I'll speak to Senator Veron first thing in the morning.'

After the meal and a wash in cold water, I reclined on a cushioned seat in the garden on my own, enjoying once again the scent of the flowers that opened themselves at night, whilst watching the ripples of the moon in the fountain. I wondered whether or not I used to do this ten years ago, and what I might have been thinking about at the time.

My mind inevitably drifted to my work.

It was reassuring to have a satisfying theory for the key in the lock, and that at last there was a new direction to explore. However, seeing Maxant's men perform so ruthlessly in the courtyard made me realize that I could not simply blunder in and accuse him of being a part of something, without first having any hard evidence. All I had at the moment was the most likely occurrence. There were still many more facets of this mystery to work out.

Tomorrow was the Blood Races. Senator Veron had sent a message for me saying that he would meet me in the morning and walk me to the Stadium of Lentus; I realized this would give me the perfect chance to speak to the other senators who were intimate with Lacanta. I would have to think of subtle ways to press them. Certainly, they would fear being quizzed by the Sun Chamber, but I wanted them to think they were not under suspicion so they opened up.

There was a knock at the main door to the house. I rose from the garden and headed inside to the hallway, noting the moonlight through the roof. If the elections were to be held after a full moon, there were only ten or eleven days to go.

Bellona had already opened the door, and she looked at me not quite knowing how to act next.

Titiana stood in the doorway, in a soft gown, waiting with that same unreadable half-smile on her face.

'It's OK, Bellona. I know who this is.'

I beckoned Titiana inside and took her hands in mine. Bellona muttered that she would prepare drinks, but I said it would be OK. 'If our guest needs something, I'll prepare it – I'm not completely useless in the kitchen. Anyway, please – have some rest.'

Bellona shuffled away out of the hallway.

'You came back,' I whispered to Titiana.

'Did you think I wouldn't?' she replied.

'You've every right not to see me again.'

She inclined her head ever so gently. 'My head appears to have been overruled tonight.'

I guided her into the garden, breathless with anticipation, and began hastily to light some of the lanterns.

'Oh, what a lovely place.' Titiana wandered around between the small, lush bushes and looked up at the sky. 'I just about remember coming here all those years ago when your father was out of the city. We sat on that fountain together.'

'You pushed me in it, if I remember correctly,' I replied.

Titiana beamed, as if all the years had fallen away. This was how I remembered her. Dark hair fell across her broad, tanned face, as she crouched down to regard the edge of the fountain pool. She ran her hand through the cold water with a child-like sense of wonder.

'Part of my hatred for you,' she began, 'was merely envy. It doesn't hurt to admit it now, but it didn't seem right that you could retain all this wealth, this property, these luxurious pleasures — and all on your own, while I had fallen so far. I built up a resentment for that.'

'I can understand,' I replied. 'Though it doesn't help you at all, I do feel bad about all of this wealth, and I intend to put the property to good use.' I quickly explained my plans for the cohort. 'But for now, it is just myself, Bellona — who is a splendid cook — and Leana, my . . . I never know how to describe her. My assistant. My bodyguard, I suppose.'

'You have a female bodyguard?' Titiana glanced up at me, a look of surprise on her face.

'You're thinking that it seems rather effeminate of me, I know, or that there might be shared attractions between us.'

Titiana turned her attention once again to the water.

'That's not the case. I like to think of us as siblings.' I explained Leana's background and how she'd helped me over the years, but it seemed impossible to sufficiently explain our bond, let alone telling her just how skilled Leana was in combat. 'In all of my travels across Vispasia, a man has never yet bettered her in a fight. I would rather have someone with those odds on my side, than against me.'

Titiana and I enjoyed another pleasant silence for a moment. Our sharing this space, simply being together, seemed enough to delight each of us.

'Was it really ten years ago?' Titiana asked. 'How far our lives have grown in different directions.'

'I know it sounds a ridiculous thing to say, but it doesn't feel as though we've really been apart.' I took a step closer and sat on the edge of the fountain. 'We get on, more or less, precisely as we used to. And I still feel, more or less, precisely as I used to.'

Titiana placed her hand on my leg as she slowly eased herself nearer to me. Both the unexpected and the desired happened: she placed her hand on my chest and moved in towards me, and all I could do was focus on her broad, sensual lips. Then I closed my eyes . . .

And she pushed me backwards into the fountain.

The cold shock of the water brought me back to my senses. Titiana laughed at me as I struggled to haul myself out, levering with my legs until I was back onto firm ground. I was soaked, my clothes sticking to my skin.

'You deserved that,' Titiana laughed, holding her hand to her mouth as if she had surprised herself. 'After all you've done, allow me that.'

Standing there, dripping with water, I drew her in close to me and she did not flinch at my wet clothing, or even tense up. She was still smiling as my hands grew accustomed to her figure, still smiling as our foreheads came together, remaining there for a moment longer.

Titiana's lips touched mine. With a lantern in one hand, and Titiana's fingers in another, I led her back through the house and into my bedroom. I kicked the door closed, placed the lantern on a table.

There, Titiana pulled up my wet shirt; she traced the lines of muscle on my body and noticed a few wounds of my own that would probably never fully heal.

She turned and raised one knee up onto the bed, in silence.

With her back to me, she unbuttoned her clothing and allowed it to slip slowly from her shoulder, down her back. Even in this light, the scar that had been wrought by the whip was painfully clear. She was waiting to see what I made of it; I closed my eyes for a moment and inhaled deeply, allowing the guilt to catch up with me. Kneeling beside her on the bed and, with my hands slipping around her front to her stomach, I began to kiss down the back of her neck, around her scar, confident that it wouldn't hurt now. Not physically, at least.

Admiring the fine musculature of her dark and sensual back, I moved around to her front and became lost once again in her body. When our flesh touched, there was no difference between us. It had been such a long time since I had felt the warmth of her skin – indeed the skin of any woman – that time lost its perspective. The taste of her body, the smell of her perfume, the soft touches from her hands: everything was worth the wait. What happened next was led by a desire to express ourselves only in our actions.

Words can only achieve so much.

Afterwards we lay in naked splendour beside each other, with the side of my head on her breast and my leg across hers, listening to the night sounds of Tryum together. We talked like we had not done for a long time: not of the arts or philosophy, or of the great affairs and figures of the city, but of trivial, unimportant things, and I felt all the better for it.

'Where does this leave us?' I asked eventually.

'As we always were: me the property of someone else, and you my escape from it all.'

'I'm happy to be your escape, but you shouldn't speak of yourself as property.'

'It is what I am in this city. What else can I be?'

'Didn't you have a dowry? You could always try to claim that back, if your husband does not respect you. I'll even help it through the courts.'

'Oh, I'm sure that's all lovely talk in your court of law,' Titiana said. 'But such freedoms seldom come to us who are not as fortunate as others. In this city, freedom is not easily affordable. Guardianship laws—'

'Went away because of the demands of the Daltan queen,' I interrupted. 'I don't want to speak badly of a marriage, but if I was your husband, you would not be considered my property. Can't you divorce if you're unhappy? I can handle the legal proceedings myself if you wish.'

'Who said I was unhappy?' Titiana sighed. 'Besides, I must think of the security of my children.'

'You must,' I conceded.

'Anyway, if you had been my husband, would you have let your father hand me over for prosecution like a common criminal?'

'I was young, and I was stupid, Titiana. I'm older now, not exactly a wise man, but with a little more experience of what's important in life.'

Somehow that left me with the vague feeling that I had lost

an argument. We lay awake indefinitely, and now and then I'd kiss whatever part of her was closest to me, and at some point I fell asleep.

The Stadium of Lentus

When I woke in the morning, Titiana had gone. She'd left no note, no gesture. There was only the vacant bed. Wondering if everything was all right, I walked into the hallway, where Leana was moving through some morning exercises. The doors were open into the garden, where the sun was glistening off the heavy dew of the plants.

'She left here in the night, if you want to know.' Leana flipped up into a handstand, her bare feet touching the wall to balance herself.

'You met Titiana?' I asked, crouching down to read her expression.

'She seemed pleasant.' Leana showed no signs of strain in her muscles.

'Pleasant?'

'Very beautiful. I did not think that you would find a truly beautiful woman, knowing how you speak when you are with them.'

'Very kind,' I said. 'Did you actually see her when she left?'

'Yes, I saw her just as she went out the door. Not wanting to wake you, like married women might do . . .' Even at this angle I could tell Leana's glance was judging.

'She is married as it happens,' I replied. 'I know it's not exactly a perfect arrangement.'

'And what does your Polla say to that?' Leana pushed herself back onto her feet with a gentle sigh.

More than your spirits would, I wanted to reply, but calmed myself. Leana was right, of course. Ultimately my actions could wreck another's home and Polla most definitely would not approve. Not out of any direct moral judgement – that was not her way – but for the long-term pain it would cause to everyone involved. 'Did you manage to talk with her?'

'Yes. Very pleasant, as I say. Though have you ever asked if it is likely that a woman would be interested in coming all the way across the city on her own merely to fuck?'

'Leana, please.'

'Have you asked yourself what she hopes to gain?'

'We have a complicated past, as you well know,' I sighed. 'Anyway, neither of us has anything to gain from this. We never really did – we just . . . I don't know. I'm not one for soothsayers and I trust the astrologers as much as I trust politicians, but sometimes it feels as if the gods have brought us together for a reason.'

Leana moved into her stretches. 'I need to find the city's gymnasiums.'

'This house isn't big enough for your exercises?'

'I need more. More weights. Competition,' she replied. 'You could at least find a few more fights for me.'

'Be careful what you wish for.'

In the gentle light of dawn, I attended to some brief administrative matters, which involved sending an update to my superiors out of the city. I always preferred to engage in desk work early on in the morning, when my mind was clear and my attention focused, before the day became too hot to concentrate.

My peace was disturbed by a banging on the door. After Bellona opened it, Senator Veron barged his way through, his face creased in delight.

'Drakenfeld!' Veron embraced me like an old friend. I smelled wine on his breath, and marvelled that he had been drinking already – though perhaps he had not stopped drinking all night.

'You're very early.' I guided him into the study. His step was lively and eager to be somewhere that wasn't indoors. 'I wasn't expecting you until a little later.'

'I'm not disturbing you, am I?' Veron laughed. 'Because it's bad luck if I did – I'm here to take you to the Stadium of Lentus.'

'No, I was only writing letters and doing my administration.'

'You Sun Chamber types . . .' Veron slumped on a seat in the corner, prodding the cushioning with admiration. 'Still, it's good to see. Nice to know we're all in reliable hands.'

'Did you have a good night?' I asked.

'I did. I met up with these two ladies new to the city. Both daughters of diplomats – old enough, in fact, to be my daughters. I impressed them with another fine social display and we all ended up in bed together. How was your night?'

I didn't question what his wife might think of the matter, but then again I wasn't exactly one to offer ethical commentary on marriages. Instead I told him what I'd seen last night with Maxant's men and the bloodbath in the courtyard.

'Yes, I heard about it. Messy business, politics,' Veron added, as if it was an everyday thing for the city. 'Any developments with regards to Lacanta's murder?'

'It's difficult to tell. You will, of course, be told as soon as I know anything.'

A smile grew on his face. 'And what about that lady of yours, the rather delicious dancer?'

'I'm enjoying her company when I can.'

'I knew there was blood in you,' Veron crowed. 'I must admit, I was getting worried for a moment. My physician tells me that it can make you ill if you don't bed others often enough. It isn't good for your soul, so the current thinking goes.'

'That's your excuse,' I replied. 'On a more professional note, I've an offer you might be interested in.'

The senator leaned forward and grew very attentive. I explained my thoughts about moving a cohort here and forming a headquarters for a more efficient operation. At the end of my little speech, Veron nodded and sat back in the chair. He declared that we had a deal. We negotiated a rate of a thousand pecullas a month for usage of my premises, which surprised even me, and he said that we could start getting things moving this afternoon — perhaps while we were at the races, which seemed a good idea.

'Though do you really want to share your house with those men?' Veron ran his hand through his hair. 'They can be quite . . . Well, you know what the lower classes are like at times. Vulgar and crude.'

'I've walked the slums of Venyn City for many years, and often chatted in slum taverns with some folk you would consider beneath you. They're just like you and me, you know; they just have less coin.'

'But having them in your own house, Drakenfeld. I mean, really.' Veron chuckled, shaking his head. 'You're a strange figure. Your father didn't like to associate with people like that will-ingly.'

'He missed out on a good thing,' I replied.

'Come on,' Veron bounded to his feet. 'If you like the lower classes so much, I'll take you to somewhere where you can stand with forty thousand of the buggers.'

*

Leana, myself and Senator Veron headed up-city, to the famous Stadium of Lentus. On our way we organized for a message to be delivered to Constable Farrum of the Civil Cohorts, explaining that they could commence moving their materials into specific rooms. I told them that Bellona was in charge of matters while I was out – and that the cohort was to do whatever she requested. I also managed to send another update to my superiors, too.

Veron spoke of the Stadium of Lentus with an affection not often heard for architecture. There were several such stadiums or hippodromes throughout Vispasia and the Stadium of Lentus was famed for its Blood Races.

A tide of people surged through the orange, sunlit streets, towards the structure that loomed over much of the city. Approaching it, people would first see a series of wide arches crowning one enormous side of the structure. The decorative stonework stretched for several hundred feet, before curving at either end. A marvel of modern engineering, there were stone vaults, walls and columns providing support; and from the top of every arch flew the banner of a black falcon upon yellow.

The stadium had been completed only one year before I left the city. It was a legacy of King Lentus, Licintius' and Lacanta's father, but it remained one of the great structures of Vispasia. Many stood slack-jawed as they stepped up to it, dumbfounded that such a building could stay up without collapsing. I counted myself among those in awe.

As we came closer, the sound of the crowd grew so loud that one could be mistaken for thinking a raging summer storm was approaching. Closer still and in the shadow of the building several female prostitutes lingered in the smaller alcoves at the base, sashaying and posing for passers-by. One furtive man in a brown tunic began chatting to a woman, before she took his hand and led him away along the dusty road. Occasionally soldiers might try to steer away such trade, but there was no military in sight just yet, and so the worst the clients would receive was the odd heckle from passers-by. Veron was cheered by their presence somewhat, declaring it a sign of a thriving economy. As far as such indicators went, I was not convinced.

Veron guided us towards a special entrance to the Stadium of Lentus, an archway covered in wonderful yellow and black tiles. Here stood soldiers from the King's Legion, their armour dazzling in the light of the sun, a sharp contrast to the purple cloth beneath. After some brief negotiations from Veron, who the military treated with a great deal of respect, we were ushered through.

'I feel vulnerable without a sword,' Leana said.

'If you'd brought it along, you'd only be kicked out by the soldiers,' I replied. 'Rules are here for a reason.'

'He's right,' Veron declared. 'The crowds get lively at times – but that just makes things entertaining. The second race in the stadium's history resulted in utter carnage between rival supporters. It was no surprise that weapons were soon banned.'

One floor up inside and we discovered dozens of stalls offering drinks, coloured flags, soothsayers offering predictions, and astrologers offering readings of various texts. One woman was selling doves for blood sacrifices to be used with the various idols beside her, in order that one might influence the outcome of the races. Another, Veron pointed out, was selling curses on leather tabs – she would apparently do more business later in the day when people were feeling bitter about their faction having lost.

'A huge amount of business is done on race days,' Veron declared proudly. 'I'm a patron of this level. I bought into a scheme when the stadium opened up and a lot of these traders pay me a monthly fee for pitching here.'

Though there were fewer people here than on the other side, the noise between the floors of the stadium was still intense, as if we were on the inside of a drum.

Leana glanced around cautiously.

'Do you see trouble?' I whispered.

She focused her attention on different parts of the crowd. 'It's hard to tell if anyone is watching us with so many opportunities to hide, though I thought such things were now behind us.'

'And so they should be,' I replied. 'I don't think anyone will start something while we're with here with Veron.'

We proceeded up another stairway and towards a rectangle of light, which led us into the stadium proper.

Leana was not impressed easily, but the look on her face was one I had never seen before.

'You Atrewens,' Veron said, 'have a wonderful smile.'

'I still don't think she's interested, senator,' I replied.

'Well, one must give these things a go . . .'

We stepped out onto one of many tiers that stretched all the way around the stadium. It was an enormous oblong, with a several-hundred-yard straight connecting two perfectly curved ends. Beneath the upper arches, which were defined against the cloudless sky, tens of thousands of people stood on tiered steps. This was a good proportion of Tryum's population – and every single one of them was making a noise. Coloured flags indicated support for the various groups of riders, and drums and horns added to the atmosphere and noise.

'Drakenfeld, were you here when this was finished?' Veron called.

'No, I visited once while it was being built, and I went to the old stadium on several occasions.'

'Yes – that place was torn down for housing in the end,' Veron said. 'Tenement buildings now stand in its place. Mind you, that old thing was quite a death trap.'

'You mean the tenement buildings are not?'

'Admittedly there has been a fire or two over the years. But what about the stadium? How marvellous is this! There's nothing quite like it in all of Vispasia.' Veron tilted up his chin, basking in the atmosphere.

I considered telling him of the hippodrome in Dalta, which was bigger than this, and featured columns made of gold as well as an extendable canvas roof, but it seemed to be splitting hairs.

Veron began discussing the rules of the coming engagement to Leana and I was pleased that she was patient enough with his attempts at charming her. He leaned towards her as he gestured to the race track below. Throughout the day, he explained, teams of riders would negotiate the track in a figure-of-eight route, making sure to avoid the spiked barriers and barbed poles along the way. Different races possessed marginally different rules, but essentially riders carried weapons and had to knock their opponents off their horses with the primary aim of finishing the ten circuits alive. If one came in the top three, a rider became a hero for the day. Whoever finished first, became a legend. Anyone could participate, and citizens, soldiers and madmen signed up throughout the day entertaining their dreams of race-track fame. To win any of the races was a spectacular feat, though they saved the most gruesome spectacles for the best professionals who came on last. Successful riders could become celebrities in Tryum, and rather wealthy to boot. For some, it was a career of sorts.

'Come,' Veron said, 'let us head further up, where things are a fraction more civilized.'

Veron promised me that he would point out senators and arrange the introductions for me, and I checked to see that the list of senators I needed to speak to was firmly in my pocket.

*

Heading towards the senators, we squirmed through the crowds, which continued to flow into the stadium, bringing with them more noise and excitement.

There must have been at least fifty senators standing before us in their fine tunics, their cloaks under one arm, nestled in shade on the one side of the stadium where the sun remained constantly behind them. I pitied those who stood roasting gently in the heat on the opposite side.

Our position was at one of the curved ends of the track, where a bold black line marked the start and finish of the race. Made of compacted sand the track was lined by yellow wooden poles. The other end of it was barely discernible, and even what was close enough to observe was almost vanishing in the shimmering heat.

After glancing at some of the faces around us – some of which I knew, some I could recall seeing from my brief walks around the Regallum area – I reached into my pocket to examine Veron's list, and scanned down the names.

Nucien Malvus was the one I desired to talk to most, and I enquired with Veron whether or not he was here.

'Oh yes, he's here all right,' Veron said. 'May I introduce you to him now? I would take great delight in seeing the expression on his face when you arrest him.'

'If you feel it necessary,' I replied. 'Though I'm not actually going to arrest him – I just want to talk.'

'It is not necessary, but it would merely be one of life's little pleasures to see his smug face confronted by an Officer of the Sun Chamber. I don't even care if he's involved with Lacanta's death.'

Veron led the way. We moved past the other senators and their guests, some of them nodding politely to me, some deciding not to meet my eye, and more than one glancing at Leana with disdain. Veron stopped before a tall, bright-eyed, long-faced and handsome individual who couldn't have been much older than me. He held himself with great posture, relaxed shoulders, straight back; he had clearly spent some time in the gymnasium, too. His tunic was cut from a fine green cloth, inlaid with precious stones, and his boots were highly polished. All in all it was far too much for a day like this, but he didn't seem in any discomfort.

I made sure my brooch of office was on full display as Veron made his announcement.

'Senator Malvus,' he declared, louder than was required, 'I wish to introduce to you Officer Lucan Drakenfeld of the Sun Chamber in Tryum. He wants to have a word with you concerning the murder of Lacanta.'

Malvus' countenance soon cooled. He examined us, the small party who had come to ruin his morning. I gestured for us to step to one side. 'Please, we can do this in the sanctuary below if you'd prefer.'

'As you wish, Drakenfeld,' he growled.

Veron took a gentle bow with his arm out wide, indicating the path for Malvus to walk. The senator strode back the way we had come while Veron merely stood there smiling. 'Enjoy, Drakenfeld.'

Nucien Malvus

In the dark, relative calm beneath the stadium, I stood a better chance of hearing what Nucien Malvus had to say about himself. On the way to the venue Veron told me what he knew of the man. Before our conversation, I already knew that Malvus was the youngest in the Senate, and only because of a quirk of law and good timing, and in no small part because of his fabulous wealth. As a result of this he often went about with the air of untouchability, Veron explained, which in turn inspired the man's attempts to steer various factions of the Senate according to his whims. Though I trusted Veron on some issues, I didn't when it came to rivalries in the Senate. There would be another side to Malvus' story, no doubt.

We walked along the neat rows of stalls, which weren't as busy now that people were filling the stadium proper. Leana stepped vigilantly behind us, ensuring we would not be disturbed.

'I was wondering when you'd come to find me,' Malvus murmured. For a supposedly arrogant man, he had become very humble in his composure.

'What makes you say that?' I asked.

'Come on – Lacanta is dead, so who would be the likely killers? Usually lovers and those closely associated with her – we are the ones dragged up before the courts, paraded about in public to have our innermost secrets aired. It's good sport for many, I'm sure – there's much pleasure to be had in watching successful people suffer.'

'You seem rather experienced in such matters,' I observed.

'I have some legal training,' he replied, 'though nothing of the calibre of the Sun Chamber.' There was a note of admiration in his voice.

'The truth remains that anyone could still be responsible for Lacanta's murder,' I said. 'It's only been a few days and the case grows increasingly complex, so I am ruling out no one.'

'If you care to share, what have you found out so far?' he asked.

'Your name in a book that belonged to Lacanta, for one thing.' I smiled at his curiosity: senators, everywhere, were after information.

Malvus didn't flinch or seem remotely surprised at my statement. 'The two of us were close – this much is probably known by several senators. I gave her the book – something she might appreciate, as she liked to read.' His words came slowly and with great consideration. 'She was ever-eager to expand her knowledge of the arts.'

I recalled there were texts other than a book of plays. 'Tell me upfront, to save us both a lot of hassle: were you and Lacanta lovers?'

'I suppose that depends on what you mean by love.' He laughed, but it was a sad noise devoid of his previous self-assurance. 'If you mean, did we share a bed? Then no, we did not. Lacanta was enticing. She was flirtatious, even, but she was always chaste – something I respected greatly. For better or worse, such qualities are to be valued in people of Tryum. She once kissed me, though — softly, briefly, on the lips, and I valued that even more.'

I frowned. 'I need you to be clear with me about this. You're telling me your relationship together was not of a sexual nature?'

'No.'

'Did you ever try to engage in sex?'

'I would have liked to,' he replied. 'There's no harm in that is there? I wasn't exactly going to push my luck on the matter and actually ask her, what with her brother being king — I value my neck too much. So I waited for Lacanta. I made my intentions obvious. I tried to seduce her with as many lovely words as I could possibly manage, but I would have been waiting a long time.'

'People have told me she was very forthcoming when it came to such matters.'

'People say a lot of things,' he snapped. 'You'd do well not to listen to people.'

'That would make my job difficult,' I replied. 'Were you the only man or woman competing for her attentions?'

'Probably not, but that doesn't mean she bedded everyone, does it?' he grunted. 'And even if she did, would that cast her in a bad light?'

'I'm not here to judge her lifestyle, I can assure you. I'd like to set her soul to rest quickly, so help me out: were you alone in seeking her affections?'

Malvus inclined his head. It was incredible how his demeanour could alter from one of extreme arrogance to something far more humble and considerate within a few sentences. 'No. There were others on the scene. I don't know if they were chosen by her for more intimate purposes, but what does it matter now?'

'It could matter a great deal,' I said. 'Were you there, that night, at Optryx?'

'I was, yes, very briefly towards the end. I couldn't stand to be there for the first few hours, not with Maxant posturing about all over the place.'

'I've heard descriptions of Lacanta seducing people in public. Is that really why you didn't want to be there?'

'Do you think I would enjoy the night if she did? Exactly. But it was one of those nights where it was important to be seen. A man of your status must know what it's like.'

'I do, yes. But whoever killed Lacanta certainly seemed to select a very public day for the occasion – almost as if the murderer intended the death to be witnessed by so many people, wouldn't you say?'

'I don't know because I'm not a murderer, Drakenfeld. Does it matter what they intended? Lacanta is dead. Gone. Contactable only through my prayers and offerings, and even then I'll receive nothing in the way of reply.'

'She may hear your prayers, though.'

'I doubt my faith in Trymus on occasion. The number of hours I've spent on my knees before one of his statues is great, but what good has it done me? I paid for astrologers and the city's finest soothsayers to help me speak with gods or to gain the hand of Lacanta, but it's been of little use.'

'Do you believe in such things?'

'Ordinarily, I would not. The gods are like parents to us, nurturing, to be respected – we bring them into our households to improve our behaviour. But on occasion one's mind needs more to cope with it all. I don't think it's a bad thing to admit that.'

A boy ran in front of us carrying a headless dove by its feet, leaving a trail of blood; he called for his father to make an offering to Trymus before the races began, and his father happily indulged his son's eagerness.

Smiling, I turned back to Malvus. 'You inscribed a book of

Locottus' plays to her. I could never get to grips with his style personally. Did you enjoy the theatre together?'

Malvus seemed less hostile to this question. 'Yes – she loved his plays dearly. She enjoyed the theatre every bit as much as her brother did.'

'Did she associate with actors in her personal time . . . outside of Regallum?'

He cast me a sly glance, uncertain how to continue.

'I've heard of her brother's admiration for the company of actors,' I said, not even knowing for certain whether it was true, but it was worth a go.

'I don't know how you found out, but no, she did not do that herself. I didn't even know Licintius behaved like that until, once, I discovered Lacanta covering up for his disappearance. It is something that would be frowned upon by many in the Senate, though I rather like the idea of a king cavorting with actors down-city. Licintius is a humble and good man, deep down. The theatre was an escape for both of them from the pressures of office. Besides, actors are rightly feared by senators.'

'How so?'

'They can control the emotions of a crowd. That's something to create envy in any politician. Now, please, are there any further questions? I would like to be back before the races commence.'

'Indeed, you're free to return whenever you want,' I said. 'We're just . . . having a conversation.'

'I'm sorry if I've been short with you. This has not been easy for me. I loved her, in my own way, but I'm not able to mourn publicly. I must deal with matters with a stone heart.'

'I understand.'

Nucien Malvus walked back towards the noise and light. At least now I knew Clydia, the young actress, had not been lying about the king. It meant she might also have been telling the truth about Drullus, too.

'Lucan.' Leana stepped alongside me. 'Do not turn around. We have people following us. We should get back up to Senator Veron.'

'OK,' I said and headed towards the outside. 'Who's following?'

'These men seem of more skill than before. Turning, watching, turning again, standing by stalls also. They are moving to keep pace, then stopping suddenly.'

'What do they look like?'

'Heavy. Possibly ex-soldiers. Clean uniform and they can afford good boots. They are much more professional than the previous types. I cannot be sure, but I would not be surprised if they are hiding weapons.'

'Do you think they could be Maxant's men?'

'I do not recognize any of them from the incident in the courtyard,' Leana said.

'Well, we have new friends, in that case,' I declared.

We took our position alongside Veron, who was only briefly interested in how things had gone with Malvus because down below some sort of ceremony was starting.

In long white robes, dozens of priests and priestesses of Trymus formed an avenue, which extended from a small gateway just out of sight from where we were standing, right down by the track.

The tone of the crowd had changed to something significantly more solemn, most people barely uttering a word.

Between the priests and priestesses, a line of figures emerged in a profoundly slow march. King Licintius led the procession; those behind him were carrying on their shoulders a platform, and on that lay the body of Lacanta, wrapped in a crimson sheet, her face painted red, her oiled hair dangling down over the edges.

A priest swung an incense burner beside her body and there were dancers in blood-coloured gowns dancing around her, twirling little arcs of cloth through the air as they spun their arms.

Following this came General Maxant and his soldiers, who took the same measured paces in a column four men wide. The soldiers took a different direction at the end of the avenue of priests and priestesses, and headed towards the centre of the track.

A low-level murmur rippled around the stadium as the people looked on. Lacanta's body was placed on the ground while the dancers frolicked around it, making beautiful shapes with their bodies, and the king stood by watching their rituals. Soldiers packed themselves in, hundreds of troops who had served Maxant and brought glory on the city. But this was not the glory they expected; this was very much about mourning Lacanta's death.

People among the crowd were sobbing, one woman nearby wailing out loud. Even the senators seemed to be stifling tears. Lacanta had clearly meant a lot to these people and I vowed once again, under the gaze of Trymus, that I would help her soul to rest easily.

I sympathized greatly with King Licintius. I knew what it was like to mourn a loved one; it must have been far more difficult to grieve in front of tens of thousands of people. And from what I had so far gathered, he was losing a great confidante as well as a sister. Despite a good proportion of the city mourning here alongside him, he must have felt very lonely indeed.

She'll Ride

After the ceremony, Lacanta's body was removed from the stadium. I remembered the king saying to me that there would be a private ceremony for her, so presumably that would not happen until later. Licintius was sitting nearby, only twenty feet away beyond the senators, in an enclosed booth lined with bright yellow cloth. Attendants stood around him, hesitant and nervous. Beside him, having brought new lands to Vispasia, the glorious General Maxant sat stern-faced, absorbing the attentions with a cool, impassive demeanour.

The noise had returned to the same ferocious timbre of before. Criers, who walked the rim of the dust track with all the swagger of prostitutes, announced the races. While the build-up continued, I contemplated the rest of the senators. Veron told me there would be a small interval between races and the day's events would continue until sunset. Five more senators from his list were present today, and there was plenty of time to question them, so we nestled right in their midst, as I was eager not to be regarded as an outside threat.

The first race began. Fourteen figures on horseback rode out into the stadium to deafening cheers. Coloured banners were waved more wildly than before; they corresponded to the coloured vests the riders wore above their breastplates. The riders did not just wear vests, however — they carried weapons, spears mainly, but a few with swords or maces. Each wore a helmet, but apart from that, there seemed little in the way of protection. This was their moment of glory and, no doubt, a moment of dread too. They each seemed to handle it in different ways, some waving, some beating the metal of their armour with the flat of their swords, others quietly absorbing the scene.

'Why are there no archers among them?' Leana asked me.

'Look carefully and you'll see there are no stirrups,' I said. 'At these speeds, archers tend to fall off quickly and end up trampled into the dust. You'll notice there's little armour, too, because it weighs too much. These fellows need to get around as quickly as possible.'

Leana said too loudly, 'Seems easy. You said these races were the toughest sport going.'

'Your servant,' a senator called deridingly, 'speaks bravely — from this distance.' A ripple of laughter spread around us.

'She's not my servant,' I replied, then turned back to her. 'The event can be rather nasty once it gets going.'

'Spirits save me, we did far more than this in Atrewen games as girls and boys,' she said with exasperation. 'We had to jump obstacles as well.' Again she spoke forcefully.

I chuckled awkwardly, not wanting to create a scene. The looks we received from the others were unfavourable at best. Insults were muttered about the 'dark foreigner' and my temper began to flare.

Veron calmed me down, and we discussed the rules of engagement: how the riders could do whatever they wanted, throw what they wanted, hit with anything; but they had to be quick, and weigh up the amount of attacks they made against their overall speed. The only rules were not to cause harm intentionally to the horses: those riders who did found themselves disqualified and paraded at the end for the crowd to jeer and hurl whatever they could at them.

The riders didn't so much line up as group together and then they started the race, thundering around the figure-of-eight in a cloud of dust. One rider received a spear to the ribs and, whether or not it drew blood, he fell off his horse and he was out of the race. The dust cloud arced along the other side of the stadium, well beyond the thick wooden poles and back around. Ahead of it came the charge of the horsemen, riding close together, throwing their weapons this way and that, with the more nimble and skilful riders out in front, away from the fray.

There were two riders, one in a red vest, the other in a blue, edging ahead of the pack, but as if to impress the king himself, right in front of us a rider in yellow threw a dagger at the red leader, striking his thigh; they both tumbled to the ground on the corner, both falling under the feet of the horses, to cheers and jeers from the various factions in the crowd.

The noise seemed to precede the riders around the stadium like a tidal roar. Dust drifted into the bold blue sky. The two fallen riders lay completely still in the bloodied dirt while a team of helpers came to clean up the mess.

Leana muttered, perhaps louder than she realized, 'Spirits save me, they're terrible riders. Bad fighters also.'

'You should keep your voice low,' I hissed. 'This is a noble sport in Tryum.'

'Drakenfeld,' someone said, 'this outsider seems to think she could do better.'

'I could!' Leana shouted back.

'Don't react to their taunts,' I said. 'Don't show that their words have any effect. They're baiting us.'

'Nonsense,' Veron interrupted with a grin. 'Leana, if you honestly think you can do better, you're more than welcome to try.'

'Tell me which way I must go, and the next time you see me will be there, in the field,' she declared, glaring at the senators behind. 'I have done more dangerous things in Atrewe as a child.'

A lot of the others were laughing at us, and let their disgust of Leana be known to all.

'It'll be a disgrace, but I'm happy to watch that happen to an outsider.'

'The woman will not even finish, let alone come in the top three.'

'I bet she buggers him at night.'

'They probably don't have horses where she comes from.'

I tried to maintain a cool and professional manner, half wishing Leana could smack one or two of them around the head.

Leana touched my arm, and leaned in closely. 'I would like to do this. If you will permit it.'

'You honestly don't need my permission.'

'But I want you to understand.'

'Understand what?'

'These people walk in small circles. Unlike those down-city, they have maybe never met anyone from Atrewe. I want them to know that Atrewens are every bit as good as the best Tryum can produce.'

'What happens if you end up injured or killed?'

'Spirits save me.' Her eyes revealed a desperation I had never before seen.

'Very well.' Turning to the smug senators, I called over, 'All right then. She'll ride.'

At least the view was good down by the side of the dirt track. The crowd was behind us, an intimidating sight, and there were a few people taking bets nearby, chalking up numbers on pieces of slate while young boys collected and distributed coins. I'd also found a decent pastry seller, too, so I munched glumly on one of his pies as I waited for Leana to emerge from what Veron lovingly described as 'the pits', where the riders equipped themselves with armour and weapons. Veron bought himself a cup of wine and rejoined me.

'I wouldn't worry,' he said, slapping me on the shoulder. 'She's got spirit.'

'She'll become a spirit if she's not careful.' I became acutely aware, yet again, of how much I depended upon Leana's skills, and how much I would miss her if anything happened out there.

'You think she'll meet her death?' Veron asked nonchalantly, as if he was talking about the weather.

'I've no idea,' I replied. 'Upstairs I made an offering to Polla and, shortly after, made a five pecullas bet. That should cover all eventualities.'

'Worry not, I'll help find you a new assistant should the worst happen.'

I opened my mouth to reply, but Veron continued, 'I'm joking, Drakenfeld. I know you're some strange unit together. What I still don't understand is, how come she's not attached to anyone.'

'She was. Once.'

'Once?'

'Remember the massacre I told you about, in Atrewe, when I met her?'

'Ah.' Veron nodded. 'Her fellow died in that?'

'Decapitated. She doesn't talk about it much, as you can imagine.'

Veron shook his head. 'Surely she could move on though, and take other lovers?'

'Even in death, Atrewens who were married are still bound. It makes things rather complicated, so I understand. Well, even more complicated than marriages between the living, that is. I'm sure she's met other men on the road with me, who she's been interested in. If I'm honest, I have encouraged her to go and have some fun with them, too, but as far as I'm aware she kept to her vows. Though I think it's a shame, given how short life can be, I respect her decision.'

'Love, eh? Almost as messy a business as politics.' Veron chuckled and we took our place by the barriers, talking to some of the race stewards nearby. Apparently two riders had died during the first race, three during the second and one more during the third, and in addition to this there had been ten further life-threatening injuries. The best I could hope for was that Leana would not join the corpses. I knew, however, that she would be seeking nothing short of a victory, and would push herself to make a point.

I suspected Veron had taken some strange delight in the whole process. It was like he was a god who arranged worldly events purely to see what happened. 'Are her people, the Atrewens, good with horses?'

I scoffed the last of my pastry before replying. 'I can't speak for her people. I don't think horses are part of their heritage in the same way as the nomads in Koton, but Leana's always been a good rider. She's never worn a saddle to my knowledge, but riding across a plain is a good deal different to riding at speed on that dust track.'

'That is a safe assumption,' he said.

'You've grown fond of Leana.'

For a moment Veron let his mask slip and I got to see the man behind. 'Every time she opens her mouth I dream of far-away lands . . . I never went on military campaigns like Maxant. Never really ventured too far across Vispasia, such is my rather dull life.

And there was a girl, when I was younger, who I once met in a tavern on the border of Maristan, and who I managed to remain attached to for a month at the most . . . She was probably the only woman I felt a genuine, deep affection for, and Leana reminds me of her greatly.' Veron trailed off and regarded the track. 'The things we can and cannot do in our station of life, right, Drakenfeld?'

It's a lot worse at the stations lower than ours, I wanted to say, but decided not to. 'It's never too late to walk down old roads.'

'It depends if one knows where those roads are to be found. I have no such maps. One gets such reflections when you get to my age, Drakenfeld. Leana reminds me of simpler, more honest times in my life – nothing more, nothing less.' Veron tipped the rest of his wine down his throat and threw the cup to one side. 'I'll tell you more about it some day.'

'At least you're kind towards her. Those other senators—'

'Oh, ignore those bastards. They'll never change. They think anything that doesn't come from within Detrata's borders is either to be feared or turned into a slave.'

A horn blew and there was an announcement by one of the criers; the crowd noise flared up once again.

'She's on.' Veron steered me further along the way to a better spot to view the race. I glanced around behind me, interested to see if any of the men from earlier were still following.

'You look as if someone's trying to kill you,' Veron said.

'No, simply taking it all in, senator. There she is!' I called out. I recognized Leana's nimble frame atop her horse. Again she had refused a saddle, wore a light breastplate with a black vest pulled over the top, as well as a steel helmet, and a sword clutched in one hand. Another two dozen riders in various colours crowded around her and she was soon lost in their energetic mass. Above them, the sun roasted the spectators in the midday heat.

'How long are they going to take until it begins?'

'Relax,' Veron said.

Another announcement, another cheer, and the horses thundered off into the distance, leaving only a cloud of dust.

'There they go!' Veron shouted.

My heart beat so fast it hurt to breathe. I waited to see what happened, but the raised dust obscured the view. Moments later, the yellow cloud arced in the distance and I saw the riders heading back towards us. Eventually, even the determination on the riders' faces could be perceived.

To my utter amazement, Leana was in the first three.

She seemed to hang back on the corner then lurch across behind the path of the leaders, undercutting them slightly; one of the others jabbed a spear towards her and she managed to lower herself forwards and yank back the spear, in a display that surprised even me. Her attacker collapsed from his horse and went skidding across the dirt before he slammed into the barriers.

The crowd hollered; the race moved on.

'Impressive stuff.' Veron seemed even more excited than me.

Again we waited, my hand tapping repeatedly on the barrier. The crowd gave off a deeper boom while the riders were out of sight and I simply hoped that Leana had not fallen.

Moments later, there she was, this time in the middle of the pack. The front rider and his horse collapsed, taking two other riders out with them: one rider slammed into a barbed post, ripping open his chest, while the rest of the pack veered around the carnage and raced off into the distance again.

'I'd wager that hurt,' Veron called, cringing. 'The best he could have hoped for was a quick death.'

The process repeated itself several times, each occasion bringing me to the edge of my senses. I was a man who appreciated logic and control where possible: my mood did not improve when matters were in the hands of the gods like this. Each time Leana passed us, the field around her had been thinned considerably, but all that mattered was that she was there.

'Oh, do cheer up, Drakenfeld. Stop looking so glum. It'll all be over before long.'

Finally, on the last lap of the race, none of the riders seemed to pay much attention to fighting each other: they were simply engaged in a sprint to the finish. Leana was towards the front of the field, but not first, and she remained fully in sight all the way to the finish, where her head was down as she crossed the line.

I cannot describe my relief or elation as it all came to an end: the crowd's energy peaked and fell, back to the background murmur. The horses slowed, the excitement died away.

Leana rode towards a man in red clothing, who shook her forearm in solidarity – I assumed he had won the race, but I wasn't yet sure. The results were recorded in a ledger and the criers commenced the announcement. The man in red came in first, Leana following only a few paces behind, before two other riders and, eventually, what was left of the rest of the pack.

'Tryum's thunder,' Veron declared, 'Cettrus the Red won the race. You remember the fellow from the party, Drakenfeld? He was only fairly new to the sport at the time, but now this will improve my credentials even further. I will be seen as an excellent judge of character. Soothsayers will soon be coming to me for advice . . .' Veron was losing himself in the creation of his own mythology.

Waving for Leana's attention, I watched her face crease in delight as the nation of Atrewe was called out by the nearest crier. She rode over to us, carefully jumped down and tied her horse. Her leg was bloodied with a surface wound across her thigh, and I helped her back through the gap in the barrier.

I embraced her hot, dust- and sweat-covered body, as she mumbled into my shoulder, 'Now at least they have heard of my country.'

'They certainly have.'

'A shame I did not win,' she replied, acutely aware that we were showing more affection now than we had ever done before.

'And a shame you bet on her winning, Drakenfeld,' Veron interrupted, and congratulated Leana on finishing an honourable second.

'Actually, I placed money on her finishing in the top three. I'm not reckless.'

'Logic prevails,' Veron smirked. 'Now, let's see if we can find Leana a decent physician. There is meant to be a fine fellow from Koton around here somewhere. They know a thing or two about medicine. He'll patch up that leg soon enough.'

Evening Games

It was enjoyable heading back into the tiers of the stadium to see the expressions on the senators' faces. Leana hobbled up the steps, injured but with her pride intact. Only one of the senators swallowed his own pride and mumbled his congratulations to her, the others remained cool and distant. Some looked as if the event had well and truly ruined their day. Two of them spat on the floor in front of us.

Even General Maxant inclined his head in our direction, acknowledging Leana's performance. The king, it seemed, maintained the same, remote gaze all afternoon.

We enjoyed the rest of the afternoon's races at a leisurely pace. I did not want to risk being followed or attacked again – particularly if Leana was partially injured, so I conducted the rest of my questioning at some speed, this time deciding to do it within the tiers of the stadium rather than by the stalls.

At the age of fifty-nine, Senator Gallus was the oldest of the suitors who attempted to charm Lacanta, but he suggested he hadn't ever been in with much of a chance. There were no games, he stressed – she was polite and affable, and did not successfully get him to vote with any particular motion, despite trying to. 'She kept on trying to stop the military from their campaigns. She didn't like war. I can't agree with such ridiculous sentiments. War is in our blood, after all.'

Senator Litren's initial bitter mutterings subsided into something sensual eventually, and he spoke of their moonlit walks, tinged with anticipation, as one of his most cherished memories of her. Senator Lobbe, a surprisingly squat man in his forties, and who walked with a noticeable limp, confessed to spending a fortune on gifts for her. But he later found out that Lacanta had given away several of them to her maids or their families. She calmed his rage when he found out, however. 'She could always do that,' he breathed, staring into the deep distance. Only Lobbe suggested that Lacanta might, on occasion, query how he intended to vote on a particular piece of legislation. A few times she hoped he would vote in favour of her brother's laws, or to smooth over some of the warmongering sentiments in the Senate, but his most affectionate times with her did not, he felt, coincide with political requests. That fact had spurred him on somewhat.

The most important part, for me, was that not one of them boasted of or admitted to sleeping with Lacanta. There was the chance they were lying, trying to conceal any connections with her, but I did not believe so, because they each confessed to desiring intimacy with her. They admitted to being rivals for her attention – and yet she had sexual relationships with none.

Yet again I felt I was on the verge of something significant. Why would Lacanta deliberately create the impression that she was sleeping around, despite being a very private and chaste woman? Perhaps there was a benefit in doing so – but why, to mislead others? I could not even make a single connection with General Maxant, either. His potential role in the murder did not seem to fit.

My eyes settled on the one man I had not yet interviewed more thoroughly: King Licintius. If he indeed played a role in his sister's murder behind the scenes, he had far too much to lose. As well as a beloved sister she was a great political ally, furthering his efforts in the Senate in a way that he could not. But if he had something to hide, why would the king insist I did what I could to find her and permit me access to the most secure building in Detrata? Nothing made sense on that front either.

The mighty general would be the next person to explore further. The fact that he had entered that room first, most likely as some part of an elaborate plan, was the road to understanding just how Lacanta had been murdered, and having seen what they were capable of, I just had to be careful that General Maxant's men did not get to me first.

We headed home before sunset. I thanked Veron for his guidance today. He remained with the other senators, somehow managing to bask in the victory of Cettrus the Red.

As we walked through the ancient streets, I demanded that Leana put her pride to one side and place her arm around me for support.

'Just so you know, if anyone attempts a fight,' Leana said, 'I am relying on you to do the work.'

'You know, I'm actually not a bad fighter. You just never let me get any blows in.'

'I will believe that when I see it.'

The journey home was uneventful. Whoever had been following us at the Stadium of Lentus was no longer here – or, if they were, they were more talented in their methods of surveillance, and they were lost in the thinning crowds. Only gentle streams of people accompanied us home, drunk on the pleasures of the races, calling out the chants from the day and wrapping themselves or each other in the various coloured banners.

The evening was as pleasant as I could have hoped for. The house was busy with three men from the Civil Cohorts, who were settling in to their new, hastily set up offices, and Bellona seemed to have developed a new-found confidence, ordering them about the place, telling them where they could and could not put their little crates of ledgers. Only three of the men were ever permitted inside at once, and late at night there would only be one man, who would remain a point of contact. Veron had also suggested constructing some kind of makeshift gaol nearby, and looked at the city plans to find a suitable location. Though I was happy to share my house with the cohort, the idea of the place turning into a prison did not particularly appeal.

Much to my delight Titiana arrived a little later, wondering how the day had gone.

Bellona cooked a meal for all of us, Constable Farrum and his men included, and we took several couches outside and dined humbly but happily in the garden. I don't think I'd been as happy in a long time, all of us there under that balmy Detratan evening, faces occasionally walking past the pools of light offered by the lanterns, talking, laughing. Titiana had lost her inhibitions about being seen with me in public, though we were not overly affectionate together. It was progress at least.

At first everyone had seemed on edge, possibly feeling some unease among these luxurious surroundings, but Leana spoke of her time in the stadium, immediately endearing herself to the gathered cohort. People began to relax and eventually a few of them told jokes and drank heavily from the jugs of watered-down wine. Bellona seemed delighted at the many compliments to her food and I heard her laugh for the first time – a warm, hearty laugh.

As for me? I did not want to interfere too much. I knew that if I spoke it might make people feel awkward or on ceremony, and I was more than happy to know that they were enjoying themselves. Their good humour would go some way to blowing away the dark clouds this house had seen with my father's debts and his suspicious demise.

So I lounged in the background with Titiana, inhaling her jasmine perfume, waiting to be alone with her.

She managed to persuade me to head out with her into the evening, to a 'tavern of her choice'.

My reaction must have been reasonably dismissive, because she started calling me 'po-faced' and 'pretentious'. I didn't mind being pretentious – there was nothing wrong with appreciating good things – but I took exception to being called po-faced.

Her teasing grew more and more immature and so I stood up – perhaps with more drama than intended – and said that Lucan Drakenfeld could drink and talk with anyone, in any place. I suspect I was too busy trying to impress her to understand what I was letting myself in for.

Secretly, I was delighted to be going out into the city with her.

The more I grew to know Titiana, the less predictable she became; but as soon as I'd realized that fact, I felt at ease with it. It was nice not to be myself for a while, to escape into being someone else. For one night it felt alluringly unsettling to let go, to be willingly guided by her hand into Tryum's darker places.

The whole experience seemed like some mythological story. I

had seen some strange sights in the underbelly of Venyn City, but Tryum could offer as much, if not more, in the way of debauched proceedings.

Colour exploded across the city. Uncertain of our location, we passed along tall, narrow lanes and compact plazas lit up by braziers and lanterns, so that shadows lurched and waned repeatedly. Cheap street performers wearing masks jumped out from alcoves and archways, chanting at me in foreign dialects. Illicit figures were pushing vials upon those who walked by, practically tearing coins from their grip so that it seemed more like a robbery than a transaction. A curse-dealer came by with leather patches on which to transcribe one's hatred of another, and there were street drummers and dancers and a dark festival atmosphere. People had painted their faces for the various gods and wore strange outfits made entirely from leaves.

Prostitutes were offering their trade from the side of the street, calling out – almost heckling – the crowds of night-goers. They were not coy about their business, either – both men and women exposing themselves to anyone who might look their way. Their hands crawled up bare legs like insects. But one might see the inherent loneliness of such a business – the vacant expression, the hollow laughter. Tonight their work possessed a raw, animalistic nature; in fact, one couple was engaged in a feral transaction up against the walls of a tavern, either unaware or delighted that they were providing a spectacle.

Titiana laughed at all the goings-on, finding wonder in the sheer variety of offerings. We continued through this dream-like neighbourhood, one that seemed utterly detached from the Tryum of daytime, and eventually down some steps, into a small underground tavern.

If all the chaos we had seen outside had been condensed into the large room, that would have been — almost — a sufficient description of the place. Surprisingly, those from the senatorial class mixing with the less fortunate didn't seem to be the Tryum way. Among the soft light of a hundred lanterns, there were battered cushioned couches, amphorae full of wine, cheap food and generally people not wearing much in the way of clothing. Drinks were thrust into my hand, and I refused them; flesh flashed before my eyes. Both women and men made passes at me, but not the kind that one could take as a compliment. Smoke whirled around my head, a heady, herbal concoction. Despite remaining sober, the rest of the evening became a fast blur of images: expressions of numb ecstasy, Titiana kissing me in a darkened corner of a dingy tavern.

At what point the ghost came to me, it is difficult to say. Titiana had gone to find more drink and I was sitting on a stool in one of the rare quiet spaces, away from the music and other people, as I tried to clear my head from the fug of smoke and stench of spilt wine. If there was another partygoer in the room, they had probably passed out, or were sprawling on a couch, intoxicated on some herbal concoction.

Into this relative calm stepped the eyeless man I had seen in the tombs outside Tryum.

His hair was unkempt, his skin pale, his clothing in tatters, yet he moved with the confidence of someone who was doing very well for himself. I rose to meet him, losing my gaze in the vacant spaces within his head.

'You are Drakenfeld?' he rasped, barely audible in these surroundings.

'What do you want?'

'My wife,' he replied.

'I'm sorry?'

'I'm looking for my wife. Have you seen her?'

'I don't know who she is, nor do I know who you are.'

It is difficult to gauge the expressions of another when one cannot see their eyes, but nevertheless he seemed disappointed. There was something about his manner, his slumped shoulders, his slightly bowed head.

'Where are you from?' I asked.

'The tombs,' came his reply. 'The mausoleums. I . . . came back from them.'

'You rose from the dead?' I asked, incredulous that the words even came from my mouth.

'I was brought back. A woman greeted me, a rich woman.' He proceeded to describe Senator Divran, and then his own life as it came back to him. He was the first to admit that he wasn't entirely certain himself. Though he had no name, he claimed to have once been an important man in the city, a politician or senior administrator; he could not remember the name of the king he served under, nor could he recall his address. All he really remembered were patchy snippets of his life, echoes of his past, but with some clarity he recalled his wife. He asked me once again for my help. He said he had heard my name mentioned about the city as someone who could help the dead.

Who was this figure? Was he a ghost? Had Senator Divran returned him from the dead? I could not say precisely, but if the latter was the case, it wasn't going to be easy to let him know that his wife had most likely died long ago.

My only suggestion was for him to go back to the mausoleums and scrutinize their facades in the hope that one of them would remind him of his wife – presuming she had been buried alongside him. He left me suddenly when he realized that I could be of little help, and disappeared into the crowd as quickly as he had come.

Had I imagined the whole thing? Had the heady smoke of the room gone to my head? It left open the question: if this ghost's, or dead man's, story was real, could Lacanta's murder have truly been a supernatural act after all? Should Senator Divran be questioned once again?

This was senseless thinking. The ghost surely had nothing to do with the murder, which, as I said to Divran, had the marks of a living human all over it. Unless hard evidence steered me in another direction, I would continue my business with the living.

Much later, deep into the night, after I had driven the ghost from my mind as far as possible, I hauled myself out of the establishment and gasped the blissful, cooler night air. Titiana kissed my face and asked if I was enjoying myself, saying that this was how she liked to spend any free time she had. I couldn't determine how truthful it was, and how much free time from her family she had.

She was drunk, she was falling over me and, occasionally, when she focused on me properly, she started to cry. Her behaviour was confusing: this was, more or less, what we'd done in our youth, but it didn't seem the same any more, it didn't seem as exciting as it used to, and Titiana wasn't upset back then. She said that this was her life now, but she didn't seem sincere about it; she said it as if it was a call for help rather than a statement of happiness.

Titiana had not sobered up by the time we returned home. She stumbled through the door and into my bedroom, where she collapsed on the bed and attempted to pull off her dress, all the while asking me to take her. She was not in control of her thoughts. With me almost sober, and Titiana in this state – nothing positive could ever come from such a union. So instead I pulled the blanket across her and kissed her brow before lying down exhausted alongside her.

As the ceiling slowly came into focus, I wondered, sadly, if the dead man would find rest tonight, or if I was right to be so sceptical of the supernatural as I had been through my life.

Suicide?

News of General Maxant's suicide reached us not long after dawn.

A messenger had contacted several senators just before midday, including Senator Veron, who was present at my house, and delivered the tragic news. It had been an odd morning: Titiana had left again during the night, leaving only her impression in the pillow, and her scent within the ruffled bedsheets.

My morning had been spent organizing the new offices of the cohort, with Veron arriving purely to order Constable Farrum about like a slave; he grew so increasingly disdainful towards the man that I took the senator to one side and spoke of the importance of these men feeling valued if they were to do a decent job. The news concerning Maxant was very clear and very simple: the general had killed himself on the beach in front of his villa — a knife to his chest, his hands around the blade — and had been discovered by his servants first thing that morning. I stressed the urgency of getting to the scene of the incident before others could disturb it too much, and Veron immediately sent for horses so that we could ride out to the coast.

I hastily scrawled a note to my superiors concerning Maxant's death, thinking it powerful enough information to request assistance; I stuffed it in a messenger tube before issuing it to one of the men from the Civil Cohorts, demanding he dispatch it immediately.

Within the hour, Leana, Veron, myself and Constable Farrum were riding out of the city at a ferocious speed.

Along the coast the wind was strong, and the skies were as usual clear and mesmerizing. Little licks of white surf littered the sea and birds sliced through the sky in all directions. There was a pungent, vegetative tang, which cleared my head. It was an invigorating change from the odours of the city.

The journey had not taken long and just after midday we came on the final stretch of road, which led to Maxant's villa. Though much of the land on the approach had been put aside for agricultural use, a few olive and fig trees were dotted about the local landscape. Either side of the road, enormous, narrow poplars reached up like the fingers of a god.

Eventually we reached Maxant's villa, a splendid, sprawling red-roofed, limestone house with several similar, smaller structures nearby. The estate was large enough that I guessed some of these may have been for religious purposes or were even purely ornamental. A soft haze had rolled in from the sea, and so his formal gardens to our right had taken on the appearance of some mythological scene. The rest of the property seemed to be in the middle of being refurbished, which was not unusual considering he had spent many of his recent years abroad on military campaigns.

One of the servants stumbled out to greet us – a pale-skinned, old, bald man wearing a grubby white tunic. With tears in his eyes he told us, much to my relief, that we were the first people from Tryum to have arrived at the scene. The servant fell to one knee after Veron announced who he was, but the senator picked the old man up by the shoulder with a tenderness that surprised me. When he began to tell us what had gone on, the servant babbled incoherently. I asked him to speak more clearly and he said, 'Thank Trymus you've come so soon. We . . . we were going mad. We don't know what to do.'

'You need not worry now,' Veron said calmly, glancing towards me. 'Please, show us the way.'

Three other servants gathered in the villa, their concerned expressions obvious: probably worried what their future would now hold for them given their master was dead. They ushered us outside, through the house itself, which was also in some state of renovation, out through the ornamental gardens and down to the beach. The servant gestured for us to stop, and he indicated the footprints in the sand. 'These are the master's steps. They lead down to his body.' My gaze followed the footprints to the high-tide mark, the sea having receded into the distance, where wading birds strode through the shallow pools.

'Where are your footprints?' I asked.

'Mine?' he asked, his eyes wide in fear. 'No, I came from another way — they are over there. That is the route I took.'

'Why did you go that way and not straight down to the shore from the house?'

'Each morning before dawn I walk the beach. When the sun rises there is little chance to stop working. I came from that direction. We do not like to disturb the firmer sand around where master likes to look. It isn't proper and it annoys him greatly.' He pointed along the shoreline. 'Those are the steps I made on the way back.'

'And it was you who sent the messenger.'

'I sent the boy with a note and some coin to go to the nearest town for help, very early on. He was lucky to find someone to send a message so soon.'

'You said it was suicide.'

'Yes,' the servant said. 'I hope I did not do wrong.'

I shook my head. 'Can I confirm you found the body before sunrise?'

'I did not hear the master return last night, but he is a man of exquisite skill and such a quiet return would not be surprising. Sometimes . . . sometimes we were going about our work and he would suddenly be there, talking to us, ordering us about. Like a spirit he could move through rooms.'

'You've not known him long have you?'

'Many years, though I have not seen him for much of this time. I help manage the estates while master is away.'

I examined the one set of footsteps, Maxant's own as he moved down the beach from the garden. I asked the others politely if they could refrain from disturbing the tracks for the time being, and so we took a long looping route to the body.

When we arrived it was clear to see that only one other set of footprints led here, along the shore – tracks that belonged to the servant. There was hardly anything to suggest signs of a disturbance. The sand here was well compacted, meaning that the wind would not create ripples – any disruption to the surface would have been by a human or animal. But there was simply nothing else.

I enquired if anyone had moved Maxant's body at all. The servant said he had pulled the corpse over onto its back to see if he was truly dead, but other than that no one had touched it.

The hilt of a blade stuck out of Maxant's chest directly over his heart, and his clothing was soaked with blood. The general had been wearing the same formal garb he had on yesterday, at the Stadium of Lentus, including his crimson military cloak. Though he had been quite a presence in life, his dead body was just like all the others, and it was a cold, grim reminder of one's own mortality.

This was such a waste of a life. The servant began weeping once again and I asked him to leave us in peace for the time being.

Rigor mortis had set in some hours ago, and Maxant's skin was currently in the process of changing colour; but none of these signs told me anything more than I knew already. We had all seen him late yesterday afternoon and now we could all see him here. If indeed this was a suicide – and all the signs did appear to indicate this – then he would have returned late from the Blood Races and in the hours of darkness seen that his own life was ended.

What reason could a victorious general – one who had been experiencing glories that hadn't been seen since the days of Empire – possibly possess for killing himself?

'Well, Drakenfeld,' Veron called over above the wind, 'what do you make of this suicide business? Maybe the general suffered from some military trauma and could no longer stand to be around. It happens to veterans, now and then, so I hear. Being around death so much can do that.'

As I crouched down over Maxant's corpse, Constable Farrum leaned in. 'I would see it as an honour, sir, if you could teach me something about the signs you're looking for on this body?'

'Oh, come on,' Veron scoffed. 'Now's not the time, surely? Let the man do his work, Farrum. We can play such games later. Besides, what's to see, other than that sword?'

'Actually,' I said, 'there is much to learn here at the scene. And I think I am starting to piece together exactly what might have happened.'

'How do you mean?' Veron asked.

'I do not believe this to be a suicide,' I announced above the sound of the surf.

Veron gave an expression of surprise. 'I'll be impressed if you can explain how it is not.'

'Constable, have a sniff of this.' I beckoned Farrum forwards, to his knees alongside the corpse, so that he could smell a dubious stain on Maxant's cloak. The constable leaned forward eagerly.

Then he wrenched his head back, creasing his face in disgust. 'Gods' breath. What on earth is that?'

'It is vomit,' I suggested. 'And you can see there is another stain on the front of his tunic, but it has been slightly obscured by the blood.'

'Some last-minute fear?' Veron wondered.

'For a man of his reputation?' I replied. 'No. I'd suggest that Maxant's body was attempting to rid itself of poison.'

'Poisoned?' Veron said. 'And then stabbed . . .'

'Indeed.' I opened up Maxant's mouth and sniffed the rancid contents. There were traces of vomit there, too. 'What a perfect location to stage a suicide attempt,' I continued. 'We have the ideal set-up: one set of footprints with no one else around, and a clear method of death. If we hadn't arrived here, Maxant's death would have almost certainly been registered as a suicide. But you see, the general once told me in person and with some conviction that suicide was a "cowardly way out" and that the gods didn't look kindly on those who took their own lives. I came here with doubts, certainly, but these were confirmed when I realized there was too little blood on the sand for such a wound. Something like this would have created far more of a mess.'

Constable Farrum frowned. 'How could it've been done? Maxant's a heavy man. No one could've just killed him, dragged his body here. I mean to say, there should be signs of some kind of effort, something of a struggle?'

'What's to say they used the beach? The murderer could have sailed here with the body. We're standing just a fraction on the other side of the high-tide mark.' I indicated the vegetative detritus. 'Yes, a small boat could easily have pulled up here some hours ago at high tide with Maxant's pre-prepared body, dumped it overboard and . . . Now here's the interesting thing. The killer could have walked towards the garden, creating the illusion that Maxant came out here himself, knowing there was no one else around and that the beach was private property. That strikes me as a very important point. It's all very well planned, but whoever had done this hadn't taken into account Maxant's vomit.'

'Vomit,' Veron chuckled grimly.

'A common problem with failed poisonings,' I observed. 'And, let's face it, poisoning was really the only way someone was going to get the better of a physically superior warrior.'

Leana said, 'The person who is doing this — perhaps they were not alone.'

'Unless they worked alone and let the tide take the boat out to sea. I'd say, though, that whoever did this must have had some level of access to the general to be able to poison him, one of his own men or a rival in the Senate, someone who may have despised his war efforts even.'

Veron scratched his head and took slow steps around the body, his cloak flapping in the breeze. 'There were several men I know who loathed the attention and favour he was getting from the public, not to mention from Licintius. Generally he was loved though. Some of the republicans secretly wanted him to lead further campaigns. No, surely not a senator. Do you think the servants could have been involved? Whenever I've known there to be poisonings, it's usually involved sneaking something into their food by the cook.'

'Not improbable,' I replied. 'Though he may not have eaten

here. Constable, do you think you could question these servants of his? I'd like to know every single movement in this house over the past day.'

'Absolutely, sir.' Farrum trudged up the beach, almost following Maxant's steps until he realized where he was treading, and then he quickly skittered further away, taking the long route to the house.

'The man's an idiot,' Veron grunted.

'He has potential if you'd let him,' I snapped, then saw the expression on Veron's face. 'I'm sorry, senator. Please accept my apologies. I'm just angry that yet another body has been found – and what a waste of life all of this is proving. Good people, with such a future ahead of them, are no longer with us.' Not to mention that yet another one of my leads had been killed.

'Think nothing of it,' Veron said sincerely.

'As for Farrum,' I added, 'he simply needs to be given an opportunity to make something of himself.'

'I've seen enough to know I should trust your powers of observation. So what are we to do about this poor fellow?' Veron gestured to the body of the fallen general. 'Perhaps it was his election rival – Maxant's speech did cause quite a ruckus. A gang member doing the dirty work?'

'Those gangs do not strike me as being as cautious as whoever did this,' I replied. 'As I said, this is all very well planned. Much, in fact, like Lacanta's murder also seemed to be very well planned.'

'You think the two incidents are linked,' Veron said.

'I'm not ruling it out,' I replied, though did not reveal my hunches about General Maxant. If he was involved in Lacanta's murder – or at the very least knew something – my job was about to get even more difficult.

Henbane

For some time I examined Maxant's body, before walking further along the shore, scouring the immediate surroundings for any signs of disturbance, or for anything that may have been dropped. Nothing would change my original theory, which seemed to be the least illogical method, of murder. Nothing indicated that this was a suicide.

We made some hasty arrangements to have his body moved back to the house by the servants. According to his staff, this was not Maxant's main residence. After the war, he had hoped to get the place into shape so he could move in with a larger household of servants. He had no wife – she had died many years ago while he was abroad – and their children had grown up and long moved from the city. Why he had little contact with his family, who could say, but I was hardly one to cast a weighty moral opinion on such matters.

Eventually his corpse was wrapped and carried inside, but I insisted the blade be left in place to be examined further. It seemed to be a standard-issue military blade, though I wondered if this was Maxant's own, or if he carried something else.

Later, we were shown a much more ornate example. It was still around twenty inches long, double-edged, but this one possessed a wonderful brown and silver pommel, with intricate craftsmanship — a far superior weapon to the one that had been found in his body. This, I felt, enhanced my original suspicions — if Maxant was going to kill himself, he would surely have used his own blade. I guessed that if he had left it here to attend the Stadium of Lentus, which forbade weapons of any kind, then he would have been weaponless at the time the killer struck.

While Veron wanted to examine Farrum's progress in interviewing the servants, I decided to explore the property with Leana. I was impressed, if not in dumbstruck awe, at the wealth on display here. Maxant had brought back treasures from around the known world: idols, trinkets, vases, bowls, objects whose function seemed beyond my comprehension. Many of them were strewn about the house, piled up seemingly with disregard, as if he no longer knew what he could possibly do with them all.

We wandered into the rear garden, which was not as tidy as the one at the front of the villa, though it was much larger.

Leana eventually stopped me, pointing to my left. There was a smile on her face. 'Spirits save us. A little yellow flower with the dark heart,' she said. 'Henbane.'

'Let me look at the leaves.' The nearest plant was a knee-high specimen with identical leaves to the one we had found in Drullus' hideout. The flowers possessed speckled yellow petals, which merged into something far darker.

'Well,' I said, 'perhaps today we may have solved one murder at least.'

'Lots of henbane plants here.' Leana gestured around us, and I noticed that they were indeed scattered about the place. 'Maxant walks in his gardens before he came to the city,' she continued. 'Perhaps a couple of leaves catch in his sandal or in his cloak and stick to him as he rode into Tryum. They fall out when he gets to Drullus' hideout. It is nothing to do with making poisons – it is his inability to keep his garden tidy.'

I weighed up the options, slowly nodding. 'We know henbane is rarely grown in this region. A man who has travelled far throughout his life would easily collect interesting species for his own gardens. In fact, there are hardly any plants growing in this garden that I recognize to be native. I can well believe Maxant killed Drullus, too. The murder was clean and professional, after all. A soldier would know how to do it efficiently. Drullus seemed to die without a struggle . . .'

'When confronted by a famous general, Drullus might have thought it futile, and simply knelt on the floor before him.'

'It might have been possible they knew each other,' I added. 'If Drullus had let him into his hideout so willingly. Did they see each other at the party? I would be inclined to think their paths crossed – somehow. Drullus' submission indicated he knew something that, ultimately, would lead to the ending of his life.'

'What could that be?' Leana asked. 'The king's relationship with Drullus?'

'We know that the king admired the actors, not that he was sleeping with one of them.'

'Maybe Drullus had seen something on the night of Lacanta's murder and had to spend his days on the run.'

We both turned to walk back through the bright garden, back into the house.

'I'm convinced Maxant was involved in the killing of Lacanta,' I whispered. 'Perhaps he did not kill her himself, but he had something to do with it. Only he could have put the key in that door. And now it seems just as likely that he killed Drullus, too – an actor who may or may not have known something about the murder.'

'The general can no longer talk to us about the matter,' Leana said.

'I'm not so sure,' I replied. 'His corpse has already informed us that his own death was not a suicide – and that, in itself, has given us much to think about. The dead may still talk.'

'You mean like my spirits?' Leana said and smiled.

I checked with the servants to see if there were any nearby villages where a boat could have been obtained, but there were none locally. It was only a hunch, and admittedly a poor one – we were, after all, dealing with killers who planned things efficiently, and so acquiring a boat at the last moment was perhaps not our killer's style.

I did not tell Veron of my conclusions that General Maxant had been involved in the murder of an actor. I wanted to keep everything close so that a solution might present itself in my own mind. Besides, I knew better than to share a secret with him.

The senator rode back to Tryum, keen to pass on the news about the murder, and for immediate relatives to be located. He took Constable Farrum, whose interviews had not revealed anything out of the ordinary, back with him. I only hoped the poor man could cope with Veron's snobbery towards him on the journey home.

Not long after, a steady trail of senators and officials from the city began to arrive at the house. A good deal of time was wasted explaining the situation to them. I stressed, several times over, that this was a murder and not a suicide, and that seemed to comfort them somewhat. My temper very nearly flared again when two of the officials refused to speak to Leana. One even refused to acknowledge her presence so I told his companions that I would no longer be able to speak to him.

It was important for me not to create a scene when I depended upon people being open to me so, to avoid going too far with my anger, Leana and I headed outside to survey the buildings on site.

There was little else to go on, and the place was becoming too busy.

Satisfied that we had learned all we possibly could, we rode back to Tryum as the sun weighed low across the landscape, bathing it in a hazy, vermilion light.

Four soldiers were waiting at my home, dressed in their civic clothing and leather breastplates rather than the considerably more intimidating metal of war.

The cohort had let them in and they were standing in the garden sipping wine. Before passing on the day's messages, Bellona whispered to me, as I passed through the hallway, that they were rather high-ranking men who had served with General Maxant.

What on earth could these soldiers want? Leana slipped quietly into her room telling me not to get into any fights, while I headed out to the garden.

'Greetings.' They turned their attention to me and moved almost in unison to line up. They would have presented a fearsome presence to any host.

One handsome officer stepped forward and introduced himself as General Maxant's lieutenant, and said that the gathered soldiers were his leading officers on the recent campaign. 'We came here to thank you.'

'For what?' I indicated for them to sit on the couches, and stood facing them with my back to the fountain.

'We heard you were the one responsible for revealing that General Maxant hadn't killed himself,' he replied. 'You argued the case against his suicide.'

'Yes, and I will argue against any cleric who wishes to record the death as otherwise.'

'It's a great honour to us,' another soldier continued. 'If he had killed himself, it would've tainted his name as well as those who followed him to the ends of the earth. It would've brought great shame upon us. You've given him honour in death.'

'I'm grateful you came here to tell me so, but I merely sought a true explanation of events. Your commanding officer has been killed, which means we now have a hunt for his murderer on our hands.'

'You'll have our assistance wherever required,' the soldier replied, and told me where they could be found should I need them. 'Say the word, need information, and we'll help.'

'Since you're here, I'd like to know if the general had any obvious or concealed enemies?'

'Every man in Tryum had a right to be envious of him,' the soldier declared. 'He led us to Mauland and back.'

Another said, 'He was loved because of his actions, because of what he'd done for us all. He gave Detrata back its reputation as a serious nation, not to be messed with. I bet every king or queen in Vispasia suddenly got worried. Licintius adored him. The Senate even more so.'

'What about his political rivals, could they have poisoned him?'

'Very probably,' the first man grunted. 'Politics isn't for the squeamish, after all.'

The conversation went round in circles and the soldiers were growing frustrated with my questioning, so I decided not to press too hard. Despite the proud manner in which they spoke about their beloved general, it crossed my mind that someone in the military could have killed him because of some personal rivalry. No doubt if I had suggested this, it would have angered them further.

After they left, I consulted the messages that Bellona had given me, only to see a royal seal on one particular tube.

Hastily, I opened it up and read that the king demanded to see me, first thing in the morning after sunrise, for further updates. The password of the day was 'Hexagon'. Sighing because we had to trudge yet again to Optryx, I put the letter down. Licintius was an impatient man, seeking answers quickly, so I could understand his frustration – especially as he'd now lost a sister and a close friend in so short a time.

In my study I began to compile my notes so as to make a clear report of events so far to the king. It was pleasant to hear the noise of others in the house. Though I did not suffer loneliness in any way, it pleased me to know I could wander out and engage in conversation on matters of the city. Besides, I remembered the mysterious stalkers who had been following us in the Stadium of Lentus yesterday – no doubt there would be others waiting somewhere, outside the walls of the property, or watching from beyond the gates.

Later, Titiana visited again and we ate olives and bread, and drank a little wine in the garden. Woodsmoke drifted on the evening air.

I began to open up about the Maxant murder and posited a few theories, none of which completely satisfied me, and her hands – without my asking – began to work on my shoulders, around my neck, soothing away the tension with every word spoken. She suggested a few ideas of her own, jokingly, though for all I knew they might have been close to the truth.

We moved to the bedroom, as we tended to do more often than not; I barely felt in control of the situation, and our passions often got the better of us. We had no direction, no future to plan for, and neither of us seemed to care in the slightest. In the light of a lantern I lost myself, enjoying her strong, gently perspiring body and forgetting momentarily all the pressures of the murders. The scent of her skin, her powerful kiss, the gentle curve of her hips, all helped me forget.

It was another hot night in Tryum. Only a stone's throw from my door, a soothsayer screamed out the misfortunes of some poor soul. There was weeping, somewhere, then the groaning of the wind as it searched through the narrow, crowded streets. Again I lost Titiana to the city, though this time I was at least awake to watch her leave me.

'Why must you go?' I asked.

'I'm a married woman. You should know better than to keep asking.'

'Perhaps one morning I might wake to find you here, alongside me?'

Titiana hesitated from gathering up her clothes. 'Perhaps.'

I lay there watching her getting dressed, observing the nuances of her mannerisms: the way she would always put on her left slipper before her right; her superb balance; the way she would carry a tiny vial of perfume to put on her wrists.

I led her to the door and she kissed my neck, slowly, before vanishing into the night.

Poison Sellers

Before sunrise I washed and, still eschewing the fashions of the city for tunics and pale trousers, donned a smart outfit of silver doublet, white shirt, black trousers and a green cloak. I spoke briefly to a young, tired man from the Civil Cohorts, who reported that there had been a few thefts in the night, and three fights, one of which ended in a death. I asked to see records of the incidents and he said he had none. Though he was not in my command, I explained that Senator Veron would ask to see all crimes logged, which seemed enough to put fear into the lad. He hastily began to write in a ledger, muttering, 'I hope he's not drunk when he comes here. He'll have us beaten.'

'Does he beat you?' I asked.

The young man nodded. 'Just the once. They say he hit a slave so badly the poor boy could hardly walk properly afterwards.'

Outside my gate, the city was already waking, the streets were not as crowded as they would become, but we didn't have the time to explore the sensual delights of the district.

Our path led directly to Optryx.

✳

We waited in a room that overlooked the royal gardens — not the same room as before, and I was not entirely certain it was the same garden as before, either. However it was a graceful room, decorated in tastes that many of the city would not comprehend. The references in the frescoes were obscure and I was not even sure I knew them all myself.

Leana and I sat for some time, in a companionable silence, which provided a pleasant opportunity to work over the nuances of the murders in my mind, trying to fathom the connections between them.

One theory was that the king ordered Drullus' murder, in order to silence the actor from spreading rumours about their relationship. It was just possible that Licintius directed his trusted general on one final personal mission. Why else would Maxant have gone there?

But at least key figures were starting to emerge — even if they were then being killed. Maxant, Drullus and Lacanta — all connected, ultimately, to the king. He had never been a consideration before — he'd been in a room full of witnesses to vouch that he hadn't been there and he, personally, had insisted that the case be solved. Admittedly, something still didn't quite sit right, but he was the only person that bound the threads together.

I could understand Drullus being eliminated, but it seemed highly improbable that Licintius would want his old friend and trusted general out of the picture, especially after what he had done for Tryum and what he could do to boost the king's own popularity. And, equally, it did not seem logical for Licintius to kill his beloved sister, a woman who was working the political scene in his favour. He needed them to help his own existence.

But if someone wanted to eliminate the king's political success . . . that could be a distinct possibility. Two key political assistants killed.

I needed to be patient. Ideas were slowly forming in my mind, and I had come far in just a matter of days. I was also still curious about the vial of my father's poison, and hoped to locate an apothecary who knew more. I would do that later today.

The sun began to rise above the rooftops, casting its long, orange light into the garden. Presently, the king entered with his entourage. Leana fell to both knees, and I moved down to one.

'Please, Drakenfeld, rise. And your personal warrior. Get up. No ceremony this morning.'

We both stood while the king seated himself on the bench, overlooking the garden, and his personal guard took up their position at the edge of the room before facing forwards. Licintius wore a resplendent purple robe inlaid with gemstones.

'Maxant, too,' he declared, and I watched his expression very carefully.

'It seems so, sir.'

'You are the one who claims this is not a suicide. That is what my staff inform me.'

'That's correct, sir,' I replied, and explained my reasoning.

For a moment Licintius remained silent, contemplating either my words or his fine garden. I, too, could not help but stare at the fine statues, ornate water features and immaculately kept plants.

'You have a fine mind,' the king said. 'Is it, I wonder, any closer to working out who killed my sister? I fear for her spirit's safety.'

'I can't be sure, sir, but I have my theories. I'm much closer than when we last spoke, but I would not yet feel comfortable accusing anyone.'

'Tell me what you know so far.'

I explained my suspicions about Maxant being the first to enter the room and, potentially, being the only man who could have placed the key in the back of the lock to make it look as if the door had been locked from the inside.

'As to why he did this, I could not say. And, I should add, that it is not certain that he did so. I would not like to accuse the dead – I merely speak in terms of the most likely turn of events.'

The king remained unreadable. 'You realize you speak ill of my own general?'

'It is a working theory,' I confessed.

'And you know nothing else?'

'I have spoken to many people already, sir, including several senators. I hope to interview more shortly.'

Licintius nodded as if I had merely confirmed something he already knew. 'Very good, Drakenfeld.' He rose and, uncontrollably, I stood to attention.

Licintius paused to regard Leana, who lowered her gaze. 'You, lady. You rode well in the stadium two days ago, didn't you?'

Leana inclined her head and replied, 'I rode for Atrewe. Sir.'

'You did your country proud. Should you find yourself no longer working for Drakenfeld, you could always make a go of things as a stadium rider.'

With that, he turned his back to us and strode slowly to the door. 'I want more answers soon, Drakenfeld. I have lost a sister and a general, and someone must suffer for these actions or I'll hear the reason why not.'

The soldiers followed him out of the room, and that was that.

It was mid-morning by the time we arrived back at my house. I was left with an overwhelming sense of desperation, as always when I was halfway to solving something. One might think that such a stage should generate feelings of optimism, but it did not, especially with the pressure of having to please the king. It didn't help that I half-suspected the king was involved in some way, and where would that leave me?

A messenger stopped by, covered in dust and sweat, having returned from one of the outposts of the Sun Chamber on the nation's border.

He left me with a note from my superiors, and I felt an immediate sense of relief. They had received my notification of Maxant's death and were mustering a small, military cell of fifty soldiers to establish itself outside the city by tomorrow morning at the earliest.

It would be discreet – this would not be a visible warning to the people of Tryum – but it would be there if I needed assistance. Details were provided for how to contact them and where they would be stationed.

I still had the apothecaries to hunt down and so searched for the list of addresses. The vial containing my father's poison was still safe, and I placed both it and the list in my pockets, before calling Leana.

Another busy day stretched ahead and together we headed through the streets of Tryum.

'What do you hope to gain?' Leana asked as we weaved our way through a crowded lane. Merchants were trying to lead their animals through, which caused quite a ruckus, and our progress was slow. 'You know it is poison, yes?'

'I need confirmation whether or not my father had acquired the vial himself.'

'It seems likely though? Also, a poisoner would not leave a vial lying for someone to find.'

'No,' I replied, raising my voice above the noise of traders calling out from the nearby stalls. 'But I need to find out what his final movements were – for my own peace of mind. I still need confirmation of his behaviour. It is important to me.'

'Has the sudden talk of suicide hurt you?'

'I just need to settle it.'

The apothecaries were scattered about the city from Regallum to Vellyum, but the first few we tried yielded no luck. Few of them dealt with poisons and not one of them had seen anyone who fitted the description of my father. As we moved from store to store, I began to wonder if my father had not purchased the poison himself but had been killed by someone else. Leana was right in suggesting that the speculation of Maxant's own death had brought about a sense of shame over my father's own death. Though Polla did not place as great a value on such things as, say, Trymus or Festonia — in Polla's eyes there is not a huge amount of difference between the living and the dead anyway — the social stigma of suicide lingered heavily in my mind.

We worked our way down-city, towards the slum districts and the poorer shops. Children ran about in rags, old women sat in the shade of awnings kneading dough, and soothsayers were exchanging glimpses into the future for coin.

'So many soothsayers in Tryum,' Leana said.

'People will resort to anything to make more sense of their own world.'

'Did you grow up believing nonsense?'

'No,' I laughed. 'In Polla's writings, she does not agree with such sentiments. Polla requires only that we try to make our own sense of what goes on as best we can, and to put our faith in the unseen forces. I'll admit desperate times might make me consider such options, but I soon regain my composure.'

Leana grunted, though I could not say whether it was a positive or disapproving noise.

The last apothecary on our list was found next to a ruined temple. Outside, two old men were naked, their bodies covered in lines of red paint, prostrating themselves before a statue of a woman, now and then throwing water and flower petals over their heads. Incense wafted around the streets, mixing with the stench of the sewers.

The shop was large in comparison to the other buildings in this neighbourhood. Inside were stained wooden floors, a low ceiling that looked like it would buckle at any moment, and crates of bottles stacked up precariously against the wall to my right. Herbs covered the walls, papers littered the floor, and there was a sense that the proprietor was about to go on the run. As it happened, he was not – a lean man with the long beard of a prophet stepped forward from a back room, and greeted us with disdain.

'I'm an Officer of the Sun Chamber. I want to ask you a few questions.'

'Sun what? Means nothing to me,' he replied with a laugh. 'That like the army or summat?'

'Sun Chamber,' I corrected.

'If you say so. Anyway, I'm busy.' His eyes didn't seem to focus on mine.

Leana stepped forward, unsheathed her sword and pressed the point into the man's grubby-looking stomach.

'Go ahead,' he grunted. 'It's not like I've got much of a future round here.'

I asked Leana to step back and continued more calmly. 'I believe my father came here and bought some wares off you.'

'I don't do refunds,' the man replied, casting a suspicious glare in our direction.

'Look,' I continued, 'I just want to know something very simple – whether or not you sold my father poison.' I gave a description of him and a rough estimate of when my father might have come here.

'Father, y'say?' The man looked me up and down before his eyes settled on my Sun Chamber brooch. 'Man came in here weeks ago wearing something that looked exactly like that.' His finger prodded the brooch and I nodded. 'I ain't so good with descriptions, lad. My memory ain't what it used to be. That's a blessing round these parts. People want to remain unknown – that's why they come to me and not the fancy places – but I remember a brooch like that all right. He didn't look much like you though.'

'Did you sell him this?' I held up the vial.

The man smirked and shuffled into his back room. A moment later he returned with a box, which he opened to reveal dozens of similar vials.

'These are mine,' he replied. 'I only keep the blue ones for poisons – to keep it separate from the other potions.'

'So my father did come here.'

The expression on the apothecary's face relaxed a little. His voice lost its bitter edge. He looked as if he felt sorry for me. 'I did sell it, yeah. But so what? I sell a lot of poison.'

'Did he come here asking specifically for this? Did he seem hesitant in any way?'

'He asked for this one, there was no doubt he knew what it was for. People don't buy that sort of thing to cure headaches, though it would do the job just as well. I know you're looking for answers, son, but you'll not find much. All I can say is that I've rarely seen a man so lacking in spirit and vitality. I put it down to age, but when a man buys poison, well . . . All you know is that someone's life is going to end, sooner or later.'

We went outside and I crouched down in the street, holding my face in my hands. A cart clattered by and the driver cursed at a passer-by. Dust rose up around me and my eyes soon began to sting. Dreary shades of yellow and brown began to merge in my blurred vision.

I could only speculate at the pressure my father must have felt to have taken such an act, to have made that decision to end his existence and take his chances with the gods.

Leana placed her hand on my shoulder and she guided me to my feet again.

'No one need know,' she said. 'You carry the shame only in your heart – others cannot see in there.'

We walked most of the way back along the backstreets of Tryum in silence. The only thing that brought me out of my glum state of mind was seeing a stand that sold a selection of straw dolls – one was very much similar to a gift I had given Titiana years ago. We had taken a ride out to the woods that day, where we camped and ate roasted meats under the starlight. Those were more innocent times.

I purchased the small doll, which was no taller than my forefinger, and slipped it into my pocket. Leana frowned at me but didn't comment, and we continued on our way.

We arrived home at dusk. I was hoping to avoid speaking to anyone, but the men of the Civil Cohorts seemed in buoyant mood.

They eagerly revealed they had caught several thieves today, and had kept an immaculate and precise record of the persons involved, which would inevitably lead to private prosecutions. Their aggressive questioning had linked two of the men back to a gang who sought to gain the blessing of a couple of senators, to get work come the election season.

Veron, who had by now returned, was delighted with this news – as he could use it for his own purposes in the Senate. Now that they had a more robust point of contact and sense of organization, they had found the citizens of Tryum wanted to bother them with all sorts of trivial matters. One reasonably well-off man had been struggling to cook his dinner, because his wife was ill, and was so panicked that he decided to reach out to the cohorts for help.

'As if we could produce anything better than sludge!' Farrum chuckled. 'I told him to bugger off in the end. Wasting our time like that.'

'People will want to look up to you all the time now they know where to come. I've had it often over the years – we are in a position to help people, so naturally they'll come to us. Don't be too harsh in judging them.'

'Aye, you're right. So any more ideas on the murders?' Farrum asked.

'Not yet,' I replied.

'Did you manage to speak to any senators?'

'No.'

I opened the door to my room and was both surprised and relieved to find Titiana sitting on my bed. Though I had hoped for solitude, her company was not a disappointment.

She asked me how my day had been and I gave her an honest assessment. Her soothing gestures and touches opened me up yet again, and when I spoke of my meeting the king she stared at me with awe.

'What's he like?' she asked. 'I think I've only ever seen statues of him, but we all know how reliable they can be. What's he like as a person? Tell me.'

Charmed by her innocence, I gave her my opinion of him – that, ultimately, he was a good person, smart and dedicated. But this time I hinted that the king wasn't being entirely honest with me about Lacanta. 'He seems to be a link, somehow, between all of these killings, this whole mess. I'm missing something, and I can almost see it – perhaps I already have, but I just need more time.'

'I can't stay for long,' Titiana whispered. 'I should have said so when you first came in, but then I saw your sad face.'

'You don't need me to moan at you all night long. I'm not ideal company right now.'

'No, you don't understand. My husband will be returning to Tryum shortly. I may not be able to come back here as easily.'

'Oh,' I replied. This was something I really should have anticipated. I searched my mind for the right thing to say, but could only mutter, 'When can we meet again?'

Titiana looked to the floor. 'I really don't know, Lucan.'

I nodded my understanding. I did not need telling twice.

Titiana gazed up, unsettling me with her focused eyes. 'I want you to know, though, that whatever happens . . . I have . . . these past few days have been—'

I placed a finger to her lips and kissed her brow. 'It's taken me all this time to finally find you again. The gods will, I'm sure, arrange for another meeting soon enough.'

'Hopefully it won't be another ten years.' She took my hand and steered me to the bed.

What followed was both intense and upsetting, both a union and a separation. Every moment, each gesture seemed to be stretched out in time; and the passion wasn't the same. There was an overwhelming sense of loss about the act – the sudden promise of her absence highlighted some other emptiness inside me.

Afterwards I watched her getting dressed, asking myself if I had wasted my time with her. I had hardly taken my time to understand the only woman with whom I'd genuinely known intimacy like this.

Before she exited, I reached down to the floor and picked out the doll from my trouser pocket. 'I bought this, earlier,' I whispered, and held it up for her. 'It reminded me of when things were a lot easier.'

Titiana took it with tears in her eyes. She kissed my out-stretched fingers and turned to go. Vaguely I wondered if I'd see her again. If these were my final acts with her, were they particularly memorable? Would she cherish anything that had happened between us?

I sat in the stillness of my room for some time, staring at the ceiling, and growing increasingly annoyed with myself for allowing my actions to get out of my control.

With a lantern in my hand I shuffled across to the corner of the room and stood in front of a small marble bust of Polla; there, I fell to both knees, placing the lantern on the tiles beside me. I had said to Leana earlier that Polla required her followers to make their own sense of what went on in this world, and that we should put our faith in the unseen forces.

'Well here I am, goddess,' I whispered, with my arms out wide and with my chest naked to her. 'Here I am, with my father bringing shame to my family, my lover having walked into the night for the final time and a murder that involves the most important people in the nation. You are no soothsayer, goddess, but my logic is failing me now. I could do with a sign, or a message. Anything.'

In the silence that answered my call, I stretched out on the floor, exhausted from the day, and stared into the warm, flickering light of the lantern, and a harsh scent came to me . . .

A Sign

I was staring sideways at Leana's boots, the floor tiles cool against my aching cheek.

'Another seizure,' she grunted matter-of-factly, placing her hands either side of my ribs. She hauled me up and onto my bed.

Feeling rather numb, I said, 'That was not the sign I was hoping for.' I grunted.

Leana gave a soft smile. 'Praying to your goddess will not help you. You have given your heart to another woman instead. Or, perhaps she has taken it of her own accord, who can tell?'

Leana moved to scoop up her cloak, which she had used as a headrest.

'How long was I gone?' I asked.

'I cannot be sure. I was in the hallway when your woman left you. I heard your foot kick the wall not long after. I do not think it was any longer than normal.'

'I should really take those herbs from the apothecary.'

'You should. And this is better, Lucan. Herbs, something real. Practical logic. No prayers.'

'You talk to your spirit gods,' I said. 'There's no difference. We each need help with what we can't see.' Leana walked to the door and I called out softly, 'I don't thank you enough for what you do.'

'I will not refuse a pay rise, if you feel guilty about it.' Leana left the door ajar as she left.

Sleep came intermittently that evening, and I was as sensitive as ever to the grinding carts and night-shouts of Tryum.

When I finally came out of my room, Bellona was standing in the hallway, having only just written a message on parchment.

'Has someone called already?'

'You were asleep and I did not want to disturb you.'

Smiling softly, she handed me the letter.

'It was the priest again,' she continued. 'I did what you said and took down more details, but he would not share that much. All he said was that he was a priest from the Temple of Ptrell—'

'Ptrell?'

'Yes.'

As in the Mark of Ptrell – the discreet, engraved mark on the wall in Optryx. At the time I had thought it a sign, a piece of esoteric graffiti perhaps, but Ptrell was such a rare god.

It was too rare for this to be a coincidence. Ptrell had some business in Optryx and I wanted to find out what that was exactly.

Leana and I both walked with haste through the streets.

'The symbol of Ptrell,' I whispered as we marched through the pale light of dawn, the smell of woodsmoke thick in the air. The city was as calm as it always was at this hour; this serene picture was how I remembered Tryum to be when I used to recall its streets. Our urgent pace seemed very much out of place with this calmness.

'Do you remember seeing the symbol of Ptrell when we were in Optryx?'

'The eye within the hand?' Leana replied. 'Yes. Scratched in the wall in a storage room.'

'Hardly anyone follows Ptrell in Detrata – I believe I said so at the time. Polla is the dominant god here, of those who blend intellectual query with matters of the gods. It just seems hard to believe that a priest of Ptrell is also in the city. What if he's connected to that sign in some way?'

Leana shrugged.

Few people were about so we had to rely on the directions that Bellona had taken, which were accurate. It took less than an hour to arrive at the priest's dwelling, a small shack somewhere among the backstreets of Vellyum. It was a very old wooden temple, which at first could have been mistaken for a tavern. A corroded brazier stood outside and there were a few food offerings and cheap jewellery draped across a sculpture of a raised, flat hand.

Leana knocked on the door of the temple with her foot, and we waited.

Eventually it opened and, smiling from the shade, out stepped a man I assumed was the priest. He wore green silk robes with fine, gold detailing, an effect that looked rather like a spider's web, and he was carrying a white staff. Wafts of incense could be smelled inside.

'My name is Lucan Drakenfeld, son of Calludian. You've called on me a couple of times.'

His face immediately showed immense relief, as if he had finally met up with a long-lost friend and any moment now he would embrace me.

'Since I learned of your arrival in the city, I have tried unsuccessfully to contact you,' he said.

'Is it urgent?'

'Not any more. I've given up hope now.'

'Maybe I can still help?'

'That is possible. I hope I did not wake you this morning when I left a message? I hoped I could reach you, since you were always out, at the early hour, but that lovely lady wouldn't let me go until I gave her more details.'

I smiled and we were led inside. The place was every bit as resplendent as the stone temples further in the city, except everything was crafted from oak and ash – statues, benches, altars. A hazy morning light fell in through wooden shutters.

The priest sat down on a chair by the window with a sigh, and he gestured for me to sit down. Leana seemed content with keeping watch by the door, though I doubted we'd have any trouble at this hour, and in this place.

Pockmarks covered the priest's face, and there was a small burn mark on his hand; that combined with the rope mark on his neck led me to believe that this man had led something of an interesting life. Everything about his expression suggested he was a man of deep serenity; his thick gold rings said he was not short of money.

We sat in silence for a while, until I said, 'I follow Polla, a sister to your rare Ptrell.'

'I always like speaking to devout followers of Polla – your hearts seem kinder than many.'

'Yours is a rare temple indeed. I've not seen any like it in Tryum.'

'Alas, this is the only one.' He gave a warm laugh. 'I have noticed that you are a busy man.'

'Being busy comes with the territory, I'm afraid,' I replied. 'Being in the Sun Chamber rather kills one's private life.'

'Your father was also a very busy man.'

'You knew him?' I leaned forward, hoping for any news of his final weeks.

'I met him, though I did not know him well enough to say we

were friends,' the priest replied. 'I met him in his offices, in fact – when I first came to ask him for help. That's why I have been trying to establish contact at your home.'

'My father is no longer with us, I'm afraid. He died some weeks ago.'

'Ah, I know this, but I was hoping I could talk to you instead. Your father had been looking into a small matter for me, but could not, unfortunately, bring it to a happy resolution in time. Then I recently learned that his son had returned. I thought that perhaps this son may know of something, or could find the time himself to look into the matter.'

I didn't want to add more duties to my day, but seeing as he was a priest of Ptrell, a god so close to Polla, it was hardly something that could be refused. 'What was the issue?'

'Many weeks ago I was hoping to set up this small temple in Tryum to Ptrell, and to establish a community of worship for him.' He continued in soft, regretful tones, the way someone speaks of a loss. 'I came here four months ago expecting two visitors to meet me on our holy day, a young lay preacher and a priestess, who had travelled from Maristan where I had been conducting rituals. We travelled separately due to our various holy commitments. Only the lay preacher arrived. The priestess never turned up.' He closed his eyes and whispered something hard to discern. 'I feared she had been caught by those foul gangs of thieves and assassins who trade in ruining the lives of others. There was talk that she might have been sold into prostitution or into the domestic slave trade, which we pretend does not go on.'

My startled expression must have been rather noticeable.

'You think you can help?' the priest asked, a sudden keenness in his voice.

'Yes and no,' I replied, my heart beating ever faster. 'Do you have paper and a quill or reed pen?'

'Yes. You would . . . like me to pass you some?' He looked as if he was humouring me.

'Please,' I replied.

'Very well.' He stood up and rummaged around in a drawer, retrieving a poorly made scrap of parchment, and then provided me with a reed pen and a tiny ceramic pot of ink.

I hastily arranged myself at his desk and called back to him. 'I need you to describe the priestess, absolutely everything you can about her, eye colour, hair, any potential places where she may have been marked by religious ornamentation.'

'Yes, well . . . She had blonde hair, if I recall correctly – though not bright blonde. A strong jawline. She would have had several earrings in her right ear to denote her relative inexperience . . .' He went on in some detail and I nodded to myself as he spoke, pausing only to apply more ink to the pen. After he finished I indicated for Leana to come over.

She strode across the room and whispered, 'What is the matter?'

'I think Lacanta's still alive,' I replied. 'We must move quickly.'

Back to Optryx

I needed more time, more clarity, and to get back into Optryx to work out what might have happened in the Temple of Trymus that night.

'I do not follow you,' Leana said.

I passed her the notes recorded only moments earlier. 'This is his description of the missing girl he was asking about. See for yourself.'

Leana held up the document and we walked a little more slowly while she read. 'Oh. I think I see now.'

'And what do you see?'

'It reads like a description of Lacanta.' She handed back the note, buried her hands in her pockets and we picked up our pace once again.

'Exactly. So, what if someone like Lacanta had come along at the right time – someone who was utterly anonymous. What if that same woman fell into the hands of the king? For months she could have been kept prisoner until the right moment. In her desperation she carves her holy symbol upon the wall. A Lacanta lookalike, this priestess could have easily been killed just over an hour before Maxant entered that temple in front of everyone.

With the body still that fresh, without stiffness having started to set in, no one could possibly have noticed that the body had been planted. What's more, guests would have seen the real Lacanta only moments before, fooling everyone into believing that the murder took place within a different time frame entirely. There is no possible way Lacanta could have been killed so quickly, and especially not behind a locked door. Furthermore, General Maxant crashes through and places the key in the lock on the inside of the door to confuse everyone. What was made to look impossible, or the use of magic, turns out to be simple to explain.'

'That must mean that Lacanta and Maxant were working together on this.'

'As was, I suspect, the king. However, if a royal is involved in such deceit and treachery – and it can be proven – we'll immediately have to call in others in the Sun Chamber, a few soldiers from our Sun Legion does not seem enough.'

Thankfully the king was not in residence. His banners were not on display by the entrance gate and the guards of the King's Legion seemed confused about whether or not I could go in, despite the fact that Veron had supplied me with the week's password. Their uncertainty unnerved me – the king had given us access, so had he suddenly declared that access revoked? Lacanta's body, we were told, was being kept in a temple further down the city, and there was an effort to steer us in that direction, but I wanted to see inside the residence. Eventually I managed to negotiate our entry, threatening to bring the Sun Chamber army.

We dashed to the chamber where I had previously seen the sign of Ptrell. Once the door was opened for me, I headed straight up to the sign on the wall: it was indeed still there, as clear as ever, an eye set within a palm. The priestess must have been kept in here for a while before she was murdered, to have taken the care to engrave it with such neatness, and so deeply, into the stone.

Aside from a couple of wooden crates and a rack of clay pots, there were few signs of use for the room. A few flecks of blood remained on the wall, which could have come from anywhere, and the floor tiles had been scrubbed — one area, near the door, even retained brush marks in the dried, dirtied water, which suggested to me that no one previously used this place at all. I enquired with the cooks and staff nearby as to whether or not they entered the room, but half of them had never seen it open, while the others merely assumed it was a storage area.

Standing in the doorway, I peered down the passage. The room was located near to the Temple of Trymus so she could have been moved there quickly and with discretion, and without coming into contact with the guests that evening. It was also close to the kitchens — and I recalled the king's physician, Yago Boll, suggesting that a small fruit knife might have been used as the murder weapon. That weapon had long since disappeared, but if it had been a fruit knife, then the kitchen was where the murderer could have acquired one.

As we left Optryx, I had the suspicion we had upset someone. Certain members of staff started to give us accusing glances, and pointed in our direction. A soldier was called over, but we didn't hang around to learn of the results.

The day had started bright, but a few hours into it clouds began to move in again, the rays of sunlight few and far between. Under such darkening skies we located the temple, on the edge of Regallum, where Lacanta's — or rather the priestess's — body was being kept.

'What will you look for?' Leana asked.

'The description we were given by the priest made a reference to several ear studs on her right ear, but none on the left – these were part of her indoctrination ritual. I want to look for the holes these piercings would have left – Lacanta would never exhibit such an unusual array of decoration because of the fashions of the city. If they are there we'll know for certain that Lacanta is still alive.'

This particular Temple of Trymus was small and had to be sought out with some effort. It was located down a narrow lane ending up at a low limestone wall, so it was a place of little traffic. The bearded head of Trymus was carved in stone above the entrance, and a large, locked wooden door stood in our way. I knocked, but there was no answer, and Leana scrutinized the rest of the building but could find no other means of entry.

The lock mechanism was easy enough to pick and, a few moments later, I pushed the door open to find darkness beyond.

Once our eyes adjusted, the light from the street was our only guide, until Leana found a candle in a nearby room that was still lit for the offerings. Where was the pontiff of the temple?

It did not take long to locate the body. It had been stretched out within an elaborate gold cot with highly polished details of fauna; precious silks had been wrapped around her body and her face had been painted red. Various faces of Trymus, carved from marble and bronze, loomed over her from the surrounding walls.

'Could you bring over that candle?' I said.

Leana stepped closer and we looked down over Lacanta's head. I lifted away her hair and examined her ears closely. The skin was not what it was, and possessed a dried, frail texture, but sure enough her right ear bore the markings I was looking for.

'They would have removed the earrings so that she bore even more of a resemblance to Lacanta, of course. Also, the priest's description of her was of someone slender, but the body we found was somewhat amply proportioned. It isn't unlikely that she'd been kept and fed for some time, I suppose? The priest said she had disappeared well over four months ago. Depending on when she was found, that remains a good hundred days of rich royal food and no exercise.' I shook my head. 'I remember the physician confessing that he'd not seen her properly in over two years – his bad memory helped convince me she was genuine at the time, unless he was in on the act as well.'

There was a sound of footsteps skidding in another room, and the rattle of armour. Someone was coming our way.

Leana blew out the candle so we were in utter darkness, but the soldiers had already entered.

'Do not move, either of you!' a voice shouted.

There were at least three men in the room. Holding my breath I heard Leana unsheathe her blade before slamming into one of the soldiers. In the clamour I drew my own and, as my eyes grew better adjusted to the darkness, I took my chances against one of the men, but merely ended up striking metal in the dark. After I heaved one of them up against the wall, I followed Leana, sprinting back out the way we came.

'The wall,' she snapped.

I sprinted after her breathless, and when we came to a wall that was about my height Leana gave me a hand to get over it, before scrambling up after me.

'They will not easily climb over in their heavy armour,' she said.

We ran without purpose or direction, losing ourselves in the crowded plazas and the hectic morning trading, turning this way and that before finally taking refuge in the shadow of a tavern.

I was exhausted and sweating; my breath came in great heaves. Leana recovered swiftly and asked, 'Who were they?'

'The King's Legion, I think.'

'Why come after us now?'

'Because someone, somewhere, has given the order for us to be stopped. I think we shouldn't really have been permitted to enter Optryx in the first place, which explains their initial confusion.'

'But the king, he said we can go there whenever we like, yes?'

'Yes,' I agreed. 'That's what he told us. But I suspect, if he now knows we're on to something, he's going to be desperate to stop us. He wouldn't dare touch me at the start of the investigation. Two Sun Chamber officials dead in the same city, a week apart? He knew that would invite the wrath of the Sun Legion and have agents, spies and officials all over Tryum. He probably thought he'd let me try to investigate as much as I could, but suspected I would not be able to solve his mystery.'

'His mystery?'

'I'm convinced that he's at the centre of this – it couldn't have been done without his knowledge. It's impossible for all things involved in this affair to have been so *without* his knowledge, and his influence or manipulation. Now he thinks we're close he will probably try to stop us, and not care at all that the Sun Legion might come. He must have assumed the crime appeared so impossible to solve that he could have his fun with me. I'm annoyed now, though. The king will eventually dispose of that body on the funeral pyre.'

'Then no one will believe you,' Leana observed.

'Once it's burned the only evidence will be for me to produce Lacanta herself.' I searched my mind to work out what my next move would be.

'Lillus,' I whispered.

'You want a haircut now?'

Getting Out

At the salon on the edge of Polyum, in front of the fabric stall, Lillus was busy berating a middle-aged woman with an incredibly weathered face and garbed in a dark shawl.

'Never do I want to see you here again!' Lillus bellowed. 'Away with you.'

'Charming the ladies as always,' I called out.

'Ah, Lucan, my boy. A pleasure to see you — though is that stubble I see? This must change.'

'I tried shaving at home, but it's not the same. What was the issue with the woman?'

'She was a witch. I caught her trying to gather human hair off a client so that it could be used for a curse. But this is not the only problem, it seems — you are troubled, Lucan. You and your friend have been running. Step into the cool shade. Drink something. Talk to me.'

'Lillus, it's an important matter,' I said. 'Do you think we could have a moment of privacy?'

He regarded me with a renewed sense of professionalism. 'It will be so.'

✶

Drinking a cooling tisane, sitting on the benches, beneath the frescoes of sporting heroes and large purple paper lanterns, I enjoyed a moment of peace to gather my thoughts.

Leana stood by the front door keeping an eye on the street and, after seeing her for the first time, Lillus informed me that his mother, too, had come from Atrewe. I told Lillus of my situation, knowing he was fantastically well connected: he was the eyes and ears of the city, and I needed them. He simply nodded, gently brushing his moustache, inclining his head now and then.

'Quite the situation,' Lillus whispered.

'We'll have to leave Tryum immediately. I need some messages putting about the city if you could manage that for me?'

'Of course, of course.'

'I would like it said that I have been called back to Venyn City on urgent Sun Chamber business, but will return shortly. Meanwhile, I would appreciate it if you contact the priest of Ptrell and let him know that the priestess was found dead some time ago. He needs peace of mind, at least, but please urge him that it's in his interest not to press the matter further.'

'This is simple enough.'

'I have a member of staff back at home, Bellona, who is a fantastic cook. Should she find herself out of a home, can I send her to you? I'll see that you're paid, of course.'

'I was thinking of branching out, as it happens, into the culinary business. That fabric stall is useless. Is she good?'

'Incredible,' I replied.

'Though my female customers are plentiful, I need more men to come here, and too few appreciate good-quality fabric. Filling their guts on nice food, however, is good for business.'

'Thank you, Lillus. I truly appreciate the favours.'

He dismissed my thanks casually. 'The least I can do. Will you return to Tryum soon?'

'I will, but I don't know how long I'll be. I need to meet up with the Sun Chamber in the safety of the countryside and wait for their guidance.'

Lillus gave a gentle grin. 'To see the boy grow is a marvellous thing.'

'Well, the boy might stop growing if the king's men get hold of him,' I replied. 'Lillus, there's one final thing, one more message. There was a woman I once knew, who I was lucky enough to meet again.'

'You found love at least!' Lillus declared, beaming now. 'Tell me of her name.'

'She's called Titiana.'

Lillus frowned. 'Describe her, if you will.'

I did, giving details of her physical appearance and of her character.

Lillus nodded slowly. 'And how did you meet her?'

'She was dancing at a tavern that Senator Veron took me to.' I told him of the evening and how I used to know her.

'My guess is,' Lillus continued, 'that she told you she was a poor lady?'

'More or less.'

'And did she dress like a poor lady?'

'Well, not quite . . . I assumed she wore her best clothing when she came see me. Lillus, please, if you know of her, tell me.'

'I don't know her, but the name is familiar to me – because she, too, works in the information business. She sometimes dances, sometimes is a courtesan. She spent some time in the theatre, learning the dark arts of acting and of disguise. She comes and goes. Information is a dirty business.'

I placed my head in my hands. 'Blinded,' I breathed.

'If Veron was blabbering about where he was going that night, it would have been easy for her to find you and make it look as if you were the one to find her. Who set her on you, is the question.'

'Probably on the king's orders,' I sighed. 'He would have sent someone to get close to me, to observe my movements. To see if I was getting close to solving the matter or still had no clue. It was a good plan, come to think of it. It meant he remained in control of matters.'

'You investigate criminal affairs,' Lillus said, 'you're not a spy. You weren't to know, my boy. You weren't the first to be fooled – you won't be the last.'

'No, but I should have known at least. I just assumed she was interested in me.'

'Again, you are not the first to make such assumptions. I have learned, over the years, that those who show the most interest are often the ones not to trust. What was that message you wanted me to send?'

'Forget about it. There's one last thing you could help with though.' Rising, I reached into my pocket and produced the sketch found within the book in Lacanta's room. 'What do you make of this?'

Lillus moved to catch the light of the sun, and scrutinized the document for what seemed a frustratingly long time. 'Clever,' he breathed. 'Forgotten language, these symbols. The old tongue, dead letters. It's the outline of one corner of our nation – the symbols spell out Detrata. The little triangles, I cannot say what they are for, but I have known them to be used to signify problems, perhaps places to stay away from.'

'I found it in a book in Lacanta's room.'

Lillus reconsidered his initial statements on the matter. 'I think she was too clever and forgot where she had hidden this. She could have others, but remembered to take those.'

'Where do you think she could have gone?' I asked.

'Where do you think?' he responded, glancing down at the map once again.

'There were books on Destos. It's a holiday area for the rich. She might have gone on holiday there as a child, but—'

'She might have fled there,' he interrupted. 'This looks like Destos now you have said the name. The coast is shaped just so . . .' He outlined it with his fingers. 'But if she has gone there, it is impossible to tell where.'

We conferred for a moment longer, but this was all I had to go on. A coded draft she'd left behind by accident.

I stood up, embraced Lillus, and thanked him for his company, his help and the favours. He said his messages would be spread quickly and with discretion, and I had to believe him – there was no one else to trust. He wished me luck and kissed my cheek.

It was mid-afternoon by the time we made our way back to the house. I seethed with anger and frustration. I had simply let Titiana walk into my life and there she was reporting my affairs to someone else. The irony of me spotting those con men in the tavern during dinner, while I was busy being conned myself, was not lost on me.

But that was not what bothered me the most.

I somehow felt that all her gestures and her words of affection had been honest. She had me seduce her all over again before she would forgive my past actions towards her. Surely she would not have bothered to go through all that effort if there was nothing genuine inside her heart?

Leana stopped me with an outstretched arm, and steered me towards a doorway of a pottery shop. 'Look,' she said. 'On the gate.'

The entrance to my gardens, some fifty paces away, appeared slightly different, and eventually my eyes settled on what it was.

On one of the spikes was a human head.

A small crowd stood before it, pointing up in disgust. With discretion we stepped nearer and I saw, glistening in the late afternoon sun, that it was the severed head of Constable Farrum.

I immediately thought of his poor family, his now fatherless children. Someone in the gathered crowd vomited against the wall and while everyone was too busy avoiding the mess, we stepped along the pathway to my house. Leana drew her sword, as did I.

The door was open, the entrance was covered in blood.

We first stepped past what I assumed was Farrum's body – he had been not only decapitated, but there were several wounds to his torso. He hadn't even had time to draw his sword before he was killed.

I closed my eyes listening for anyone else in the house, but it seemed utterly silent. Under the open-roofed hallway, by the central pool of water, we found another dead man from the Civil Cohorts – his head, too, had been cleaved from his body, which hung half in the water, half out. His uniform was soaked and his severed head floated by his feet. Further into the study, two more men from the Civil Cohorts had been slaughtered, their heads still attached this time, but with several abdominal wounds. Bloody footprints trailed all around my house, slick on the tiles. There was so much of it here, it seemed impossible to gauge a sense of what might have happened.

Leana dashed from room to room, stealthily checking whether or not there were any more bodies. I stood aghast at the carnage.

'No one else so far,' she said. 'Not even Bellona. Perhaps she has escaped?'

'I hope so,' I replied.

Leana moved to the open doors to the garden, while I took a look around: nothing had been disturbed from my study. Books remained on the shelves, papers piled neatly where they had been left. Leana called out my name and I ran outside into the garden.

She cautioned me before I stepped out into the sunlit space, shading my eyes.

'Oh, Polla . . .' I breathed, my voice catching in my throat. 'Oh please, Polla. Please, no . . .'

I fell to my knees.

There, hanging by her neck from the edge of the rooftop, was Titiana. She, too, had been cut open and blood had pooled beneath, glistening in the light.

I am not ashamed to say I wept then – tears of rage and of despair. I heaved myself to my feet, dragged a couch up to her body and climbed up to cut the rope connecting her neck to the masonry.

Her beautiful face was covered in bruises, her eyes shut to the world.

Leana helped me lower her body to the ground.

I collapsed next to Titiana's lifeless form, cradling her head, smelling her blood-soaked hair. I kissed her forehead, and rocked back and forth without a clue what to do next.

Leana stood over me, silhouetted in the blinding light.

Time seemed to lose all consistency, but when my control over myself returned I knew that I could not stay there holding her for all that long.

I wrapped Titiana's body up in one of my finest cloaks, cleaned her face of blood, and left her in the garden along with a hastily prepared offering to Polla – hoping that it would be enough to see her through to the next realm. I kissed her lips one final time and forgave her – as she had forgiven me – for any of her actions that may have compromised my investigation. Now was not the time to bear grudges.

After changing from my blood-soaked clothing, and washing my hands and face, Leana and I quickly packed a few belongings and prepared to leave. I was about to step out of the door when she called me back once again. I dreaded what she might have found.

However, she had discovered Bellona hiding in a cupboard, huddling in shocked silence. Bellona did not say a word at first, but she had not been harmed and for that I was immensely relieved.

Eventually, she managed a whisper. 'The soldiers came. King's men. They dragged the lady into the house. They said where is he, where is he, and she screamed she didn't know. I hid here and closed my eyes . . .'

'It is OK.' Leana held her so she might be soothed, and gave me a look of desperation that I shared with her.

But we urgently needed to go.

Leana lifted Bellona up to her feet. I gave her directions to Lillus' salon, and told her that he would look after her. 'Be strong. And for your own safety, you must be quick,' I added. 'Do you understand?'

She squirmed a nod, tears still streaming down her face. I wished I could guide her there myself, but I no longer had the time.

After she gathered her belongings, I guided her to the door and placed a small purse of coins in her pocket. 'Tell him what happened, but tell him I'm safe.' We steered her down the path and she wailed when she saw Farrum's head on the gate.

Leana grabbed a shoulder bag of her belongings and I picked up mine.

With our swords visible, we marched down the blood-splattered path, past Farrum's severed head, and into the streets.

Finally confident we were not being followed, we proceeded

through the backstreets, navigating our way towards the South Gate, through Vellyum and then Plutum, losing ourselves in the intensity of the crowds.

I felt numb. My mind was a mess and sweat streamed down my face. I couldn't bring myself to say anything to Leana. The vision of Titiana's hanging body could not be released from my mind. Why did she have to die? Was her death a warning to me, a way to make me fall apart?

I vowed to myself, in the presence of Polla, that her death would not go without justice being served.

As we saw the limits of the city approach, the high wall that kept separated the urban sprawl from the countryside, Leana took me to one side. 'If the king looks for us, he will have let these soldiers on the gate know about us.'

I looked around, trying to read the crowd for any followers. 'That's a good point. We should find a cart — a heavily loaded one, or possibly one that stinks.'

'You want us to ride on a cart?'

'No, underneath it. If it's not worth the hassle, the soldiers won't bother searching it and will wave us through.'

We waited for the better part of an hour until a trader came along the road, taking out rotting manure from the city stables to spread on the farmland beyond. I offered him ten pecullas — five now and five on the other side — which wasn't much as far as bribes went, but he was poor enough for it to make a difference. His wide cart reeked, but we climbed underneath, hanging on to the timber frame as the horse plodded on. The cobbled road tipped us this way and that, violently lurching over any potholes, and soon we found ourselves approaching the city walls.

The cart rolled to a halt and my arms were already starting to ache. I closed my eyes and prayed to Polla that we would not be found. Voices came, one of them the farmer's, the other probably that of a soldier. A foul liquid dripped through the cart and onto my sleeve.

What was taking so long?

A few pairs of boots shuffled back and forth around the cart.

Eventually a whip cracked, the horse plodded forwards, the cart rolled on. I breathed out a sigh of relief as we passed the South Gate and continued rocking along the South Road out of Tryum. I held on for what felt like hours, but in reality was far less than that. We tipped up at an angle as the horse took on a hill, and it was only when we crested it and levelled out that I called out to the farmer.

The cart rolled to a halt. We came out from underneath. I brushed myself down and paid the farmer, who continued on his way. The South Road was busy with trade and travellers, and at the base of the hill stood the contained mass of Tryum. Optryx remained a bright palace on the horizon: if the king was in there, I would find him. But not yet, not now – first I had something else to do.

A Meeting

We walked for miles that afternoon, trudging only for a little while along the main road, but then out onto dusty tracks to avoid any incident. Clouds provided enough cover from the sun, making the journey bearable.

It was early evening by the time we reached the nearest settlement, a small town called Festellum. We found a small tavern with a tiny top-floor room and pretended to be a simple couple on our way to the city. It was a sparse place, with far fewer furnishings than my own home, but at least we could rest in relative peace.

Accustomed to Bellona's fine cooking, I was disappointed in the tavern's offerings, but Leana pointed out that we were lucky to be alive and should be grateful we still had our heads to eat with.

She had a point.

That night Leana took to the floor. 'I am now used to soft furnishings. It is not good for the soul. You have the bed.'

I lay staring at the ceiling for some time, incredibly exhausted – in body and mind – from the day's events. I tried to make sense of what happened. It took me a long time to dismiss the image of Titiana hanging there, devoid of life. It seemed wrong that someone so vibrant and energetic could be so . . . still.

In my mind I turned over what Lillus had said to me, reflecting on my moments with Titiana. It seems my ego had got the better of me. I genuinely believed that her affections for me had been sincere.

Anyway, the answer would never come, and there was no way to find out. All I had was my investigation, and my determination to find the one thing that could prove my theory about Lacanta still being alive: Lacanta herself.

A thoroughly deep sleep came laced with melancholic dreams, which seemed to linger on during the first hour of the day. Eventually I couldn't recall precisely what they were about, only that there was a racing chariot and a falcon circling in the sky above it. Perhaps if we came upon a Detratan mage or a priestess on the road it would be worthwhile checking if there was some hint buried within the hazy images.

The sun had not quite risen and already we were preparing to leave the settlement. After acquiring food from the tavern kitchen, and a crude map from one of the other guests, we managed to buy two mares from a young couple who were heading into Tryum and needed the money.

As dawn broke, there were already many travellers on the road, mainly traders, though a few priests – and I thought again of the poor priestess who had never made it to her temple.

So many people go missing each week it is easy to become complacent: but I make sure I never do, conscious there is always a loved one, someone who cares, someone whose life will never be quite the same again.

We did not arrive at the station post until the middle of the afternoon, exhausted from the heat and dust of the journey.

Away from the main road the landscape had been unforgiving, and I was relieved to enter a small copse of trees and see the small, round, crenellated building, in which the Sun Chamber agent would be stationed.

It was not widely known that these structures existed, let alone were inhabited. It was hidden among old poplar trees on the side of a small valley and we could have had trouble finding the place. There was a small stable behind the building, so any passers-by who strayed this far from the road would probably dismiss it as a farmhouse. Yet that stable was constantly active with the horses of messengers and officials passing back and forth, and a gentle river of information was always flowing.

With immense relief we dismounted, tied our horses and banged on the door. It opened up, and an elderly man questioned who we were, so I told him.

'Ah, of course, Drakenfeld,' the man declared, before turning inside. He waved over his shoulder for us to follow. 'Drakenfeld, the young officer from Tryum. Knew your father well. Sadly I couldn't make the funeral, but I did visit his body. A letter you sent came through here not long ago. You're not following it up, are you? We dispatched the messenger on a fresh horse, so he was as quick as any messenger in Vispasia.'

'I'm confident the letter got to its destination, but I'll not be around in Tryum for the reply, unfortunately.'

'Trouble?' he asked.

I gave a nod.

'Which is why you're here?'

'Correct again,' I replied.

'Right you are. I'm Trajus, by the way. Retired officer – used to do what you do, but find myself more suited to being behind a desk these days.'

'I'm not sure being behind a desk would ever suit me.'

'I was like you, son, but when you get an arrow lodged in your leg and a wound that never quite heals, you don't get much choice in the matter.' Trajus moved back to his seat and relaxed into it with a thunderous groan, which he seemed to enjoy. The place was modestly decorated – bare stone walls, with a stove and a few plain chairs, desks and benches. One workbench was littered with papers and scrolls, while in the corner of the room stood a small bust of Polla, with beads and necklaces draped over her. In my head I briefly requested her blessings.

'Now, what course of action would you like?' Trajus asked.

'It's a serious situation. I'm going to need an urgent message dispatched to my senior officers – have any soldiers been stationed nearby?'

'Two dozen Sun Legion veterans on the other side of those trees.' Trajus gestured towards the window.

'Really? I saw nothing on the way up.' I looked across to Leana, but she shrugged.

'Then they're doing their job properly, son. No one's supposed to know they're here. Not even I know what they're here for.'

'That might be my doing – or at least I hope it is. Please, can you take me down to see them?'

The disappointment was apparent in Trajus' face. 'I'd just got settled in my chair.'

Trajus limped at a frustratingly slow pace through the afternoon sunlight, leaning on his stick for support. Eventually, through the yellowing poplars and down a small country track, we arrived at a dip in the valley, a natural shelter carved out of the land itself. There were no tents, just a smouldering campfire in front of a small, crumbling barn overlooking the valley.

'Where are they?' I asked.

I heard the clamour of armour – and some brief, sharp orders being issued from up the slope. Silhouetted against the bright sky were the two-dozen men, sheathing or lowering their weapons almost in unison.

'Trajus,' a voice called down, and a figure gestured towards us with the tip of his blade. 'Who are these people?'

'I am Lucan Drakenfeld, Officer of the Sun Chamber.'

'Is that so?' the voice called back. 'Then we have business with each other, Lucan Drakenfeld.'

The figure marched down the hill and into focus. I could hardly believe my eyes. Looming over me in his resplendent uniform was an old friend.

'Maxin Callimar?' I called over. 'Is it actually you?'

'You were always getting into trouble, Lucan, even years ago.'

Callimar strode into view smiling – a good deal older, flecks of grey in his beard, his nose even broader than it used to be, those brown eyes more penetrating than before. His skin had been darkened by a lifetime under the Vispasian sun. His hair was still raven-black, though, and he'd put on a lot of muscle mass over the years. We embraced, and I felt the iron grip of his veteran arms.

'What are you now, a captain?'

'General,' he said laughing. 'One of ten in the Sun Legion. And you've come a long way since I trained you, so I hear.'

We took a step back so we could assess each other better. We'd known each other in Free State where Sun Chamber officers had to undergo a stint of military education. We became close friends for that brief time, the way a young and older man can do: me eager to learn, him eager to talk over a cup of wine.

'Time's been kinder to you than it has to me,' Callimar said.

'I don't do half the things you lot do.' I indicated his fellow veterans, who were stepping down slowly from the slope. 'What good fortune that they sent you.'

'Fortune hasn't much to do with it. Our unit had been ensconced in a small town a few hours from the border of Maristan when there was news that some Lucan Drakenfeld character wanted help. I'm hardly likely to leave a friend standing, especially one like you.'

'I'm relieved to find a friendly face out here.'

'Sounds serious.'

'It is.'

'Come, then. Trajus, please, we'll be fine from here. Thank you for bringing him and his colleague down.'

Trajus muttered something before shambling back up the slope to the station post, while Callimar placed his arm around me and steered me towards the barn. It felt good to be among friends, to have someone from the Sun Chamber back me up in what had to be done.

We walked back to the quiet shelter of the old limestone barn. I introduced him to Leana, and was a little surprised he made no comment on the fact that I had chosen a female assistant.

We sat inside on rough wooden benches while his veterans set off in small teams around the hillside. Callimar offered us a cup of water, which was gratefully received.

'So, friend,' Callimar said, 'what trouble have you found for yourself this time? The details I was given were hazy at best.'

'It's King Licintius,' I said.

Callimar's face darkened and his expression grew more serious. 'Go on.'

'He's staged the murder of his own sister, Lacanta, arranged for a priestess to be killed in her place, and tricked the whole city into believing his sister had been killed. In fact, the whole of Tryum believes the king to be in mourning for Lacanta, but I'm convinced she's alive.'

366

Callimar grunted a laugh of disbelief. 'That sounds like a lot of effort.'

'There's a lot more I'm trying to connect. General Maxant has been killed, but I believed him to have been involved in the staging of Lacanta's murder, too.' I explained how Maxant had been the first one on the scene, the only one who could have put the key in the lock on the inside; the connection between him and the actor, Drullus, and the leaf of henbane. 'And we found Maxant's own murder staged in a similar manner – people were led to believe one thing, though quite another in fact happened.'

'And you investigated all of this, Lucan?'

'I did. The king permitted me access, but I don't believe he wanted me there – another senator called me to the scene that night – but the king couldn't get rid of me, not so soon after another Sun Chamber official had died.'

'A unit far bigger than my men would have been dispatched in an instant,' Callimar said.

'Exactly – and he also had to create the illusion that he was interested in seeing Lacanta's supposed murderer caught. It would have looked strange otherwise, but he was no stranger to acting, it seems. He put on quite a show of making me welcome. He must have been very confident in his own plans, but he now knows I'm on to something. He's grown desperate. The King's Legion will be out looking for us.'

Callimar waved his heavy hand dismissively. 'City troops will be lazy. We've hidden right in front of their noses and, if they come for you, we'll keep you concealed.' Callimar frowned momentarily. 'Your father – he was the official who died, wasn't he?'

I nodded and took another gulp of water.

'Lucan, I'm truly sorry. I hope Polla does her best for him.'

'Thank you.'

'Are these accusations enough, do you think?' Callimar asked. 'What solid evidence have you found?'

I mentioned the priest's descriptions of the missing priestess, and our verification of the body. 'Of course, the body will be burned before long,' I continued. 'They have to give the impression the funeral rites are being conducted in accordance with Trymus' own laws.'

'Why would he have gone to all this trouble?'

I shrugged. 'That's what I've not yet worked out.'

'Looks like we'll have to find Lacanta, in that case.' Callimar grinned. 'Good luck with that.'

'It might not actually be too difficult . . .'

Callimar seemed confused. 'And what makes you say that?'

'A hunch.'

'A hunch, he says?' Callimar chuckled to Leana. 'Where do you think she is hiding?'

'Destos,' I declared, and added, 'possibly.'

'Has she gone on holiday?'

'Something like that.' I described my discussions with Lillus, and produced the map. 'Admittedly it's not much to go on, but Destos is near enough to Tryum that, if she is working with Licintius, he can see that she is well looked after. But it's far enough that she might never be found. Destos is also where the wealthy go to escape Tryum – she may have a fondness for it from her childhood, and know it reasonably well. More importantly, it's safe.'

He scrutinized the map and didn't seem much impressed by it. 'This map is useless, as far as maps go. You think she'll be in a safe house?'

'I suspect it will be large enough to house her and some form of protection,' I replied. 'I can't imagine she'd hide out in a cave, not after she's spent her life in Optryx. We must examine all the major properties in the region.'

'In that case, we might need more than my men. I can arrange that – auxiliaries in Maristan can do the grunt work, and those on the border can be here by nightfall.'

'If it can be done quietly, all the better. Military movements on the border could cause all sorts of problems. We'll need scouts and agents, lots of them.'

'All easily arranged. Sixty miles to the border, which is a day's ride for the best of our riders. It could be two or three days before we start to see some real military presence. We're not restricted by time are we?'

'I don't know. The king will probably think I'm still in the city but, even so, he might see more assistance is sent to wherever Lacanta is hiding. And if we find her, we'll need her to remain alive. She must be prevented from killing herself or from being put to the sword. Only then can the picture become complete. We need a confession and there's still so much that I do not know.'

Callimar reflected on the subject for a moment, rubbing his jaw. 'I'm guessing this wasn't the homecoming you had in mind.'

'You could say that.'

'Then you'll need a stronger drink than water,' he replied, standing up. 'I'll fetch some wine.'

That night, while messengers and riders were moving across the countryside, quietly altering the destiny of nations, I bedded down in the barn in the company of two veterans. We talked for a while about politics and joked about Sun Chamber administration. Stories were exchanged and there was a light-hearted effort at one-upmanship. Because I was well educated, one of them then asked me if I believed it was possible for one of his former lovers to have successfully placed a curse upon him, and I said honestly that I had never yet seen evidence of a curse working. It seemed to ease his concerns, though I did not want to ask him what he had done to receive one in the first place.

Eventually, Leana and I were left alone. As we rested there were other soldiers patrolling the local terrain to make sure we were kept safe, and it was the first time in a long while I had felt relaxed enough to think clearly. Exhaustion overwhelmed me, so much so that once I had laid down with Leana watching over me, my head wouldn't come back up. For a moment I thought another seizure was coming, but I remained quite awake and mentally alert. Meat was being cooked on a nearby fire sheltered by the ruined door of the barn. A few more of the veterans returned to tell jokes.

I wanted to join them. To be in better spirits.

It must have been my new-found freedom that made me think obsessively of Titiana that night. Given the pace of my exit from Tryum, I had not really had time to come to terms with what had happened. I had not shed a single tear at my father's demise and yet the short intensity of my relationship with Titiana — something born of passion — combined with this sudden calm, all seemed to drag me into a deep misery. All my frustrations and rage were focused onto King Licintius.

The Search

The morning passed uneventfully and so Leana took the opportunity to work with me on my sword skills. There were no wooden practice swords so I kept alert and impressed myself by managing to deflect the majority of her blows.

'I could have killed you twice,' she declared afterwards.

'I coped better than usual in that case.'

She grunted either satisfaction or dissatisfaction – I could never quite tell, even after all these years together.

A little before noon, another rider returned, on a fresh horse, having ridden through the night. While the horse was rubbed down, the messenger, showing no signs of struggling after a lack of sleep, revealed that our requests were being put into action. Our superior officers were discreetly journeying to the region. Auxiliaries were being smuggled across the border and into Detrata. The wheels of the Sun Chamber moved quickly, subtly, but to a startlingly efficient degree.

The makeshift camp was packed away leaving no trace of anyone having being there, and that afternoon we set off in a north-westerly direction, through the rolling hills. Three other groups headed along different roads, mainly to keep our numbers down to a minimum so as not to attract too much attention.

Our group followed a trail near an aqueduct supplying Tryum, but at a distance – keeping the structure in sight at all times as a navigational aid.

The following days were among the most frustrating and dull I had ever experienced. Time seemed to stretch out due to my impatience, and the vast and sun-bleached landscape expanded to the horizon without varying, rarely promising anything to break up the day.

Our journey took us through farmland first, then wilder grass-lands and forests that banked up steep inclines. I hadn't noticed it in the city, but here were the subtle changes of nature that indicated the turn towards colder weather. Certain plants were flowering, other kinds had died, and the leaves were becoming speckled with brown, as if autumn was some disease.

Our days were long and uneventful. During this time, Leana had made something of a friend in Callimar. They talked of combat technique and weapons, topics for which I could muster little interest. He was keen to learn the arts of Atrewen killing and Leana grew very talkative, to a surprising extent. Killing was something that was occasionally necessary, but I preferred it that people remained alive – these two, however, talked with noncha-lance, perhaps with little regard for the shattered families or ruined futures that death could bring to the living. It was the way of a warrior and I accepted that.

I accepted, also, that I was no warrior.

'You two seem to get on well,' I said to Leana, lingering at the back of the train of horses.

'We do. He will share wine with me and treat me as an equal. A nice change from Tryum.'

'Tryum had citizens from all over the known world,' I pro-tested. 'You could share wine with all sorts of people.'

'Your idea of "all over" is very different from mine,' Leana grunted. 'Some people would share wine with me down-city. Up-city they treated me like a trinket. They just stared. In Venyn there were plenty of people from the south, from Atrewe and beyond, many different cultures, and many of them were successful people also. Here it is less so – the only people who hold power in Detrata are from Detrata. I grew tired of the comments, Lucan. I grew tired of the staring. Tryum is not the marvel you think it is.'

As for my own relationship with Callimar, I had grown up significantly from my days in the academy. Back then he had much to teach me, both officially and unofficially, and our friendship was one of those best left in a certain time and place, but nothing could be achieved by revealing such sentiments. I was polite and courteous to him, but found our conversations strangely lacking in substance. Memory might also have exaggerated those more innocent times back then. It seemed to me that, if not careful, one could romanticize the past beyond all recognition.

The nights were cooler, but the midday heat was still powerful. We wore light hooded cloaks for shade, and I worried for the health of our horses. We camped under the stars with a soldier on sentry duty. I volunteered to do the job myself, rather liking the idea of staring into the indigo sky as dawn broke across the grassland, but Callimar insisted a military man do the job. Perhaps I would have been more interested in the poetry of the landscape than where a particular threat may have been coming from, but I happily took my sleep anyway.

We were not, to our knowledge, being followed and we had not, to our knowledge, been seen by anyone other than traders, villagers or those toothless priests who crawled across the countryside searching for gods that I'd never heard of.

After two nights the landscape changed again to endless acres of farmland and plantations, indicating that we had finally arrived in the region of Destos.

'You'd better be sure she's here,' Callimar whispered to me.

'You already know I'm not,' I replied.

'I've not told the others that.'

At a small hamlet, which formed the hub of the local agricultural community, we managed to purchase maps from a family in need of coin. With a necessary lack of subtlety, we quickly gathered what little information we could about the region, where the larger villas were likely to be, whether wealthy people from Tryum owned any land, where small settlements were, and so on. We covered half the region's hamlets in a day.

As we moved on, an agent of the Sun Chamber caught up with us, having received a notification about our mission. Callimar seemed to know him well enough, which put me at ease.

An expert in the region, he had discovered the whereabouts of three large villas not marked on any map, nor did they seem to be known to locals. The villas were away from a road, hidden by geography and at the far end of the region, by the coast. Callimar arranged for the agent to try to reach the others of the Sun Legion, who had headed out in slightly different directions, and for us to reconvene at a specific point along the coast.

But that night we lay under the stars, the nearest town being miles away. Beneath their cloaks, the soldiers' armour reflected the warm light of the campfire, a stark contrast to the darkening skies around us. Callimar stood on the edge of our small encampment, regarding the distance with his usual stern expression.

Deeper into Destos

We were up before the sun, making our way deeper into Destos. In the morning we investigated two villas a mile apart from each other, both sprawling complexes fit for a royal, but we found no signs of life. The first villa had been put up for sale but no one had made a claim for it, while the second was in the hands of a retired general who only used it on occasion. We searched each property but there were no signs of anyone living in them. They were splendid places and it seemed such a waste for them to stand empty.

In the afternoon we met up with a scout and reached the third property of the day, smaller and tucked away in a copse. I approached the main entrance with the scout, with Callimar, Leana and the others around the other side to see if anyone made an exit. Yet its inhabitants were a wealthy couple who used the place as a holiday home, and their story stood up well.

On the slow trek away from the property, my heart began to sink. We could search these places for ever and still find nothing. Callimar said little, but his expression revealed a growing scepticism, one that I was starting to share myself.

*

Another cool, uneventful evening followed, but by morning the agent had connected with our camp. He spoke of a property on the coast, concealed under a cliff-face. He had spotted movements of what looked suspiciously like soldiers in disguise making their way to and from the place the previous afternoon, yet nobody local knew of any owners.

We followed the agent's lead and rode towards the coast and, along the way, met up with a large group of Callimar's veterans. Our small force grew to twelve.

This was not the Destos I remembered. It was supposed to be lush and vibrant, a playground for the rich of Tryum. Some of the grasslands we went through had been tortured by the sun over the past few weeks, leaving dried-up riverbeds and wilting plants. Some farm dwellings had long been abandoned. There were large villas that had fallen into ruin, paint cracked, materials stolen for rebuilding elsewhere. Even the isolated, more cultish temples had fallen into disrepair — it was no way to treat a god, whatever one's persuasion. These were symptoms of the state of Detrata and made the sentiments of senators who yearned for the old days understandable, if unreasonable.

We reached the coastal track in late afternoon, with the Ferrous Sea to one side as calm as could be and sandstone cliffs directly below us. Our agent told us that we only had a short way to go. The path wound down through large gorse bushes dotted with yellow flowers, and eventually our procession came to a halt.

Callimar rode back towards me. 'How do you want to play this one, Drakenfeld?'

After a moment's reflection, I said, 'The most important thing of all is that Lacanta remains alive. If she sees several soldiers running towards her, there is always the risk that she may take her own life. What's your view?'

'She'll have protection. We should wait until nightfall, examine if there are any guards, eliminate their threat without drawing attention, and break in to the villa. If she's there.'

I turned to the agent, a tall, skinny fellow in sand-coloured clothing, who had a cool, detached expression. He replied, 'I'll go down and survey the situation again. Expect me again at dusk, no sooner.'

'Good.' To Callimar I said, 'Whatever we plan, I'd prefer it if we could keep the killing to a minimum.'

'As weak a disposition as ever, eh, Drakenfeld?' Callimar chuckled and held his arms wide like a bargaining merchant. 'We'll try. But sometimes a little blood is unavoidable.'

With no campfire, and hidden well away from the road, we waited for the agent to return. Callimar possessed a remarkable talent for making himself and his veterans invisible. It was a lot cooler here with the breeze washing in from the sea and we ate uncooked, meagre rations. Callimar had requested noise be kept to a minimum and we occupied ourselves with nothing but quiet contemplation.

As the sun slipped from the sky, I felt the chances of bringing the murders into the light were going with it. We had trekked halfway across Detrata on a whim because of a book I'd spotted on Lacanta's shelf. It was a thin connection, but I had nothing else to go on. The grim faces of the soldiers made me wonder if we had all been wasting our time.

'Someone approaches,' called a voice.

As expected it was the agent, who dismounted with a sense of urgency and marched directly towards me, surrounded by the others.

'What have you seen?' I asked.

'At least two soldiers walking the perimeter of the property,

and someone I believe to be female standing in the gardens looking out across the sea.'

'You believe to be a female?'

'Yes. Her form was feminine, but her hair had been cropped.'

'A woman trying to disguise herself,' I wondered aloud, growing more excited at the prospect.

A Cliffside Villa

Night came and we moved down the hill towards the villa —
myself, Leana and the veterans, who were all prepared for combat
with their armour strapped tightly and clutching short swords.
The road sloped gently at first, before turning into a dirt track
taking a more precarious zigzag down towards the sea. There
were cart tracks here, indicating regular traffic, perhaps for food
or supplies, or even an important guest or two.

Swiftly, we spread ourselves out into a thin line, three veterans
hurrying ahead, and the rest of us deliberately lagging behind.

Down through the trees I could see that the location below
was precisely as the agent described. It was one of the most wonderful places imaginable. The light of the moon indicated where
the sea ended and the cliff-side gardens began, but the tidal roar
seemed to come from everywhere. The building itself was a large,
square whitewashed structure, with a gap in the middle for more
formal gardens and a fountain, the top of which we could see
easily from our elevated approach. The cliffs extended up either
side and, out to sea, stood an outcrop of rock that looked like
the arm of a god reaching for the moon.

Towards this serene retreat, a second faction of the veterans abandoned the road and slunk down between the trees, heading for the rear of the property. That left Leana, myself, Callimar and one other soldier. We left the track and headed around to a side wall. I heard a muffled noise to one side, but then nothing more.

Moments later, one of the other veterans trotted towards us holding a blade. 'From a guard, now dead. It's a Detratan short sword, standard military issue.' He threw it to one side.

'It's definitely her then,' I said, with more belief than ever.

We waited for the other veterans to confirm that all the guards had been dealt with, before moving on to gain access to the property.

All the soldiers headed around to the front and shortly would set to work busting down the double doors. Meanwhile, myself, Leana and Callimar scaled one of the rear walls using rope. I must admit I was not as agile as I used to be and, with every lurching grip of the rope, I could sense Leana's disapproval.

I landed inside, just about avoiding a large rose bush, and stepped into the wide ornamental garden. We drew our swords, and walked towards the rear of the villa, when I heard an explosion of wood. Screams came, followed by the emergence of several cloaked figures who came dashing towards us. They stopped running and looked around, some with panicked expressions; a few of the others tried to hide their faces from view. The rest of the soldiers filed in behind them and formed a long line with their swords at the ready. The gathered throng realized they were surrounded and there was nowhere for them to run.

I stepped forward. 'My name is Lucan Drakenfeld, Officer of the Sun Chamber, and this is General Callimar. I believe you've just met his Sun Legion veterans. A woman known as Lacanta, sister to King Licintius, is being kept hidden among you. We wish for her to be handed over immediately.'

No one answered. Callimar marched forward and grabbed a middle-aged man, who fell to his knees so Callimar had to drag him along on the grass in front of the line of captives. 'Right, let's not piss about!' Callimar shouted. 'If no one answers us, this one loses a hand. If no one answers again, he loses a foot and so on. You get the idea.'

Wearily I asked the question once more, and again no one said a word.

Callimar wasn't bluffing: under the moonlight, he knelt beside the man, whose hood fell back to reveal a gaunt, pale face. Callimar stretched out the man's arm, pressed his hand down on the grass and, with two hefty chops, hacked into the arm.

The man wailed in agony, collapsing sideways as his blood surged across the grass. Callimar reached back to grab the man's foot, and pulled it aside with phenomenal strength, toppling him, still screaming, onto his back.

'Ask again!' Callimar shouted.

So I asked my question again.

At this point, a woman in a shawl moved forward and pleaded with us to stop. 'He meant no harm. Please, just leave him alone.'

I marched over to her and pulled back her hood. The woman's hair had been cut short not that long ago, and I was struck by how startlingly similar she was to the murdered priestess.

'Lacanta,' I breathed.

We assessed each other, neither of us having worked out what we'd do should this situation arise. Relief overwhelmed me. This supposedly dead woman had filled my thoughts and defined my actions ever since I had returned to the city. Now here she was.

Leana stepped in alongside me, pointing the tip of her sword at Lacanta's face. 'Let's question her inside.'

Lacanta stared defiantly along the blade.

'Callimar,' I called back. 'We need to ensure any accomplices are kept somewhere safe for now.' I faced Lacanta, still talking to him. 'We're going to take her into the house.'

Lacanta regarded me with nothing but a cool, distant fury.

We discovered a pleasant room inside the villa. The doors opened to face the sea, and a soldier stood guard outside to prevent anyone escaping.

I let Lacanta feel free enough to recline on a couch, while I paced around the room scrutinizing the trinkets, goblets and other tableware, marvelling at the objects. The villa was every bit as resplendent on the inside as it was on the outside, with a breathtaking level of detail on everything, from silver cups to carved chairs.

Leana drew up a chair alongside Lacanta, then lit a few candles and lanterns nearby. She moved one nearer the table in order to cast a light on the royal face. Again I was taken aback by how much she resembled the priestess.

'Did he have to cut off his hand?' These were the first words to come from Lacanta's lips, addressed to any one of us in the room.

Clearly she had been used to making decisions. Her voice was strong yet soothing, her pale green eyes rather disarming. There was a beguiling quality to her face; it was one of striking symmetry and balance. The words and descriptions of others had led me to form opinions of her personality and of her tone. I had fabricated her entire character in my mind, but now there was the need to start all over again.

'I didn't think he would cut it off. You know soldiers.' I inched away to examine the frescoes on a wall. Another silence passed. I was happy to let any impatience get the better of her.

'What will you do with me?' she asked, watching the silhouette of the soldier outside the doors.

'We must wait and see,' I replied. 'You were involved in the murder of an innocent priestess. Yet your brother has done a splendid job in fooling the city and the Senate of Detrata into thinking you were very much dead. To my understanding and experience, the law is not clear on these matters. Alive or dead you are, however, physical evidence of the dishonest actions and words of a king, to his people and his Senate, so you will return at some point to Tryum. You might find you're not as popular as you were when you had been supposedly killed.'

The sea continued to churn at the cliffs below, booming into the distance.

'For now, we have plenty of time to process the strange actions of your brother. His lifestyle was certainly interesting; his activities rather curious, as were his strange antics down-city.' I stared at her more closely, and recalled Drullus. 'Not to mention his lover.'

She was visibly taken aback by my comment, so I stayed with that line of questioning.

'Of course you know all about that, don't you?' I said. 'You've had a while to become familiar with it.'

'I've no idea what you're talking about.'

'The actors told me everything, Lacanta, all the details – so there's no point in denying it. You'll only waste our time.'

'And how could actors have possibly seen anything?' Lacanta fell silent, before muttering, 'We were so careful. No one could have seen a thing.'

I frowned at that, trying to discern her meaning. 'Does the name Drullus mean anything to you?'

'Nothing at all.'

Confused, I began to analyse her words. Lacanta thought I was talking about something else entirely – not the king's relationship with Drullus, but of another relationship. By a quirk of fate, she'd just made a confession about something I had never thought to question.

It slotted in with so many other things: the fact that neither of them had married; that Lacanta pretended to bed other people, but never actually went through with it; the reason she had taken part in the staging of her own death. It had never occurred to me that, one day, Lacanta may have wanted to return to Tryum, albeit in a different guise.

'Drullus was an actor that the king associated himself with – you know, on his trips down-city. He confided in Drullus. He told him about your relationship with each other, and Drullus in turn told me.'

She shook her head. 'Drullus is just a nobody. How could he have known? Licintius would never have said anything to a mere actor.'

'It's called incest, Lacanta, no matter how you dress any of this up.'

Lacanta could no longer meet my gaze.

'This is what you planned,' I continued. 'You hoped to return one day, with a different hairstyle, new clothes, perhaps different jewellery and make-up. Combined with another name, you hoped that no one would notice.'

Still she said nothing; still she avoided my eye.

I crouched down beside her, and searched for a more gentle approach. 'You saved yourselves for each other, isn't that right? You were fooling a city so that you could get away with your illegitimate love. And you killed a poor innocent priestess to dupe a nation.'

'You shouldn't be so smug,' Lacanta snapped.

'Meaning?'

'We had help,' she replied.

'I imagine that it's the kind of task that cannot be done alone.'

'No, you don't understand – we had help.' She paused. 'From a Drakenfeld.'

Lacanta gave me a suddenly confident look, not quite a smile – something more sinister than that. My heart sank and I closed my eyes for a moment, but there was no avoiding it. At the back of my mind there had been a nagging doubt about how my father had come into so much money, a doubt that also led me to think that he may have found the missing priestess and was the reason she remained missing.

'So now what will you do?' Lacanta sat back and took on a different, more arrogant manner entirely. Here she was, back in control, the one with power. 'Will you want to implicate your precious, beloved father in all of this? It will ruin his lovely reputation. It will ruin your delightfully honest family name. And do not think I won't mention it to as many people as I possibly can.'

'Tell me what he did.'

I knelt beside her, allowing her to continue, almost at a whisper.

'We needed a body in place of mine,' she said, 'someone who looked like me. Who better than someone who deals in such matters as missing people, skilled in the knowledge of how easy it is for people to disappear from the city. Someone who, on occasion, locates them on behalf of others.'

'An Officer of the Sun Chamber,' I breathed.

'Your father was badly in need of money. In exchange for supplying us with someone who might look like me, we would give him ample amounts to pay off his debts.'

Which explained the sudden arrival of money.

'It took him many weeks until we could find someone who would fit. He killed himself not long after. The quiet, moralistic ones are the worst – one never quite knows how they will react under pressure.' Her face became more spirited now, her voice warmer, kinder. 'But it does not have to be this way, Drakenfeld. We can both take our secrets with us. No one has to know any of this. You can leave here now and no one need ever know about the shame on your family. You will have my word on that.'

Questions and Waiting

The veterans took it in turns to watch Lacanta, though I respected her right to privacy — she said it was indecent for a woman of her position to be stared at by such men and she was right. So Leana handily volunteered to spend the night in Lacanta's room, watching over her. We cleared her room of her possessions and anything that could be used as a weapon. A dagger was found beneath her pillow.

Nearby I noted another three books on Destos, one of which was a more detailed piece of travel writing, though much like the one I had seen in her room in Optryx. Was one of these the object removed from her room, leaving a mark in the dust? Concealed in another book was yet another piece of paper, with more clear and obvious script than the paper I'd originally found, but it was updated and much easier to follow. This time there was no doubting it was a map.

Without Leana present I was careful to use the apothecary's herbs I'd brought with me. The tisane certainly calmed my mind enough for me to have faith in herbs for a night — it made a change from having faith in gods so that they did not punish me. On deeper reflection, Polla might have agreed. The herbs might not always work, either, but since I had been taking them regularly I had not experienced anything notable in my sleep. The world was full of uncertainties but, thankfully, for the first time in a long while my seizures were the least of my concerns.

Sleep came easily. It was peaceful and deep, the best for weeks. I woke up refreshed and saw everything with a heightened sense of clarity.

After an initial debate between myself and Callimar, we decided to wait a couple of days in the villa with Lacanta while our agents did their work. If there had been regular contact between the property and the king's men, then our soldiers would intercept any carriages or horses travelling to the property. At first it seemed strange that Lacanta had brought such a small entourage with her, but perhaps she had wanted as few people as possible knowing the plan.

The men with her, it transpired, were all eunuchs. We only found out when one of them stripped himself naked before Callimar's men and pleaded with them not to hurt him. A lot of people who find themselves in captivity tended to do that when they had run out of options and become desperate.

We permitted Lacanta to walk in the gardens, both inside the property and out, with an armed escort. There was no reason to be needlessly cruel while waiting for her sentencing. Whenever she did, however, I decided to accompany her. Sometimes people would tell me strange things when they were more relaxed and sanguine about their fate. Her talent for conversation, when she opened up to me, was beguiling. It was obvious she was far more well read than myself, so before the beautifully serene view I merely let her talk more so that I might learn one or two things about the gods and the stars.

The conversation turned again to my father's involvement, and she asked me how I could so easily bring shame upon my family.

I reminded her that it was not I who brought the shame in the first place, and that I forgave him.

'Polla, I'm sure, will see that my emotion is kept out of such decisions when the time comes. Besides, given there is shame in my family, it only seems fair to correct that. Polla would approve. I hope.'

'What is so special about your goddess that makes you regard her so highly?'

'Nothing, I suppose, which is exactly why she is special. She encourages me to cast light into dark places, to investigate matters in the physical plane as best as I can, to the best of my abilities and to the benefit of Vispasia. She enables me to think on my own, to question everything. We respect our gods and goddesses like we would our own parents, but Polla seems to be a goddess whose advice is constantly effective. Her scriptures are practical, not judgemental; her priests and priestesses full of useful advice.'

'She sounds far more pleasant that Trymus. His priests seem more concerned with perpetuating his own glorious myths and moral absolutes than with advice.'

'You spoke of shame on my family,' I said, 'but do you have no shame about your sexual unions with your own brother?'

I expected her to say nothing, to look away, but instead she began to justify her actions. 'We shared a mother and a father – it hardly seems much of a bother to share a bed as well.'

'The gods disapprove,' I replied. 'The laws of nature disapprove. But, more importantly, the laws of Vispasia also disapprove.'

'Laws and gods . . . they do not understand matters of love. Our union was one of deep affection, full of tender and caring gestures. How many marriages in the city can claim such enjoyment? Not that many, I'll wager. How many women can claim to be so happy? Again, far too few. We have always been close, Licintius and I. The first time we slept together, it felt so perfectly natural – the most natural thing in the world, in fact. We merely had to create the pretence that it was not going on.'

'I could never connect your very austere room, and the fact that no one could actually claim to have been sleeping with you, with the reports that you flirted with everyone around you, and led a rather wild social life. It simply made no sense.'

'Well, now you know,' Lacanta said.

'It's such a shame that an innocent priestess had to lose her life over it. So many people have ended up dead because of your actions.'

'Who else?' she asked, quite surprised.

'You realize General Maxant is dead?'

'No . . . No, I didn't. What happened?'

She could have been lying about her ignorance, but I told her anyway – that he was murdered, that it was staged to look like suicide. I admit to still not knowing why Maxant died. My suspicions were that the king had silenced his general for knowing too much, but there was no proof of this.

Lacanta told me that she did not know Maxant well enough, but he seemed an honest if somewhat dull person. 'Hardly a man one could have a meaningful conversation with,' she said. Lacanta received little contact from Tryum and knew nothing of what was going on there. I tried to question what the arrangement was between her and her brother, how often they might meet up, but she was not forthcoming on the details.

In the end the clouds began to move in, bringing in a gentle, sideways rain that I first mistook for sea spray. Our conversation had, for the moment, reached an end. Together we headed inside.

The Sun Chamber Commissioner

Five long, repetitive days later we received notice that one of the most senior Sun Chamber officials was already on their way to the villa from Free State, and they would arrive the following evening.

Upon receiving the message, Callimar looked at me and muttered, 'You realize I've never even met a Sun Chamber commissioner, let alone worked with one?'

'Well, don't look at me like that,' I replied, 'neither have I.'

'Why are they sending her and not an administrator, or a commander?'

I shrugged. 'Maybe they fancied a holiday in Destos.'

We waited another six days, as it happened, due to the rough weather around the coast. The storms were glorious: forked lightning ripped between clouds in the late afternoon in a way I hadn't seen for years. However, the mornings were deceptively calm, allowing me to wander the local paths and discovering several plants that Lacanta said grew only in this region.

No incidents had occurred with her: she had been an intelligent and polite companion, and not at all as I had expected. It was obvious to see how she would have worked her brother's policies through the Senate so effectively, and made the hearts of many a senator skip a beat or two in her company.

On the morning of the sixth day, an entourage of Sun Chamber officials and soldiers were spotted approaching, so Callimar — strangely nervous — arranged for his veterans to tidy the place up as if it was on military parade. We saw to it that Lacanta was put in her room with two guards; her eunuchs, too, were under watch.

The rest of us stood on the front lawn, looking up to the dirt track, waiting for the arrival of our officials.

Eventually, they came: there must have been twenty horses at least riding down to meet us, with a dozen soldiers on foot. On the horses rode officials in resplendent Sun Chamber robes: largely black or dark colours, but with bold, yellow detail, and a huge embroidered golden sun upon the chest and back. They passed the line of trees and down into view, the officials at the front riding towards where we were standing.

One woman raised her palm for the entourage to stop. A man behind slipped off his horse and moved around to ease her down to the ground. She must be the commissioner.

After she had dismounted, the others followed suit. Two women and four men, each of them much older than myself, stepped in alongside her, each garbed in their fine silken robes of office.

The commissioner stepped forward to greet us. She was a woman of at least fifty years, with a good posture and ferocious, dark eyes. Her shoulder-length grey hair contrasted with her tanned skin; her nose and face were broad, and she had clearly become used to a good meal or two in later years.

'Which one of you lot is Lucan Drakenfeld?' she called out above the noise of the sea.

I stepped forward and descended to one knee.

'Oh do get up, Drakenfeld,' she said. 'You're the bloody reason I've come all this way. Save the ceremony for Free State.'

'Thank you for coming so soon, ma'am,' I replied.

She waved away my politeness and regarded the villa. 'Does this place have couches? Does it have a stove?'

'It has both,' I said.

'Good. My arse is sore and I've not had anything decent to eat since we left land.' She stormed inside, the others following in a long, equally glum chain. I suspected I was not the only one who didn't like travelling by sea.

We commandeered one of the studies, which did not have too many scrolls or books — but there were chairs and desks, which was enough to claim this as a base for operations.

I stood before the group of officials and the rather miserable commissioner, who introduced herself as Commissioner Tibus, third in rank of the entire Sun Chamber. Like Callimar, I had never met someone so senior, and I found myself quite nervous. It didn't help that her temper could have been improved.

I set out the scene for the officials, starting with the night back at Optryx where Senator Veron summoned me because of the murder of Lacanta, sister of the king. I took her step by step through my findings and methodology, discussing the trail down-city to investigate the actors, Drullus' death, my observations around the king's residence, discussions with other senators, the picture of deceit that had been cleverly built up over a long period of time, Maxant's death and, finally, the missing priestess of Ptrell — whose symbol I had seen in Optryx.

Commissioner Tibus regarded me without expression as I continued. I said I had confirmed that the body of the priestess had piercings, but that wasn't enough to go on, which was why the only proof was to track down Lacanta herself. Which is, I concluded, why we were all here, and I informed them of what Lacanta had told us so far — largely of her relationship with Licintius.

Commissioner Tibus nodded. 'Is there anything else?'

'There is, ma'am.' I took a deep breath before revealing my father's role in the set-up: that he supplied a lookalike for Lacanta so that everyone could be fooled, and that he did this to pay off his gambling debts. I concluded my story with Licintius' soldiers creating carnage in my home and our hastily arranged exit from the city.

'Licintius was obsessed with the theatre,' I added, 'and only now do I realize that everything had been staged, and he was busy scripting my own story.'

'The theatre, indeed.' Tibus whispered to one side, 'I never did have him down as a man of taste.'

'I suppose at first he had not wanted me there. But, as long as I was investigating the case — visibly — and trying to solve a murder that never actually happened, I was helping him to demonstrate his innocence. So long as I didn't make the connection, I would have been a boon to his case. He welcomed me there, but he had people watching my every move. He probably relished his own theatrics, attending public events lamenting Lacanta's death . . .'

Commissioner Tibus cleared her throat. 'Well now, have you anything else to add to this saga?'

'Only that for my family's role in this affair,' I said, 'I apologize. To you and before the wise gaze of Polla.'

Each of the gathered Sun Chamber officials regarded me with a cold stare; some made notes, others whispered something to the person beside them. I could not read the situation at all.

'Now you're quite sure of Calludian's — your father's — involvement?'

'I am, unfortunately.'

'Such a shame.' Tibus shook her head. 'He was a good one. Didn't we pay him enough?'

'As I said, he formed a habit for gambling – he had huge debts.' I left out the question of how my brother might have led him astray.

'So it goes,' Tibus declared. 'Still, that business could prove rather tricky to cover up. It won't go down well, I can assure you. That said, having the man's son expose him does seem to put a nice, honest spin on the matter.' Some of the officials nodded in agreement.

I had no intention of being seen as someone who exposed him; my father ought to be remembered for all his good points.

'Is Lacanta here still?' Tibus demanded.

'Yes, we've looked after her well. Someone remains with her at all times.'

'Good. I'll want to see her later. She must remain alive if I'm to bargain with Licintius. We must tread carefully – Detrata has a vicious streak of nationalism in it, more than any other nation in Vispasia. If we try to arrest Licintius outright, they could see it as a threat, and I daresay that will raise the chances of separatism from the Royal Union. Which we're honour-bound to prevent, lest anyone forget.'

'What should our next move be?' I asked.

'It's a tricky thing, dealing with royals,' Tibus said. 'It is through national donations that the Sun Chamber does so much. Yes, we help facilitate stability and trade, and all of those pretty things we say to each other when we're in council; but generally speaking we are meant to help kings and queens. The law is designed around the protection of such individuals and their property. We're not really supposed to arrest the buggers.'

'Ah,' I said, fearing that Licintius may go unpunished for the sake of diplomacy.

'So then,' she continued. 'I think that it is best this business be dealt with by Detrata's own Senate, and in Tryum. But we must present Licintius to the Senate in such a way that they can sentence him appropriately. These two siblings — do they claim to love each other?'

'As far as Lacanta tells me, they're obsessed with each other. They'd have to be to go to such great lengths.'

Tibus shook her head. 'In that case, we must send an army to the gates of Tryum and demand that Licintius present himself before his own Senate. Showing that Lacanta is alive — and more importantly showing to the people of the city that she is alive — will hopefully be enough of a combined threat so that he gives in to our demands. It will be a humiliation for him. We leave first thing in the morning. We will send word immediately to drum up auxiliaries from Theran and Maristan to accompany whatever we can send up from Free State. We'll not need more than two thousand soldiers — we're not starting a war. At least not yet.'

My eyes widened at the reality of bringing the Sun Legion to the gates of my home city. 'What if Licintius doesn't give himself up?'

Tibus gave me a big grin. 'He will when Tryum's cut off and under siege,' she said. 'There's nothing like a starving populace to make a king come to his senses.' She turned to one side and called back, 'Let it be known widely that Lucan Drakenfeld's work has shown excellence, and guts, the likes I've not seen for a good long while. More of this, please.'

Commissioner Tibus stood up with a groan and placed a palm on her lower back, rubbing it vigorously. 'But may Polla bless us — we are about to bugger with Vispasia's political fabric and unleash Polla knows what devilry onto the continent if we're not careful. Hopefully only just a little blood will be spilled if

Detrata can be left to settle its own affairs. Makes the job rather unpleasant otherwise.'

Tibus marched to the door and the others rose to follow, but she paused in the doorway. 'Now then, young Drakenfeld – I take it Callimar's soldiers haven't yet scoffed all the food?'

It took a little over a week to muster the necessary forces to march on Tryum. During that time we ate and drank, pillaging the stores in nearby villages and gathering the rations brought up from the boats. Commissioner Tibus and Callimar took it upon themselves to plan the assault on Tryum, and questioned me on its potential points of weakness.

'It's difficult,' I replied. 'There are a good number of loyal and patriotic soldiers based there, and the walls are high, wide and engineered to withstand an attack.' Though I was momentarily relieved not to have the responsibility of decision-making, I felt that I wanted to argue against the siege: to negotiate, to find a non-violent solution to the whole matter. 'It does not seem fair that a city will suffer because of the lust of two people.'

'It's about more than that,' Tibus declared. 'It is about punishing a king who has deceived his own people. If the people suffer, too, then they'll blame the king. Anyway, such a man is not fit for rule, though that decision is for Tryum to decide for itself – all we need to do is help that along. Besides, worry not, Drakenfeld. Hopefully it won't come to that. I've already sent agents into the city to see about bribing members of the King's Legion. Loyalty to gold is often stronger than that to a royal.'

The officials who came with her seemed to have little to say on the matter. Though apparently soulless and without much in the way of personalities of their own, they were adroit planners and would consult Tibus on every point of the forthcoming military operation, as well as hypothesizing over the political consequences. Letters and riders were dispatched with surprising regularity.

I merely contented myself with taking it in turns with Leana to watch over Lacanta, who now seemed to have accepted her fate. When there were just the two of us, she would talk quite openly: when others were around, she kept her thoughts to herself.

Eventually the time came for us to move out. Two small, barred wagons had been brought for Lacanta and her eunuchs, though she had one vehicle to herself. These mobile gaols were cushioned inside, and possessed a roof, so they were not entirely humiliating. It was, however, a world away from what she would have been used to as a royal. Once they had been marched to the top of the slope, the eunuchs were crammed into the other carriage. The huge trail of Sun Chamber officials, soldiers and prisoners eventually rolled up the hill and started on the long journey towards Tryum.

Siege Conditions

Two thousand soldiers marching towards my home city was a breathtaking sight. Through the dry grasslands that stretched for miles around the city, a handful of Sun Legion soldiers marched alongside auxiliaries from the neighbouring countries, following the line of aqueducts. Maristanian troops, it seemed, were only too keen to lend a hand in humiliating their ancient rivals.

Cavalry, spearmen, archers, engineers, siege towers and artillery troops armed with both stones and bolts, were all united under the banner of the Sun Chamber, a flaming sun emblazoned on black cloth. Dredging up a cloud of dust, this slow tide of violence trickled across the landscape. The sky remained cloudless all day.

'This is all your doing.' Commissioner Tibus rode up next to me to admire the view, munching on an apple.

I opened my mouth to say something, but I didn't know how to reply.

'I was joking, Drakenfeld,' she added. 'Well, partially anyway. It takes one Sun Chamber officer to bring a common thief to justice, but it takes an army to force a king to submit, such is the nature of power. Two thousand soldiers is not that many, but we need to show the likes of Licintius that we mean business. If he protests, like he did with our initial envoys, we can always summon more. We'll tell him that.'

'Have our agents been at all successful inside the city?'

'We've not heard back from them, so we must assume otherwise. Our envoys were turfed out without being given a proper hearing – that's a slap in the face to the Sun Chamber right there. Licintius knows the law, oh yes. He knows what to expect.' Tibus threw away the core of the apple and turned away.

Merchants – those who had not heard the news or noise of an advancing army – scattered from the roads to the city, drawing their horses across farmland at a rapid pace. A few people lingered to watch what was going on, unaware that their home city was about to be under siege. The gates to Tryum were closed and soldiers were lining the walls to the city. Behind us, the camp was being set up for a long stay.

Meanwhile, all the rest of us could do was wait.

A night passed while we waited for messengers to continue back and forth, for diplomacy to have its opportunity. The messengers had been perfectly clear: the king was to surrender himself for questioning on behalf of the Sun Chamber's highest authority. The Senate would take charge of affairs for the matter to be resolved. Whether or not Licintius passed this message on to the Senate was another matter.

Day came again, and traders or travellers who wanted to flee the city were driven from the city's gates without repercussion. Tryum was sealed. Small packs of cavalry rode around the city enforcing the blockade. Entry was forbidden by order of the Sun Chamber and it was at this point that Commissioner Tibus informed me that the river route towards the sea would shortly be blocked, too. All of this was to add pressure: to force Licintius to open the gates to the city and hand himself in.

Later, wondering vaguely how long it would take for a city to
starve, an idea came to me. I rode over to find Commissioner
Tibus, who was in her leather command tent along with Callimar, and I made a proposition to them.

The three of us walked back out to the viewpoint, looking
down on Tryum.

'I don't want my people to go hungry,' I said.

'No one wants that,' Tibus agreed. 'What's your idea, Drakenfeld?'

'It's in everyone's interest for this whole thing to end as soon
as possible. Well, that can be two ways – either Licintius hands
himself in or we break down the walls or gates and march in to
collect him.'

'Stating the obvious, Drakenfeld . . .' Tibus wiped her brow
with her handkerchief, looking increasingly annoyed with the fact
that I'd dragged her out into the heady sunlight.

'Not entirely. The first point may never happen, but I believe
there's a short cut to the second version.'

'Which is?'

'The aqueducts.' I gestured to the spectacular works of engineering that supplied Tryum with fresh water from the hills and
mountains. 'We can make our way into the city, through an aqueduct. There's hardly been any rain around here over the past few
weeks, except a storm that passed over Tryum – not the hills.
There are access points throughout the structures, aren't there?
Admittedly it could be some distance between them – but there
will be a way inside them. I know of at least one point where the
walls were broken and in need of repair. A tiny force can sneak
into the city while no one even realizes. I know those streets
better than anyone here, and I know my way around Optryx, too.'

'You want to lead a band of soldiers through one of those
things,' Tibus said. 'I like it. General?'

Callimar smiled. 'I'll not let you go in alone and have all the fun. Who can we take with us?'

'A unit to go after the king and a unit to open the gates,' Tibus declared, commandeering the plan. 'We could do with bribes being arranged where possible – and a couple of agents doing the dirty work. As young Drakenfeld keeps reminding us, non-violence is the key – all of this is a gesture and a threat, nothing more. We don't depose kings in these circumstances; we let the bodies within the nation decide on the best course of action.'

Callimar added, 'We could arrange for a decoy on the opposite side of the city – move a few siege weapons into place, to look as if we are planning to gain entry from another gate. While the city's forces are all looking in one direction, we'll crawl in through the other.'

I took a deep breath, relieved that my whim was not as ridiculous as I had first imagined, and that the people of Tryum might not have to go without food after all.

We spent the morning resting in anticipation of the forthcoming operation, then later that afternoon Leana and I headed out on foot with fifty infantrymen and two of our engineers, short, cheerful and intelligent men who couldn't stop arguing with each other. While the heat was beginning to fade, we set out on our route away from Tryum, heading along the largest-looking of the aqueducts, looking for a point of entry or a weakness that could be exploited. The aqueducts around Tryum were two centuries old, the engineers explained, designed at the start of the Detratan Empire, and formed the blueprint for the structures that today littered Vispasia. Each one was fundamentally the same and each shared precisely the same incline for the water to flow.

We only had to march for less than half an hour until our engineers located what they thought was the best way in. To gain access to the deck, which carried the water, we had to climb up onto the upper tier of two immense rows of stacked arches. At the top we would find one of hundreds of manholes, but it would not be easy for fifty-something people to climb up. Instead we marched to where the aqueduct collided with a hillside: there the tunnel would continue for a short way through the land itself.

The ascent took another half an hour, owing to the temperature and having to navigate past the overgrown gorse bushes that blighted the hillside. Eventually, we all made it. Tryum stood in the far distance and the square manhole was right before us. We shuffled forward in single file, the engineers, Callimar, Leana and myself at the head of the line. A small wooden hatch, about three feet wide, covered a slightly raised square hole. The engineers opened it up with so little trouble I wondered why we needed them to come along. Soon torches were lit and brought forward.

Leana volunteered to go down first. She did not take the rope she was offered, but nimbly climbed down and dropped the couple of feet until she made it to the water deck, where she made only a shallow splash.

'It is all right,' she called up. 'There is little water down here.'

Callimar followed her down using a rope; I passed him down a torch while he was halfway, and he took it inside. After Callimar, I sat up on the side, dangling my legs in, then tentatively grabbed the rope, easing myself down onto the water deck.

Inside was aged stonework, a low curved ceiling above us and beneath our feet the flat bed where the water flowed. Unsurprisingly it smelled of damp, and a thick, viscous slime coated the sides. We moved forward to give room for the others as they climbed down, many of them bringing torches with them. Soon the tunnel had filled with soldiers, the clamour echoing for some way. Callimar issued orders for silence, which was not easy for those wearing armour.

I stared at the blackness beyond, thinking of the couple of miles of this we would have to negotiate, but Leana nudged me forward, having acquired a torch of her own from one of the others.

'Come,' Callimar whispered. 'It's time you showed us around your city.'

The journey in the dark took much longer than I thought. We tried not to stumble or make too much of a noise. The darkness ahead was punctuated only by thin slivers of fading light that managed to work around the wooden manhole covers, but as dusk came we could rely only upon the torches.

A good hour into the journey, my pulse began to race: we could hear the noise of soldiers outside Tryum's walls, or perhaps it was the noise from within Tryum; it was difficult to tell. All I knew was that we were nearing our destination, the heart of Tryum itself.

Callimar called back behind him and fifty short swords were at once unsheathed.

It took a little while until we reached the broken stonework of the aqueduct deep inside the city. There remained a shattered hole to one side and I peered through the gap up at the stars now starting to define themselves above the city. Immediately to one side was a rooftop, and down below the streets were eerily empty. Our torches were extinguished and left standing upright within the channel of the aqueduct. One by one we climbed down onto the next rooftop, jumped down onto a lower one, then down onto the street, where we immediately split into much smaller groups.

The plan was to go about the city unnoticed enacting three

tasks. Twelve of us, myself and Leana included, would make our way to Optryx. Around twenty soldiers would head independently towards the gates of the city, while the remainder hung back should the first operation fail. They would then see that the gates could be set alight or bribes could be given to various members of the King's Legion.

With spectacular professionalism, everyone disappeared into the night. Meanwhile, I regarded the streets, staring at the vacant benches outside a tavern, at the temples with their doors closed. There appeared to be so few people, and those who we passed were almost scuttling about the city with a furtive purpose, or were simply drunk.

Tryum's silence permitted us to hear the roar of the soldiers outside. I hoped the commissioner would keep to her word, that the noise was a simple distraction and not an effort to gain entry into the city through violence.

I led the group through the Polyum district, and eventually Regallum. The huge Temple of Polla, with its torches either side of the wide staircase, was a beacon on a night like this. We hurried along under Polla's gaze, keeping close to the walls and remaining as much as we could in shadow. A soothsayer shambled into my path and I nearly knocked her to the ground; her one eye regarded me as she let me know what she thought of me. I apologized and ran to catch up with the others.

The road to Optryx was devoid of life and, as hoped, there were few soldiers around. Many of them would have been required to attend to the threat from the siege. The four guards standing to attention on the portico walked out to intercept us, only to find themselves immediately overwhelmed. Callimar and another Sun Chamber soldier immediately gained the better of them. They were struck down before they could draw their weapons, bodies dragged to the other side of the street where their throats were cut to make sure. Blood seeped across the paving stones.

Another handful of soldiers from the King's Legion came out to investigate. Seven of our group diverted their attention while Callimar, Leana, myself and two others slipped around the perimeter of the courtyard inside the gated entrance. Those engaged in combat drew the king's soldiers well out of sight. Meanwhile, we headed around the side, avoiding the main entrance.

We breached the first of many ornamental gardens, careful to remain quiet. I checked back but it seemed no one had followed us. Starlight had grown brighter, and there was a beautiful fragrance coming from the plants around. Had it not been a mission of some urgency, it would have been pleasant to have remained longer to explore this place.

Needing any point of entry, we headed towards a slight glow from one side of the palace: it was an open door with a couple of candles lit inside.

We burst in and startled three people, two men and a woman, all of them naked on one of the tables in a dining room, alongside the light of a lantern. Callimar immediately claimed a position of authority and demanded that they answer for themselves. The woman sheepishly drew up her dress from the floor and begged forgiveness. One of the men slunk into the darkness in one corner, where he began weeping; the other stood trying to cover himself up.

The woman, who must have been a good ten years older than I was, was senior to the two, much younger, male servants. She pleaded with Callimar not to say anything to get her into trouble. The general kept his cool and ordered them to get to their own quarters immediately and say nothing, otherwise he would report them.

They all sprinted out into the gardens in various states of undress, leaving us with a way into Optryx. Callimar said, 'The things people do to occupy themselves in a siege.'

I laughed, reached to put out the flickering lantern when that harsh smell suddenly came to me . . .

Leana was standing over me, explaining something to the other soldiers in the darkness.

'What the hell is wrong with him?' someone said.

'Seizures,' she declared. 'An innocent thing. It is nothing to worry about.'

'He's cursed,' one of the others called. 'Tainted. I've seen it before.'

'Devilry,' said another.

'He was like an animal.'

Callimar snapped back at them while Leana helped me to my feet. My muscles ached. 'I don't care what's wrong with him — touched by a god or otherwise, right now we're here to hunt Licintius.'

There it was: the glares of the soldiers, the deep look of distrust, fear. Even in the poor lighting of the room, it was obvious how their faces had creased up in disgust. The sense of shame was overwhelming. That same look in Callimar's eye, too — someone who regarded me as a friend. A deep and awkward silence pervaded while I regained my composure.

'We continue,' I said.

Callimar nodded, but it took a moment until the others would follow.

'Where do you think he'll be?' Callimar snapped.

'He could be anywhere,' I replied. 'The temple, a room of contemplation, a war room — he might not even be here at all.'

'He will be,' Callimar said. 'Someone like Licintius won't be on the front line – he'll be skulking here, biding his time. He's probably too shocked to do anything.'

The residence was practically empty. What should have been a bustling place of servants, administrators, clerics, priests and traders seemed eerily silent. Voices echoed down the corridor and we would instantly look for an alcove to hide in. No lanterns had been lit and so Optryx remained in utter darkness.

We checked the various bedrooms and then those meeting rooms where I had conversed with Licintius. There was a small amount of activity in the kitchens, but when I noted several crates being carried down the corridor it occurred to me.

'He's planning to flee,' I whispered.

'Coward,' Leana replied.

'We'll stop him,' Callimar said. 'Don't forget, the rivers are blockaded out to sea, so he won't get that far.'

We continued with even more urgency, working our way deeper into the heart of the royal residence.

A cluster of soldiers spotted us in the corridor: we tried to get out of sight but they sprinted after us, their armour clamouring down the passage.

'We'll keep them back,' Callimar said. 'You go on. We'll catch up.'

I didn't need telling twice. Callimar and his men formed a line, each taking a fighting stance, waiting for the king's soldiers. Upon hearing their weapons starting to clash, Leana and I dashed through familiar halls that lined the way to the Temple of Trymus.

We paused as we saw the temple doors open.

Licintius.

He froze, just for a brief heartbeat, as he saw us. He dashed towards nearby doors. Two soldiers followed him out of the temple and remained to confront us; Leana slammed them both to one side, before she cut one of them across his throat, and sliced the back of the other's knee where there was no armour.

Sprinting across the dark, ornate hall, I called for Licintius to stop, but he continued to open the opposite doors and went through them.

Leana then caught up with me before running ahead through the doors and into the adjacent corridor, in pursuit of the king.

I turned the corner in time to see her whip her blade low through the air, clipping Licintius' heels.

The king collapsed face forward to the ground. Leana stood back for me to descend upon him. I arrived at his sprawling form, pressed my fingers into his throat and looked fiercely into his eyes while heaving deep breaths. Sweat poured down my face. From the look in his eye, both of us knew all I had to do was squeeze on his throat and that would be the end of it. I wanted to – for all he had done.

But no. A violent resolution might have felt satisfactory for a fleeting moment, but I represented the Sun Chamber, and followed Vispasian laws, those of a dignified culture, and I would not regress to the ways of some northern savage.

'Get him out of the way, in there.' Leana pointed to the nearest door. 'It is out of sight. I will check the other guards quickly before they recover and bring attention.'

I opened the door to a side room, which turned out to be an office of some description, then threw the king across the floor, gently closed the door, and watched over him, in an angry silence, waiting for Leana to return.

A Time for Answers

Eventually Leana came in and closed the door behind her. 'Both now dead. I hid the bodies in the temple.'

She lit one of three candles on the desk, while I regarded Licintius once again. In his boots and a dark green outfit that seemed more suited for travelling than the business of state, he looked like a man who had other plans tonight. I reached down to grab his hair, pulled him up onto his feet and shoved him back into one of the fine leather chairs.

The tip of my sword touched his throat. 'We have your sister, Lacanta, alive and outside the city walls.'

'Oh spare me any lectures.' Blood trickled down his grazed cheek from where he had fallen. 'I heard from your messengers, and I cannot exactly miss the army that is currently trying to gain access to my city.'

'It's only a matter of time before they get in. The gates will be opened one way or another and, very soon, they'll march Lacanta back along the roads chanting that she's alive and that you, Licintius, deceived the people of Tryum. Your subjects will soon learn to despise you.'

'So she's alive,' he said, showing more calm and control. 'That should be a time for rejoicing, surely?'

Smiling at his audacity, I said, 'She's admitted everything, Licintius, so there really is no point pretending otherwise. You'll just make yourself look even more foolish.'

He grunted a laugh.

'You really had me running about this city, didn't you.'

'I would have had you killed right at the start if I'd known how annoying you would become. The Sun Legion have come to my door anyway, so what does it matter now?'

'Every move I made while still alive contributed to your deception, didn't it?'

Licintius shrugged, seemingly oblivious to his situation.

'A man who sleeps with his own sister. The gods would be appalled.'

He glared at me. Once I would have been nervous at such a stare, but not now. 'When you spoke with Lacanta, did she mention a certain Drakenfeld senior?'

'She did. I've already brought up the matter with my superiors. If the subject is aired, then so be it. It is better to have such things out in the open than burning into my guilty conscience for the rest of my life.'

'What a sanctimonious bastard you are. How noble of you. How moral,' Licintius spat. 'What now?'

'We wait it out,' I replied. 'The gates will open soon. The soldiers from the Sun Legion will do their business. My superiors will take over the reins. I can finally get some sleep.'

'What about me? What will happen to me?'

'You'll be put before the men and women of the Senate, where the evidence will be presented. It will be up to your senators to show mercy or not.'

I explained what was known and the process of how his crimes had been exposed. In the end it couldn't be helped: I had to ask about Titiana.

'Who?' he asked.

I described her in more detail, every word of it almost sticking in my throat. 'I know that she was working for you.'

'Titiana . . .' Licintius said. 'Oh I bet you thought she loved you? How sweet of you. Yes, I wanted someone who knew you, ideally someone who could get close to you, but to find someone like her, skilled in the arts of subterfuge – that was fortunate. Senator Veron talks so much it was easy enough to find a place to arrange a chance encounter. Your history together was perfect. She loathed you at first, but then tolerated you, so I understand. The moment she told me all I needed to know . . . Well, one must eliminate all trails. I suppose it is only fair to let you know she never actually loved you, Drakenfeld. A man needs to know such things.'

I said nothing, simply staring at him, analysing every minute alteration in his expression to see if he might have been lying.

'What a sentimental young fool you really are.'

Leana placed her hand on my shoulder while I saw Titiana's hanging body in my mind once again. I considered striking Licintius down, or at least smacking the hilt of my sword across his forehead.

But dignity must be maintained.

There were still many questions that needed answering and over the following painfully slow hours of darkness I decided to try my luck seeking explanations from the king. Tiredness might have brought out a side of him that wished to tell the truth.

'I was impressed by the way you staged Maxant's death,' I began. 'Quite the masterpiece – poisoning him like that, arranging it to look as if he had killed himself. I know how you did it, I just don't understand why you did it.'

'You've worked out this much already,' the king sneered. 'Are you sure you cannot work out the rest?'

'I have my theories,' I said. 'That you had Maxant killed by some skilled assassin because he had done your dirty work and knew too much for your comfort. Perhaps you did the job yourself, if you could manage to escape the palace – you managed to sneak down to see those actors often enough. He was the one, after all, who probably killed the priestess in the temple – on your behalf. You could have had an argument with him; perhaps you never told him why he had to kill the priestess until then. I can imagine all sorts of scenes between the king and his favourite general.'

'Vispasia is better off with him dead. He would have wanted to lead his soldiers across to Maristan if he had the chance. You come here making your theories, but you have no idea about the tide I was holding back. With Maxant among them, those in the Senate would willingly revive the Empire. They'd want us to invade any nearby nation in a heartbeat. I was keeping Detrata in the Union.'

'Forgive me for thinking you not the most trustworthy person in the building. So are you admitting you killed him?'

Licintius shrugged off the question.

'Somehow,' I continued, 'you managed to get poison into his food or drink, and he threw it up over himself, didn't he?'

'Unreliable things, poisons,' Licintius said. 'Who can say how he ended up consuming such a nasty substance?'

'I know he killed Drullus, too, but I don't know why that poor actor had to be caught up in all of this.'

'Young Drullus had played his final role.'

I tried to work it out for myself from those few words. 'I think I get it now. He was a mouthy disturbance to make people think he had something to do with Lacanta's death. You hired him to do that, to be a clever distraction for whoever investigated the matter, to attract attention down-city. One last role to act.'

'He was a delightful actor, but then I knew sooner or later you might find him. Could he keep a secret? I didn't want to find out. How did you ascertain that Maxant killed him?'

I explained about the fresh henbane leaf Maxant had somehow brought with him to the city. 'And, of course, I only found that out because Maxant himself had been killed. So many deaths, Licintius. You've caused so much pain.'

'Ah, but my hands did not kill the priestess or Drullus. And you are forgetting one rather valuable thing. There is no law against a king ensuring that people are removed if they pose a threat to him,' Licintius muttered. 'That is our privilege. We are immune to common murder laws, as anyone could be a threat to us. Who are you to argue whom I find to be a threat or otherwise?'

The sun was about to break free of the rooftops when shouting could be heard, repeated constantly: 'Lacanta is alive. Your king has deceived you! Lacanta is alive. Your king has deceived you!'

The voice sounded a little frailer than I had hoped, possibly after having repeated the message a thousand times throughout the city. I could imagine Lacanta in her caged carriage being hauled through the streets for everyone to see. It would have been a deeply embarrassing and humbling moment for her. Now that it had all ended, I felt an overwhelming sense of exhaustion wash over me.

Licintius was asleep in his chair; Leana stood behind him with her blade.

'I'll go out and see what's going on,' I said. 'Will you be OK?'
Leana nodded.
'Try not to kill him.'

'You would not mind if I did,' she replied.

'No, I suppose this time I wouldn't.'

When my name was called loudly from the corridors I ran towards the source. Sun Legion soldiers rushed in. The gates of the city had been opened before dawn and our forces marched into the city. Only a hundred people had died in the confusion: many of Tryum's own soldiers had been bought off, but a few others foolishly followed the king's word rather than coin.

After the initial position had been secured, hundreds of soldiers filed in and escorted Lacanta's rolling cage through the streets as the news was called out. Apparently people gaped in awe: this was the first time many of them had even seen the king's sister, who was all the more famous since her staged death.

Lacanta and her eunuchs were paraded like the spoils of war through the city to Optryx. She remained outside the residence while soldiers began searching the premises – and that was what brought them here, to me.

I told them we had Licintius; they told us that Callimar and all his men had been found dead.

Poor Callimar had done so much to help me. Was it wrong of me to feel a little relieved at the fact that their knowledge of my seizures had died with them?

The whole process continued at breathtaking speed. Commissioner Tibus came personally to address the king and placed him under arrest. I'll never forget seeing his expression falter just the once at the acknowledgement of what might happen to him.

While our military personnel filled the residence, Licintius was taken to a safe room where he could be placed on suicide watch until his trial. A message went out to every senator of Tryum that by Vispasian, not Detratan, powers, an emergency session of the Senate would start within the hour. Attendance was mandatory.

However, what Licintius had told me was already starting to haunt me. If he wasn't bluffing and he was removed from control of the nation – with a warmongering senate taking control – just what would that mean for Vispasia? What if Detrata without Licintius then wanted to pull out of the Union, the very thing that the Sun Chamber worked so hard to bind together with its law? Ultimately, in some roundabout way, I could be responsible for that. The thought did not sit well with me.

Bad Memories

Many of the Sun Legion's forces and auxiliaries were present in the upper city, maintaining order surrounding Lacanta's carriage. There had been one crazed attempt at freeing her from a fanatic, but he had been killed on the spot and disposed of without further comment. No one else tried after that, though thousands wanted to see her in the carriage.

I gave my statement to the men and women of the Senate, the enormous domed building situated in the heart of Regallum. Veron was sitting in the front row, and made a brief wave before he maintained his serious countenance. Several rows of benches extended back behind him, each filled with senators.

It seemed strange to repeat all that I'd done in front of the gaze of Licintius and Lacanta, both bound and heavily guarded. Her expression was empty, her shoulders were stooped, and her skin grubby from travel across the country. In her simple dress she must have felt humbled, having previously been someone used to looking more glamorous in front of the senatorial class.

So I told my story, from the locked temple through to Maxant's body on the beach. My father's role as an accomplice was discussed, much to the surprise of those gathered there. After about half an hour, Tibus took over again and proceeded with the prosecution. Knowing that the spectacle could go on for hours – for this was just as much a theatrical production as a legal debate – I decided to leave, barely caring what would happen to Lacanta and Licintius.

My job was done, I was exhausted. I wanted to go home.

My property was vacant and had long been cleaned of corpses, so I sat alone by the fountain in the garden, staring at the spot where Titiana had hung. Sunlight streamed in over the roof of the house, and I basked in the sultry evening warmth. This place contained so many memories for me, so many happy occasions from my youth, all the way through to that horrific departure.

Leana stood over me.

'Do you mind if I ask you something?' I asked.

She shrugged.

'Forgive me for bringing it up, and I apologize if I offend, but how did you manage to cope with your husband's death, all those years ago?'

I was wary of bringing up the subject. Over the years I'd gleaned only that Leana's husband – she never told me his name – had died while protecting a prince as the wars raged throughout Atrewe.

'What makes you think I cope with it?' Leana replied.

'I can't pretend that Titiana's end hasn't somehow wounded me inside,' I whispered. 'I don't mean to even compare it to what you had – it's trivial, in relation, but it still hurts.'

'Of course it will,' Leana said softly. 'It is fine to feel pain. You want words of advice, Lucan?' She looked at me sincerely.

I nodded.

'It will hurt you whenever you think of it. But soon you will think of other things and the hurt will not strike you as often.

But it never goes and it is foolish to pretend otherwise.' Leana placed her hand on my shoulder. 'I am sorry for your loss. I grieve with you, my friend.'

Senator Veron was the first to come and find us and I was glad to see another friendly face. He told me that he had 'acquired' my house after the king had ordered my property forfeit when I left the city. He had not done anything to it yet, except clean it up.

'I was preserving it for you,' he said, and I genuinely believed him this time. 'But it seemed to be filled with foul spirits after what we found when we arrived. Some people tried to blame you at first – since you were the one who had gone missing. I knew better than that, and argued your case. It's all yours if you still want it.'

'Thank you, Veron.'

'Don't hang about here, Drakenfeld. The bad memories will eat at you. Stay at my place. My wife is still out of the city and I have plenty of wine for company. If you want, I'll buy this place off you and turn it into something without such memories. It could even become a prison to go with a new batch of cohorts.'

'That's a kind offer.'

'Of course it is. Look at what you've done, at all you've been through. Come back to mine. I'll see you're looked after well.'

'What did you do with Titiana's body?'

His expression softened and he sat beside me on the edge of the fountain. 'We burned her in a multi-god ceremony. We had a few priests of different temples. Her and the cohort – all of them were sent off together. It must have been a terrible sight for you to discover in your own home.'

That statement didn't warrant an answer. 'How did it go today?'

'He's dead,' Veron said. 'Licintius is dead and it took us six hours to arrive at that conclusion – rather short by our standards. It helped that Lacanta admitted much of it. She could hardly not, given that her being alive contradicted any possible defence.'

Veron told me that the king was not charged with the murders of the priestess, Drullus and Maxant, nor for the gods-angering relationship between brother and sister. Instead he was executed for willingly deceiving his Senate and his people.

For treason.

'He was dealt with in the same way as all those who commit such a crime, and beheaded. His execution happened in the Senate gardens, so at least he had a nice location for it. I'll show you his head later if you want. It's on a spike outside the Senate building.'

'Thank you, but no,' I replied. 'I've had quite enough of it all. What about Lacanta?'

'She has been exiled from Detrata for a period of ten years.'

'Really?' I asked.

'Yes. After you left, Licintius claimed that he acted alone, that Lacanta was merely following her king's orders. He said he'd personally banished her from the city, and that everything was his responsibility.'

'I guess he really must have loved her,' I said, 'to spare her life like that.'

I wondered just how much of that was true, knowing how smart Lacanta was in conversation. Her excellent mind could equally have helped in the planning. It was frustrating that Licintius could not be held to account for the actual murders because at the heart of all of this was the priestess: a young woman who had come to an exciting city for a new start, only to be held captive and ultimately killed so that a brother might be able to marry his own sister. Drullus and Maxant's deaths were more pointless acts, more lives erased for the hope of a corrupt love.

And Titiana, of course.

'Come on.' Veron stretched out his hand. 'Let's not linger here with our bad thoughts.'

Veron pulled me up, and he embraced me. 'It's good to see you again, friend. I had run out of people with whom to get drunk, and I don't wish to end up drinking alone like some poor drunk!'

Getting Away

We spent just the one night at Senator Veron's immense house. He was kind enough – though the more cynical might say he had his own career prospects in mind – to invite the other senior Sun Chamber officials to spend the night there also, and there were more than enough rooms to go around.

The dinner was sumptuous – big pheasants, fat fruits, exotic spices and tender rice. I suggested to Leana that this was a welcome break from being out on the road and she replied merely that I would become spoiled once again by such luxuries. Perhaps she was right, but tonight I dined heartily and didn't feel guilty in the slightest.

While Leana found herself a quiet spot in Veron's residence to pray to her spirits, I was able to speak in private with Commissioner Tibus. We sat on resplendent couches in an elegant office, while more and more people filed into Veron's house. The noise of distant chatter grew quite overwhelming. He had even brought in a pipe player to entertain his guests.

'Commissioner,' I said, 'I don't know if it is too soon to ask, but I would be grateful if you could help me to find a posting outside Tryum. There's nothing here for me now.'

She gave me a look of sympathy. 'We thought this might be the case, and it's just as well, Drakenfeld.'

'Why so?'

'Look at it this way – you've just unseated a bloody king and changed this entire nation. Word has reached me there are still a few royalists who are unhappy, even though they voted with the majority of the Senate. I would not be surprised if blood gets spilled on that Senate floor before too long. Worry not,' Tibus continued. 'I'll see to it that you don't hang about long. We'll have need of that mind of yours in darker places than this.'

'That sounded almost like a compliment.' I smiled.

'Oh, Lucan Drakenfeld.' She placed one firm hand on my shoulder. 'I'm not made of iron. If I have been harsh, it is for good reason. You see, your actions are likely to leave Detrata without a king – as a republic, for the time being. That could have ramifications across Vispasia.'

'How so?' I asked, fearing that I already knew the story.

'Imagine if a nation could successfully rule itself without a king once again. Imagine how that would be received in nations close by. If Detrata can do it, why not Maristan? Vispasia is a Royal Union, after all, and even the Sun Chamber depends upon the blessings of royal blood. How will the continent organize itself without royal rulers? This is not to say it can't, but such issues have been preoccupying my mind of late. Needless to say, many of us in the Sun Chamber will remain in Tryum for the time being, for diplomatic reasons. It's probably for the best if you're kept away for a while. But let it be known far and wide that your actions here have been of exceptional quality. I would say that your father would be proud, but that doesn't quite seem to possess the same meaning any more.'

'Not especially.' The guilt of what might happen to Vispasia was already starting to churn inside me.

'Don't boast about this,' she cautioned. 'Your work is to be commended but, as I say, people might not appreciate all you've done in the long run. You might not appreciate it yourself in a few years, but at least you've done the right thing.'

Senator Veron barged into the study with a jug of wine in one hand and a cup in the other. 'Don't boast about it?' he declared, grinning. 'The man's famous. Think of all the parties you'll be invited to! Think of the women and men who will fall at your feet. People will speak about this for years to come. Now both of you, none of this whispering, not tonight. Vispasia can wait another evening. Come and join the celebrations. I've at least a dozen senators who want to shake your hand, Drakenfeld, and I promised them I could make that happen. One of them is a powerful lady, recently divorced, if you find yourself in the mood for climbing social ladders.'

'Celebrations?' Tibus asked, rising up from her chair. 'Is the death of a king a time to celebrate?'

'That depends who you ask, my dear commissioner. Many have come tonight to celebrate a liberation, of sorts. Judges, senators, clerics, even the city censor, they're all here. The republicans are jubilant. We'll need to organize a consul for the short term. I might run for such a position myself, come to think of it. That's worth a drink or two, surely?'

Tibus gave a heavy sigh and smiled. 'And so it goes . . .'

I did not have the heart to tell Veron I would be leaving the city, not just yet, so instead I took his jug of wine, poured myself a cup and, with his arm around me, joined the others.

The following morning Leana and I readied to leave Tryum. Veron seemed genuinely distraught that I was going and I had to admit I felt sad myself. In a short period of time I'd grown fond of him, even though there was much about his character that I hoped I might change. I said I'd try to visit or, at the very least, write to him. There and then he wrote me a credit note and a down payment in coin for my property – a sum that I felt was more than it was worth, but he waved away my efforts to negotiate him down. He said a pleasant goodbye to Leana and for the first time there was no hint of lust in his manner.

Commissioner Tibus and the entourage of Sun Chamber officials gave us something resembling a sending off, lining up in Veron's ornamental gardens to bid us farewell. In front of the others, Tibus handed over to me an exquisite leather wristband, the kind given to victorious generals by their kings or queens. On one side was a golden head of Polla and on the other the burning star of the Sun Chamber.

'A token for your efforts,' Tibus declared.

'Breathtaking craftsmanship, commissioner. I don't know what to say.'

'And those horses, over there, are for the road.' She indicated the two handsome brown mares standing outside the gate. 'Head to Bathylan, on the border of Detrata and Koton. I'll see to it that you receive more instructions soon, and we'll send on your salary.'

Tibus called for Leana, surprisingly. Leana stepped forward, only to receive a similar leather bracelet to mine. Instead of Polla's head, the silver detailing on it was completely different. 'For assisting young Drakenfeld in this whole debacle, and for helping to capture Licintius,' Tibus said.

Leana seemed genuinely shocked and gratefully received the wristband. 'Where did you find this?'

'One of our men asked a few questions and ran to locate an Atrewen craftsman first thing this morning, to reset it with Atrewen icons. Drakenfeld told me of your background, so Polla would be of little use to you. Not much in the way of a reward, forcing our gods upon you, is it? I'm sure Polla would think of it that way.'

Leana smiled and thanked her once again.

And that was that, no grand ceremony, no big parade. We gathered what possessions we had and walked down the long path of Veron's gardens.

We stopped off to visit Lillus, and to see if Bellona was there and coping well. She already had her stall out selling all sorts of pastries and delights. When she saw us she seemed over-whelmed with joy and ran around the front of her stall to embrace me.

She stepped back all of a sudden, full of apologies for being so forward.

'Don't worry,' I laughed. 'I'm happy to see you again.'

Lillus stepped outside at that point and I said to Bellona, 'Is this man looking after you?'

'Looking after her? Already she is looking after me!' Lillus rubbed his stomach. I knew exactly what he meant. 'Besides, she is doing a much better trade than that nonsense fabric seller. People want to eat while they wait, not fondle cloth.'

I had a private word with Lillus, thanking him for his efforts, and he congratulated me on the case.

'It is a shame about your father,' he added, shaking his head. 'Sad that I did not know such things myself. I knew he was a different person, yet still, yet still . . .'

'It was hidden from everyone in the city, bar Lacanta and Licintius,' I replied. 'One other thing — I don't suppose you know where my brother went when he left the city, do you?'

'No, sadly. Why?'

'I'd like to track him down eventually, to see what's become of him. But it's not important.'

'Lucan, there is one final thing,' Lillus said. 'I have only heard this through . . . my usual networks . . . but the republicans are going to run the nation for a while.'

'That's right.'

Lillus nodded, in the way that said he knew far more than me. 'Go on . . .'

'My sources have heard many things overnight. The glories of Mauland have inspired a significant number of senators. There has been talk in taverns, between dozens of them, that they wish to expand our borders, to give more land to the army, and to—'

'Reclaim the glories of old,' I replied, repeating only what had echoed in the city during my short time.

Lillus gave a sad smile. 'It will happen sooner than you think, too. The humiliation of being surrounded by an army has only worsened things. They are hungry for foreign blood and they want out of the Union.'

'How many senators are involved?'

'More than one hundred. This might be the end of Detrata being part of the Union.'

'Is it my fault?' I asked. 'By removing Licintius, have I made it easier? Have I wrecked the Vispasian Royal Union?'

'Do not burden yourself with these questions. You let a nation make its own mind up on the treatment of their king. You merely provided justice for the dead. This militaristic streak is nothing new. It has always been here, and it may have happened eventually anyway. Who can say, for that path has now been closed.'

My time in this city was over; we had to move on.

We stocked up on some of Bellona's snacks for the road, said our goodbyes, and continued on our way out of the city. The departure was a much more pleasant exit than hanging underneath a dung cart, though this time I felt nauseous for other reasons.

Tryum presented itself to us one last time and I tried to absorb it all, for who knew what state I'd find it in the next time. The East Road was rammed full of traders and travellers, the city still in the process of opening up after the siege. On one side a wood yard was opening its gates for the day while next to it a stone-mason sat chiselling at his bench. Overhead a skein of geese swooped by, making quite a racket, while two oxen lumbered into view as a priest struggled to pull them along the busy road.

The steps of a temple belonging to Festonia were being washed clean of pink and red petals, the colourful flowers sailing for some distance down the road, and a couple of dogs came by to drink the blessed water. The shrine to one side was overflowing with wax from the candles. I could smell all sorts of spices from a cooking pot and, as we passed the taller, poorer buildings, dyed cloth was being stretched out to dry between them. In a way, it was heartening to see that so few lives had been disrupted by recent events. Kings and queens may fall, but cloth still needed to be dyed.

We exited Tryum and the countryside opened up, leaving my mind free of the wonderful distractions that the city offered.

There remained unanswered questions about what precisely happened, such is the way of this job, and these matters would give me plenty of agitation on the road. That I had unseated a king and, potentially, opened the continent to new tensions was unexpected and undesired. Had I made things worse or had the right thing been done? Lillus' words provided some comfort.

There was also the ghost of the dead man looking for his wife — my perspective on the world had changed greatly. Somehow one needs to see such beings with one's own eyes in order to believe — my mind had been forced open, and I lived in a world in which anything now seemed possible.

Many more questions concerned Titiana, admittedly — and whether or not she actually loved me. I had only the king's word that she did not, and Titiana had not exactly been the most reliable of people herself. I did not know how the king had found her, nor how they conspired against me, but they were both intelligent, manipulative people, while I had been blind to it all.

Perhaps Leana was right, and I was too trusting.

Titiana must have felt something for me; those intimate moments between us could not have all been an act. At least one kiss came from her heart and was not part of some trade I was unaware of.

It seemed to me the more one picks at the fabric of our world, the less one really understands it. For many people it remains better for their conscience to know as few facts as possible, to shy away from the difficult questions — in fact, to place those questions in the hands of our gods. As much as I respect Polla's will, and as much as I look to her from time to time for guidance, it strikes me as more than reasonable to try to find answers to these matters myself — even if the answers that reality provides are not always comforting.

My goddess, I'm sure, would approve of such an attitude.